The yellowbacks... classics of popular fiction

The yellowjackets or yellowbacks were a great series of bestselling adventure and crime thrillers that had its origins in the mid to late 19th century following on from the 'penny dreadfuls'. They virtually began the mass market revolution of the early 20th century with a clear standard format and imprint/series livery (what would today be called branding). Hodder & Stoughton published the yellowjackets in two main series with series run dates of: 1923-1939 and later 1949-1957.

As the tagline ('where thrillers really began') on the back cover implies, the imprint and series focused on thrillers that were the bestsellers of their time. This current reissue or retro revival if you will, brings back many of these masterpieces, now classics in their own way and extends it further by including key titles from that period that were either great crime or thriller or even general commercial fiction (including sub-genres of noir, horror, gothic, romance, westerns, etc.) influences of their time. There are some perennial favourites and many rarities either lost or not easily available being revived in the current series. Writers and characters ranged from adventure heroes like Bulldog Drummond, Allan Quatermain, Richard Hannay or the Saint through thriller grandmasters Edgar Wallace and E. Phillips Oppenheim, crime and mystery maestros like Patricia Wentworth, GK Chesterton, Agatha Christie and the Detection club, to western and swashbucklers like Zane Grey, Max Brand, Captain Blood and even romance or general fiction classics like Hermina Black, Denise Robins, Marie Corelli or Stella Morton. These were books that had storytelling at their heart and always entertained.

The yellowbacks had both hardback (with varying design elements) and paperback (which built the series look) versions with the latter still carrying the imprint 'yellowjacket'. The current reissues pay tribute to both and use an amalgam of elements from both editions while retaining the complete yellow (or 'mustard-plaster') livery with the author's name in blue beveled type with a 'simulated emboss' effect and a white outer 'outline', and the book title in black. These reissues retain the distinctive size of the original mass market paperback and follow the three main category variations—the thrillers (crime, westerns, mystery, adventure) had blue lettering for the author's name, while Romance and softer general fiction had red; and other categories like humour had green.

For more detail and a full list of titles visit https://www.hachetteindia.com/home/yellowbacks

THE DEDUCTIONS OF COLONEL GORE

THE DEDUCTIONS OF COLONEL GORE

Lynn Brock was the pseudonym of the Irish writer Alister McAllister, who moved to England and wrote a series of mystery novels featuring Colonel Gore which became popular in the 1920s and 1930s during the start of the golden age of detective fiction. He also wrote several plays under the name Anthony Wharton. He was educated at the National University of Ireland, where he served as chief clerk between 1908 and 1914. During the First World War he served with the British Army in the Machine Gun Corps.

THE DEDUCTIONS OF COLONEL GORE

Lynn Brock

Bonus Novella:
Too Much Imagination

hachette

The Deductions of Colonel Gore
First published in the UK by Collins in 1924; and in the US by Harper's in 1925. Re-published as *The Barrington Mystery* by Collins in 1932.

1

The texts in these editions in most cases have been reprinted as is, with minimal editorial changes and by and large no bowdlerizing for political correctness; though in some editions, a few words and phrases considered archaic, or those considered offensive now, along with archaic punctuation may have been modified in places to make the text more accessible to today's readers. The narratives, language, beliefs, social mores and/or cultural depictions, in these volumes are a reflection of their times and must be viewed as such. They may also contain certain cultural, racial and gender prejudices and stereotypes that may be outdated or clearly wrong then and wrong today; but their removal would be tantamount to claiming these prejudices never existed. The Publisher does not endorse or support those depictions or stereotypes; and these books have been made available for a discerning audience that will read it for entertainment value and a chronicle/record of popular fiction of past times.

Cover design by Priya Singh adapted from the original classic yellowjacket by Hodder & Stoughton.

Cover illustration by Ishan Trivedi.

Series note: Some of the books in the series (unless otherwise credited) may have cover or inside illustrations from the original yellowbacks or early editions, and while full restoration has been attempted, some images may be grainy or faded due to the condition of the original material. The end notes or bonus material or blurb details may have been sourced from the public domain or free use publications such as Wikipedia and attribution is hereby made also allowing similar free use reproduction from here. Sources requiring further specific attribution may write in and further detailing and/or corrections shall be made in subsequent printings/editions.

Reprint specifications may be subject to change including but not limited to finishes, paper, colour sections.

ISBN: 978-93-5731-123-6

Hachette Book Publishing India Pvt. Ltd.
4th & 5th Floors, Corporate Centre,
Plot No. 94, Sector 44, Gurugram - 122 003, India

Typeset in Electra LT STD 10/12.5 pt by Manipal Technologies Limited, Manipal

Printed and bound in India by Manipal Technologies Limited, Manipal

MIX
Paper from responsible sources
FSC™ C043100

CONTENTS

The Deductions of Colonel Gore

1

FOR just a moment following the sound of the door's closing behind her husband's entry Mrs Melhuish's profile remained downbent in abstracted calculation to the bridge-block in her lap. A small forgetfulness, natural enough, perhaps, in a hostess's last half-hour of anxiety before a duty dinner of importance. Yet, even twelve months ago, Sidney Melhuish remembered with passionate resentment, that absorbed, adorable little face would have flashed round, even in such an anxiety, in eager welcome to his coming. As they noted and weighed the momentary delay, his rather cold eyes hardened. Then, swiftly, they averted themselves. When Mrs Melhuish raised to him an expression of good-humoured perplexity, he was mildly absorbed in his finger-nails.

'What a nuisance, Sidney. Mr Barrington has just rung up to say that Mrs Barrington can't possibly come. Frightful earache, poor thing. I've been trying to work out my table. Do come and help me.'

Her air of charming, unruffled dismay was candour itself—beyond suspicion. And yet Melhuish was aware that for an instant as she spoke her smiling eyes had repeated once more the question they had asked of his so often of late. But of the hideous, the incredible suspicion that lurked behind it his clean-cut, gravely-smiling face betrayed no slightest hint as he moved behind her chair to inspect the much-altered plan of the dining-table which was drawn on the bridge-block.

For a moment or two they considered it in silence.

'If I had had even another quarter of an hour's notice—I know Beatrice Colethorpe would have stopped the gap for me. But even the amiable Beatrice would kick at a dinner-invitation of twenty minutes.'

She turned—Melhuish observed how instantly—as the door of the drawing-room reopened and Clegg announced the first of the evening's guests.

'Colonel Gore.'

No moment of feigned abstraction now—no summoning of her forces—no steadying of her nerves to meet his glance. Instead, a quick smile and gesture of vivid, frankest pleasure, in which his poisoned thought detected relief and eager escape from the danger of being alone with him.

Gore's lean brown face reflected the cordiality of his hostess's greeting, as she rose and went to meet him with outstretched hand.

'"Early", you commanded me. Therefore I have obeyed. Not too literally, I hope.'

Mrs Melhuish laughed as her hand slid into a clasp of fraternal heartiness.

'Well, as you have kept us waiting for three years, I think we may acquit you of undue precipitation.' She turned to her husband. 'This, Sidney, is the one and only Wick.'

Gore's twinkling gray eyes ran over his host in swift appraisement as they shook hands. In the four days for which he had been installed at the Riverside Hotel he had contrived to learn a good deal about Barbara Melhuish's husband, and that swift, straight, shrewd glance of his assured him at once that his informants had not been mistaken. A bit frigid, Dr Sidney Melhuish—a bit solemn, perhaps—but one of the right sort. Steady, clean eyes—steady, clean mouth—plenty of jaw and chin. A man that knew his job and knew he knew it. He grinned his charming grin and took the hand of Pickles's husband in a grip of steel. Thank the Lord, *she* hadn't made a mess of it, as so many of the Old Lot had somehow contrived to do.

'I know you very well by repute, Colonel Gore,' Melhuish smiled cordially—few men could resist Wick Gore's grin. 'Indeed, it is only with the utmost difficulty, I assure you, that I refrain from addressing you as "Wick" straightaway.'

'Why refrain?' twinkled Gore. 'Especially as I may confide to you that I have been in the habit of addressing your wife as "Pickles" since she was able to throw dolls and bottles and things at me out of a perambulator.'

'Now, now,' expostulated Mrs Melhuish. 'No indiscretions, please.'

'I apologise. I must remember that now I find you with a husband who believes not only that you are perfection, but that you always were.'

But his little pleasantry had somehow fallen flat, he perceived—as little pleasantries sometimes did. Melhuish, he divined, was a man to whom little pleasantries must be administered cautiously; no doubt, too, in three years of matrimony the light-hearted Pickles had acquired some of the seriousness of mind becoming to the wife of a rising physician.

'I *must* get my table right. Do come and help me,' said Mrs Melhuish hurriedly, returning to her diagram. 'Mrs Barrington has developed bad earache and can't come. We have just seven minutes to divide four women neatly and tactfully amongst five men. Let us concentrate our three powerful intellects. There—now I've drawn a nice new table. The blob at the top is Sidney.'

Gore glanced down at the first design, thus abandoned.

'Barrington is coming then?' he asked.

Mrs Melhuish nodded her golden head abstractedly.

'Mrs Barrington insisted upon it, he said. Ah—I've got it.' She scribbled some hasty initials. 'There's no help for it, Wick. You must divide Sylvia Arndale with Sir James. There—!

She held up her revised scheme for her husband's consideration, and, when he had approved it with his grave smile, flitted from the room to superintend the rearrangement of her cards. It was nine years since Gore had seen her; but she had changed, he reflected, as he attended upon her exit, very little; if at all, for the better. Pickles must be just thirty now. Thirty . . . Extraordinary. His mind flashed back to the night of her coming-out dance—November, 1910. Twelve years ago—incredible. Ah, well—those days were done with, and the Pickles of them. With the faintest of sighs he turned to rejoin the lucky beggar who had, somehow, succeeded in capturing that airy miracle and putting it in charge of his socks and his servants and his dinner-parties. A good chap—a good-looking chap—a chap, perhaps, a tiny shade too old for her, but in every way plainly to the eye a chap to make her as happy and contented a wife as—well, as any intelligent wife was likely to be made.

'You know most of the people who are coming to us this evening, Barbara assures me,' said Melhuish.

'All, I believe, except Barrington. I knew Mrs Barrington, of course, very well in the old days—when she was Miss Melville. She married just after the war, I think?'

'Yes.'

A certain quality in the monosyllable attracted Gore's attention.

'Successfully, I hope? What part of the world does Barrington come from?'

'Jamaica, I believe.'

Gore grinned.

'Sounds like sugar. Money to money, I suppose. Always the way here in Linwood. Simply revolting the way it breeds in hereabouts. No chance whatever for the deserving poor, is there? I suppose old Melville came down with thirty or forty thousand at least?' He sighed. 'Lord—who wouldn't be a son-in-law . . . in Linwood?'

For a moment Melhuish was absorbed in adjusting the rose shade of a light to his satisfaction.

'As a matter of fact,' he said, with that curious dryness of tone which his guest had already noticed, 'I understand that the Melvilles disapproved of the marriage and made a very small settlement. Mr Barrington is a patient of mine—Mrs Barrington too, indeed. But I cannot claim what one would describe as an intimate acquaintance with either of them personally. My wife, no doubt, can tell you all about their affairs. As you are aware, of course, she and Mrs Barrington are very old friends—'

He paused. His smile was formally courteous, but unmistakably resolved to discuss Mrs Barrington and her husband in no further detail.

'Right, my good man,' reflected his insouciant guest, without resentment. 'Keep your poker down your back if you think it makes you more impressive. A little bit sensitive, are you, because people are old friends of your wife's and not of yours? Myself included, perhaps? Well, we've got to talk about something. Let's try golf.'

But Melhuish, it became clear at once, regarded golf merely as an inducement to walk six miles on Sunday afternoon. Cheerfully Gore tried the by-election of the preceding week, fishing, the Panel System, and the Navy cuts. Mrs Melhuish returned to find the two men staring at the fire with the apparent conviction that in all the universe it alone held for them a common interest.

'I *did* tell you, Wick, that Sir James Wellmore is our *piece de resistance* this evening? Or did I? At any rate he is. We are awfully proud of him. He's our show patient.'

'You have met Sir James before, of course?' Melhuish asked.

'Once or twice—in the deplorably long ago—when he was not yet Sir James. When we were stationed out at Fieldbrook Barracks in nineteen-thirteen—just before we went to India—I remember he dined us and danced us and shot us in the most princely way. His first wife—she was still alive then—had, I recall, a penchant for the Services.'

Mrs Melhuish flashed a little teasing smile at him.

'If I am not mistaken the present Lady Wellmore was addicted to the same pleasant vice in those days. Or was it the younger Miss Heathman who was the attraction?'

Gore's teeth showed beneath his trim little wheaten moustache.

'How happy could I have been with either,' he laughed lightly. 'I believe I *did* miss the chance of my lifetime then. Someone told me last night at the club that Angela Heathman's income at present works out at just a shilling a minute. I've never stopped thinking about it since. If I hadn't gone off so hopelessly, I—by Gad, I believe I'd chance my luck now.'

'My dear Wick,' laughed Mrs Melhuish, 'Miss Heathman lives in the fourth dimension nowadays—or somewhere where there are better things than marriage and giving in marriage. Quite a difficult proposition, I should say, for a mercenary adventurer—even if he still has the smile of an angel and, still, no perceptible symptoms of a tum-tum.'

As their eyes met in smiling mutual approval, it seemed to Gore that nothing of their old camaraderie had faded, after all, in the passage of all those years. They had always looked at one another and chaffed one another just so, shrewdly yet with conviction of absolute understanding and sympathy, since the days when he had been a Harrovian of unusually misguided enterprise, and she the twinkling-legged bane of her nursemaid's existence. It was pleasant to be back, if only for a little while, in one's own country, and to find that one's old place was still there, waiting for one. The chilling disillusionment that had invaded him steadily during the four days since his return was forgotten in a soothing content. From the radiant, piquant face of his hostess—smiling at him precisely as it had smiled at him twenty-five years before amongst the branches of forbidden apple-trees, with one eyebrow slightly higher than the other— his eyes turned to absorb the effect of the warmth and colour and dainty comfort of the big drawing-room that was her setting. And as they turned they met the eyes of her husband.

There was a moment of silence, and then Gore said, brightly, that it had looked quite like snow about five o'clock that afternoon. With that opinion the Melhuishs agreed, Mrs Melhuish with sparkling vivacity, her husband with considered conviction, as Clegg reappeared to announce the arrival of Mr and Mrs Arndale.

'Good Lord,' thought Gore, as he reared his graceful and admirably-tailored person from the most comfortable chair he had sat in for nine years. 'The man thinks I'm an old flame of Pickles's. I know he does. That's why he has been watching me like a cat, is it? Fi-fi. Tut-tut. Pickles, Pickles . . . I hope I have not been mistaken in you?'

But no trace of these interior misgivings was visible as he shook hands with Cecil Arndale and his pretty, plump little wife. They, too, were part of the Old Days and the Old Lot— Sylvia Arndale and Barbara Melhuish were first cousins, and Cecil Arndale and he had been at Harrow together, though nearly three years separated them—and their pleasure at the meeting was as manifest as his own. In sixty seconds Mrs Arndale had reproached him for calling on two afternoons on which she had been out, informed him that she had made fifteen people buy his book, and secured him for dinner next day and a dance in the following week.

'I went to see your film twice,' she pouted, 'and there you were, standing with hundreds and dozens of dead antelopes and things stacked all around you—and I never got as much as tsetse-fly's whisker out of the lot. I shall never forget that you sent Barbara all those lovely stickers and beads and things as a wedding-present, and forgot me—me, who was once more than a sister to you—absolutely. Never, never.'

'My dear Roly-Poly,' grinned Gore placidly, 'you forget that I sent you a very beautiful and costly flower-bowl when you *were* entitled to a wedding-present—which was, pray recollect, four years before I became a movie-star—'

'For Heaven's sake,' cried Mrs Arndale, 'don't remind me how long I've been married to Cecil. It's not fair to him, poor dear. It embitters me so, and he has a perfectly ghastly time when I'm embittered.'

Cecil Arndale laughed—a little foolishly, as he had always laughed, his rather prominent blue eyes glistening slightly in his large, brick-red face. He had grown fat, Gore observed—much too fat for a man of thirty-nine—and his fatness accentuated that slight weakness of mouth and chin that had always marred his good-humoured, healthy, conventional good looks. His laugh faded again instantly into abstraction; his blue eyes stared vacantly across the room, while his lips twisted and puckered and smoothed themselves out again restlessly. Too much food, Gore conjectured—altogether too much drink—too much money—too easy a life of it. Poor old Cecil. He had always threatened to go soft. With some little difficulty Gore suppressed the recollection that this hefty, healthy six-footer had spent the war in England, and, incidentally, doubled during it the fortune which he had inherited from his father. Well, someone had had to stay at home and build ships. Besides, Arndale had married in 1915. And anyhow all that was his own affair. Gore, who had been through the business from start to finish, was not disposed to overrate the advantages to be derived from that experience. He wondered a little, none the less, just what the plump, outspoken little Roly-Poly had thought, privately, of her spouse's devotion to his business—say, in March, 1918.

'How's your brother?' he asked her. 'I fancied I caught a glimpse of a face that might have been his—brought up to date—passing me on the Promenade in a most vicious-looking two-seater. But I haven't run into him yet, end-on, so to speak—'

'Bertie? He lives just beside you. You're staying at the Riverside, aren't you? He has a flat in Selkirk Place at present—just across the way . . . at the other side of the Green. Number 73. You'll find him there any morning up to lunch-time in bed.'

'Still unattached?'

'We hope so.'

'What does he do all day?'

Mrs Arndale shrugged her pretty shoulders.

'He plays a good deal of golf, I believe—races a good deal—hunts a little. If he happens not to be away, and if it's too wet to do anything else, he runs down to the Yard in his car, smokes a cigarette, and runs back to change. I have calculated that on an average Bertie changes seven times a day.'

'Oh, then he's attached to the Yard now, is he?'

'Cecil says so. I suppose Cecil knows. It's his Yard.'

Arndale came out of his abstracted silence for a moment.

'Bertie's all right,' he said. 'Bit of an ass about women, that's all.'

'We all are, thank Heaven,' smiled Gore—'er . . . until we're forty . . . or . . . er . . . thirty-nine.'

Arndale's eyes regarded him blankly.

'Eh? Thirty-nine? No. Bertie's nothing like that. . .' With a visible effort he concentrated upon his calculation. 'Bertie's thirty—or thirty-one. Why, hang it, old chap—*I'm* thirty-nine.'

He smiled vaguely and strolled away. Gore caught his wife's eye.

'What's the trouble, Roly-Poly?' he asked bluntly.

She shrugged.

'Heaven knows. Cecil's always like that now . . . I'm frightfully worried about it, really. It's not money, I know. We're simply revoltingly well-off. . . It's some sort of blight. . . something mental.' She smiled wryly. 'Sometimes I think it's I who am responsible for it . . . of course I've always known that I'm not *the* right person . . . And yet we get on quite well. . . He's quite fond of me, really, in his way . . . Oh, don't let us talk about it any more. Let's talk about you. It's so absolutely ripping to see your old phiz again, Wick.'

As she patted his arm with a little impulsive gesture the door reopened and Clegg announced the guests of honour.

'Sir James and Lady Wellmore and Miss Heathman.'

While the Melhuishs chatted for a moment with the new arrivals Gore took stock of them with something like dismay. Wellmore, whom he remembered as a brisk, cheerful, keen-eyed middle-aged man, looked now every day of a tired, peevish, short-sighted sixty-five. Lady Wellmore—could that large- bosomed, broad-hipped, triple-chinned woman be the Phyllis Heathman of the old days? And that sallow, weary-eyed, bony- necked female with the nervously-flickering smile—could that be the once really quite pretty Angela? Good Lord.

His hostess's voice claimed his attention.

'You have met Colonel Gore before, Sir James, I think.'

Wellmore's tired eyes rested on the younger man's face perfunctorily, as he allowed his flabby, damp hand to be shaken.

'Yes,' he said briefly, 'I remember you. Nineteen-thirteen. You were stationed at Fieldbrook Barracks. In the Westshires. One of the prettiest shots I ever saw. Been in Africa, haven't you? Wonder you didn't stay there instead of coming back to this filthy climate. My wife has your book. But I've no time to read books. Never had.'

He passed on towards the fireplace and bent to warm his hands at the cheerful blaze wearily, his back to the room. Chairman of the United Tobacco Company—owner of three millions—master of six thousand lives—he could afford to dispense with ceremony.

But Lady Wellmore was graciousness itself. She had simply *revelled* in his book—especially the parts about the pigmies—she considered the parts about the pigmies perfectly *fascinating*. And the film—perfectly *wonderful*. She had been absolutely *thrilled* when dear Barbara had told her that she was to meet him again that night. She rounded him up in a *cul-de-sac* formed by a small table, two chairs, the flank of the big piano, and her sister.

'Angela, have you forgotten Colonel Gore? He has been regarding you with the most reproachful of eyes.'

Angela Heathman smiled nervously and held out a languid hand. At close quarters the sallow, haggard weariness of her face, with its drawn lips and shadowed eyes, was still more noticeable. Beside her sister's florid exuberance her faded thinness was accentuated painfully. Her smile faded, her eyes looked beyond him in brooding abstraction. She said nothing— withdrew her hand listlessly, and appeared to have forgotten the existence of the people who surrounded her.

'Nerves, poor thing,' Gore reflected. 'Another of 'em that doesn't know why she was born.'

As a silvery-toned clock somewhere in the room chimed eight fleetly, Clegg announced the last guest.

'Mr Barrington.'

For a moment the hum of voices died. The man who had entered surveyed the occupants of the room with smiling composure as he moved towards his hostess.

'My wife has charged me with the most abject of apologies, Mrs Melhuish. She had hoped until the last moment to be able to come.'

'We are so sorry,' Mrs Melhuish assured him. 'But it would have been folly for her to have ventured out on an evening like this. Of all afflictions in the world, I can imagine none worse than earache.'

'Dreadful. Quite dreadful,' Barrington agreed. He included Melhuish in his smile. 'However, she has retired to bed with a large supply of aspirin tabloids at hand . . . How are you, doctor? Worked to death, I suppose, as usual? I see you rushing about in that big car of yours from morning to night. Lot of sickness about, isn't there?'

'Yes,' said Melhuish simply.

Not a brilliant conversationalist, Dr Sidney Melhuish, Gore reflected—an exceedingly dry stick indeed. No one could suspect him of shyness or nervousness; his clean-cut face was as cool as a chunk of ice. Just one of those men who just didn't want to talk most of the time and wouldn't. Grim-looking chap, when his mouth set. Sort of chap that would look at your tongue and tell you you had six months to live and touch the bell for his man to show you out. Poor Pickles . . . What sparkling conjugal *tête-à-têtes* . . .

And yet, a moment later, when Melhuish crossed the room, Gore caught a glimpse of another man—a man whose kind. wise eyes and almost boyish sincerity and simplicity of manner ! and gesture brought a faint flush of animation to Angela Heathman's apathetic face as he smiled at her. No doubt she, too, was a patient of his. For that matter, as far as Gore had been able to discover, everybody in Linwood was, though it was only four years or so, he had learned, since Melhuish had purchased an old and decaying practice and installed himself in that most conservative of Westmouth's suburbs, a stranger and an interloper. True, he had brought with him from Bath, where he had been in practice for several years before the war, a reputation for brilliance, especially in heart cases. But Gore knew the stiff reserve and suspicion of Linwood too well to believe that a reputation for anything in the world acquired anywhere else in the world could influence it in the least. Something—something which no doubt Pickles had found out for herself—there must be in this difficult husband of hers that was not vouchsafed to the common or garden general practitioner . . . Something, for instance, that had been able to win for him not merely the patronage but the friendship of a man|

like James Wellmore, whose sole standard of judgment was value for his money.

His eyes returned to the shrivelled, peevish face of the tobacco magnate, bent obstinately on the fire, its underlip protruding sulkily as he listened to something which Barrington was saying to him. There was no trace of affection, paternal 0n otherwise, in his expression just then. Indeed as Barrington moved away from him towards Mrs Melhuish, Wellmore turned to look after him with an unmistakable scowl until, detecting Gore's interest in him, he switched his erring gaze back to the fire once more.

'I have succeeded in finding that cutting for you, Ml Barrington,' said Mrs Melhuish.

'How kind of you to have remembered,' replied Barringtoi displaying his small, even teeth in a smile of open admiration He was an extraordinarily handsome man, Gore admitted ungrudgingly—quite the handsomest man he had seen for some time—with some quality of charm that lay deeper than the perhaps slightly theatrical effect of his dark aquilinity and reckless gray eyes. Thirty-five at most, broad-shouldered, slim-flanked, easily—a *little* too easily, perhaps—sure of himself, he was one of those men at whom no woman could look without interest or without the awakening of her oldest and strongest instinct. Already Gore had noticed with amusement that, as he moved across the room to his hostess, the regards of the other three women had followed him with a speculative intentness. And that the charms of this smiling Adonis were not lost upon Mrs Melhuish herself was no less evident. Her colour had brightened beneath the flattery of his look; her poise and intonation as she spoke to him were tinged with the subtle challenge of her sex—the indefinable yet unmistakable blending of defiance and invitation that—by a cynic as hardened as Wick Gore—could be taken for nothing but. . . well, what any chap with two eyes in his head would take it for. Miss Pickles hadn't changed *all* her spots, then—for all the rash vows of holy matrimony. Still a flash of colour and a sparkling eye for an agreeable-looking young fellah. She had always preferred 'em dark . . . and a bit hooky about the beak.

'I put it down somewhere,' said Mrs Melhuish, glancing about her. 'Now . . . where . . .? Oh, yes. I remember.'

She moved to the piano, and picked up an envelope that lay on some music. Barrington took the envelope from her smilingly, opened it, glanced casually at the newspaper cutting which it contained.

'Thanks so much,' he said, as he replaced the cutting and put the envelope away in a pocket. 'As a matter of fact I had rather thought of running up to look at another shoot in that part of Wiltshire this week.'

'Really?'

Mrs Melhuish's colour had forsaken her now. Her eyes consulted with anxiety the little Sevres clock on the table beside Gore, rose to his brown, hard profile, and rested there for a moment warily. He stood but an arm's-length from her; but he was listening with the most flattering of attention to Lady Wellmore's views upon the sinister aims of Labour. The slightest movement of her golden head showed her her husband and Sylvia Amdale grouped by the big chair near the fire into which Wellmore had subsided with a yawn. At the other side of the room Arndale struggled feebly with Miss Heathman's vagueeyed listlessness, pausing between each laborious effort to regard a water-colour above her head vacantly. Mrs Melhuish's hand strayed to a bowl of chrysanthemums by the piano, touched a great gold and russet bloom caressingly.

'If the door is shut, go away,' she said softly—almost inaudibly. 'I may not be able to manage tonight. I will ring you up tomorrow at eleven if not.'

Barrington bent to examine the gorgeous blossom.

'It will be open,' he smiled.

His reckless eyes dwelt in hers victoriously for an instant. As she turned to introduce him to Gore, Clegg appeared once more, slightly flushed and seven minutes late.

'Dinner is served, madam.'

2

It was, it appeared, Sir James Wellmore's inviolable rule to get out of his bed at seven o'clock and get into it again before midnight, and at half-past eleven he and Lady Wellmore departed in an immense limousine. Miss Heathman, silent and vague-eyed to the last, accompanied them; the big house on the Promenade of which she was the capricious mistress, lay on the Wellmores' homeward way across the Downs to their palatial mansion at Bishops Leaze. The Arndales had gone away before eleven o'clock hurriedly, disturbed by a tele- phone-message requiring, Gore presumed, Mrs Arndale's immediate return to some urgent trouble of the baby, with details of whose incredible brilliancy of intellect and beauty of form she had regaled him at intervals during dinner. It was twenty minutes to twelve when he and Barrington made their adieux to Mrs Melhuish and went down the stairs accompanied by their host.

As Clegg helped him into his overcoat, in the hall, Gore glanced at the artistically-arranged trophy which occupied the wall space between the hall door and the door of the dining-room. His wedding present made, he reflected, quite a decent display, the two befeathered Masai head-dresses and the scarlet-and-ochre magic-mask forming an effective centre to the design. The shaft of one of the Wambulu spears had developed some mysterious breed of worm some months after its arrival, Melhuish told him, and had been replaced by a new one.

'Hope your maids aren't curious about cutlery, doctor,' Gore grinned, as he accepted a light for his cigarette. 'I mean—those hunting spears are probably quite safe. But those little arrows—and the knives—Well, I think I inserted lavish warnings in the packing-cases. I hope I did.'

Barrington fitted a cigarette into a long amber holder. 'What?' he asked. 'Bad medicine, are they?'

'Possibly very nasty indeed,' said Gore—'some of them.' He touched the beaded sheaths of two small knives, crossed to form the lower point of the trophy. 'These two little brutes, for instance . . . I shouldn't mind betting that if you were thoughtless enough to scratch yourself with one of these—even after three years—something exceedingly unpleasant would happen you in the next few minutes. I've actually seen a poor beggar die in less than two minutes from a prick of one of those little throwing-knives . . . Die most untidily, too.'

'What's the poison?' asked Melhuish, with professional interest. 'I remember now that my wife did say something about the cautions you sent her. But I'm afraid we had both forgotten all about them.'

'It's a root called "nmakato." Not in the B.P., I rather fancy, doctor. We didn't succeed in seeing the root itself. As a matter of fact, the old witch-doctors who distill the stuff are rather reticent about little trade-secrets of that sort. I saw the flowers of the thing, though—yellow—not unlike our gorse, both to look at and to smell. They use the flowers to make wreaths for their young women when they retire into seclusion to think over the joys of matrimony for a month or so before they plunge into them.'

He held out his hand. 'Well, we shall meet again, doctor, no doubt.'

'You haven't decided yet how long you'll stay in Linwood?'

'Some weeks, at any rate, I hope. Good-night.'

'You coming my way, Colonel?' Barrington asked, as the hall door opened to let them out into the foggy dampness of the November night.

'I'm at the Riverside,' Gore replied. 'Just across the way.'

'Oh.'

Barrington turned to his host.

'Good-night, doctor. I shall run in and see you tomorrow or next day. I've been sleeping a lot better since I cut tobacco right out. But I still get those nasty twinges . . .'

Melhuish nodded gravely.

'Come and see me. I hope you'll find Mrs Barrington's earache better when you get back. Please tell her how sorry we were that she was unable to come.'

'I will. Good-night.'

'Good-night.'

The two departing guests sauntered side by side for a few yards, chatting desultorily until their paths diverged—Gore's towards the hotel, the lights of whose upper windows were visible through the branches of the trees in the Green, his companion's along the deserted vista of Aberdeen Place, at the end of which the Corinthian façade of the club rose palely in the glare of the arc-lamps in the Mall.

'My old heart's worrying me a bit,' Barrington explained. 'I've had to cut out most of the joys of life—temporarily, at any rate.'

Gore murmured sympathetically.

'Bad luck. You're in good hands, though.'

'Melhuish's? None better. You a bridge player?'

'Incurable.'

'Then I expect I shall run into you at the club.'

'I expect so. Remember me to your wife, won't you? She and I are very old friends.'

'Indeed? She'll be delighted so see you any afternoon you care to run in. Hatfield Place—Number 27. Don't forget.'
'Twenty-seven. Many thanks. Good-night.'

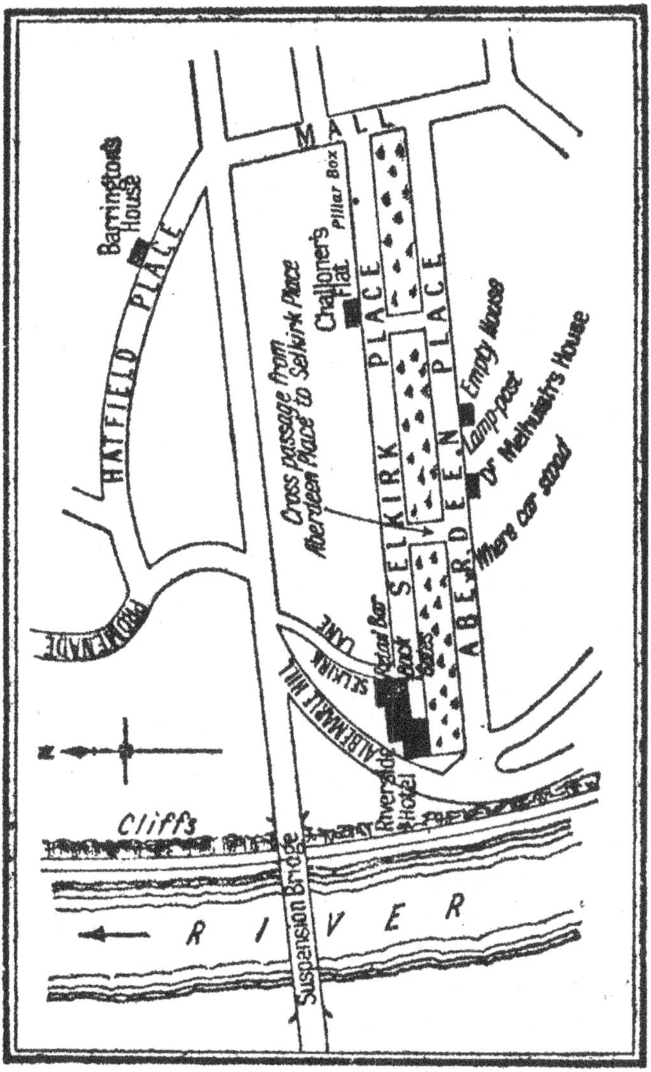
MALL
Barrington's House
HATFIELD PLACE
PROMENADE
Pillar Box
Challoner's Flat
SELKIRK PLACE
Cross passage from Aberdeen Place to Selkirk Place
ABERDEEN PLACE
Empty House
Lamp-post
Dr Melhuish's House
Where car stood
SELKIRK LANE
ALBEMARLE HILL
Riverside Hotel
N
Cliffs
Suspension Bridge
RIVER

'Good-night, Colonel.'

The two parallel rows of tall houses which formed Aberdeen Place and Selkirk Place respectively faced one another, at the distance of a long stone's-throw, across the Green—a pleasant strip of ornamental garden enclosed by railings for the exclusive use of residents, and running the entire length from Albemarle Hill at the western end to the Mall at the eastern. For convenience' sake two transverse passages of roadway divided the Green into three detached sections, roughly equal in length. Gore's path from the Melhuish's house to the back entrance to the Riverside Hotel—the front entrance was in Albemarle Hill, overlooking the river—lay along one of these two cross passages, and when he had parted from his fellow-guest, therefore, a very few steps interposed between him and Barrington the railings of the middle section of the Green and the shrubs and trees which formed, inside the railings, the ornamental border of the garden. Happening to glance backwards, however, for no more particular reason than that his ears had informed him that the retreating sound of his late companion's footsteps on the pathway had ceased abruptly, he caught a glimpse of Barrington halted beneath a lamp, facing another man—taller, and wearing a light-coloured raincoat—the sound of whose voice, raised, it seemed to Gore angrily, reached his ears indistinctly during the instant for which he slackened pace to look back. Afterwards he recalled that in that brief instant he had wondered a little from where that taller, raincoated figure had emerged; since, while he had lingered chatting with Barrington not a soul had been in sight in Aberdeen Place against the glare of the Mall. He was to recall, too, that something in the build and size of the second man had suggested Cecil Arndale vaguely—but just how vaguely or how accurately he was afterwards quite unable to weigh. These particular speculations, to which at the moment he attached no importance of any kind, were destined subsequently to assume one of very serious concern to him. For, in fact, as it proved, that hurried, careless, backward view of Barrington, partially blocked out by the laurels, yet unmistakable, was the last he was to see of him alive.

He went on his way, turning left-hand as he reached the roadway of Selkirk Place, which terminated in a cul-de-sac at the pillared gates admitting to the grounds of the Riverside. Beside the gates a three-storied red-brick building, comprising a retail-bar on the ground floor with some living-rooms used by the staff above, formed the rear of the hotel, connected with the main block facing the river by the annexe in which Gore's suite lay. The bar, a discreetly-managed, quiet little place, unexpected in that exclusive residential quarter of the suburb, catered principally, Gore surmised, for a regular little clientele of chauffeurs and coachmen from Selkirk Lane. The lane which branched off northwards from Selkirk Place at its doors was bordered by stables, most of them now converted into garages, and provided, no doubt, a considerable number of such customers.

But at that hour the bar had long closed its doors for the night; the wan illumination of an arc-lamp suspended above its portals accentuated its effect of cold inhospitality. One window of the seven that looked up Selkirk Place was still, however, lighted up. A shadow moved across the yellow blind as he passed—possibly the shadow of the tawny-haired Hebe who presided over the bar, and of whom Gore had caught glimpses as she went to and fro across the annexe between her domain and the main building of the hotel. Rather a pretty little thing, he had noticed, if somewhat excessively embellished; not too severe, either, to refuse a smile in return to his 'Good-morning' or 'Good-afternoon.' Betty, he had gathered, was her name— Betty Rodney. Rather a pretty name. He yawned, crossed the grounds, and was admitted into the annexe by the night porter.

'I want to get a couple of letters off in half an hour or so,' he said, when the man had roused his sitting-room fire, 'if you'll leave the door into the gardens open for me, I'll stroll up myself and drop them into the box in Selkirk Place, when I've written them.'

Left alone, he manufactured himself a modest whisky-and-soda and seated himself to compose with its aid and that of a very terrible pipe, applications for two vacant positions for either of which, it seemed to him, he might hope to be considered as eligible as the next fellow. One was the secretaryship to a small London club devoted to the consolation of the Very Poor of the Services; the other the secretaryship of a golf club in Hampshire. A cheerful fire glowed and crackled soothingly; there was no other sound to disturb his efforts at ingratiating composition. Presently he finished his drink, knocked the ashes out of his pipe, refilled it, and slewed round in his chair to regard the fire-irons thoughtfully. On the uppermost page of his writing block the words—

'RIVERSIDE, HOTEL,
'LINWOOD, WESTMOUTH.
'*Nov.* 6,1922.

'GENTLEMEN,—'

lay reproachful and forgotten.

'If the door is shut, go away. I may not be able to manage tonight. I will ring you up tomorrow at eleven if not.'

That was what she had said, furtively, nervously, under cover of the clumsiest interest in the chrysanthemums. And Barrington, as cool and cocksure as be-dam, had said, 'It will be open.'

What door? When was it to open? What the devil did it mean?

What the devil *could* it mean? Was it possible that, in her own house—under her husband's very nose, Pickles—the

Pickles whose image, idealised, no doubt, in parts, yet always extraordinarily vivid, had cheered him and bucked him up and made him feel a bit better in even the darkest hours of the past nine years—was it possible that *she* was playing the rotten, silly old game—carrying on with that sleek-headed— Gore's private surmise used at that point an epithet of Anglo-Saxon vigour which it instantly deprecated. No. The thing was incredible.

Incredible—unthinkable. A bit of a flirtation, perhaps—perhaps not even that. He drew a breath of relief to find his loyalty to the Pickles of the old days still staunch enough to hold her clear in the face of any suspicion, however insidious.

Straight as a die she had always been—in everything. It wasn't possible that she could have changed—could have become one of those treacherous, loathsome little cats whose exploits filled the papers nowadays. There was some quite simple explanation of that remark of hers about the door. There must be. It was pretty rotten of him to have believed anything else for a moment, he told himself—the sort of thing one might expect from some half-baked young cub eager to sniff out filth in every corner. He turned, rather peevishly, in his chair, took up his pen, dipped it in ink, and resumed his correspondence with determination.

The son, the grandson, and the great-grandson of soldiers, he had found himself at his father's death a subaltern in his father's old regiment, with exactly two hundred a year in addition to his pay. To most people, since the average income of the men in the Westshires was some ten times that amount, such a position would have appeared embarrassing. He had contrived, however, to endure it with fortitude, aided by a practically imperturbable smile, a useful dexterity in all sports and pastimes beloved of youth, and a quite special brilliancy as a polo-player—an amusement which he had pursued, unavoidably, on other people's ponies for the greater part, but to the great glory of the Westshires. In the year 1912-13, the year in which he had obtained his company, he had been, with one unpublished reservation, as blithe and contented a young man as was to be discovered in the length of the Army List. The reservation was Miss Barbara Letchworth—better known to her intimates as Pickles. But of that fact Wick Gore took very great pains to ensure that neither she nor anyone else should have the slightest inkling. To the day in 1913, when he went out to drink three cups of tea and eat eleven sandwiches and take a cheerful farewell of Miss Letchworth—then one-and- twenty or thereabouts and horribly sweet in cool, fluffy, summer things—preparatory to his departure to India, that extremely intelligent young woman had no faintest suspicion that night and morn for three whole years past he had cursed, for her sake, the day on which he had been born—born, at all events, to two hundred a year in addition to his pay.

From India the battalion had gone, very abruptly, to France in 1914. In the course of the following four years Pickles had written quite a number of charming letters to Captain, Major, and Lieutenant-Colonel Gore successively, accompanied by superior brands of cigarettes and sundry strange garments, each of which he had worn solemnly at least once. A year on the Rhine had completed his military career. Chance had thrown in his way an offer to form a member of an expedition to Central Africa; he had accepted the offer eagerly, sent in his papers, and disappeared for two years. A pleasant twelve months in Rhodesia, where his book—the record of the expedition's adventures and discoveries—had been written, had induced him to consider seriously the project of setting there permanently.

But at that point a childless and long-widowed aunt had chosen to die and leave for distribution amongst a horde of nephews and nieces a very considerable portion of the money which her husband had extracted from a small colliery in the north. Gore's share in this good fortune, long despaired of, had amounted on final examination, to an income of three hundred and fifty pounds a year. Two days after his forty-second birthday he had landed in England, spent a week interviewing solicitors and tailors and such things, and, bored to extinction by a London which seemed to him entirely populated by Jews, had fled westwards in search of such of his kith and kin as still survived.

The Riverside Hotel had commended itself to him as a headquarters for various reasons. Its advantages for that purpose had been in no way discounted by the fact that the entrance to the very comfortable private suite with which the management provided him lay within just one minute's walk from a certain hall door in Aberdeen Place which bore the plate of Dr Sidney Melhuish.

On the very afternoon of his arrival in Linwood, as he returned along Aberdeen Place to the hotel, he had caught a glimpse of a slim figure in moleskins as it disappeared through that hall door. A quite amusing acceleration of his heart-beat had been perceptible for some moments. The same amusing symptom had manifested itself when next morning he had rung up Mrs Melhuish from the Riverside and heard, for the first time for nine years, her voice say, 'Yes?' He had found the operation of breathing troublesome for an instant—an instant so long that she had added: 'Who is speaking, please?' Quite amusing. Especially in view of her placidity when at length—after nine years—he had replied, a little curtly, 'Gore.'

There had been a silence, and then a calm, unsurprised 'Gracious. Why, you said you were going to stay in Rhodesia for ever and ever.'

And then:

'I'm so sorry. But my husband has just come in for lunch. I must fly. Can you ring me up this evening . . . about seven? I shall be—'

And then, of course, after nine years, the exchange had cut off.

But her invitation to dinner had made up a good deal for that first flat disappointment.

'Do come early, like a dear,' she had said. 'We want to have you to ourselves for a few minutes. Sidney is pining to meet you. You'll love him. He's just the darlingest old thing in the world.'

He recalled now exactly the inflection of her voice as she had said that—

With fresh determination he dipped his pen once more in ink and after the word 'Gentlemen' wrote the words, 'I beg to apply—'

It was then five minutes to one.

It was twenty-five minutes past one when he stamped his two letters. He slipped into an overcoat, and let himself out into the chill clamminess of the fog. The pillar-box for which he was bound lay half-way along Selkirk Place, a couple of hundred yards from the back entrance to the Riverside. At the gates he paused for a moment to light a cigarette, and observed that the window above the bar was still illuminated. As his eyes rested on it, the yellow blind was drawn a little aside, and someone feminine—the tawny-haired Miss Betty Rodney, he presumed—was visible for a moment, peeping down at him.

No doubt Miss Rodney's attention had been attracted by the halting of his footsteps beneath her window at that hour. He went on his way towards the pillar-box, reflecting, perhaps not entirely originally, that in general and in particular women were curious things.

3

Mrs Melhuish had switched off all the lights in the drawing-room save two beside the fireplace when her husband re-entered the room, and was lingering, he perceived, merely to say good-night. She turned at his entrance, smiling through a little yawn.

'Well. . . what do you think of Wick? Quite a dear, isn't he?'

Melhuish nodded.

'I like Gore very much indeed,' he said sincerely. 'I wish that we could have provided a rather more amusing evening for him.'

'It was not exactly a giddy party,' Mrs Melhuish confessed. 'However, we'll get something a little brighter for him next time, Are you sitting up, dear? I hope not, after your wretched night last night. I heard you coming in at a quarter-past four . . . bad boy.'

'A haemorrhage case . . . one of Mrs Ashley's maids.'

'Oh.'

There was a little pause. He wondered if tonight again she would contrive to evade the good-night kiss which was for both of them, now, an ordeal dreaded and avoided when avoidance was with even a pretence of decency possible. But he stood between her and the door. Tonight no escape was possible; the ignominious, hateful farce of their day must terminate in that elaborately casual contact of her cheek with his, cold as ice, burning like hell's fire. He read the pitiable hesitation in her eyes, yet, even in his pity of it, would not spare her or himself. His cold scrutiny rested mercilessly on her face until it was raised to his.

'Good-night, Sidney.'

'Good-night.'

'You are quite pleased with everything? Sir James's congratulations upon my cook were really quite embarrassing.'

'Everything was admirable—as it always is.'

She swept him a little mocking curtsey, and was gone.

He stood where she had left him until he heard her bedroom door close remotely, then glanced at his watch and moved to the fire, to stand before it, considering. Five minutes to twelve. How long would he wait tonight?

It had been a little before one when he had heard her go downstairs that night—the Monday night of the preceding week—that seemed to him countless centuries ago. The hour of meeting had been altered for Friday night to a quarter-past one. At least a whole hour lay before him—a whole hour to watch drag by, minute after minute, listening in the darkness, writhing in self-contempt, aware that beyond the wall that separated her room from his, she, too, was waiting and watching and listening in the darkness—hating him because, on his account, she must lie there for that never-ending hour before she could safely creep down the stairs. Yes, he reflected grimly, at moments she must hate him. Hate him because she feared him, because he stood in the way of her pleasure, because he was what he was—her husband. That thought still appeared to him ludicrous, though for a whole week now he had known beyond all doubt the amazing truth of her treachery to him. Even at the end of that week of devastating certainty he was still unable to look at her face without stupefied wonder at its self-control. It seemed impossible that a spirit so courageous as hers, so defiant of obstacles, so intolerant of pretence, could conceal a bitter hatred so smoothly. And yet . . . what hatred could be imagined more bitter than that of a woman for a man who stood between her and the man of her—

Of her . . . what?

Desire . . . Passion . . .? His soul laughed at the bare thought of the words in connection with her. Caprice? A prettier word— probably a more appropriate one. At heart he guessed and dreaded a stronger and more dangerous driving-force than these behind her betrayal of him—a craving for the things he himself had proved incapable of giving her—the gaiety and grace and thousand dancing, laughing sympathies of youth. From the very beginning she had teased him on the score of a seriousness which, he was himself well aware, was prone to heaviness. From the very beginning he had seen that inevitably his professional work must separate them—seclude him from great tracts of her life, as it must seclude her from the principal business of his. Youth for Sidney Melhuish had been a phase of single-minded purpose and strenuous preparation for its achievement. Youthfulness he had laid aside deliberately at the threshold of a career which for him, over and above the possibilities of material advancement, was a mission—a consecration to the grimmest, most desperate of crusades against the most ruthless and invincible of enemies. Gaiety and grace were for those others, he had told himself, who neither saw nor heard nor heeded . . . until they had need of him and his kind. He had envied them a little at odd moments—pitied them a little— wondered at them a little—been always much too busy to feel the need of attempting to imitate their decorativeness. The attempt in any case would have been, he knew, a futile one. His lips twisted wryly now as, staring down into the fire, he recalled his wife's efforts, in the first tentative days of her life with him, to teach him to dance—

She had striven, too, to teach his mind to dance, he knew, in those first days—striven to infuse him with some tinge of the agreeable ephemeral interests which were the life of the set from which he had isolated her temporarily during their brief engagement, but which, he had quickly perceived, would always remain her tribe and her world. But he neither shot nor fished nor hunted. Theatres and novels held for him the faintest of appeals. The allusive tittle-tattle of her friends—light-hearted young people of both sexes possessed of an abundance of money and of leisure, who visibly resented his silent seriousness—bored him. At the end of a year his wife had frankly confessed him, as a social ornament, hopeless.

'I do believe, Sidney,' she had said one afternoon, when his unexpected intrusion from the consulting-room had dispersed one of her bridge-parties precipitately, 'that the only purpose for which you believe human beings are provided with tongues is as an aid to medical diagnosis. Do you know that for seven minutes you stood here, in your wife's drawing-room, without speaking, or even attempting to speak, one single word? I timed you by the clock.'

'Well,' he had urged, 'they wanted to go on playing bridge.'

'No. They had stopped—when you came into the room.'

'Well, why did they stop when I came into the room?'

'Because they all think you disapprove of women playing bridge in the afternoon.'

'I do,' he had said simply.

At that she had laughed until her eyes had streamed tears. But there had been no more afternoon bridge-parties at 33, Aberdeen Place. That incident, he supposed, had marked in all probability the definite point at which she had admitted to herself that her marriage had been a mistake . . .

That had been two years ago. Had this business with Barrington been going on then, for two whole years—unsuspected for all that time—so unsuspected that in the end they had thought it safe enough to risk these meetings at night in the dining-room of his house. A serious risk—since she must have realised that at any moment a telephone-call might awaken him and bring him downstairs to discover them. But no doubt they had long grown to believe that there was no risk whatever—no need for even the most elementary precaution against surprise.

How many nights had they met so before that Monday night of the preceding week on which, by the merest of chances, their secret had been revealed to him? The tyre of a belated taxi-cab had happened to burst just outside the house, and the report had awakened him—to hear, a few moments later, the door of his wife's room open softly and her footsteps steal past his door. Minute after minute he had waited, at first drowsily, then with surprise, until at length uneasiness had induced him to go downstairs in search of her. Fortunately, his slippers had made no noise on the thick carpet, for they had come out of the dining-room as he reached the drawing-room landing. A man's voice, unrecognised at first, had brought him to abrupt halt.

'Friday, then. Same hour?'

'A quarter past one,' his wife's voice had answered cautiously. 'A quarter to is too early.'

The man had laughed.

'Your dear hubby has forbidden me late hours, you know. Bad for dicky hearts. However—'

He had recognised the voice then. Barrington. While he had stood in stupefaction the hall door had been shut stealthily. In an instant his momentary fury had chilled to ice. The brain and nerves that had never failed him had recovered their aplomb, had decided upon the simplest, surest road to vengeance. He had turned and crept barefooted back to his bedroom—to lie awake till dawn, perfecting his plan, devising means against all possible mischance.

And yet his plan had miscarried. On Friday night Barrington had come tiptoeing along Aberdeen Place at the appointed hour, clearly visible from the upper front windows of the house to eyes that watched for his coming. He had come up to the hall door, but had gone away again almost immediately, pulling the door to behind him cautiously—it had been left ajar for him, evidently. No footsteps had crept from the adjoining bedroom. There had certainly been no meeting that night.

Nor on the next, nor on any of the following nights—unless one had taken place last night during his absence on the case to which he had been called out a little before two o'clock in the morning. Six nights of fruitless waiting, of coldly-raging fury that listened in the darkness until the silence of the house was as the roar of thunder. There was no certainty that he would come tonight, either—that he would come for a month of nights. No matter. On the night on which he did come he would pay for all those others . . .

Clegg's respectfully reproachful cough behind him roused him from his thoughts. He bade the man good-night and went upstairs slowly to his room. Did the servants know? Had they, too, grinned and leered at him all that time behind his back for a poor blind simpleton? Probably. In Clegg's eyes, too, he told himself now—too late—he had detected the question that had lurked in his mistress's. 'Does he suspect? Does he know?'

Patience. His turn to laugh would come—if not tonight, one night.

For a little while he moved about his room, making the noises for which her ears listened. He caught a glimpse of his face in a mirror as he switched off the lights—absorbed, the eyes narrowed, nose and lips pinched, a crease between the eyebrows—a tell-tale face, the face of a watching, waiting sneak. He swore viciously beneath his breath, and in the darkness began to tear off his clothes. Damn them—let them go their way. They should not pull him down with them.

He groped for his pyjamas, and remembered then that the night before the cord had slipped through at one end and that in his impatience with it when he had returned in the small hours of the morning he had pulled it right through and tied it about his waist on the outside. But it had been restored, he found, to its proper place—almost certainly by her hands. The same misadventure had befallen him on his honeymoon, one night in Venice. He remembered the adoration with which he had watched her little fingers rescue the errant tape with a hairpin, deftly . . .

He seated himself on the bed with smarting eyes and strangled throat. Was it—*could* it be too late? Was nothing left of the dream? Had he lost her utterly? Impossible—impossible— impossible. He didn't—he couldn't believe it. In the morning, before she went downstairs, he would go into her room and face the thing with her—holding her hands—smiling at her—her friend and confidant. Even if she loved this other man—he could bear to know that, he told himself, if she did not conceal it from him—even if she loved him, they would face the difficulty together—talk it over—calmly and wisely. Somehow the trouble would pass, if they faced it together . . .

Presently, shivering in the damp air that came in through the open windows, he got into bed. But the sirens were busy now on the river, as boat after boat hooted its slow way down the tortuous, narrow channel on the tide. He lay there, wide-awake, listening to them, wondering if she, too, heard them.

He had not heard the door of her room open, nor any sound of her passage across the landing—merely the creak of a stair—a stair, it seemed to him, of the second flight from the landing. The tiny noise, almost imperceptible, awaited for so many nights, stopped his heart for a beat. The guile that had once more all but eluded his vigilance shocked him violently, hardened his mood to stone again. What stealthy pains must have gone to the noiseless opening of her door, the crossing of the landing, the descent of the stairs, step by step—until that small, dreaded sound had brought her to abrupt halt, listening with straining ears to discover if it had betrayed her. How had she learned this minute, patient cunning? How had she concealed it from him?

He was out of bed now. When he had opened the door and listened for a moment, he switched on a light and dressed himself in the clothes which lay always in readiness against a night-call. His long fingers adjusted his collar and tie with the careful neatness with which they performed the task every morning. He smiled sardonically at the thought that without his collar and tie, a husband, however injured, started at a disadvantage if his wife's lover happened to wear one at the moment of *dénouement.*

He felt no anger now, none of those vague, futile emotions which were the stock-in-trade of the wronged husbands of convention. His mind held but one thought, one desire—the successful accomplishment of that entry of absolute surprise. He switched off the light again and went softly down the stairs.

On the drawing-room landing he paused to lean over and look down into the hall. The subdued radiance of the light in the fanlight, left on always at night, showed him the lower portion of the dining-room door. As he had expected, the door was shut, though already, at the distance of two flights of stairs, the subdued murmur of voices was audible through it. He went down another flight, with increased caution, and on the first landing—that outside the morning-room—came in view of the dimly-lighted hall. To his amazement he saw, standing just inside the open hall door, Cecil Arndale.

He halted, dumbfounded. Was it possible that he had been mistaken? Had it been Arndale's voice which he had heard that Monday night? Had it been Arndale whom he had seen come and go on Friday in the moonlight? No. There was no likeness whatever between the voices of the two men—no likeness whatever between their figures—no possibility of such a mistake. Besides, at that moment, a man's voice was speaking in the dining-room. Arndale obviously could hear that voice too. He was listening to it, his eyes fixed on the dining-room door, so intently that not even for a moment had they turned towards the darkness of the staircase. For that moment of surprised surmise, Melhuish made no movement forward or back. The maddest, most ludicrous of conjectures had flashed into his mind. Was it possible that there were two of them—and that somehow they had both come on the same night?

'My God!' his senses asked of themselves, 'am I mad? Is this I who am standing here on this landing outside the morning-room thinking this thing?'

He heard his throat produce a dry, inarticulate gasp—an attempt to call out Arndale's name—as he began to descend the stairs towards him. At that moment, however, without having heard him, at all events without a glance towards him, Arndale went out, leaving the hall door ajar behind him. The murmur of the voices in the dining-room had risen abruptly in pitch. Almost instantly its door opened and Barrington came out into the hall.

'Absolutely out of the question, my dear child, I assure you,' he was saying, as he drew on a glove. 'I'd do it if I could—for your sweet sake . . . But in times like these I simply can't afford philanthropy. A thou. That's the best I can do for you, my dear. Come—it's well worth the money—a clean sheet—no skeleton in the closet to worry about, eh? Think how nice that would be to waken up to in the morning.'

Melhuish had retreated stealthily the two or three steps which he had descended towards the hall, and stood flattened against the *portiere* of the morning-room door, the glowing end of his cigarette concealed behind him. His wife had come out from the dining-room now, though, since she stood facing towards the hall door, he could not see her face. But her voice, when she spoke, contained a hard, desperate anger of which he could not have believed her even serenity capable.

'What a scoundrel you are,' she said contemptuously. 'I wonder how many unfortunate women you have played this game with . . .'

'Well'—Barrington shrugged smilingly—'that is really beside the point, isn't it. Think it over, my dear. I'm quite sure that if you think it over, calmly and without temper—temper, by the way, does not become you, little Babs. You look quite thirty-five tonight—'

He paused abruptly, went to the hall door, opened it, looked out for a moment or two, closed the door almost to, and came back towards her.

'Bit risky leaving that door ajar,' he said easily. 'The bobby on the beat might be curious enough to come in and have a look round. Awkward, that. Better have the hinges, or whatever it is that makes the row when you close it, attended to, hadn't you, before our next midnight conference . . . Or better still, come across with that thou . . . and let us cut the midnight conferences right out.'

'You promised—you gave me your solemn word that if I made you those four payments of a hundred and fifty, you would give me back my letters and the other things—'

'I know. I know, my dear. Why remind me of my absurd impulsiveness. Forget what has been said—concentrate on the fact that what I say now is . . . a thou.'

'You never meant to keep your promise then?'

'Yes, yes, yes. Until I realised how foolishly impulsive I had been in asking for six hundred when I might have asked for ten.'

'I see. And so it will go on, you think. You think you will always be able to bleed me—that I shall always be coward enough and fool enough to pay this blackmail?'

'Hush, my dear child . . . Hush, hush.'

'It *is* blackmail. . . nothing more or less . . . You are nothing more or less than a common blackmailer—a blackguard that preys on wretched, foolish women who—'

He held up a hand, unruffled, smiling, yet menacing.

'My darling child . . . what an ugly vocabulary you have acquired of late. No, no, no. Let us be polite. Let us not be melodramatic. Let us be quite sensible. Above all, let us not shout . . . at half-past one in the morning. Besides, we really have nothing more to say to one another, tonight. I feel that. I am very sensitive to such impressions. You require, I feel, time to reflect. Tomorrow—or perhaps next day—when you have thought things over quietly and sensibly, you will send me a good-tempered little message to say that—'

'No,' she cried vehemently, forgetting caution. 'This is the end of it. I will have nothing more to do with you. I knew that you were a scoundrel—an unscrupulous blackguard. I know now that you are a liar and a cheat as well. I will have nothing more to do with you. Do your worst—I don't care what it is. Nothing could be worse than what I have gone through already.'

'Worse for yourself, you mean, my little Babs—don't you? But what about poor hubby? What would poor straight-laced, stick-in-the-mud hubby say, suppose someone were spiteful enough to—'

His suave, sneering voice was silenced abruptly. Mutely, savagely, she had struck him a swinging buffet on the mouth that had jerked his head back and sent him stumbling against the long oak settle at the opposite side of the hall.

'Damn you, you little devil—you'll pay for that.'

He stooped to pick up his fallen hat, tossed it on to the settle, and turned then again to her threateningly. She made no attempt to retreat from him as he moved towards her, but stood against the wall beside the door of the dining-room defiantly, one hand behind her.

'You horrible cad,' she panted, 'how dare you even speak of my husband? How dare an evil, hateful thing like you even think of him? Listen . . . I have done with you. I don't care what happens. Before you leave this house you shall give me those letters . . . or I swear to you I will take them from you. Mind . . . I have warned you . . . Don't tempt me too far . . .'

He eyed her for a moment, calculatingly, from behind his insolent smile.

'Sorry, eh? Threats, eh? I see. Well—'

He turned, as if to pick up his hat, but swung round again instantly with such treacherous swiftness that she could not elude him. His hand caught her wrist, twisted something from her grasp. He released her again then, stepping back and watching her warily as he laughed derisively.

'Take care, my dear . . . take care. That temper of yours will get you into serious trouble if you don't keep it under. Ugly words are hard enough to bear, but I draw the line at poisoned knives absolutely. I take it that you realise that this interesting little instrument *is*—or was at one time—poisoned . . . and that you realised, therefore, that if you had succeeded in giving me a jab with it, as you attempted to do just now . . . I say, as you attempted to do just now—'

He glanced over his shoulder quickly towards the hall door, then turned back to her again.

'I thought that door moved. The wind, I suppose. Yes, my dear. You must try to keep that temper of yours under control. Nasty thing, murder, you know—or even attempted murder. You don't deny, then, that you knew this knife was poisoned—that the slightest prick from it would probably do me in in a few minutes? You understand, don't you, why I am impressing these facts on you—facts which, I am afraid, it is going to cost you a great deal more than that thou we spoke about just now to induce me to forget. . . after all. Meanwhile—until that happy termination of a really quite seriously unpleasant incident is reached—I think I shall keep this little plaything as a souvenir. You'll remember that I have it, won't you? And what it means? Good-night, my dear. Think over things calmly—take two days to it—three if you don't feel sensible enough at the end of two—and send me a little message to say that you feel disposed to talk business—not sentiment. Shall we say now—in consideration of the little occurrence just now—two further instalments of two-fifty, eh? Good-night. My love to hubby. Think *how* nice it will be to have no more secrets from him—to feel that you are really and truly worthy of his love. Sweet dreams . . .'

He slipped the knife, which he had inserted carefully in its beaded sheath, into an inner pocket, kissed hands to her airily, and went out.

One thing only was clear to Melhuish, as he watched his wife rouse herself after a moment and shut the hall door with elaborate pains to subdue the protest of its stiffness; she must tell him her story unasked—without compulsion—without the least suspicion that he had spied upon the secret which she had chosen to keep from him. The very caution with which, after that display of reckless bravado, she strove to stifle the sound of the door's shutting was eloquent enough, significant enough. Already, rather than face his discovery of her secret by him, she had resigned herself again to the indignity and misery of purchasing this scoundrel's silence with regard to it. That alone was certain and definite—she desired . . . as strongly as that. . . that he should not know.

In the astonishing impressions which his ears and eyes had conveyed to his brain during those five or six minutes, tortured doubt still writhed hideously. But the fierce words which had followed that furious blow had assured him of one thing at least—not all of her was lost to him. His mind, agile and decisive in all other emergencies and dilemmas of his life, in this, the gravest of them, refused to move, refused to formulate any coherent thought or purpose save that one immediate need. She must not find him spying on her, lurking there in the darkness. He must have time to think, to realise, to recover judgment and balance, before her eyes met his. She had gone into the dining-room, to extinguish the lights there probably. Before she came out again he must reach his bedroom. The third stair up from the drawing-room landing had creaked as he had come down. He must be careful when he came to it.

4

The fog had grown so dense that, glancing across towards Aberdeen Place as he went on towards the pillar-box, Gore could distinguish nothing of the house to which his eyes had turned instinctively save the blurred illumination of its fanlight. Afterwards he recalled sardonically that his imagination had busied itself then for some moments with a charming, enviable picture of the happiness of the man of whose honourable, useful, contenting work that blurred light was the signal. Oddly enough, the figure which came out of the fog to meet him, just as he dropped his letters into the box, proved to be that of the very man of whose felicities, conjugal and otherwise, he had just been thinking.

'Hallo, doctor,' he said cheerily. 'No rest for the wicked then, tonight again?'

'No.'

'You getting back now—or just starting out?'

'Getting back,' Melhuish replied, as Gore, having turned about, fell into step beside him. 'A Mrs MacArthur rang me up to go and see her little boy. I've been attending him for a mild attack of gastritis. You don't know the MacArthurs, do you? They've only recently come to live here in Linwood.'

'MacArthur? No. Filthy sort of night, isn't it? Sort of night I should simply hate to be dragged out of bed if I'd once succeeded in getting there, personally. But I suppose you doctor-men get hardened to it. Why . . . that's Cecil Arndale, isn't it?'

The eyes of both men had converged to a tall figure in a light-coloured raincoat which had emerged hurriedly from a house some twenty yards ahead of them, and, after a quick glance in their direction, had set off at a sharp pace towards the Riverside, growing rapidly indistinct as it receded into the fog.

'It *was* Arndale, wasn't it?' Melhuish asked abstractedly. 'His wife's brother has a flat in one of these houses—Challoner. You probably remember him?'

'Bertie Challoner? Oh, yes. I remember Bertie very well indeed. An ingenuous youth. Yes. Mrs Arndale told me this evening that he had a flat somewhere along here. Seventy-three, she said, I think.'

The hall door from which Arndale had issued reopened as they reached it, and a large young man emerged from it so hastily that Gore and his companion only escaped collision with his formidable bulk by a fraction of a second. Recognising Melhuish, he laughed shortly and irritably.

'Hallo, doctor. That you? Where's that brother-in-law of mine got to? Oh—there he is. Hi! Cecil . . .'

But Arndale had now reached the end of Selkirk Place and was visible there for a moment in the light of the arc-lamp over the bar, before he turned to his right hand up the lane and disappeared. Bertie Challoner replaced his pipe between his teeth resentfully and turned to regard Melhuish's companion with an indifferent curiosity which changed abruptly to enthusiasm.

'Why . . . Great Scott!' he exclaimed, 'it's—'

He held out expansively an immense hand which Gore, recalling in time the trials of strength of other days, took very cautiously.

'It is,' he said. 'How are you, young fellah?'

'Fit. Come in and have a little drink. You must. I only heard tonight that you'd come home. I've been away for a few days. Come in and have a little drink, doctor, won't you?'

'Thanks, no, Challoner. I don't think so. Good-night. Goodnight again, Colonel.'

'Good-night, doctor.'

Challoner's gaze followed Melhuish's retreat for a moment or two before he turned to conduct Gore into his elaborately-equipped bachelor quarters on the ground floor—one of the flats into which Number 73, like many others of the big houses in Selkirk Place, had been divided since the war.

'Stiff old stick,' he muttered, with a grimace. 'Can't think why Pickles married him. You dined with the Melhuishs tonight, Arndale told me. That's a comfortable chair. I couldn't believe Arndale when he told me you had come home. Cigarettes? You look fit. How's things? Come back for good?'

'Not sure,' smiled Gore. 'England on a night like this is not alluring.'

'Filthy, isn't it? Enough to make a chap commit murder or suicide or anything, to look out there into that mouldy Green in a fog like this. You're staying at the Riverside, I hear. You look fit.'

'Thank you, Bertie. As that is the second time you have made that remark in sixty seconds, I presume I must regard it as deserved. As a matter of fact, you will be glad to learn, I *am* perfectly fit.'

Challoner smiled vaguely—indeed he had made no pretence whatever of listening—threw, considering the hour, a surprisingly large quantity of coal on the fire, stirred it noisily, sighed, and subsided into a big chair and a silence which became at length embarrassing. His healthy, brick-red face, good-looking in a rather massive, heavy way, boyish still in repose despite its owner's thirty years, assumed an expression of gloomy anxiety as its smile faded. Something had occurred to upset Master Bertie Challoner recently, Gore decided. He looked most unmistakably peeved and worried of mind.

'Look here, my dear chap,' said the visitor, preparing to take his departure. 'I'm sure you're wanting to get down to it, aren't you? I'll run in tomorrow morning sometime—'

But Challoner was visibly distressed by this reflection upon his hospitality.

'Not at all, not at all. I'm simply delighted to see you, Wick—you know I am. Go on—sit down again, old chap. I'm—I'm just a bit worried about something, that's all. Don't you bother about me. I shouldn't turn in for another good hour or so, anyhow. What sort of an evening did you have at the Melhuishs'? Pretty deadly, eh? Old Jimmy Wellmore, I hear—and the gashly Angela. I say, isn't she a weird old thing? I simply can't stick her. I'll swear she drinks or dopes or something.'

'You have a bad mind, young fellah,' grinned Gore. 'You always had. What a shocking thing to think of a lady who—well, she couldn't be your mother, I suppose, but at any rate she is sufficiently mature to claim your respect.'

Challoner laid aside the extinct pipe which he had been regarding for some moments with intense displeasure, selected another from a crowded rack, and blew into it exhaustively and morosely.

'I bet the old thing dopes,' he said doggedly. 'She's as yellow as a Chink. Weird old frump . . . Gets up at three o'clock in the day, Sylvia says, and floats round in a dressing-gown until she goes to bed again, playing with those filthy little yapping dogs of hers—things like that ought to be put into a lethal chamber . . . How d'you think Pickles looks?'

He replaced the pipe in the rack, lighted a cigarette, and flopped into his chair again disconsolately. 'This,' Gore reflected, 'is a little trying. I must get away before he unburdens his soul. A woman, of course—one of these fair creatures he's got in a row on his mantelpiece, I suppose.'

Aloud, he said, with decision, 'Very nice indeed. Quite the nicest person to look at I've seen since—well, since I saw her last, I believe. You got a game leg now, old chap?'

Challoner nodded absently.

'Bit. Had a baddish crash in nineteen-eighteen . . . What'd you think of Melhuish?'

Now a young man of Bertie Challoner's type must indeed be disturbed of soul, Gore told himself, if he declined an opportunity of dilating upon a game leg attributable to his share in the greatest of wars. Why this persistent desire to return to the Melhuishs' and their dinner party?

'Melhuish? Very nice. Very nice indeed. Not precisely . . . er . . . gushing. But a topping good chap, I should say.'

'Oh, he's all right, I suppose. Damn supercilious smile. Gets on my nerves. Sort of "You poor unfortunate ass, what *are* you alive for?" sort of smile. Not that I pretend to be exactly one of your brainy kind. I'm not.'

'No,' murmured the guest sympathetically.

'Still, just because he's a bit of a dab with a stethoscope, I don't see that he need treat every one who isn't as a worm. I bet Pickles often wishes she'd married old Cecil, after all.'

Gore deposited the ash of his cigarette in an ash-tray very, very carefully.

'Yes?' he said encouragingly. 'For a moment it had occurred to me to think of another substitute for her actual choice . . . Yes?'

'I suppose you know that Arndale *was* deadly keen about her, don't you?'

'Well, no. I can't say that I had known that. Though I suppose one may assume fairly safely that most of the young fellahs—*and* old fellahs, for that matter—in this part of the world—'

'Oh, yes. But old Arndale went all out for her, you know, until he found he hadn't a show. He was absolutely silly about her. You ask Sylvia. Sylvia knows jolly well that he only married *her* because she was such a pal of Pickles's. It's a fact. She'll tell you so herself without a blink. Of course Sylvia's my sister, and all that—and she and Arndale get on all right, as it has turned out—I mean, everything considered. But if you ask me, if it came to picking Sylvia or Pickles out of the water, tomorrow—well, I bet old Sylvia would feed the fishes.'

Gore smiled pleasantly and still more encouragingly upon this most candid of brothers.

'This,' he said, 'is most interesting. May I ask when this tragedy of unrequited love . . . came to a head, as it were?'

Challoner considered.

'When? Oh . . . it was going on for a couple of years before Arndale married Sylvia. Nineteen-thirteen-fourteen-fifteen . . . just before the war and during the first year or so of it. I remember Sylvia used to tell me about it in her letters when I went to France first. Both she and Pickles were rather fed up with Cecil because he hadn't joined up, I remember.'

Gore examined one of his host's cigarettes critically.

'These look about eighteen bob a hundred.'

'A quid,' said Challoner laconically. His guest sighed enviously and replaced the cigarette in the miniature silver trunk from which he had incautiously taken it.

'In another, better world, perhaps. In this, not for me. I'll smoke my old dhudeen, if I may.'

As he filled his pipe his eyes strayed again to the photographs on the mantelpiece—most of them feminine and picturesque, he noted appreciatively—and rested for a moment on that of a pretty if rather dejected-looking young woman in riding-kit which occupied a place of honour.

'I recognise some old friends among your little picture-gallery,' he said casually. 'That's little Ethel Melville in breeches, isn't it?—I beg her pardon . . . Mrs Barrington, I should say. Trying things, breeches, you know, Bertie. Very few of 'em can stand 'em. By the way, I met her husband this evening at the Melhuishs'.'

Challoner's big flaxen head swung round towards him sharply; his face had flushed a deeper shade of brick-red.

'Barrington?'

'Yes. Extraordinary good-looking fellah. Don't think I've ever seen a handsomer man in my life. Comes from Jamaica, doesn't he?'

'So he says.'

The visitor surveyed his host's profile thoughtfully. It was at that moment a profile of remarkable expressiveness.

'Yes? You think . . . er . . . that he doesn't?'

'I think,' said Challoner surlily, 'that if Barrington says he comes from Jamaica the chances are ten to one he doesn't. I think that. And I'll tell you another thing I think about Mr Barrington.'

He had risen to his feet again and was gesturing with a vehement hand.

'I think he's a damn scoundrel, Mr Barrington. I *know* he's one. I'm not going to tell you how I know it—or just what I know of him. All I say to you is this, Wick—and it's straight from the horse's mouth—don't you be taken in by that smarmy swine. Don't you have any truck with him, if you can help it. Keep clear of him. I tell you he's a real rotten bad 'un.'

Challoner's blue eyes were aglitter with anger now. His big blond head thrust forward, as he spoke, with a threatening belligerence. It was very clearly evident that he disapproved of Mr Barrington for some reason utterly and entirely.

'What does he do?' Gore inquired, after a moment. Quite unconsciously his eyes had strayed again to that large photograph which occupied the place of honour in the collection on the mantelpiece. A possible explanation of Master Bertie's vehement depreciation of Barrington had occurred to him.

'Do? Nothing. Nobody knows who he is, where he comes from, or anything about him. He was down at Barhams, at the Remount Depot, for a bit during the war—and then he turned up here again afterwards—managed to screw himself into the Amdales' set somehow. You can see for yourself what a plausible, come-hither sort of swine the beggar is—got to know every one here in Linwood—through the Arndales—got hold of Miss Melville somehow, and persuaded her to marry him— after her money, I needn't tell you. Though he got a bad drop there . . . And now . . . well. . . there he is—the kind of vermin no decent person would touch with a forty-foot pole if they knew what he really was—and yet, because he's been clever enough to bluff 'em he's a pukka sahib—and because he swindled Miss Melville into marrying him . . . all these silly asses here—people like the Arndales and the Melhuishs and the Wellmores, and so on—they all have him in their houses—allow him to run round with their womenfolk—golf with him, and play bridge with him at the club—and other little games afterwards—at his house. I could tell you a thing or two about that little sideline of his . . . If he asks you to drop in one night at Hatfield Place for a little game, Wick, my boy . . . you just go home to bed. You'll find it cheaper.'

'Dear me,' sighed Gore, 'I do hope that if I ever have a wife, no bad-minded young man will fall in love with her.'

Challoner flushed again—a fine, deep warm crimson, this time. Touched.

'You think I'm piling it on, Wick, because I don't like the chap.'

'Great Heavens, no.'

'Yes, you do. I can see you do. But by God I'll, tell you this much—if *you* knew what *I* know about Barrington—if he had tried to do to you what he has tried to do to me—if you had even an idea of the kind of blackguard that fellow is—you'd take a chance and do him in. I'm not joking. I'm not joking, Wick. I give you my solemn word—if I had the chance now, this moment, to blot him out—safely—to rid that dear little girl whose life with him is—'

He broke off abruptly, let the big clenched hand which he had shaken angrily, drop to his side, walked to the door of the room and came back.

'I'm talking a lot, old chap,' he said, with an unsuccessful attempt at a smile. 'Too much. I know what I've said won't go beyond you. It isn't that I should be afraid to say anything I've said to you now to Barrington's face any time—if it was merely a question of thinking of myself. But . . . he'd take it out of other people—if he heard. Just wash out what I've said. I'm a bit on the raw edge tonight.'

Gore rose.

'I believe you've known me for some little time, young fellah,' he said with mild reproach. 'Now, get to bed. You've been thinking too much, young Bertie. You were never meant for that sort of thing. Night-night.'

Challoner eyed him moodily for a moment.

'Well, I'm damn glad to see *you* again, anyhow,' he said at length. 'I'll walk down to the end of the road with you.'

They sauntered down Selkirk Place in the fog, arranging a morning's golf. Challoner's two-seater had gone into dock that afternoon with a big-end gone, he explained; but any of the boys would run them out the three miles to Flax ways.

'Thursday, then. I'll pick you up at the Riverside. There—' He took a hand from a trousers-pocket to wave it resentfully towards the red-brick building in front of them. 'Just to give you an idea of the sort of swine Barrington *is*. There's a little girl who looks after that bar down there. You may have seen her about the Riverside . . . Rather a pretty little thing—?'

'Miss Rodney?'

'Yes. That's her name. Betty Rodney. Brains of a chicken, but not a bad little thing if chaps like Barrington would leave her alone. Well. . . mind, this is quite between ourselves. I just happen to know. He has got that poor little kid into trouble. That's the sort of cur he is. I used to notice him hanging about round here late at night . . . I noticed his car first. He used to leave it just about here—I wondered what the devil he was up to at first, until one night, about a month ago, I heard him whistling up at her window. She sleeps over the bar, you see. And she came to that side-door and let him in. Silly little idiot. I believe she was to have been married to some chap or other, before Barrington came along and cut in. Now—well, I expect that's off now. Suppose they'll fire her from the Riverside, too, when they find out.'

'Oh,' said Gore, 'so that's the sort of gentleman Mr Barrington is. That's very interesting. You're quite sure about this girl, Bertie?'

Challoner laughed impatiently.

'Sure? I bet she's expecting him now. That's her window where the light is. It's always lighted up the nights he comes along.' He laughed sardonically. 'Though she won't see him tonight, I fancy. Oh, yes. I've been keeping a pretty close eye on Mr Barrington lately. I know what I'm talking about. Look here. If you don't believe me—I'll whistle under that window now. You'll see what happens. I know what I'm talking about, believe me.'

'My dear Bertie, I'll take your word for it—'

'No. I just want you to see for yourself. Get out of sight though. She'll look out of the window when she hears the whistle. I want her to come down to the door. Let's stand here. She can't see us here from the window.'

His big hands urged the reluctant Gore into the angle formed by the railings of the section of the Green abutting on the hotel-grounds and one of the pillars of the gates admitting to them. Then he whistled softly. A large, very wet drop fell from an overhanging branch upon the nape of Gore's neck and descended inside his collar. The dead leaves collected under the trees inside the railings and in the angle of the roadway by the gates emitted an odour of dismal dankness. The trunks of the trees looked disagreeably slimy. The fog smelt and tasted of decaying vegetation. One of Gore's still new evening-shoes had pinched him a good deal during the evening and was pinching him quite uncomfortably now. Its toe stirred a little mound of leaves collected against the foot of the gate-pillar with some impatience.

'Gone to bed and forgotten to switch off her light, old chap,' he said. 'Serve us right. Let's get to bed.'

A small glistening object, revealed by the disturbance of the leaves at his feet, had attracted his attention—the vague attention of a sleepy man awaiting against his will the *dénouement* of a rather silly practical joke. As he stooped idly to pick it up, he heard the door beside the bar open cautiously and straightened himself again as Miss Rodney came into sight round the angle of the wall and halted abruptly upon perceiving him and his companion.

Challoner smiled at her grimly.

'Good-night, Miss Rodney. Not in bed yet?'

She hesitated, plainly disconcerted; then decided upon haughty flippancy.

'Looks like it, doesn't it, Mr Challoner?' she said tartly, and disappeared, remembering, however, to close the door as softly as she had opened it.

'You see,' said Challoner.

'I see,' said Gore. 'Though I'm bound to say that Miss Rodney's little amoors leave me cold.'

He yawned without the faintest attempt at concealment as he stooped and picked up the little glistening object which had attracted his attention amongst the leaves, and twiddled it between his fingers. Challoner however, displayed no resentment of his indifference nor any eagerness to adopt his advice as to getting to bed.

He stood frowning, apparently lost in thought, until Gore turned to leave him.

'I say, old chap,' he asked abruptly, 'what time was it when you broke up at the Melhuishs'?'

'About a quarter to twelve.'

'Barrington left then—at a quarter to twelve?'

'Yes. He and I came away together. Why?'

'Nothing. I just wanted to know. Was he walking, or driving?'

'Walking. At least I saw no car about, when I left him in Aberdeen Place.'

'Oh,' Challoner said musingly, 'then he must have gone home on foot from the Melhuishs'—and taken his car out then . . . It was after one when Arndale said he saw it in Aberdeen Place.'

Despite his sleepiness and his aching toes, Gore's interest in Mr Barrington's nocturnal wanderings revived sharply.

'In Aberdeen Place?' he repeated.

'Yes. Arndale told me he saw it there then—somewhere near the Melhuishs' door. He must have gone home and taken it out—if you're sure you didn't see it there when he went away from the Melhuishs' with you.'

Gore was to discover subsequently the reason for which the hour at which Barrington had reached home that night and taken out his car was of such interest to his companion. For him, at the moment, the point possessed no interest whatever beside the information that Barrington's car had been in the neighbourhood of the Melhuishs' hall door at the hour at which Arndale apparently had seen it there . . . after one o'clock. So he had gone, then—and found the door open, presumably . . . Left his car near the door, too, to advertise the affair to anyone who might happen to see it and recognise it... as Arndale had done—

'Well, good-night, Bertie,' he said curtly, and turned so that his companion might not see his face.

'Good-night, Wick. Mind—mum's the word, old chap.'

Gore crossed the hotel-grounds, and, finding the door of the annexe still open, gained his own quarters that way. Before he took off his overcoat one of the hands which explored its pockets mechanically drew out the small object which he had picked up near the gates. He stared at it in astonishment. It was a little hide knife-sheath, thickly ornamented with coloured beads— exactly like the sheaths of those two little Masai knives which had been included in his wedding-present to Pickles, and which he had seen a couple of hours before hanging in Melhuish's hall.

He examined the thing carefully. Obviously it had not lain for any length of time amongst the damp leaves in which he had discovered it. It appeared to him too improbable a conjecture to surmise that chance should have brought to that spot—a bare hundred yards from the other two—a third such sheath. Common sense assured him that there was no third sheath—that this was one of the two which he had touched with a finger to draw the attention of Melhuish and Barrington to it.

How, then, had the blessed thing got out of Melhuish's hall, across the road, and into that heap of leaves in the comer by the gates?

And the knife that should, for all prudence sake, have been in the sheath—where was that?

For a little while he pondered over the matter drowsily, half-minded to go out again and look about for the knife. But it was now getting towards half-past two. He smoked a final cigarette before his dying fire cheerlessly, and went to bed.

5

He lunched next day with some friends out at Penbury, and was subsequently inveigled into participation in a hockey-match, in the course of which an enthusiastic curate inflicted such grievous injury upon one of his shins that he was compelled to abandon his intention of walking the four miles back to Linwood, and returned a full hour earlier than he had expected, in his host's car. A page stopped him in the hall of the hotel to deliver a message received by telephone at two o'clock. Would Colonel Gore please ring up Linwood 7420 immediately upon his return, as Mrs Melhuish wished to speak to him urgently. Mrs Melhuish had been informed that Colonel Gore was not expected back until five o'clock, and had seemed annoyed, the page said. He had personally undertaken, if Colonel Gore returned before five, to ask him to ring up Linwood 7420 at once.

'Urgently . . .' Gore repeated to himself, as he limped to the telephone-cabinet. 'Urgently . . .?'

An odd premonition of misfortune chilled him momentarily. The cheerful activities of his afternoon, the mob of light-hearted young people in whose company he had spent it, had banished most of the rather gloomy pessimism which had clouded his morning. But it was with an anxiety which he was quite unable to control that he awaited the reply to his call—an anxiety which increased sharply at the first sound of her voice.

'Is that you, Wick? Can you come across here—now—at once? I must see you. I can't explain over the phone. Can you come?'

'Of course. My collar is a ruin—my boots are unspeakable—I've been playing hockey—'

'Never mind. Never mind. Don't wait to change. Please come at once.'

'Coming right now.'

The dusk was deepening to darkness as he limped down Albemarle Hill and up Aberdeen Place to the door of Number 33. It opened to admit a patient and let out another as he came up to it. Melhuish's busy time, of course—from two to six—the hour at which he would be out of the way... Gore's depression deepened a shade.

He waited in the hall for a moment or two while Clegg ushered the incoming patient into the waiting-room and summoned from it the next in turn for the consulting-room. His eyes strayed to the trophy on the wall facing him, and instantly his memory recalled the sheath which he had found the night before by the back entrance to the Riverside. One of the two knives which had formed the lower apex of the trophy was missing. How the blazes had its sheath found its way to that heap of leaves?

'Mrs Melhuish is in the morning-room, sir,' said Clegg, pausing as the elderly lady whose name he had called emerged slowly from the waiting-room on the arm of a companion. 'That door, sir, on the first landing. If you would kindly go up, sir.'

The room was in darkness when Gore entered, save for the glow of the fire before which she sat in a low chair, leaning forward, her chin cupped in her hands. She looked up eagerly.

'Shut that door, Wick,' she commanded. 'And then come and sit down here. I want you not to look at me. That's why I've switched off the lights. I'm in a most shocking mess.'

He obeyed her silently, seating himself, when he had shut the door, so that he, too, faced the glow of the fire.

'I rang you up,' she said, after a moment, 'because I thought it just possible you might be able to help me out of it. Jolly cool, I expect you'll think. But even if you do, I know you'll listen to me. I simply must tell someone about it. And I could think of no one but you.'

'Carry on,' he said quietly. 'What kind of a mess is it? Money—or a man?'

'Both,' she said curtly. 'It's simply a shocking mess.'

'Told your husband about it?'

'Heavens, no.'

'That's bad. Why not?'

'I couldn't. I've tried to screw myself up to do it—to tell him everything. But I can't. I know he'd never forgive me . . . in his heart . . . even if the outside of him pretended to forgive me; He's the best—the noblest man I have ever known. You can't know, Wick, how good and fine he is. But. . . he'd never forgive . . . this.'

'Rot,' said Gore succinctly. 'Piffle. Humbug.'

She made a little wretched gesture.

'Ah, you've no idea what an idiot I've been, Wick.'

'I wonder.'

'You wonder?'

Her face turned to him sharply in the twilight.

'No, no,' he assured her quietly. 'No one has told me anything. My wonder is merely the result of my own, I'm afraid, rather impertinent observation . . . and, if you'll permit me to say so, your own infernal carelessness, young woman. I heard—you really compelled me to hear—a remark which you made last night, practically in my ear—not to me—but to . . . er . . . someone else.'

'My God!' she said in alarm, 'you heard—What did I say?'

'Er . . . something about a door, which might possibly not be open, you thought, but which Mr . . . er . . . the gentleman to whom you made the remark . . . seemed to think *would* be open.'

'My God!' she said again, her hands twisting nervously. 'Did Lady Wellmore hear?'

'I hope not. I think not. Though that's not your fault. Then, the man is Mr Barrington?'

'Yes.'

There was a silence. Gore rose to his feet abruptly, walked to the door, and flooded the room with light.

'Well, Pickles, all I have to say to you—and I prefer to say it to your face, please—is this. You're the silliest kind of silly ass. Mind—I know very little about this chap Barrington—can't say I care much for most of what I do know. But if he were the best man that ever stepped—and he isn't that—I should say just the same thing to you. Sorry I can't be more sympathetic. I presume you expected I should be. But, as a confidant of illicit love- affairs, I'm afraid I'm rather a wash-out.'

She turned back upon him with a movement of exasperation.

'Oh, don't be a fool, Wick,' she said sharply. 'Good Heavens . . . I'm not that sort of idiot.'

'Not that sort of idiot?' he repeated. 'Then may I ask what sort of idiot you are?'

'Sit down. Don't fidget about that way. I'll tell you the whole thing—right from the beginning . . . It began this way. I met Mr Barrington four years ago . . . and . . . well, I had an affair with him . . . I didn't know Sidney then—I hadn't met him. He had only just come to Linwood, and I hadn't come across him. If I had . . . well, this would never have happened . . .'

'Suppose . . . er . . . we keep to what did happen . . .?'

'I met Mr Barrington—he was Captain Barrington then—at a gymkhana got up by the Remount Depot people at Barhams. There was a Remount Depot out there, you know. He was stationed there then—in the summer of nineteen-eighteen.

He won all sorts of things that afternoon—he's a magnificent horseman—and, well, I was introduced to him and fell in love with him on the spot—that's the long and the short of it—over head and ears the very first moment he spoke to me. You don't understand that sort of thing. I know it will seem just silly to you—'

'No, no, no. I've known it to happen before. Carry on.'

'Well, it lasted for just five months—'

'Five months is quite a long time. And then . . . it stopped?'

'Yes. Something happened—and suddenly I saw what a frightful idiot I had been. It stopped then—very abruptly. He went away for a bit—when the depot was broken up—in the January of nineteen-nineteen. Then, a few months later, when he had been demobbed, he came back here again . . . to live. He had a flat at first in York Gardens, until he married and moved to Hatfield Place. He married Ethel Melville that spring—the very week I met Sidney. Of course I had to come across him. I couldn't avoid it. I had known Ethel Melville all my life, and of course I had to call and dine with them and ask them to dine here, and so on. He was always at the Arndales' house . . . In fact I ran into him and Ethel everywhere I went. However, he was always just polite—you know?—just like any other man one met. I thought at that time that the whole thing was done with—that he had done with me. But he hadn't. He hasn't. And that's the mess.'

Gore shrugged his shoulders.

'I suppose I'm more stupid than usual, or something. What, in the name of Heaven, *is* the mess?'

'I'm not going into lurid details, Wick. You've got to try to understand that girls—even girls who are supposed, by misguided people like yourself, to be quite nice girls—are liable to be swept off their feet absolutely . . . if they happen just to have the bad luck to come across . . . a certain sort of man . . . the sort of man that Mr Barrington is. You can understand yourself, can't you . . . that he is the sort of man who would sweep a girl off her feet?'

'Yes, yes.'

'When I say sweep off her feet . . . I mean . . . well . . . the limit. You're such an old dear that I know you'll hardly believe that I could be capable of the limit. I'm afraid I am . . . or rather, was. At any rate . . . on a certain night in December, nineteen- eighteen, I got as near to it as doesn't matter—with Mr Barrington's kind assistance. Don't look so unconvincing, Wick. I know you're shocked to the marrow . . . However . . . there it is. By the merest fluke, I stopped there and had a good look at things. And nothing happened. Which was a jolly sight more than I deserved. Delightfully candid, am I not? I assure you there isn't another man in the world upon whom I would inflict my candour so lavishly . . . if that is any consolation . . .'

'Good. Let's get to the 'osses.'

'Well... as I say . . . nothing did happen. But nobody, you see . . . as things were . . . would believe that. That's the trouble. Most of it, anyhow. I was fool enough . . . mad enough . . . to stay a night at a hotel at Bournemouth—with Mr Barrington . . . just before Christmas, nineteen-eighteen.'

Gore stared at her blankly.

'Hell, Pickles,' he said at length softly, 'what did you do that for?'

'I was infatuated with him, then. That's the only word for it. I adored him—I thought of nothing, cared for nothing, wanted nothing . . . except to be with him. It seems extraordinary to me now . . . but—Well, that's what happened, anyhow. I stayed a night at the Palatine at Bournemouth with him . . . as Mrs Barrington. If you care to take the trouble to go down to Bournemouth and ask them to let you look at the register for the date December 17th, 1918, you'll see my beautiful handwriting. He was clever enough to make me sign— Trust him.' 'But . . . how the . . .?' Gore burst out after some moments of silent consternation.

'How did I manage it? Oh, it was quite simple. I was still V.A.D.-ing at Lucey Court then. They thought I had gone home for the weekend. He had intended that we should stay the whole weekend at Bournemouth, you see. However . . . we didn't. As I say, by the mercy of Providence, I had the sense to stop and take a good look at things just in time . . . Mr Barrington included. He lost his temper . . . and I had a glimpse of what he was like . . . really . . . I came home next day.'

'Look here,' said Gore desperately, 'I *must* smoke a pipe. If I don't I shall start in to break up the furniture or something.'

'Yes, yes. Give me a cigarette. You're sure you shut that door properly?

'. . . Well, I thought I had done with him—though, of course, I feared all along that he might have kept my letters. But time went by, and—you know the way things that have happened dull off and stop worrying you. I had met Sidney. . . that helped me to forget about things I didn't want to remember, too . . . We were married for a whole year before anything happened to make me in the least uneasy. And then one day Mr Barrington rang me up and said, "I want to see *you*. I shall be on the Downs, somewhere along the avenue, at half-past two. You'd better come along and see me." Of course I refused at first, and, of course, in the end I got frightened and went. He was very hard up—that was his story at first. . . quite a polite, apologetic sort of story. Could I lend him a hundred pounds? I lent him a hundred pounds. Then I lent him another hundred. Then he asked for two hundred. I made a fuss—not that the money mattered so much, but because I had begun to realise by that time that he was not simply borrowing money from me, but demanding it. However, I gave him the two hundred—and, of course, he saw then that he had me—that I was afraid of him. And so it has gone on ever since, for two years. I think he has had about fifteen hundred pounds altogether, so far. Fifteen or sixteen, I'm not sure which. Sidney never dreams of asking me what I do with my own money . . . but of course I've been jolly careful in drawing the cheques for the money I paid away that way. So that I can't be quite sure now myself. But it's fifteen hundred at any rate.

'Then I thought that if I gave him a really large sum, in one lump, he might be persuaded to give me back my letters. The letters are the trouble, you see. He said he would if I gave him six hundred. I agreed to that—that was about a fortnight or so ago. I agreed to make four payments of a hundred and fifty each, spread over two or three weeks. I was afraid to draw out so much money at once—because, of course, he insisted on being paid in cash.'

'He would,' Gore agreed grimly.

'He insisted also on coming here to the house at night for the money. Of course, like a fool, I consented to that too, in the end. Though I might have known that his idea was to use that, afterwards, as an additional hold over me. But I gave way to him. I would have agreed to anything to get my letters back and have done with it. He came three nights and got a hundred and fifty each time. Last night he came again—I gave him the last hundred and fifty, and then he refused to give up the letters after all—said I must give him another four hundred— My God, Wick . . . what am I to do? What *am* I to do? It's killing me. I shall go silly if it goes on much longer.'

He made no reply for a little space, stifling an inevitable inclination to sit in judgment and to consider what this ugliness just revealed to him meant to him rather than what it must have meant to her who had lived with it for two years. It was no moment for sentiment or for virtuous comment, he reminded himself. Facts were facts and must be faced—however ugly and disillusioning. Had he got all of them, even yet?

'The letters are . . . very awkward?'

'Very. Those I wrote to him after the episode at Bournemouth especially.'

'You mean . . . a third person who read them would realise that the Bournemouth episode had taken place?'

'Yes.'

'Um. Well, then, you've got to get them back, that's clear, somehow. Unless you face the music and tell your husband? . . .'

She shook her head.

'No. I'd rather kill myself, Wick. In fact, I've been seriously thinking of killing myself all day.'

He grinned.

'The more seriously the better . . .'

'No. I'm not merely talking about it for the sake of talking about it. I'm not that sort, Wick. I could do it quite easily. Sidney has plenty of things in his consulting-room. All I have to do is sneak his keys. After all—what is it—to kill oneself? What is anything—if you once make up your mind to it? Things seem big and imposing and terrible and difficult . . . just to think of. But when you come to do them, they're just a little movement of your hand or your tongue or your throat . . . nothing. Who, to look at *me*, would think for a moment that I could deliberately try to kill someone else? No one. And yet I did try, last night—tried deliberately. I didn't succeed, as it happened. But do you think it seemed anything to me while I was trying to do it? Nothing. The simplest, flattest thing in the world. My dear man, if I once make up my mind to do myself in, I shall do it like a bird. And about the best thing I could do, it seems to me.'

'Yes, yes. However—to keep to brass tacks. Do I understand you to say, seriously, that you made an attempt to do Mr Barrington in last night—while he was here—in this house?'

'Yes. I tried to stab him with one of those little poisoned knives—you know . . . the things you were talking of to Sidney last night in the hall . . .'

'*What?*'

'Yes. I heard what you said to Sidney. I was on the stairs, just outside this room, while you were talking about them. I remembered, then, afterwards. If I had been just a shade quicker . . . well, I suppose I should have been in gaol by this time. But I should have got my letters and burnt them. There would have been plenty of time—at least I thought there would have been— before anyone came down and found him in the hall . . . All the night. And so Sidney would never have known. I meant just to give him a scratch. I heard you say a little prick would be enough. I should have had to fudge up some story—but I'm quite capable of *doing* that.'

Her matter-of-factness staggered him. He drew a long breath. 'Phew . . .'

For a little while he paced to and fro between the fireplace and the door.

'What happened? He took the knife from you, I suppose?'

'Yes. I was trying to get it out of the little cover or sheath or whatever you call it . . . behind my back. And he grabbed my wrist and took it from me.'

'Did he take it away with him?'

'Yes.'

'The knife *and* the sheath?'

'Yes. Both. He put the knife into the sheath before he put it into his pocket. Why?'

'Because, last night, about a quarter-past two or thereabouts, I found the sheath lying on the ground among some leaves, over there beside the gates leading into the hotel grounds. He must have thrown it away when he got outside. No, though. He had his car outside—just near your hall door, by the way—'

She uttered an exclamation of dismay. Then her eyes hardened in suspicion.

'How do you know that? How do you know his car was there?'

'Arndale told Challoner he saw it there a little after one o'clock . . . and Challoner told me . . . and Heaven knows how many other people since. However . . . to return to this confounded sheath. Barrington wouldn't take his car over there into that corner, would he? That's the one direction he wouldn't take it. To get to Hatfield Place from here, he'd go along Aberdeen Place or Selkirk Place—I don't know, though. Perhaps he went up that lane over there at the back of the hotel, and chucked the knife away as he passed the gates . . . into the Green. Yes. He might have done that. Though why exactly he should throw the knife away . . .'

She shook her head with conviction.

'No. He wouldn't throw it away. I'm quite sure of that. He put it away in his pocket carefully before he went out of the hall. He intended to keep it—he told me so—to hold it over me. I know he meant to keep it. I can't think how you can have—You found only the sheath?'

'Only the sheath. Of course the knife may have been lying about there, too, somewhere. I didn't see it. But then I didn't look for it. Of course I ought to have. I'll go across there now and have a look round. Hasn't anyone noticed that the beastly thing is missing from the hall yet, by the way?'

'Yes. Clegg noticed it this morning. I heard him telling Sidney about it as he was going out after breakfast.'

'Didn't your husband wonder what had become of it?'

'No. He merely told Clegg to ask the other servants if they knew what had become of it. I don't suppose he'll ever think of it again. He never worries about things of that sort. If he does, well . . . no one knows anything about it. It will be only another lie for me. That's nothing. I'm an expert liar now.' 'There's only one kind of liar, Pickles—and that's a damn bad one. I present you with that precious chunk of wisdom free gratis and for nothing.'

She laughed bitterly.

'My dear man, do you think I believe for a moment that Sidney doesn't know I've told him heaps and heaps of lies? Do you think anyone could deceive Sidney? You just try. He isn't a dear simple old Muggins like you, whom any woman or anyone could bamboozle. If you knew what agony it is for me now— downright agony—to look him in the face—'

'But. . . you don't think he knows anything about this entanglement of yours with Barrington, do you? Not that that wouldn't be the very best thing that could possibly happen—'

'I don't know,' she said miserably. 'Sometimes—sometimes I catch Sidney looking at me sometimes so oddly . . .

'Then I persuade myself that it's impossible . . . that if he knew anything, he'd say so at once and have it out with me. I don't know what to think. I just keep on trying not to think— trying to wriggle along somehow . . .just like a worm wriggling in clay . . . blind . . . not knowing whether it's being watched or not . . . crawling round and round in the old bit of mud. I know I'm bound to get caught in the end. I jolly nearly got caught last night, as a matter of fact. I had hardly got upstairs to my room, after Mr Barrington had gone away, before I heard Sidney go downstairs and go out. I suppose—I hope—someone had rung him up on the telephone . . . He has a night-telephone in his bedroom, you know . . . though I didn't hear the bell ring. He made no reference to his going out at breakfast this morning . . . naturally I didn't either. But I was simply scared stiff when I heard him leaving his room. I thought he must have heard us talking in the hall and got up and dressed—perhaps to follow Mr Barrington—'

'What time was that? When did Barrington go away?'

'I'm not sure. About half-past one or so, I should say.'

'How soon after that did your husband go out?'

'About ten minutes afterwards, I suppose. Perhaps not quite so long.'

'Oh, well then, I can tell you where he went. I met him last night about twenty-five minutes to two over in Selkirk Place. I'd gone out to post some letters. He told me that he'd been called out to some Mrs MacArthur's little boy . . .'

'Oh,' she said, relieved. 'Then that's all right. Another day to live. Hip-hip-hooray.'

'Oh, damn it, Pickles,' he muttered unhappily. 'Pull yourself together.'

He seated himself again and chewed the stem of his pipe in silence for a little while. Outside darkness had long fallen. Better go back to the hotel and get his pocket-torch, he reflected, before he began hunting about for the knife. If Barrington had thrown it away—it was quite possible that second thoughts had induced him to do so—the knife and sheath might very well have been separated, either in the air, or by collision with the ground or a tree or the railings. Possibly the knife had fallen in the Green inside the railings. It would be a simple matter to climb the railings in the darkness; fortunately they were of no great height.

But—what a mess . . .

And what an escape . . .

Suppose she *had* succeeded in giving the brute a jab, or even a scratch, with the thing— Suppose he had died down there in the hall, as that Masai boy had died—thrashing about on the ground in agony, shrieking— She had never even thought of that, apparently—had fancied, probably, that death would come to him noiselessly and without warning. Good Lord—what an escape for her . . .

He turned *to* look at her, discreetly, as she sat leaning forward, staring at the fire, her chin again gathered in her hands. Deliberately he tried to take an impartial, dispassionate view of her, to eliminate the special, mysterious, incalculable quality of her that had, as long as he could remember her, made her for him . . . different. But even as he strove to strip his witch of her magic, he realised how potent it was—how little a thing that could be amputated by cold-blooded common sense or colder-blooded morality. What she had just told him ought, both common sense and morality assured him, to have almost completely obliterated her glamour for him. As a matter of fact, it had not affected it in the very least. He had simply perceived for himself once more the familiar fact that, in a human system of values—and Wick Gore was a very human person indeed— not the thing done, but the person who did it, mattered.

Her inappropriateness to the part which she had played in this disconcerting narrative of hers was almost ludicrous. It would have been difficult, he told himself, to have imagined a more perfect type, a more satisfying presentment—so far as externals went—of the absolutely 'nice' young married Englishwoman. From the tip of her sprucely-waving golden head to the toes of her smartly-sensible shoes, her orderly freshness and daintiness were without blemish—an estate of jealously-guarded, minutely-vigilant propriety—sweet, sound English womanliness, scrupulously-groomed, meticulously decked for the afternoon. And yet, behind that secure, orthodox façade of 'niceness', these tempestuous passions had swirled and eddied—eddied and swirled now. He was too shrewd to be far misled by the casual, stereotyped phrases of the modern young woman's dialect. Beneath them he had had skill enough to detect the stir of the oldest, starkest of human stresses and strains. Love and Hate and Fear had had their way with her. That little mouth, whose lips were set now so coldly, had all but given the kiss of final surrender to one lover, all but betrayed another. That little hand, whose slim fingers upheld her chin childwise, had all but dealt murder. Amazing! And yet he was not amazed—save, indeed, by the knowledge that nothing she could do would ever amaze him in the least.

She turned to him at length, impatiently.

'Can't you suggest *anything*, Wick? I don't care what it costs—so far as money is concerned—so long as I get those letters of mine back. Couldn't you—wouldn't you see him, and try to force him to give them up? I mean—you're a man. You might be able to frighten him . . .'

'I'm perfectly willing to try, of course,' he said gravely. 'Though frankly it seems to me that even if you do get your letters back, he'll still have you in a very nasty place. That hotel-register down at Bournemouth, for instance? . . . How do you propose to get rid of that? Suppose, even, that he does actually part with your letters—what's to prevent his coming along to you the very next day and saying, "Look here. I want another five hundred. If I don't get it, I'm afraid your husband's going to find out that you stayed at the Palatine Hotel at Bournemouth on such-and-such a date as my wife." Well . . . what are you going to do then?

'However . . . I'll see the gentleman, if you wish, and have a preliminary talk about the matter with him at any rate. It may do some good . . . or it may do quite a lot of harm. What's his number in Hatfield Place? Twenty-seven, isn't it?'

'Yes. When will you see him?'

'I can go and see him now. Ring up first and find out if he's at home—and go round straightaway if he is.'

'I wish you would, Wick,' she said gratefully. 'You *are* a dear old thing. It would be such a relief if I could know that there was even a chance of escaping from this nightmare before I go to Surrey.' 'You're going away to Surrey?'

'Yes. Tomorrow. I'm going up to the Hescotts for Georgie's wedding. Of course I could cancel it. But Georgie would be most frightfully hurt. She was one of my bridesmaids, you see— And, of course, we've always been tremendous pals. I was so sure that all my troubles were to end last night. Do you really think you could see Mr Barrington this afternoon?'

'I'll go and ring him up now, if I may. Where's your telephone?'

'I'll show you.'

She rose to her feet, visibly consoled by relief from the despair of inaction.

'If you don't see him this afternoon—'

'I'll see him some time today. You may rely upon that.'

The murmur of voices on the stairs halted him as he opened the door.

'The Barracombes,' said Mrs Melhuish impatiently. 'Barracombes?'

'General Barracombe's girls. They live next door.'

Two fashionably-attired young women appeared in breathless excitement.

'Barbara, dear,' exclaimed one, 'such a dreadful thing has happened poor Mr Barrington! Janet and I have just found him sitting in his car, just outside our door . . . dead.'

'At least we're nearly sure he's dead,' broke in her sister. 'Your husband has gone out to him. We came at once to get him to go out. Isn't it dreadful? Of course, he may be only unconscious—he may have had a fainting fit or something like that. My dear, I'm positively shaking all over. It gave me such a shock. You see, we spoke to him—at least Hilda spoke to him, and he didn't answer. And then I thought he looked queer, somehow . . . and I got up on the footboard and touched his arm. I saw then by his face—'

Her sister checked her. Mrs Melhuish had gone very white suddenly and caught at a chair to steady herself.

'There—now we've frightened you, rushing in this way. Perhaps it *is* only a fainting fit or something like that. Though I don't think so. Do you, Janet?'

'No. I touched his hand. Oh . . . I shall never forget how deadly cold it felt. I'm sure he's dead.'

She shuddered luxuriously, rearranging her furs.

Mrs Melhuish had recovered her composure now.

'How dreadful,' she murmured. 'This is a very old friend of mine . . . Colonel Gore.'

The two young women—they were obviously the kind of sisters who existed in duet—produced beaming smiles of perhaps a second's duration, and then eclipsed them again to a becoming solemnity. Janet Barracombe stole to the door to peep down into the hall from behind the *portière*. Her sister stole after her.

'They're bringing him in,' she whispered, absorbed.

'Bringing him in?' Mrs Melhuish repeated faintly. Her eyes sought Gore's, flickered to the two figures at the door, returned to his.

'His pockets,' she whispered. 'Try. The inside ones.'

He nodded and moved towards the door.

'He had a bad heart, poor chap, I believe,' he said quietly. 'They may want a hand to carry him in.'

He shut the door of the room behind him as he left it. But the Barracombes were not to be denied; he heard it open again before he was half-way down the stairs to the hall.

'Looks as if the Lord did take some interest in our little affairs after all,' he reflected to himself grimly.

But he was to revise that impression, as events proved, somewhat extensively.

6

The weight of their burden had obviously proved too great for Melhuish and Clegg, and the latter was examining one of his hands ruefully as his master bent over the figure stretched temporarily on the long oak seat near the hall door. Melhuish looked up as Gore approached them from the foot of the stairs, stared a moment as if surprised by his appearance, then nodded a grave greeting and lowered his eyes again to the face that looked up at him with a hideously distorted grin. A glimpse of that face rendered the question on Gore's tongue unnecessary. The glassy, staring eyes, the lips drawn back in a dog-like rictus that showed all the even white teeth, were beyond all possibility of doubt those of a dead man. Yet, because he could think of nothing else to say, Gore asked the question.

'Is he dead, doctor?'

Melhuish nodded again gravely.

'Yes, poor fellow. I suppose the Barracombes have told my wife, have they?'

'Yes. It has given Mrs Melhuish rather a nasty shock, I'm afraid. Heart, I suppose?'

'Yes, yes,' said Melhuish, turning to shut the hall door. 'He lived on the edge of the precipice, poor fellow.'

'He's dead right enough, sir,' said Clegg respectfully, as Gore bent to touch the hands that lay slackly yet rigidly on the dead man's tweed overcoat—hands whose coldness he was to remember presently. 'You could tell that quick enough if you had to carry him, sir. More than I could manage, sir—what with only one good hand and a weak back.'

He exhibited his left hand, maimed by the loss of three fingers.

'A trench-mortar did that for me at Fleurbaix, sir. Blew our officer's head right off, it did, and—'

'If you'll kindly help me, Colonel,' said Melhuish, 'we'll take him out to my consulting-room. Not that I can do anything, I regret to say. But he can't remain here, poor fellow. Just a moment. I have a patient out there. I'll get rid of him first.'

He disappeared for a few moments, then returned shepherding to the hall door with mild suavity an apoplectic-looking elderly man, whose eyes bulged curiously as he passed the figure on the oak seat.

'Yes . . . heart. It was liable to happen at any time. I've been attending him for the past year or so. Indeed he was probably on his way to me this afternoon. His car was just outside my door. You'll see it as you go out.'

The patient produced a hoarse grunt from a vast, creased red neck.

'Umph . . . umph. No man in his senses ought to drive a car with a bad heart. Madness. Asking for trouble. Danger to every one else, too. Wonder you allowed it, Melhuish.'

'I quite agree,' said Melhuish. 'Quite. But he was an extremely difficult patient, poor fellow. Well, I hope you'll have no more trouble. I don't think you will, with a little care. Mind this weather, won't you. Very treacherous, these raw evenings. Good-bye.'

Gore heard the quiet, grave voice remotely only, and as a background to his thoughts—busy thoughts just then—thoughts that had insisted most disconcertingly upon returning almost two years to an evil-smelling mud-and-dung hut on the beaten clay floor of which a Masai boy had lain grinning up unpleasantly at the light of an oil-lantern. His forehead puckered as he stared at the distorted face before which, in obedience to a gesture of Melhuish's, he and Clegg had formed a hedge as the departing patient had passed it. Something in it—something in that dog-like baring of the gums—had stabbed his memory sharply to wakefulness. A suspicion that hardly dared yet to whisper itself, that was still vague to the point of absurdest incoherence, was fumbling at the door of his consciousness. Involuntarily his lips twisted in a grimace of dismay, as if his nostrils had scented once more the rank stink of that oil-lantern.

'Looks horrid, don't he, sir?' murmured the manservant sympathetically. 'Looks as if he'd been in agony o' pain, like, when he died, sir, you'd say. When I was in France, sir, I see'd once—and I expect you see'd it yourself often enough, sir . . .'

The hall door closed and Melhuish came back to them, with the quiet, cheerful earnestness of his profession in the presence of death.

'How long do you think he has been dead, doctor?' Gore asked, as casually as he could contrive.

'How long? I should say about half an hour—or perhaps three-quarters of an hour. Not longer. Not perhaps so long.'

'Must have been that at least, sir,' said Clegg. 'The lamps of the car weren't lighted. Mr Barrington would have turned them on when it came on dark, wouldn't he, sir—I mean if he was alive then?'

Melhuish smiled gravely.

'Clegg has the logical mind, Colonel, as you perceive. Though, personally, I should be inclined to believe that the last thing poor Barrington did was to switch off his lights. The tail-lamp was burning.'

'So it was, sir,' said Clegg, a little crestfallen.

'Yes. I should say from half an hour to three-quarters. Now, if you'll kindly give me a hand . . . How many patients waiting, Clegg?'

'Two, sir. Mrs Lauderdale and Admiral Parsons.'

'Very well. I'll see them in the dining-room. Get the lights on there, will you.'

'Yes, sir.'

They carried the dead man out to the consulting-room and laid him on a couch, Clegg following them a few moments later with the gray Homburg which had been left behind in the hall.

'Looks as if it had been in the mud, sir,' said the man, as he laid the hat on a chair beside the couch. 'Not hardly dry yet, the mud. Mud on his overcoat, too, sir. Looks as if he'd had a fall, poor gentleman, somehow.'

He lingered with the stolid, morbid curiosity of his kind, eyeing the still form on the couch as if by staring at it hard enough he could induce it to reveal the secret of the trick of being dead. Melhuish, who had gone to wash his hands with professional carefulness in a little cupboard opening off the consulting-room, returned to find him examining the dead man's hand.

'His hand's a bit scratched, too, sir. I'd say he must have had a fall by the look of—'

'Never mind that now, Clegg,' said his employer good-humouredly. 'Get me Mr Barrington's house on the telephone. Say I wish to speak to Mrs Barrington.'

Gore had touched with a careful finger the mud-stains on the brim of the Homburg hat, and had turned then to regard those on the dead man's overcoat and trousers.

'He *does* seem to have had a tumble, doesn't he?' he said musingly.

Melhuish shrugged his shoulders.

'Possibly. Certainly not recently. Yesterday, perhaps.'

'Curious that he should have died just outside your door, doctor.'

'Curious?'

'Curious, I mean, that his life should have lasted sufficiently long to bring him just to your door—to the spot to which he had set out to come.'

'Oh.'

Melhuish's gravity had relaxed. His smile of polite agreement conveyed that coincidences of that quite unprofitable sort held no great interest for the scientific mind.

'As a matter of fact he didn't quite reach my door, poor fellow. His car was actually outside the Barracombes' door. Well, I suppose I must go and ring up Mrs Barrington. We can only hope that she has been in some measure prepared—'

Clegg reappeared at the door.

'Mrs Barrington is not at home, sir. I've asked her maid to hold the line in case you wished to speak to her.'

Melhuish nodded and left the room. For a moment Gore feared that the servant's curiosity would induce him to linger at the door. But Melhuish's retreating voice summoned him away.

'I shall want the car in ten minutes from now. Tell Rogers, will you?'

There was no time to lose. Already Gore was busy at his task, hurriedly but methodically investigating the contents of the dead man's pockets. At the very outset of his search he found an envelope which, after a hasty glance at the newspaper-cutting inside, he secreted in one of his own pockets. There were, however, no other letters or papers of any kind. He rearranged the clothes carefully—disappointed since, now, the recovery of the letters would probably prove a still more difficult and delicate business to handle—yet relieved that he had at least recovered that compromising newspaper-cutting. As he restored the overcoat approximately to the folds in which it had lain when Melhuish had left the room, one of his hands touched accidentally one of the cold hands that rested on the rough tweed. A little splinter of thin glass, dislodged from beneath the cuff of the sleeve, attracted his attention. He drew up the cuff and saw that the glass of the wrist-watch beneath it had been broken. Broken, apparently, at twenty-three minutes past one—for the hands of the watch had stopped at that hour.

He remained so, bent over the still figure of the enemy who had held her happiness in a strangle-hold, holding back the cuff, considering. Barrington had certainly had a fall at some time so recent that the mud-stains on his clothes and his hat were still, in places, partially undried. There was mud, too, on the hand to whose wrist the watch was attached—mud, and a long, angry-looking scratch. Mud on the right hand also. He had had a fall, then—when? At the time at which the glass of his wrist-watch had been broken—twenty-three minutes past one? Curious that in all that time—over four hours—since twenty-three minutes past one until the Barracombes had found him at a quarter to six—he should have continued to wear a muddied hat, a muddied overcoat, muddied trousers, muddied boots— should not have even washed the mud from his hands. Curious, certainly. A very curious neglect, indeed, for a man of Barrington's smartness of appearance. For nearly three hours of daylight he must have gone about with those disfiguring mud-stains . . . Dashed odd, that.

His eyes returned to the distorted, agonised face. In some cases, he supposed, heart disease did end in an agony terrible enough to twist the lips of death in such a snarling grin—to set the eyes astare with such a horror. It was possible, he supposed. His knowledge of such matters was too slight to afford him any certainty upon the point, one way or the other. Melhuish—who must know his business—who, it seemed, was regarded as an expert in heart-diseases—had said definitely and explicitly that the man's heart had killed him. He had been attending Barrington, apparently, for heart-trouble for the past year— doubtless had examined him several times—knew all that could be known about his heart. It seemed impossible to believe that he could have been mistaken.

'But suppose,' that insidious, fumbling suspicion whispered, 'suppose he *is* mistaken. Suppose this man died, not of heart-disease half an hour or three-quarters of an hour ago—but in a very different way—at twenty-three minutes past one last night. Suppose that. Suppose he fell in the mud at twenty-three minutes past one last night—dead. Suppose he came by that ugly-looking scratch on his hand in a struggle with someone—someone from whom he was trying to take a sharp-pointed little knife which would make just such a scratch quite easily. Suppose, after that, he went out into the fog and darkness and fell . . . as he was going towards his car. Look at those mud-stains. Some of them are dampish in places—but the majority of them are bone dry. Would they have dried that way in four hours of a damp winter's afternoon? No. But they *would* have dried that way in sixteen hours. Feel his hands—icy cold—stiff as stone. Do a man's hands chill and stiffen that way in even three- quarters of an hour from his death? No. But they would in sixteen hours. Look at the man's face. Where have you seen a dead man's face like that before? Remember. Suppose someone went out and found him lying there in the mud and put him into his car and drove him off—'

But there, as Melhuish returned to the room, Gore's mystified speculations interrupted themselves abruptly. The doctor was plainly perturbed.

'Mrs Barrington is away, it appears,' he said gravely. 'She left her house late last night, and has not returned since. Very awkward.'

'Very,' Gore agreed. 'The servants have no idea where she can be found?'

'No—as far as I could discover from the very stupid woman who spoke to me on the telephone . . .'

'What will you do? Ring up some of the relatives to come along here?'

Melhuish shrugged.

'Well . . . that, too, is very awkward. I think I told you last night that Mrs Barrington's marriage had not altogether met with her family's approval. As a matter of fact, I understand that she has not been on speaking terms with any of them since. I should hardly like—as you can understand—'

'Quite,' Gore nodded. 'Barrington has no relatives living in the neighbourhood?'

'I have never heard him speak of any.'

Melhuish reflected for a moment.

'I wonder, Colonel, if you'd mind very much going to 27 Hatfield Place and trying to find out whether they can't give us an idea where Mrs Barrington is to be found. The woman I spoke to was almost inaudible . . .'

'Certainly. With pleasure, doctor.'

'I'm awfully sorry to trouble you. I should go myself at once if I hadn't two patients waiting. But I must see them. You could ring me up from Hatfield Place, perhaps—?'

'Very well.'

'Thanks.'

At the door Gore turned.

'If by any chance Mrs Barrington should arrive while I am there, before you come—?'

'She is a friend of yours?'

'She *was* a very great friend of mine.'

'Well, then, I leave it to you, Colonel, to tell her as gently as possible.'

For a fraction of a second Gore hesitated.

'If she should ask the cause of death . . .?'

Melhuish had bent over his writing-table to make an entry on a memorandum-block. He raised his head at the question, and for a moment the two men's eyes met.

'I should just say "Heart", if I were you. It will probably be unnecessary to go into any details—Mrs Barrington knows that this was likely to happen at almost any moment. However—in case it should be necessary—her husband died of syncope . . . following on myocarditis . . . resulting from acute disease of the coronary arteries.'

His quiet voice divided the verdict into three little layers of precision calmly and deliberately. If he was mistaken in that verdict, he had no slightest suspicion of it; that, at least, seemed certain. Nothing could have been more reassuringly definite and convinced than his clean-cut, clever face with its unswerving eyes and uncompromising lips.

'Thanks. Syncope—myocarditis—diseased coronary arteries.' Gore memorised the details. 'I'll just run up and say good-bye to your wife, and then go across to Hatfield Place straightaway.'

'Many thanks.'

In the narrow passage outside the consulting-room Gore halted. The passage was the continuation of the hall, and from it he could see the Barracombes moving towards the hall door slowly in colloquy with Clegg. No doubt they were endeavouring to extract from the man the fullest possible details of the tragedy—details which he was supplying, as his illustrative gestures showed, with dramatic zest. The three figures came to a pause half-way along the hall, and Gore, having no mind to encounter the curiosity of two bouncing young females just then, and realising that he was likely to be detected by them loitering in the passage, turned about to retreat again for a moment to the shelter of the consulting-room. As he pushed open the door, Melhuish, who had apparently been kneeling on the floor beside the couch, rose to his feet abruptly. So abruptly that the lens which he had been using escaped from his hand, and that he was obliged to stoop again to retrieve it.

Gore's nerves tautened. He divined instantly that Melhuish had been using the lens to examine the scratch on the dead man's hand. What had he made of it? Why had he been so startled at being disturbed in his examination? Why had he waited to make it until the instant he was left alone?

7

His smile of apology for his sudden intrusion was, however, tolerably natural and convincing, he flattered himself.

'Some people in your hall. . . Do you mind if I let them get out?'

Melhuish laid the lens on his writing-table with a somewhat ostentatious carelessness.

'Those two girls? Rather overpowering young women? You hadn't met them before, I suppose. I dread them. The general's a cheery old fellow. An indifferent general, I understand. But that's a normal condition of British generals, apparently.'

He went to the door to look towards the hall.

'All clear now, Colonel, I think.'

'Good. Sorry to have disturbed you again.'

'Not in the least. I was merely having a look at that scratch on poor Barrington's hand. One has to be careful, naturally.'

'Of course, yes.'

'It's merely a superficial scratch. No significance whatever.'

'I see. Well, I think I'm safe now, doctor. Ah, there is Mrs Melhuish . . .'

She had come down the stairs and was standing in the hall looking towards them, her golden head agleam beneath a cluster of lights. Hurriedly Gore detached himself from Melhuish, aware that the latter was following him slowly, but hoping for time to say just the one word for which he knew she was waiting. As he reached her, however, the door of the waiting-room opened, and a weather-beaten, bearded little man, with a pair of blazing blue eyes, emerged puffily. Mrs Melhuish bowed.

'How do you do, Admiral?'

'That's what I've come here to find out, Mrs Melhuish—if I can do it before midnight. How long more does that husband of yours mean to keep me shut up in this chamber of horrors, I should like to know? . .

Gore's chance was gone. He swore softly as the hall door closed behind him. From the post office in the Mall, however, he rang up Linwood 7420, and heard instantly, to his relief, her voice say: 'Yes? Who is speaking, please?'

'Gore.'

'I knew you would ring up. Well?'

'Nothing, except a newspaper-cutting. I have that. When can I see you? What time do you start for Surrey tomorrow?'

'My train is at twelve-thirty. I shall be here all the morning.' He reflected that Melhuish would be out of the way then, going his rounds.

'Very well, I'll go round at half-past ten. By the way, is anyone likely to be listening in?'

'No. Not here.'

'Good. What clothes was Barrington wearing when you saw him last?'

The question plainly puzzled her . . . or alarmed her . . . for there was a silence before she repeated the words.

'Clothes?'

'Yes. Evening clothes?'

'No. A dark suit—dark brown, I think—and a tweed overcoat. Why?'

'I'll explain when I see you. He had those . . . papers . . . with him?'

'Yes.'

'Loose—or in some sort of package?'

'In a large envelope.'

'Oh! Then there were not a great number of. . . papers?'

'There were originally. But these are the ones he kept.'

'And he had them with him last night. You actually saw them?'

'Yes. He always took care to let me see them. He used to read me extracts from them sometimes. Not last night . . . but . . . usually.'

'But you're quite sure that what you saw were the papers— or some of them—those we want?'

'Absolutely sure.'

'I see. Well, I can't explain very well until I see you; but I'm afraid, Pickles, it's going to be awkward.'

'They must be somewhere in his house—in some desk or drawer or something. I've thought of that. If they are, I'm done for. If Ethel finds them—Someone coming—Sidney.'

The receiver at the other end was replaced hurriedly. He waited until the exchange cut off. It was useless to wait longer, since he had not told her that he was speaking from the post office in the Mall. In any case there was nothing more that could be prudently said over the phone.

Barrington had changed into that brown suit, then, in the interval between their parting in Aberdeen Place a little before twelve and his return there some time round one o'clock. At what hour exactly had he returned there? Why the deuce hadn't he found that out from her?

Wait, though—she *had* told him the hour. She had said that Barrington had gone away about half-past one. Half-past one— If she was correct in that belief, then he had simply worked himself into a damn silly fuss over nothing. In that case the glass of the watch couldn't have been broken by a fall at twenty-three minutes past one . . . last night. That idea was all moonshine. Barrington had had a fall at twenty-three minutes past one that afternoon, that was all there was to be said. How or where—that didn't matter to *her.* Had had a fall, muddied his clothes, damaged his watch, and—it must be so—scraped his hand. Had had, possibly, a severe fall, and had been too badly knocked about by it to bother about his clothes. Had had, possibly, a fall severe enough to hasten his death . . .

His relief was so intense that he uttered aloud a little laugh that moved an observant newsboy to disrespectful parody. Amused, Gore stopped to buy a paper from the lad, whose demeanour changed instantly to the most respectful politeness at the prospect of business. As his hand went into his trousers-pocket in search of a coin, it came in contact with the envelope which he had transferred to it hurriedly in the consulting-room, and he took it out to place it in a pocket of greater safety. He remembered then the hastily-seen words written in the margin of the newspaper-cutting, and when he had secured his paper and paid the boy, moved a few steps forward to the nearest street-lamp to read them.

'Tonight. One.'

He had gone to her, then, at one. That fitted in with Arndale's having seen his car near the house shortly after one. Had he stayed a whole half-hour? Run the risk of discovery for a whole half-hour? Or *had* he gone away, after all, say, a minute or two before twenty-three minutes past? Gore's brief-lived cheerfulness subsided into uneasy doubt. He went on his way across Linwood Gardens to Hatfield Place wrapped in such dejected absorption that it was not until he reached the steps of Number 27 that he realised that one of his hands still held, in addition to his evening paper, a handful of loose coppers and silver and the envelope containing the newspaper-cutting.

For if there was one thing of which he was certain with regard to this most infernal mess in which Pickles had involved herself, it was that her husband had, for his own reasons, deliberately lied to him when he had said that the scratch on Barrington's hand possessed no significance. Of that Gore had no doubt whatever. If ever a man's eyes had said, 'I am lying, and you know I am lying, and I know that you know it,' Melhuish's eyes had said so then. *Why* had he lied? What reason *could* induce any medical man in his senses to do such a thing wilfully—to burke wilfully the real cause of a man's death—to risk wilfully exposure, the loss of his reputation, of his professional honour, of his profession itself—if not a criminal prosecution and its penalty? Common sense answered inevitably: to save himself or someone else from a worse danger? And from that it was but a single step to the unavoidable conclusion. Rightly or wrongly, Melhuish suspected that his wife's hand had been responsible for that scratch.

Well . . . if he knew enough about her relations with Barrington to suspect *that*, it hardly seemed worth while to bother about a few letters, did it? In any case, it seemed to Gore, Pickles was—to use her own dialect—pretty well done for. 'Damn it all,' he reminded himself sharply, 'it's quite possible that she may be arrested within the next twenty-four hours for the fellow's murder, if what I think and what I believe Melhuish thinks, is true. Do you realise that? Arrested for murder—lugged off by the arm by some big lout of a policeman—snapped away from all her life that has been like a flower snapped off its stem—done for —*Jini*— Arndale saw Barrington's car there last night and recognised it. How many other people saw it there and recognised it? For that matter how many other people know all about her affair with Barrington from beginning to end? Once let someone get wondering about that scratch on his hand and whoosh—the whole pack'll be after her . . .'

But, then, where the devil had he been all that time, Barrington? Where the devil had he been hidden from the time he had died until the time when those two girls had found him sitting there in his car in the darkness, dead? Who had brought him back to Aberdeen Place that afternoon? Certainly neither Melhuish nor Pickles; that was sure. Who then? Some other silly ass like himself whom she had persuaded to help her out of the mess?

The idea at first seemed ludicrous—grotesque. And yet as he knocked at the door of Number 27, it became abruptly the most probable and likely idea in the world. For he recalled just at that moment that just at that critical hour of the preceding night just such another silly ass *had* been in Aberdeen Place—close enough to the hall door of Number 33 to see Barrington's car waiting near it.

He turned and stared through narrowed eyes at the lights that twinkled beyond the trees of Linwood Gardens. For the first time the unbelievable thrust certainty in his face.

Cecil Arndale . . . By God. So she *had* done it.

8

He became aware that the hall door had opened behind him, and turned to find an elderly parlourmaid regarding him with tight-lipped sourness.

'Good-afternoon. Has Mrs Barrington come in yet?'

'No, sir.'

'Dr Melhuish has asked me to find out, if possible, where Mrs Barrington is at all likely to be.'

'No idea, sir.'

'No idea at all?'

'No, sir. For all we know, Mrs Barrington may not be coming back. Nothing would surprise us that happened in this house.' Gore's shrewd eyes took stock of the woman's respectable aggrievedness.

'It is exceedingly awkward,' he explained. 'No doubt Dr Melhuish told you over the telephone that Mr Barrington died this afternoon?'

She nodded silently. The fact appeared to possess no interest for her.

'Mrs Barrington may *not* be coming back, you think? Have you any reason to think that she intended to remain for any length of time?'

She shrugged, looked first to right of her and then to left and then down her nose, after the manner of her class, plainly struggling between a desire to air her grievance, whatever it might be, and to give no information about anything to anyone.

'She went away late last night, I understand? You realise that it is extremely urgent that we should ascertain where she is at once?' His hand went into a pocket significantly.

'May I ask your name, sir?'

'I am Colonel Gore. I am a very, very old friend of Mrs Barrington's.'

The maid's hard features relaxed into a bleak smile.

'I thought I recognised something about you, sir. You don't remember me, I suppose. You wouldn't, after so many years. But I was pantry-maid, sir, at Downs Lodge with Lady Harker, the time you and Mr Louis Harker and Mr Cecil Arndale blew up the harness-room, showing the coachman your experiments with your chemicals. I was watching the whole thing from my pantry, sir, that day. Flora was my name then, sir, though I had to change it to Florence afterwards, because of ladies I've been with not thinking Flora suitable to my station.'

Of Flora the pantry-maid of Lady Harker, Gore retained no faintest recollection whatever. But the blowing-up of the harness-room, and his share in the personal consequences of that exploit, he recalled very distinctly.

'My goodness!' he exclaimed, shaking this old acquaintance warmly by the hand, 'I *am* a silly ass. I *knew* I'd seen you somewhere, but I couldn't—Well, well, that was a good old bust-up, wasn't it?'

She ushered him into a sitting-room off the hall, and there, when they had chattered for some moments of things and people of other and better days, she unburdened her soul readily enough of the trials of the present—trials so grievous that her box was packed and all her preparations made for departure from Mrs Barrington's employment.

Stripped of her aggrieved comment, the facts were these:

Mrs Barrington had left the house about eleven o'clock on the preceding night, and had not since returned. Where she had gone Florence could not say. But why she had gone, Florence could, and did say very explicitly.

On the afternoon of the preceding day a gentleman had called to see Mrs Barrington. Florence did not know his name—he was not, it appeared, one of the gentlemen who visited the house regularly—but he was a big, tall, handsome young gentleman with very fair hair, and she had seen him often driving his motor-car 'like mad' about Clifton—always beautifully dressed. While this ornate caller had been with Mrs Barrington in her drawing-room, Mr Barrington had come in, and there had been a row for which Florence had no adjective but 'shocking!' The young gentleman—whom Gore had no difficulty in divining to have been Mr Bertie Challoner—had gone away; but the row had continued, upstairs in Mrs Barrington's bedroom. When the housemaid had gone into the room some time later, Mrs Barrington had been crying on her bed, with her eye and all one side of her face bruised black and blue.

Naturally Mrs Barrington had not gone out to dinner at Dr Melhuish's. But Mr Barrington had. He had come home about twelve o'clock—(Florence herself had been asleep then, but cook had heard him)—and had gone out again a little before one, not to return. He had made no inquiries of the servants as to Mrs Barrington's whereabouts. Florence was of opinion that he must have expected that Mrs Barrington would have left the house before he got back from Dr Melhuish's. What else could he expect after what had happened before he had gone out?

'And if you ask me, sir, back to this house Mrs Barrington won't come—unless hearing Mr Barrington's dead brings her back. But I may say, sir—and it's only fair to myself—that, come back or not come back, I'm leaving today, sir, with my wages or without them, and my box is packed and ready to go with me. Because I've always been in nice, well-behaved places, and in any case the hours that is kept here and the noise there is at night never suited me. Gentlemen coming in at one and two in the morning, three or four nights in a week, to play cards and drink more than's good for them, and talking and laughing all night so's a person couldn't get a wink of sleep till four or five o'clock in the morning. More like a gambling-hell, it was, sir, than anything else, lately. And so me and cook's said often to one another. I'll be only too glad to get out of the house and have no more trouble on account of it. I'm sorry for Mrs Barrington, sir, because I know she's a lady, and I know of her family and have been with friends of her family since I was in service first, sir, I may say. Every one hereabouts knows that Mrs Barrington's family was a very good family, sir. She was a Miss Melville, sir, as, of course, *you* know. But she ought to have been able to manage her house as a lady's house, and not allow gentlemen drinking and playing cards till all hours of the morning.'

She and cook and Emily were much perturbed by the possibility of being summoned as witnesses to a possible inquest. Cook and Emily had felt so depressed by their forebodings that they had gone off to the pictures to try to brighten themselves up.

'I shouldn't think that you need be in the least anxious about that sort of thing,' Gore assured her. 'Poor Mr Barrington's heart has been in a very bad way for a long time back. Dr Melhuish tells me that he has been liable to die at any moment for some months past. Now, let me see. Mr Barrington got back about twelve, you say. And went out again?'

'Yes, sir. He went out again a little before one, cook says. She's got dreadful weak nerves, cook has, being a stout woman as always have weak nerves, if you've noticed, sir, and she was so upset by what happened in the evening that she never got a wink of sleep all night. She heard Mr Barrington going out again just before one o'clock, with whoever it was came in with him.'

'Oh. Then someone came in with him at twelve o'clock?'

'Yes, sir. Some man, cook says. She heard them talking here, and there were two glasses with the decanter and the siphon on that table this morning.'

'And then—they both went out again just before one?'

'Yes. Cook heard Mr Barrington going up to his room, and he must have changed his clothes, for Emily found his evening-clothes this morning in his dressing-room. And then they went out by the back way to the garage, cook says, about one, sir, or a little before, and went off in the car.'

'How long did Mr Barrington stay out then?'

'Well, he didn't come back again, sir, after that.'

'You mean—last night?'

'I mean—at all, sir. The first any of us heard of him since that was when Dr Melhuish told me on the telephone he was dead. I can tell you, sir, *that* coming on top of mistress's going away at eleven o'clock at night without a word to any of us, and not coming back—well, it was a bit too much for me, sir. I just sat down today and wrote out my notice, and then went and packed my box, and I'm going at eight o'clock, sir, soon as some of my things as were with the washerwoman come back, if you'll excuse me mentioning them, sir. You can understand, sir—?'

'Yes, yes. Naturally you must all find it very upsetting. Still, I hope you'll stay at all events until Mrs Barrington returns. Er . . . the garage is at the back, then?'

'Yes, sir. It's only a small place. Mr Barrington had only a small car, sir, as I suppose you know.'

'The car did not come back last night . . . or today?'

'No, sir.'

'Did *not*?'

'No, sir. We were on the look-out for it, of course, all day, on and off. But it didn't come.'

'Mr Barrington's chauffeur? He didn't see it either . . . today . . . or last night after Mr Barrington took it out?'

'Mr Barrington had no chauffeur, sir. Anything that was done to his car in the way of cleaning or suchlike, mending it or that, he used to get Mr Harry Kinnaird's chauffeur to do it for him. Mr Harry Kinnaird used to allow his man to do it in his spare time. A very nice young man, sir, and very clever at that sort of work, I believe, and always willing to oblige anyone. So Mr Barrington used to make use of him that way. Mr Harry Kinnaird's garage being the next to ours, sir, in the lane at the back.'

'However . . . you're sure the car didn't come back?'

'Quite sure, sir. There's nothing new about that, sir, as far as that goes. I mean, Mr Barrington's being away for the night. We're used to that, sir.'

'I see. He was frequently away for the night?'

'Often, sir. Two or perhaps three nights in the week.'

'With the car?'

'Sometimes with, sir—sometimes without it.'

'Any idea where he was in the habit of going?'

The elderly Florence compressed her thin lips primly.

'Well, sir . . . we've had our ideas . . . but he's dead now, and there's only One has any right to judge him now.'

'Yes, yes. Quite, quite. Er . . . perhaps Mrs Barrington has gone to stay with friends?'

'Mrs Barrington has very few friends now, sir, that you'd call friends. However, I'll bring you the card tray, sir. Perhaps that will help you. And then perhaps you'll excuse me, sir. I think I heard my laundry coming back.'

Left alone with the card tray, he selected some dozen names with which he installed himself at the telephone. His inquiries were made with extreme caution and without revealing his own identity; it appeared to him under the circumstances neither necessary nor prudent to publish Mrs Barrington's prolonged absence from her household nor the fact that he, personally, was in search of her. As a matter of fact, however, he found no difficulty in satisfying himself that none of the people whom he had selected had the faintest idea of her whereabouts. He was about to abandon his quest and ring up Melhuish to inform him of its fruitlessness, when another name—not amongst those which he had collected from the card tray—suggested itself.

Mr Challoner, as it happened, was at home, and answered the call with an extremely ungracious 'Hallo.'

'Oh. That you, Bertie? Gore at this end. I say, old chap, I wonder if you can help us. We're trying to get hold of Mrs Barrington. I don't suppose you've heard yet . . .'

'Yes. I heard just five minutes ago. I met Miss Barracombe running round spreading the news.'

'Oh. Well, I've been ringing up all sorts of people to try to find his wife. Melhuish asked me to. She's not at her house, you see. I'm speaking from there. I thought perhaps you might be able to . . . er . . . help us.'

'I?' said Challoner's voice stiffly. "*I've* no idea. Why the deuce should I?'

'Oh, sorry. Right. Thanks.'

'But... I say, Gore—just a moment. Why ring *me* up? Why should I know where Mrs Barrington is?'

'I've been trying every one I could think of, my dear fellow. Sorry to have bothered you. I'll have a go at someone else. It's deuced awkward, you see, that she should be away, just now. Well, I'll have a go at someone else . . . Good-bye, old chap.'

'Good-bye.'

Gore smiled faintly at the angry truculence of that 'Good-bye.' A singularly ingenuous youth, Master Bertie Challoner.

'Bet he's telling her *now* we're looking for her,' he thought, as he rang up Linwood 7420.

'That you, doctor? No luck so far. What? Oh . . . you're bringing him here? Shall I wait? Yes . . . certainly. Very well. I'll tell the servants. Yes. Right.'

Bringing him there . . . Well . . . why hadn't Melhuish brought him there at once—instead of carrying him into the consulting-room at Aberdeen Place and carrying him out again—if the man had died as he had said he had expected him to die? In the blindest darkness he could have told that he was dead. What need to take him in, then, to examine him? To give him time to see those two waiting patients? Perhaps. But Gore thought not. He knew of a more urgent need than that—a need that had to see, before other skilled eyes saw it, perhaps, what it expected to see.

'You're mad,' said Gore's common sense. 'You've worked yourself into such a state now that you *can't* think straight. The man daren't do it. He daren't attempt such a bluff. Why, that servant of his twigged something fishy about Barrington's look straight off—twigged that he'd fallen—twigged the scratch on his hand. If a servant could twig it, Melhuish must know that anyone may twig it. He'd never try on such a bluff. He daren't. That scratch means nothing—that's the fact of the matter. You're simply allowing your imagination to twist things so as to make them fit into one another. . .just because you're in a funk about a woman who doesn't care a hang about you . . .'

He was quite unable, however, to decide which belief he really and honestly held at that moment. One seemed as convincing as the other. He abandoned his speculations with some irritation, and went in search of the parlourmaid, to consult with her as to such simple preparations as appeared necessary.

He had returned to the sitting-room, and was awaiting Melhuish's arrival there, when the sound of a car stopping outside the house brought him to the window, the blind of which had not been drawn. A smartly-figured young woman, visible for a moment against the lights of the vehicle as she paid her fare, came hurriedly up the drive, and admitted herself with a latchkey. The mistress of the house had returned, then.

So Challoner had known where she was to be found, and had told her. Well . . . that was *their* affair. She had got back in time—that was the important thing. The less talk there was about the Barrington *menage* for the next three or four days, well. . . very much the better for every one concerned.

Mrs Barrington's face was still concealed by a thick veil when he met her in the hall, but he recognised her voice at once. Although nine years had elapsed since their last meeting, she displayed neither surprise, pleasure, nor emotion of any kind upon seeing him.

'Don't expect a broken-hearted, tearful widow, Wick,' were her first words, as their hands touched. 'I'm no use at pretending. I don't feel anything. I'm not going to try to pretend that I do. Where is he? Still at Dr Melhuish's house . . . or have they brought him here?'

'Melhuish is bringing him here . . . They are probably on the way now. Your maid knows.'

'Oh.'

She stood for a moment looking at her hands in silence. Then with a sudden movement she raised her veil.

'Look,' she said. 'He did that the last time he spoke to me.' Her voice rose to sudden passion. 'Now... can you understand?'

Gore made a little gesture of deprecation.

'Hadn't you better go straight up to your room?' he urged gently. 'Much the best thing. Look here—let me ring up your mother and your sister for you . . .'

'If mother or Elsa come to this house,' she cried angrily, 'I shall walk straight out of it. You understand?'

'Well, but you must have someone to look after you,' he protested—'some woman. If you won't have your own folk . . . what about Mrs Melhuish? You and she used to be tremendous friends, I remember. I'm sure she'd—'

'Mrs Melhuish?' she laughed impatiently. 'Why on earth should she come here? Of all the people in the world I *don't* want to see— You don't know how amusing that suggestion of yours is, my dear Wick.'

'But you must have someone to look after you,' he repeated. 'You can't be left to the mercy of servants.'

'Oh, don't talk nonsense,' she said hardly. 'I can look after myself. I don't want anyone—*anyone.* I just want to go right away from here for ever and ever, and never see anyone or anything connected with Linwood again. That's all I want. You don't know, Wick—you've no idea what I've been through during these three years for which I've been that man's wife. You think you know me, that I'm the Ethel Melville you remember nine years ago. I'm a very different sort of person, now, Wick, I assure you. I've learned a thing or two about life since those days. I can look after myself.'

She changed the subject with a gesture of the gloves which she had drawn off as she spoke. 'Is it true that you were at Dr Melhuish's house when he was found?'

'Yes. I happened to have called—'

'Those awful Barracombe girls found him sitting in the car, didn't they?'

'Yes.'

'He was dead when they found him . . . or did he die in the house?'

'He was dead when they found him. You . . . er . . . you knew, of course, that his heart was in a bad way? . . .'

'I knew that he had been going to Dr Melhuish about it. I guessed that it must be something serious. But he never told me anything about himself.' She smiled again bitterly. 'I used to try to find out things for myself in the beginning. But it didn't pay. How grey you've grown at the temples, Wick. But you've kept your grin—and your figure. Still a bachelor?'

'Alas! Er—you'd like to see Melhuish when he comes? Or do you think you need?'

'Well... do you think it's necessary? I've no idea what I'm expected to do. I don't want to see him if it's not necessary. I don't suppose he'll want to see me either. He disapproves of me, I know. Indeed, I've no doubt that he and his wife have told you so already.'

'Gracious, no,' Gore assured her hastily. 'What an absurd idea. On the contrary, they were both most awfully put out, I know, that your earache prevented your going to them last night. Mrs Melhuish—'

'Oh, hang Mrs Melhuish!' she cried out angrily. 'Hang the whole lot of them. Cats. Treacherous, spiteful cats, that's what all these Linwood women are. Wait until they find out about this black eye of mine. I suppose it will be all over the place tomorrow. Wait until they get hold of it. *Then* you'll hear them howling and squalling. For two pins I'd just walk out of that door again into a taxi and drive to Broad Street and clear out by the first train I saw for anywhere, for good, and leave them to it.'

In a tolerably wide experience of his fellow-woman Gore had learned at least the wisdom of silence before her wrath. This most unconventional of widows was, he perceived, on the edge of that condition which privately he described as 'jumps.' He said, 'Now, now,' soothingly, pulled down her veil adroitly, took her by the arm, and led her to the foot of the stairs.

'Florence,' he called.

The parlourmaid's head, as he had expected it would, came over the balusters.

'Er . . . do you know what hot-water bottles are?'

'Yes, sir,' replied the woman in surprise.

'Well, go and make two of 'em as hot as hell, and get them and your mistress into the same bed as quickly as possible. Got that?'

When the woman had descended to the lower regions he said peremptorily, 'Up you go.'

Mrs Barrington burst into tears distressingly; but she went.

Gore returned to the sitting-room and stood there for a little while looking at a small pedestal writing-table which occupied one of the corners by the window. Possibly there—in one of those little drawers, those infernal letters had been kept. Well . . . they were not there now, nor anywhere in that house; so much appeared certain. At all events those which really mattered. Quite possibly the others were there still. Pleasant for Mrs Barrington when she found them . . . and for Pickles. Deuced awkward that they should be on such bad terms as they appeared to be. However, those other letters, it seemed, were not serious . . . or so serious.

But if Barrington had not returned to the house after that stormy interview in the hall at Aberdeen Place, what had become of the letters that did matter? He had had them with him there; Pickles had been quite definite upon that point at any rate. What had become of them afterwards?

There, at once, he came once more to a standstill. Had Barrington got into his car and driven himself away to some night-haunt of his? Or had someone else driven him away? Driven him away, hidden him and his car somewhere until darkness had fallen that afternoon, and then driven him back to Melhuish's door and left him there, to be found, as in effect he had been found, by some curious person?

Looked at that way, side by side—considering the improbabilities and difficulties of the second supposition, the first appeared immensely the more likely. If it were the correct one, then the sole hope of recovering the letters lay in finding out where Barrington had spent the night and the greater part of that day—questioning. Heaven knew how many people as to how he had spent his time and where he might be expected to have left behind him a bundle of letters. A pretty job to undertake. One might as well start in to look for a flea in a crowded church. Not that that or any other job would trouble one much if one could only be sure that that scratch on Barrington's hand had nothing to do with his death or with Pickles. That was *the* thing that mattered. Blow the letters. The fellow was dead— probably the letters would never be heard of again.

On the other hand—that someone else who might be supposed to have driven Barrington away and brought him back again so mysteriously—who was he?

Melhuish himself? Melhuish had certainly not brought him back. He had been in his consulting-room, there could be no doubt, from two to six that afternoon, as on all other afternoons of the week save Sundays. If it was not he who had brought Barrington back, almost certainly it was not he who had driven him away. It was impossible to suppose that he would have been mad enough to enlist a confederate to do half of so desperately dangerous a job for him.

Arndale? There was no getting away from the fact that Arndale *did* fit into that second supposition dismayingly. On the spot at the critical moment. Pickles could probably twist him round her little finger. Just the rather weak, good-natured sort of chap that would allow himself to be persuaded into helping a woman out of a fix.

Here followed an interval during which Gore debated with himself quite unprofitably as to the motives which had induced him to behave in that weak, foolish way also. But eventually he picked up the thread of his argument once more at a point a little farther on.

Someone—some man—had come in with Barrington at twelve o'clock . . . who was *he?* Barrington must have met him on his way to his house from the Melhuishs'. Instantly Gore's memory flashed back to the tall figure in a light-coloured raincoat which he had seen for a moment through the laurels of the Green, halted beside Barrington's in the light of a lamp in Aberdeen Place, just after their parting. He had thought at the time that the wearer of the raincoat was Arndale, he remembered. Arndale had certainly been wearing such a coat when he and Melhuish had seen him come out from Challoner's flat. Was Arndale, then, the man whom the cook had heard come in with Barrington, who had talked over a whisky-and-soda with him for an hour or so, and gone out with him again just before one o'clock . . . in the car?

Blazes . . . it *did* fit.

Gore caught just then a glimpse of his reflection in the mirror over the fireplace, and made a rueful face at it. The second supposition looked altogether too like the correct one, after all—so like it that the thumb of one of his hands, which had been rubbing the pad of his second finger thoughtfully, flicked the chances of any other supposition's being the right one into the *ewigkeit*.

Footsteps rasping on the gravel of the little drive distracted him from his reverie. He glanced out through the window and saw the headlights of a large car drawn up before the gate. Mr Barrington had come home.

9

'Colonel Gore, sir?' inquired the elderly chauffeur to whom he opened the hall door.

'Yes. That Dr Melhuish's car? Oh, there is Dr Melhuish. I'll go down.'

Melhuish was removing the rugs which had covered the occupant of the back seats of the car during the brief journey from Aberdeen Place. He turned his head as Gore came out through the gate.

'Mrs Barrington has got back, I hear. Have you seen her?'

'Yes,' Gore answered, wondering a little who had given him this piece of information. 'I've persuaded her to go to her room.'

'Good. Which floor is he to be taken to?'

'Second.'

Melhuish considered for a moment, his eyes fixed on the headlights of a car drawn up some thirty yards away before the gates of the next house. He turned to his chauffeur.

'Go and tell Mr Harry Kinnaird's man I want to speak to him for a moment, Rogers, will you. He's there, beside that car.'

The elderly Rogers—a converted coachman, obviously—turned a dogged, dubious muzzle towards the blinding beam of the headlights at the next gate.

'I don't think that's Mr Kinnaird's car, sir. His is a Daimler. That's a Sunbeam, by the look of her.'

'Go and do what I've told you to do,' said Melhuish curtly.

'Fearful old humbug, that chap of mine,' he explained coldly, when the man had gone upon his errand. 'He is constitutionally incapable of tightening a nut until he has argued for twenty minutes that it can't possibly be loose. I've been trying to get rid of him for twelve months, but he simply refuses to go. We shall want a third to help us up those stairs, I think. I'm afraid I shall have to enlist your services again, Colonel, if I may. Awfully sorry to give you so much bother. But old Rogers is absolutely useless except at meal-times.'

This sudden outburst of loquacity terminated as abruptly as it had begun, and the two men waited in silence by the car, concealing the back seats from the possible curiosity of the passers-by. No one, however, paid the slightest attention to that portion of the car, which lay in an obscurity rendered still more secure by lights in front. As they waited Gore puzzled his brains in the effort to imagine how his companion had learned so extraordinarily quickly that Mrs Barrington had returned. That problem was still, however, unsolved, when the argumentative Rogers returned, accompanied by a smart, youngish man in the breeches and leggings of his calling.

'It weren't Mr Harry Kinnaird's car, sir,' said Rogers in morose triumph. 'It's Judge Thornton's car. I knew it were a Sunbeam. I could tell it weren't a Daimler, anyways.'

Melhuish, ignoring his difficult retainer absolutely, addressed himself to his companion.

'I wonder if you'd mind very much giving us a hand for a moment or two. We want to carry poor Mr Barrington in and get him upstairs. I'm sure Mr Kinnaird will not make the least difficulty. I'll go in and explain to him presently.'

'Mr and Mrs Kinnaird are away, sir,' said the man civilly. 'They went to the south of France the day before yesterday. But, of course, I shall be only too pleased to do anything, doctor.'

His glance weighed Gore's figure quickly and approvingly.

'I think this gentleman and I can manage all right.'

The parlourmaid, carrying a hot-water bottle in either hand, met the cortege in the hall, but retreated discreetly before it up the stairs at a gesture from Melhuish. She alone of the household witnessed the curious indignity of its master's ascent of the stairs. She stood, a mute, accusing sentinel, before a closed door, and watched his passage unblinkingly, bestowing upon Mr Kinnaird's chauffeur a bleak smile of recognition, her fingers assuring themselves of the propriety of the spruce cuffs which, together with cap and apron, she had assumed since her mistress's return. Noting these additions to her attire abstractedly as he went by her, Gore concluded that she had probably thought better of her decision to depart. Vaguely, for Mrs Barrington's sake, he hoped that she had, since she appeared a decent, sensible sort of woman despite her grumpiness. Little did he think then that those tight, straight lips of hers were to utter the one word that was to solve the riddle of her master's death.

But at that moment his attention was absorbed by the discovery, revealed as soon as they had entered the lighted hall, that the mud-stains on Barrington's clothes had disappeared. Melhuish, who had ascended the stairs in advance, carried the dead man's hat. So that it was not until they reached the bedroom where he awaited them that Gore perceived that it, too, had been brushed clean. There another still more significant fact leaped to his eyes, as the body was laid on the bed. The wrist-watch had disappeared.

Not a flicker of an eyelid, however, betrayed the sharp alarm that stabbed him like a knife at this confirmation of his worst fears. Nerves and brain that had acted like lightning in all the tight places of forty-two years, acted like lightning in this one. Melhuish meant to put up a cold bluff. Very well. There was just one thing to do: sit tight and let him get on with it.

He straightened himself and looked at his watch.

'Well, it seems rather a heartless sort of thing to think about, doctor, but I'm supposed to dine with the Wellmores at eight. By the time I get back and change—'

Melhuish nodded.

'Thanks very much. I'll look after things here.' He nodded too, pleasantly, to the chauffeur, who stood by the door, awaiting his dismissal. 'That's all, thank you. Much obliged.'

'Not at all, sir,' said the man civilly. 'Though it's the last job I ever hoped to do for poor Mr Barrington. He died very suddenly, doctor?'

'Yes. Very suddenly. But he had had a long warning.'

'Heart-disease, sir, hadn't he? He used to tell me that his heart kept him awake at night a lot.'

'Yes, yes.'

'Good-afternoon, doctor.'

He saluted smartly and left the room a little behind Gore, who had taken leave of Melhuish with a nod and a smile. Gore waited for him in the hall, under pretence of surveying himself in the mirror there.

'Er . . . you used to look after Mr Barrington's car for him, I think?'

The man, who had been about to pass on with a smiling 'Good-afternoon, sir,' stopped.

'Yes, sir. I used to clean it for him and do small odd jobs. Mr Kinnaird allowed me to do it in my spare time.'

'Yes. So I understand. Er . . . Mr Barrington used his car a good deal at night, didn't he?'

'Well, yes, sir, he did a good deal, I believe.'

'Have you any idea where he used to put it up when he took it out at night?'

The chauffeur stared, obviously puzzled as to the purport of this interrogatory.

'Well, no, sir. I can't say that I have. I used to hear him taking it out late at night—our garage is the next to his, you see, sir, in the lane at the back. And sleeping there, of course I've heard him often going out at night in his car. But—no—I've no idea where he used to take it.'

'I see.'

'I shall be very sorry for my own sake that he's gone, sir. It'll mean a big loss to me. Especially now when I've been docked of half my wages for perhaps three or four months to come.'

'How's that?' Gore inquired, as they went down the drive.

'Oh, well—you see, sir—Mr Kinnaird may be a millionaire, and I believe he is, but he's a precious tight 'un with the money—'

'Only those that haven't got it aren't,' smiled Gore.

'I agree, sir. Still, it's a bit thick cutting thirty shillings a week off your chauffeur's wages when you're spending perhaps a hundred a week or more in the south of France. Now, isn't it, sir? Yes, I'll miss poor Mr Barrington's quid a week badly. I heard his car going out last night about one o'clock. I little thought it would be the last time I'd hear him going out with it.'

'Well, well,' said Gore, 'it's a difficult world. You never know what's round the corner, do you?'

The chauffeur smiled.

'Shouldn't mind that so much, sir, if there weren't such a lot of corners.'

The hall door of Number 27 opened, and the parlourmaid came out hurriedly on to the steps to peer towards the gates.

'Is that you, Fred?' she decided to call out. 'The doctor wants to know if you'd leave a note for him at Coggan's—the undertakers—you know? In Victoria Street. It's in a hurry. He didn't know that I was the only one in the house except the mistress—'

'Certainly,' said the man obligingly, and touched his cap to Gore as he turned away. 'If you should happen to know of anyone who wants a man, sir, I've driven most kinds of cars.

Had six months in shops. Perhaps you'd remember my name, sir—Thomson? . . .'

Gore promised to remember, and went off towards the Riverside hurriedly. He glanced at his watch. Just comfortable time. For the first time for two hours he realised that his shin was aching like the devil.

10

At twenty-five minutes past ten on the following morning he was standing at the door leading out into the Riverside's gardens from the annexe, watching his friend the page-boy perambulating two yapping and beribboned Pekinese in a drizzle that threatened to develop speedily into a downpour. Would he or would he not go? It was true that Melhuish would be out on his rounds, but he might easily learn that Colonel Gore had called again to see Mrs Melhuish. Two visits in less than twenty-four hours—he might well begin to wonder what the unduly sociable Colonel Gore was up to—even if he didn't know. If he did know—and Gore had awakened that morning with very little doubt upon the point—well . . . the situation was even more uncomfortable.

So far as Gore could judge, now, what had happened was this. On that Monday night Arndale had met Barrington in Aberdeen Place at—say—a quarter to twelve, had gone with him to his house in Hatfield Place, remained there until nearly one o'clock, and then gone out with him in his car. So much seemed beyond doubt. Conjecture supposed that they had parted then, but that Arndale had somehow guessed or known where his companion was going. Quite probably Pickles herself had supplied the information, suspecting that Barrington might attempt the very trick which, in fact, he had attempted, and thinking it advisable to have a powerfully-built and devoted admirer handy in case of such need. Arndale, then, had followed Barrington to Aberdeen Place, and had been waiting outside when Barrington had come out. There had been a quarrel. Barrington, the smaller of the two men, had taken the knife from his pocket—perhaps for purposes of intimidation rather than with any intention of actually using it. There had been a struggle for it, and somehow the blasted thing had scraped Barrington's hand. Probably it was the fact that Barrington had died of heart-disease. Shock—fear—violent exertion—any of these might have proved the last straw. If he had begun to scream, for instance, Arndale might have stunned him to unconsciousness; but there would, almost certainly, have remained some tell-tale evidence of the heavy blow necessary to produce that result. No. Barrington's heart had killed him.

Realising that he was dead, what would Arndale have been likely to do?

His first instinct, naturally, would be to clear off and leave the beggar lying there. But then there was that scratch on his hand to think about. He would say to himself: 'They'll examine that scratch. They'll find out that it has been made by some poisoned weapon or something. They may find out quite easily that a poisoned knife had been taken from the Melhuishs' hall. They'll find Barrington with his car here, a little way from the Melhuishs' house. They'll get on to the Melhuishs'. Pickles will give the show away in the end and admit that Barrington was there with her, and that I was waiting outside for him.' Having thought all that—probably with someone else's assistance— though Cecil Arndale had always been quite capable of thinking very prudently and quickly where his own safety or comfort had been concerned, Gore remembered—he had picked Barrington up, out of the mud, put him into his car, and driven him away—

At that point there was a break in the story. It was difficult to imagine where the car and its dead owner had remained hidden all that night and the greater part of Tuesday. Difficult— but not impossible. It was simply a question of supposing Arndale to have known of a place where they might be safely hidden.

Well, then, as soon as darkness had fallen on Tuesday he had driven Barrington back to Aberdeen Place and left him there. Quite an excellent idea, that, to leave him at the door of the doctor who had been attending him—as Arndale could hardly have avoided knowing—for heart-disease, and who would be prudent enough not to draw awkward attention to a scratch on one of his hands. Why? Because the doctor, also, knew how Barrington had come by it.

That seemed to Gore an inevitable conclusion. Melhuish had had a hand in the business. Melhuish knew that Arndale had had that scrimmage with Barrington—had come out, say, four or five minutes after Barrington had left his wife, and had seen the two men struggling and Barrington fall. Either he had known before he came out, or he had learned from Arndale *when* he came out, that Barrington had been with his wife. Arndale, Gore felt pretty sure, would give Pickles away without hesitation if it came to explaining the very awkward position in which Melhuish had found him then. But it seemed much more likely that Melhuish knew all about Barrington's visit to his wife that night before he came out. It was too curious a coincidence altogether that he should have followed Barrington out so quickly.

Wait, though—he had been called out by a Mrs MacArthur. Well, he might have known *and* have been called out.

Melhuish, then, had helped Arndale, probably, to decide upon the plan which had been adopted, on the understanding that he himself would manage all the rest if Arndale got the body back, next day after dark, to his hall door, or so close to it that he would certainly be the doctor to be called out to it by whoever found it. Arndale had driven the car away. Melhuish had gone off to the small boy with gastritis.

The story halted in places—there was that awkwardness about the unknown hiding-place—it supposed extraordinary nerve and will on Melhuish's part—nerve and will which had, no doubt, overpowered such doubts and fears as Arndale might well have felt. But, on the whole, the bits of the story fitted. And it was the only story Gore could think of, of which the bits did fit, or anything like fit.

The knife and its sheath . . . what about them? There, too, for instance, the story halted pretty badly. The scrimmage must have taken place in Aberdeen Place, probably near the car, which would have been drawn up against the kerb of the footpath. Even if, in the course of the encounter, Arndale, in his anger or his flurry, had thrown the knife away from him, and thrown it with such force that it had crossed the roadway of Aberdeen Place and hidden itself inside the railing at that side of the Green, no man on earth could have thrown the sheath to the place where it had been found. As he stood at the door of the annexe, Gore's eyes measured the distance. The width of the roadway in Aberdeen Place—say, fifteen yards. The width of the strip of Green—say, twenty yards. He took the little limp, featherweight sheath from his pocket and weighed it in the palm of his hand. The page-boy had disappeared indoors. He threw it across the grass with all his force, and measured the distance of its flight as he went to retrieve it. About nineteen yards. Absolutely out of the question that anyone could have thrown it thirty or thirty-five.

Then, the knife itself? What about *it?*

Before breakfast that morning he had taken a mashie and two ancient golf-balls out into the grounds of the hotel, played the balls carefully over the railings into the Green, and climbed over after them. In half an hour's energetic patrolling to and fro in the likely regions of the dank little enclosure he had found, however, nothing more lethal than a decayed corkscrew. He had made, then, an exhaustive search of the hotel grounds in the neighbourhood of the gates by which he had found the sheath, but without result. That part of the story, too, remained, then, vague.

Then, Arndale had told Challoner that he had seen Barrington's car near the Melhuish's door shortly after one o'clock. Would he have made any reference whatever to Barrington or his car if, only an hour or so before, he had played the part which the story supposed him to have played? Hardly. No doubt he had gone into Challoner's flat, after disposing of the car and Barrington for the night, in order to have, afterwards, an explanation to give of his having been in the neighbourhood of Aberdeen Place at that hour on that night, suppose anyone should have happened to see him and recognise him. The last thing in the world he would think of doing would, surely, be to make any reference whatever to having seen Barrington's car.

Stop a bit—

It was probably at that precise moment that it occurred to Gore for the first time that Challoner, too, might have had some hand in the business. Not in the actual performance of it, but in bridging that difficult gap between the time at which Barrington's car had left Aberdeen Place on Monday night and the time at which it had returned to it on Tuesday afternoon. Challoner had a car, and, presumably, a garage for it. If he had a garage, it would almost certainly be quite near his flat—probably in that lane at the hotel end of Selkirk Place. There were plenty of garages there. And on that Monday night his car had not been in its garage; he had said that it had gone into dock on Monday afternoon with a big-end gone. On that night, that garage, a minute or so from Aberdeen Place if it was situated in the lane, had been empty.

Challoner and Arndale were brothers-in-law. Challoner's views and feelings with regard to Barrington were clear enough. If Arndale had gone into his flat and told him his story and said: 'I'm in a devil of a fix, Bertie. Your garage is empty,' would Challoner have refused him the use of it?

Why . . . perhaps—nay, in all probability—Mrs Barrington had been there in Challoner's rooms at the very time. There could be no doubt that she had left her house that night on account of the row of the evening—the row of which Challoner had been the cause, if the grumpy, but obviously truthful, parlourmaid was to be believed. What was the obvious—the only conclusion? She had gone to Bertie Challoner—to his flat—and had remained there. Had been there when Arndale had been there—had heard his story—had, by her very presence if not by actual words, persuaded Challoner—if he had needed any persuasion—to become his brother-in-law's confederate in getting rid of the dangerous, hated thing that waited outside for disposal. Deserted as both Aberdeen Place and Selkirk Place both were at night, that conference must, for prudence sake, have been a hurried one. The less time given to Challoner to think, the more likely he would have been to act rashly. Arndale had probably obtained the key of his garage from him without the least difficulty, driven the car to it, and locked it up for the night. Then he had returned to Challoner's flat—probably to say that there had been no hitch. It had been about twenty minutes to two or thereabouts when he had come out of Challoner's flat again so hurriedly. Gore estimated that would allow, from the time of Barrington's death at twenty-three minutes past one, seventeen minutes for all that had to be done. Quick work—but if there was anything certain, it was that, if the job had been done that way, it had been done quickly. Challoner's garage *must* be supposed to be quite close to his flat; that was essential. If it was in that lane, the thing was as plain as a pikestaff.

Why not go and find out, now, on his way to Aberdeen Place? He looked at his watch. Half-past ten exactly. It would take perhaps five minutes to find out if Mr Challoner had a garage in the lane.

As a matter of fact it took just a minute. A shirt-sleeved young fellow hosing a van informed him at once that Mr Challoner's garage was the first on the left from the Selkirk Place end of the lane.

Plain as pikestaff.

It has been said that Wick Gore was a very human person. As he went past the pillared gates of the Riverside's back entrance again, he smiled grimly yet not unkindly, at the spot where he had found the sheath of the Masai knife.

'There . . .' he would have said, if he had spoken his thought just then aloud, 'all you have to do is to reason out logically what must have happened and stick to it. It seemed impossible that that confounded sheath could have got there into that corner. But . . . I stuck to what I reasoned *must* have happened— and there . . . it's as clear as daylight. Arndale took the knife from Barrington and kept it. It is now either in the river, or buried somewhere. The sheath probably remained in Barrington's other hand. Well, then, when Arndale was driving the car and Barrington to the garage in the lane, just as he got here, outside those gates, he saw the sheath . . . either still in Barrington's hand or fallen on the floor or the cushions of the car. On the spur of the moment—he was just then driving the car round a sharp, narrow corner—he snatched it from Barrington's hand or wherever it lay and threw it away and believed he had thrown it inside the railing of the Green. But as a matter of fact it fell short . . . by the gate-pillar there, where I found it. If you ask me why he kept the knife and threw the sheath away, I reason thus. He meant to get rid of them both, and to get rid of them separately, and to get rid of them as soon as possible. So he began by getting rid of the sheath at once. It might lie for years amongst those bushes inside the railing before anyone saw it. And even if they did see it, by itself it wouldn't matter in the least.

There you are— It's perfectly simple—provided you reason logically, and stick to what you've reasoned, and don't get guessing about things blindly because at first they don't seem to square up all right. Perfectly simple—and quite infallible—provided you stick to it.

It was therefore with curiously mingled feelings that he beheld, as soon as he entered the hall of 33, Aberdeen Place, the second Masai knife replaced beside its fellow at the bottom of the trophy, sheathless indeed—its point being protected merely by a piece of cork—but unmistakably the fellow of its neighbour.

Clegg had opened the door to him, after some delay, with a countenance in which a dejected gravity struggled with a profuse perspiration. The large trunk which he had apparently just carried down the stairs and deposited in the hall was accountable, it seemed, for both.

'Sorry to have kept you waiting in the rain, sir. I'm just bringing down Mrs Melhuish's luggage. Mrs Melhuish is leaving us today for a week, I'm sorry to say, sir. This house is a different place altogether, sir, when the mistress is away. She's in the morning-room, sir, if you'll go up.'

'Thanks, yes,' said Gore, still unable to remove his eyes from the trophy. 'I see you've stuck a cork on one of those little knives I sent home to Mrs Melhuish. What's become of the sheath?' 'I don't know, sir,' the man replied with wrinkled forehead.

'It's got lost somehow. Somebody must have knocked against the wall in passing and loosened that knife from the little hooks. I missed it from the wall yesterday, and it wasn't until this morning one of the maids found it under the coat-and-umbrella stand. I've searched high and low for the little case as was on it, but there isn't a sign of it anywhere about. Only thing I can think of is, one of the girls must have taken it on account of the beads on it. Girls is funny about things like that, sir. Anything with a bit of ornament or beads or anything of that sort, sir, some of them can't resist it. They *must* have it.'

'So you've stuck a cork on the point.'

'Yes, sir. I thought it safer, after what you were saying to the doctor the night you dined here, sir, when you were going out.'

'Quite right. In the morning-room, you say? . . .'

Mrs Melhuish rose hurriedly from the writing of a telegram to greet his entry.

'Well, Wick? No luck?'

'No, I'm sorry to say.' He took the envelope containing the newspaper-cutting from his pocket and handed it to her. 'Except this.'

She tore the envelope into tiny fragments, dropped them into the heart of the fire, and watched them burn.

'You saw Mrs Barrington last evening?'

'Yes . . . for a moment.'

'Do you think there is any chance *of your* getting those letters out of her, Wick? I mean—it seemed to me, if you offered to help her to go through her husband's papers— I'm sure she'd probably let you do it. Women hate papers and business and all that. . . and she has no men-folk. I'm sure you could persuade her to let you do it. You couldn't mistake the envelope. It's a very large, thick buff envelope—folded over—I mean—I don't suppose for a moment she'd let you have it, if she had the faintest idea what was in it. But you could manage to prevent her knowing . . .'

He had watched her face closely; but the candour of its anxiety was unmistakable. She had, then, not the slightest doubt that Barrington had gone home when he left her—not the slightest suspicion that she herself could have been responsible for his death. Well, *that* was an immense relief, anyhow.

'That's quite a good idea,' he said slowly. 'But the trouble is, Pickles, that those letters of yours are not at Hatfield Place.'

'Then, where are they? How do you know they are not there?'

'Because Barrington didn't go back there when he left you. I don't know where he *did* go. But he didn't go back to his house. That's a certainty. We've got to find out where he did go, before we can hope to get hold of that large envelope, I'm afraid. And that's not going to be easy, perhaps.'

'Oh.' She seated herself, and after a moment said again uneasily, 'Oh.'

'However, you mustn't worry too much about the letters, you know. It seems to me quite possible—supposing that he has left them locked up or shut up somewhere—Heaven knows how many establishments he has been running . . . it seems to me quite possible that you may never hear another word about them.'

'No, no . . . I shall never have a moment's peace—'

'Oh, yes, you will. Good Lord, Pickles . . . well, I suppose one oughtn't to say such a thing, but, hang it all, if I were you, I'd go down on my knees and thank Heaven for having done what it has done for me . . . without expecting anything more from it. He's gone. I'll risk it and say, "Thank God." Don't worry about the letters. I'm not a miracle worker, but I'll do my best. Now, look here . . . I want to know about this confounded knife. It was found by a maid under the coat-and- umbrella stand in your hall this morning, Clegg told me just now. How did it get under the coat-and-umbrella stand? That's what I want to know. Any idea?'

She had flushed up angrily.

'Really, Wick— I do wish you wouldn't question the servants. What on earth will Clegg think?'

'Clegg? Clegg will think that I'm a silly old bloke fussing because a bit of his wedding-present to the mistress of the house has been lost. That's all. I'll try to bear it, if you'll tell me how that knife got under that coat-and-umbrella stand.'

She made a little gesture.

'You aren't an absolute ass, Wick . . .'

'Thanks. That is to say . . . you think I am right in supposing that your husband put it there . . . to be found by the maid? . . .'

'He must have found it in one of Mr Barrington's pockets,' she said anxiously. 'I suppose he doesn't want me to know that he found it there. And so he put it under the coat-and-umbrella stand for the maids to find . . . At all events, that's the only thing I can think . . .'

It was, Gore admitted to himself, as he stared at her troubled face, quite possible that Melhuish had found the knife in one of Barrington's pockets before he himself had had the chance to search them—probably while he was examining him in the car. Of course, if that were so, that . . . well, *that* altered the story altogether, so far as Melhuish's part in it was concerned, at any rate. If that were so . . .

'Look here, Pickles . . . I want you to tell me again—exactly—what happened on Monday night when you saw Barrington. I want you just to answer my questions, and not bother to think why I ask them. If I'm to get hold of those letters for you, I must have the facts exactly. That's what it comes to. Now, will you just be as accurate as you can for about three minutes? It had been arranged that Barrington was to come to you at one o'clock. At what time *did* he come . . . exactly?'

'Just a minute or two before one.'

'Sure?'

'Yes. I looked at my watch before I left my room to go downstairs. It was one o'clock exactly then. When I got downstairs, I found that he had come a minute or two before.'

'How did he get in? Had you given him a latchkey?'

'Yes. He insisted on my giving him a latchkey. But I told him not to use it. I hadn't expected that he would come before one.'

'Where was he when you went down?'

'In the hall, waiting.'

'Alone?'

'Yes . . . of course.'

'Then . . . you talked to him . . . in the hall?'

'First in the dining-room. I gave him the hundred and fifty pounds there . . . and then he refused to give up the letters unless I gave him another four hundred.'

'Then you had a row about that... in the dining-room?'

'First in the dining-room, then in the hall.'

'How long altogether? I want you to be as accurate as you can about this. How long was he here—altogether?'

'About— Oh, I can't say exactly.'

'A quarter of an hour?'

'Longer than that, I think.'

'You think? Half an hour?'

'Not as long as that. No . . . not as long as that.'

'Twenty minutes?'

'Yes. I suppose about twenty minutes.'

'So, then, he went away about twenty minutes past one?'

'Yes, I suppose so.'

'Have you any reason—any reason whatever—to suppose that anyone was waiting for him—outside?'

That question startled her.

'Waiting . . . outside?' she repeated sharply. 'No.'

'There was no one waiting outside for him—so far as you know?'

She hesitated.

'I don't think so. Though I remember now that he did look towards the hall door when we were in the hall. He said he thought it had moved, or something like that. But then he said it must have been the wind.'

Wind? Had there been any wind on Monday night? Gore thought not. There might, of course, have been some through-draught.

'Do I understand that the hall door was open while you were talking to him in the hall?'

'No. Not open exactly. But not quite shut to.'

'Was it like that during all the time he was here?'

'Yes. I asked him not to shut it quite to, when he came in, because it makes a fearful row when you shut it. A sort of squeal. The hinges are very old or rusty or something.'

She turned her face again to him suddenly, as a thought occurred to her.

'Oh, yes . . . and I remember now . . . when we went out to the hall at first, he said that it was very risky leaving the door like that, ajar, because a policeman might see it open and come in. It had blown open a little then, so there must have been a wind—'

'It had blown open a little when you came out into the hall from the dining-room?'

'Yes.'

'Hum. And then he said he thought the wind had opened it?'

'No . . . not that time. That was after he had closed it to. He closed it to the first time, when we came out into the hall first. And then, while we were in the hall, he said he thought the wind had moved it again . . .'

'So that . . .'

Gore fell to silence abruptly, then, after a moment, repeated a question which he had already asked—this time very deliberately.

'But, as far as you yourself know, Pickles, there was no one waiting outside for Barrington?'

The intentness of his air plainly mystified her. If Arndale had been outside—perhaps right up against the hall door and listening—it had not been at her invitation at any rate.

'No. Why do you ask me that again that way?'

'Don't bother about that now. Did Barrington look out, when he thought the door had moved . . . either time?'

'No, I think not. I'm not sure. He just pushed the door to the first time, I think. The second time he did nothing.' 'When he went away, did he shut the hall-door behind him?' 'He pulled it just to, and I shut it a few moments later.' 'You heard no voices outside?'

'No. Why? Do *you* think there was someone else with him, Wick?'

'Never mind what *I* think. *I'm* asking the questions, Pickles. You're sure—once more—that Barrington had your letters with him when he left you?'

'Of course, yes.'

'Don't be impatient. I've nearly finished. And the knife?' 'Yes.'

'And the sheath of the knife?'

'Yes.'

'And the hundred and fifty pounds?'

'Yes.'

'In notes?'

'Yes.'

'When he took the knife from you, was it in its sheath . . . or out of it?'

'In it. It stuck, and I couldn't get it out behind my back.' 'You're absolutely certain of that?'

'Absolutely. *He* took it out of the little case then, and looked at it, and then put it back in the case and into his pocket.' Gore drew a long breath of great content.

'Good. Barrington went away at twenty minutes past one. You shut the hall door. What did you do then . . . exactly?'

'I went into the dining-room for a moment, switched off the light there, and then went up to my room and undressed—very quietly, I needn't tell you. I was just getting into bed when I, heard Sidney go downstairs and go out.'

'What time, please? How long after Barrington had left you . . . exactly?'

She knitted her brows in the effort to remember.

'I really can't say, Wick. I was perfectly wretched and worked up—'

'Five minutes?'

'Longer than that. About ten minutes.'

'Not a quarter of an hour?'

'No. About ten minutes.'

'So that, if Barrington went away at twenty past one, your husband went out at half-past one?'

'Yes. I think so. I can't be sure. I was too frightened and miserable to think about the time. You must understand that, Wick.'

'Yes. Good. You sleep at the front of the house?'

'No. My bedroom is at the back—behind Sidney's.'

'So you don't hear noises in Aberdeen Place?'

'Not unless they're very loud noises.'

'Good. What's the row between you and Mrs Barrington?'

Again she hesitated, puzzled.

'How you jump about. . . The row? About Bertie.'

'Bertie Challoner?'

'Yes. Bertie has been making a fool of himself with her, rather . . . taking her about. . . and making us all uncomfortable. Well . . . Sylvia and I found her actually having tea with him in his flat one afternoon about six months ago . . . and Sylvia went for them . . . You know what Sylvia is when she gets going. Of course Bertie got up on his back legs, and there was a jolly old row for about ten minutes. Sylvia hasn't spoken to her since—or to Bertie. I—well, of course, Bertie is my first cousin, and I'm very fond of him. And, of course, I took Sylvia's side—probably said a good deal more than I should have said. Rather amusing that must be for you . . . now that you know all about *my* glass-houses. However . . . that's the row.'

'But she was to have dined here on Monday evening—'

'Oh, yes . . . we're quite polite to one another. I had to be—you can guess why. Besides, I didn't want to drop her altogether . . . because nearly every one she ever knew *has* dropped her during the last year or so on account of her husband. I've been sorry for her. We've had her to dine here with us occasionally, and that sort of thing. But I know she has hated me like poison ever since that flare-up in Bertie's flat. Not that I think for a moment that there was anything serious in the affair . . . so far.

Bertie isn't a bit that sort. He thinks she's a martyred saint. . . and all that sort of thing. He's rather a nice boy, Bertie.'

'Well, I think that's all I want to ask you about. Oh . . . this thing?' He put his hand into his pocket and took out the little beaded sheath. 'What are we to do with this?'

'Burn it,' she said promptly.

'Once more—you're absolutely certain that Barrington took the knife *and* the sheath away with him when he left you?'

'Absolutely. As certain as I am that Sidney must have found the knife in his pocket.'

He considered that.

If Melhuish had found the knife in Barrington's pocket, he must have said to himself—supposing that he knew nothing of Barrington's visit to his house at one o'clock nor of the supposed encounter with some supposed third person who had waited outside—he must have said to himself, 'Now, how the deuce did this thing get into Barrington's pocket? Either he must have pinched it from my hall, or someone else must have taken it from my hall and given it to him. When *could* he have pinched it himself? Why should he have pinched it himself? He *didn't* pinch it himself; someone else gave it to him. Who?' If Melhuish had not been able to guess who, would he not certainly have taken steps to find out? Questioned his servants and his wife? Of course he would. But he hadn't done that. No—he had been able to guess. If he had not been able to guess, would he have hidden the knife for a maid to find? Would he not have simply replaced it in its place in the trophy? But he hadn't done that. He had invented this way of explaining the knife's absence from the trophy during the preceding day. Why? To destroy, as far as possible, any possible association of the knife with Barrington. Why, again? To destroy, as far as possible, any possible association of Barrington and the knife with . . . the one person for whom he would have been likely to have taken such cunning pains—his wife.

He turned to Mrs Melhuish.

'There is one more question, I find, Pickles. On Monday night, while Barrington was with you, did you notice anything—anything whatever—that might lead you to believe that your husband or anyone else in this house knew that he was with you? Anything whatever?'

It was a moment before she spoke, hesitatingly,—

'The only thing,' she said at length, 'is Sidney's going out.'

'But we know why he went out. Mrs MacArthur, or whatever her name is, rang him up to go and see her little boy.'

'She rang him up, yes. But he didn't go.'

'Didn't go?' he repeated.

'No. I met Mrs MacArthur shopping this morning, and she apologised to me for having rung him up at that hour, and said she was so glad he hadn't gone, because her little boy had been so much better next morning. When I came in I went straight out to the consulting-room and looked at Sidney's diary—you know? . . . the book he enters up his visits in.'

'Well?'

'Well . . . at the end of the space for Monday he had begun to make an entry—and then he had scratched it out—very carefully. But I got a magnifying-glass and had a good look at it. He had written something there at the end of the space, and scratched it out.'

Gore raised his eyebrows and let them fall expressively. 'Where does this Mrs MacArthur live?'

'In Vyford Place.'

'Vyford Place? Where's that?'

'It's one of the new roads—beyond the college.'

'Beyond the college . . .?'

He made a hurried calculation. If Melhuish had gone out at half-past one, he could certainly not have walked to any road beyond the college—interviewed a small boy afflicted with gastritis and an over-anxious mother—and walked back again to Aberdeen Place—all in ten minutes. Forty minutes work at the very least. Yet, he had been back in Aberdeen Place at twenty minutes to two at the latest...

Of course, he might have taken a taxi—both ways. Even then he couldn't have done it in ten minutes. And the chances of picking up a taxi in Linwood at half-past one in the morning were about the same as those of finding a tank in Piccadilly Circus at noonday . . .

'Hell, Pickles,' he said softly. 'That's queer. Look here—how long was your husband out . . . exactly? . . .'

But while she still stood frowning, he turned and picked up the little beaded sheath hurriedly, as the door behind them opened and Melhuish came in.

'Finished already, Sidney?' Mrs Melhuish asked, with extraordinary composure, as the two men exchanged good-mornings.

'No. I'm afraid I may not be able to get back to take you to the station, Barbara. I thought I had better let you know in good time. They want me to go out to Mrs Larmour's to meet Sir John Taylor in consultation at a quarter to twelve.'

His smile said, 'I've come back to say good-bye to my wife'—just that and nothing more. There was nothing to do but make the most graceful exit possible, and, as quickly as possible, Gore made it.

11

He went down to Cleveport by a midday train to lunch, golf, and dine with a married cousin, and—it must be quite frankly admitted—dismissed Pickles and her affairs almost completely from his mind for nearly twelve hours. The greatest anxiety of the business had been laid to rest; Pickles had had no hand, wilfully or accidentally, in Barrington's death. She had been— miraculously—extricated from her troubles and difficulties at their blackest hour. The thing was done with. As regarded the letters, he felt pretty sure that she had heard the last of them. They were not at Hatfield Place; there was no necessity to worry about Mrs Barrington then. Supposing that someone did find them wherever else Barrington had left them, what likelihood was there that that someone would ever think of making trouble for Pickles on the head of them? No doubt the world did contain a certain proportion of blackguards of Barrington's particular type. But only an almost grotesque pessimism could reckon that the person into whose hands the letter would stray that way, accidentally, would be another individual of the same kidney. Gore was not inclined to be pessimistic just then. The certainty that Pickles was clear of the greater danger, and the fact that the wet, depressing morning had given way to an afternoon of crisp, brilliant sunshine, had indeed so strongly influenced his spirits that, after a very little reflection, he had abandoned his carefully concocted 'story' root and branch, lock, stock, and barrel, and decided to devote his attention to playing the kind of golf which he knew a plus-two cousin would expect from him.

The 'story,' it appeared to him now, had been the figment of a most amazingly distorted imagination. Barrington had died just as he had appeared to die, of heart-disease, on his way to visit Melhuish professionally. No doubt his fall, however it had occurred, had knocked him about severely. Heaven knew, too, how he had spent the night. He had died, at any rate, just as he had been liable to die at any moment.

Melhuish had found the knife in his pocket when he had examined him in the car, and must have believed that, somehow, Barrington had contrived to pinch it. Perhaps, for a moment, he had thought that the scratch on Barrington's hand might have had something to do with his death. At any rate, as nine men out of ten would have done under the circumstances, he had decided, since the man was dead, to avoid any trouble about the knife by concealing the fact that Barrington had stolen it. And so he had invented the idea of leaving it somewhere about for one of the maids to find.

It was possible that he had suspected, and did still suspect, that there had been something—some furtive connection—between his wife and Barrington. But that he actually knew anything definite regarding it, Gore doubted now altogether. As to that telephone call of Mrs MacArthur's, Melhuish had gone out intending to go and see the child, but had probably failed to get a taxi, and, knowing that the boy was in no danger, had decided against a long walk on a nasty night for nothing, and had gone home again. His own words had been: A Mrs MacArthur rang me up,' not 'I have been to see the little boy of a Mrs MacArthur.' Gore was pretty certain about that; for he remembered that it had occurred to him at the time that this Mrs MacArthur lived in Selkirk Place and that Melhuish was then still on his way to her.

As to the knife-sheath—well, that, too, was perfectly simple, after all. After leaving Pickles, Barrington had gone, in his car, up the lane at the end of Selkirk Place, bound for wherever he was bound for. He had said to himself: 'Better not keep that knife, perhaps. It's really no use to me—poisoned, too, and dangerous. *My* business never comes to producing proofs. So long as she knows I can say that she tried to give me a jab with a knife, that's all I want.' So he had thrown the knife away. Then he had thought better of it, and had got out of the car and looked about for it. He had found the knife itself, but the sheath had come off it. While he was still looking for the sheath he had probably been disturbed. It would have been just then—say, just at half-past one—that Melhuish had come out from his house. If Barrington heard the hall door of Number 33 opening—had seen it opening, as he could have seen from that corner, looking across the Green—he would get into his car and clear out. And so the sheath had remained behind, to be found where it had been found.

All the rest of the story—all that about Arndale and Challoner and all the rest of it—seemed now the most amazing moonshine. It amused Gore to perceive how curiously his judgment had been warped by the desire to translate an ordinary death into a murder, to fasten the murder on someone, and to run that someone down. The ease with which facts had permitted themselves to be twisted so as to support an entirely erroneous theory impressed him sardonically. How many times in courts of justice, he asked of his rather abashed common sense, had the things one called bald, hard facts, absolutely misled juries— juries summoned specifically to do the thing which he himself had done gratuitously, to fix the blame on someone, and, despite themselves, determined to do it.

He got back to the Riverside about eleven o'clock that night, and over a pipe and a drink decided to write Pickles a line to her Surrey address, to ease her mind about things generally. He felt just then like cheering people up. His visit to Cleveport had been an entirely soothing success—not least because the plus-two cousin—off his game, of course, but playing quite scratchy stuff—had ended but one up on the nineteenth green. He had met several old friends, fixed up several days' shooting, been appointed godfather, had a mild but quite sparkling flirtation with a charming little widow during dinner, and encountered some marvellous Westmouth cream—that most contenting of sherries. So he made a long arm for his writing-case, cocked it on a knee, and began his letter of good cheer with light-hearted fluency.

'*November* 8, *1922*.

'DEAR PICKLES,—Just a line to ask you not to worry in the least about those foolish questions of mine this morning—or *anything*. You need have no anxiety whatever about the discovery under the coat-and-umbrella- stand. I have thought the thing over very carefully, and—'

A slight sound behind him disturbed him at that point. He turned in his chair and saw, framed in the doorway, the tawny-haired Miss Rodney, surveying him with a smile intended, he divined, to invest her uninvited appearance in his sitting-room with a quality of vivacious feminine playfulness. To that kind of playfulness Gore had, at ordinary times, no violent objection. But, since it was getting on to midnight and he had lived for some little time in a wicked world, the smile with which he greeted this unexpected apparition was correct to the verge of fatherliness.

'Not in bed yet, Miss Rodney?'

She laughed, and flashed a look at him from beneath her eyelashes.

'Every time you see me you say: "Not in bed yet, Miss Rodney?" Can't you think of anything else to say?'

'Had I said that to you before?'

'As if you didn't remember. And that's just what I've been wanting to talk to you about ever since—you and your friend Mr Challoner. I saw a light in here as I came along the passage. So I said to myself: "I'll just pop in and pluck *that* little crow with him." But I've disturbed you. Writing to your best girl, I suppose. My eyes—what a swanky dressing-gown. Now, if you wanted to be a sport, you'd offer me a very, very, very good cigarette.'

'Dear sportive, giddy little kitten,' mused Gore. 'Too many teeth. Too little chin. Cute as a pet fox. What's she after?'

He supplied the best cigarette at his command, however, and lighted it for her politely. She blew a little cloud through experienced nostrils, and then seated herself on the arm of a chair.

'You're older,' she said pertly, 'when one looks into your face for a bit.'

'The shorter the bit then,' he laughed, 'the younger I remain.'

'Is that a hint to me to clear out?'

'My dear young lady, I had no hope whatever that you would remain.'

Her eyes hardened; her whole expression changed with extraordinary promptness. A kitten with ready claws, this.

'Don't think I want to force my company where it isn't wanted, please. I just want to ask you a simple question. And I'll be obliged if you'll answer it.'

'With pleasure, if I can.'

'Well. . . what were you and Mr Challoner doing on Monday night hanging about there at the gates? Perhaps you'll kindly tell me. Because I'm anxious to know.'

'Did we hang about? Or rather—did we seem to hang about? How thoughtless of us. We were not planning a burglary, however—merely, as far as I can recall, parting till the morrow.'

'That's a lie,' she said coolly. 'And you know it is. Which of you whistled—you or Mr Challoner?'

'Did we whistle?'

'One of you did. Which of you? I want to know, please.'

'Obviously. You can understand then, how natural it is that I should want to know why you want to know.'

'Because I want to know what you and Mr Challoner were doing there.'

'I have already told you that I parted from Mr Challoner there. I had been in his rooms, and he walked with me as far as the gates of the grounds.'

She eyed him sullenly for some moments in silence.

'You won't answer the question I've asked you?'

'I *have* answered it, Miss Rodney—twice, I believe.'

She threw her cigarette into the fire angrily.

'Well, you may be as glib and as smart as you please, but I tell you I'm going to know the meaning of you and your friends hanging about that way at night, watching and spying on people. If you won't tell me, I'll go to Mr Challoner and ask him. And if *he* won't tell me, I'll go to Dr Melhuish and ask him. And if *he* won't tell me, I'll complain to the manager and have it stopped. You'll see.'

'My dear Miss Rodney,' said Gore suavely, 'I assure you you are labouring under some most extraordinary delusion.'

'Oh, am I, indeed?'

'I assure you.'

'Well, then, why did I see you twice on Monday night, waiting about there at the gates? I saw you there just after half-past one—and I saw you there again at half-past two, with Mr Challoner. Why did I see Dr Melhuish there at half-past one, too, just before I saw you? What's the game? Come on. Say it out. And let's have done with it.'

'We have done with it, Miss Rodney, so far as I am concerned. If you imagine that I entertain the least interest in your private affairs—I mean, beyond the interest which is their due—you are absolutely mistaken. To state the matter quite concisely, I don't. Another cigarette? No. They *are* pretty bad. Goodnight.'

Before his adroit manoeuvring she had retreated slowly to the door.

'All right,' she snapped. 'But if there's any more of it, I'll complain to the manager. Understand that. He'll soon put a stop to your molesting people.'

She waited for his retort, but as there was none, flounced out into the passage and went off towards her sleeping quarters, leaving Gore to shut his door and return to contemplate his fire dubiously.

Melhuish, according to this account, had been 'hanging about' by those gates just before he himself had gone out through them on his way to post his letters. At half-past one, she had said—probably a vague estimate of the hour, approximate merely, yet, as it happened, accurate enough.

For he recalled that, having stamped his two letters, he had looked at his watch and had seen that it was twenty-five minutes past one. He had felt suddenly disinclined to go out into the fog and damp again, and, having decided not to post his letters that night, had lighted a pipe and smoked for a bit, thinking about things. Finally he had changed his mind again, decided that his letters ought to go that night, put on an overcoat, and gone out—as nearly as he could now reckon, at 1.35 or a very little later. Melhuish had been nowhere in sight then. Of course there had been a pretty thick fog—

He remembered then that the blind of that lighted window over the bar had been drawn a little aside, and that someone had peeped down at him as he halted to light a cigarette. Naturally enough the girl had been curious, if Melhuish had been 'hanging about' there a couple of minutes before—

It had taken, say, two minutes or three to reach the pillar-box. At 1.38, then, he had met Melhuish by the pillar-box. Say two minutes later, at 1.40, they had seen Arndale coming out of Challoner's flat. Yes. That fitted. Beginning from the other end, it fitted too. At 1.20 Barrington had left Pickles. Ten minutes later Melhuish had gone out, at 1.30.

But that allowed Melhuish no time to 'hang about.'

Well, allow for a difference of clocks and watches. Allow Melhuish five or six minutes to 'hang about'—

What had taken him across there to that corner, by the gates? What *had* he been hanging about there for? Waiting for Barrington? Had he, as Pickles had originally feared, followed Barrington—seen him go in to this girl—waited for him to come out? Had he followed Barrington knowing that Barrington had just come from his own house—knowing that he had been with Pickles—knowing what had passed between them—knowing everything?

Or had he merely seen Barrington's car and wondered where Barrington was? Perhaps Barrington had moved the car from Aberdeen Place, where it had stood apparently while he had been with Pickles, and had left it at that corner while he was with this girl.

But why should Melhuish 'hang about' wondering where Barrington was—unless he had some special reason beyond mere idle curiosity . . . a thing unlikely in a man of Melhuish's stamp?

Devilish odd that he should have been there—at that spot where the sheath had turned up.

Suppose he *had* followed Barrington, knowing that Barrington had those letters of his wife's— Hell—

Suppose he had waited outside until Barrington had come out from this Rodney girl, and had demanded them. Would a threat of exposure have scared Barrington into giving them up? Wouldn't he have simply defied Melhuish? Might not that scrap which the 'story' had supposed to have taken place over in Aberdeen Place with Arndale, have taken place in that corner by the gates . . . with Melhuish. Suppose Barrington had shown fight, and taken out the knife—

Gore turned his back on the fire, plunged his hands as far as they would go into his trousers-pockets, and informed the hearthrug solemnly that he was damned.

Perhaps this girl had seen the scrap. Perhaps she suspected that it had had something to do with Barrington's death—perhaps knew that it had— Perhaps she had come in just now to try to get some information out of him— Jolly—

It was absolutely ridiculous. Here he was again, back in a muddle of confused suspicion—trying to twist a few miserable, maddeningly inadequate facts into another 'story' as absurd as that which he had abandoned for good and all that morning. What was it? What was this obsession that had him in its grip—that refused to allow him to let this sleeping dog lie? Did he or did he not believe that Barrington had died of heart disease—was it impossible for him to answer that simple question to himself?

He seated himself and, having torn up his uncompleted letter to Pickles, threw it into the fire and fell to meditating upon this curious vacillation of his judgment with regard to the whole affair. It occurred to him after some moments, as a species of relief from formless thought, to make a diagram—a kind of temperature-chart, which would exhibit concretely these strayings to-and-fro of his conjecture; and after some consideration he evolved the following graph, designed to record the varying phases of his opinion with regard to that definite question: 'Do I believe that Barrington died of heart disease and from no other cause, or do I not believe it?'

Starting from the blankness of mind indicated by 'No record,' he divided the progress towards certainty into the stages 'Surmise,' two degrees of Suspicion, Belief, and Certainty. *Minus* degrees of the same kind would indicate the stages to Certainty at the other end of the scale—that is to say, in this

B d. (h.d).

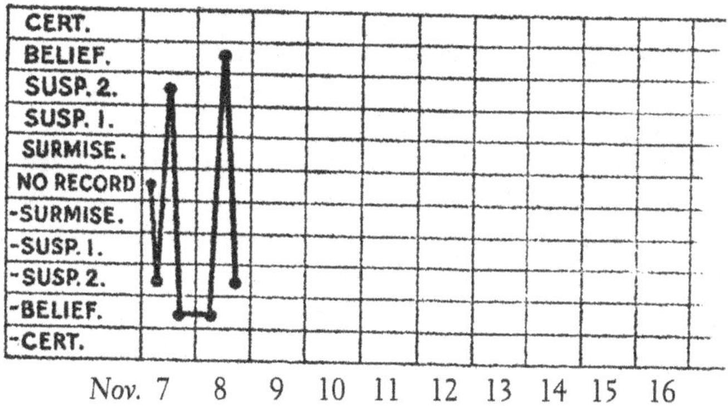

particular case, certainty that Barrington had not died simply of heart-dis- ease.

He traced the 'curve'—one, certainly, of sufficiently acute aberration—for November 7th and 8th. From 'No record,' it sprang to the strong suspicion of his first view of the dead man's face, and the scratch on his hand; from that it sprang to a suspicion that had been almost belief that Melhuish's verdict of heart disease had been the right one; from that it jumped to a belief that had been almost certainty at the other end of the scale, marking the discovery that Melhuish had brushed the mud from Barrington's clothes and taken away his wrist-watch; so it had remained overnight until that morning when it had leaped to absolute belief that the 'story' was all moonshine; and now it had dropped once more to the strongest of suspicions that another 'story' no less sensational, lay behind the affair.

Having considered this edifying product of his intelligence for some little time, he made three similar graphs illustrating his speculations with regard to the three people, one of whom, it seemed, or had seemed, must have been, wilfully or accidentally, responsible for Barrington's death if natural causes had not been responsible for it. Then he decided to make a fifth graph, to be used—if occasion should arise, for some possible fourth person. And having got as far as that, he ultimately decided to make one for every person who, to his knowledge, had been connected with Barrington in any way whatever.

This proved a longish job; but the task interested him. Many of the graphs, of course, remained blank and curveless; the great majority of the names which his memory collected from the preceding forty-eight hours or so appeared so absolutely improbable that he was almost disposed to omit them. But the strain of doggedness in him refused to allow him to abandon his design. It would be curiously interesting, he reflected, if by chance someone of those improbable persons should prove in the end—if there ever was an end—the key to the riddle. Not that he seriously anticipated any such dramatic *denouement*. He had at that moment very little doubt that either Melhuish or Arndale, or both, had had some sort of scrap with Barrington, and that in the course of the encounter Barrington's hand had received a scratch which had been at least partially responsible for his death. The details persisted in remaining bafflingly obscure. Little discrepancies of time and place intruded themselves irritatingly. But the central fact appeared to him beyond all doubt or question. Barrington's death lay between Arndale and Melhuish.

He had tossed the diagrams to the hearth-rug as he had completed each. He gathered them up now in a jumble, as they came to his hand, and made a key list, numbering the graphs to correspond with the numbers opposite the names on the list respectively—twenty names in all, including that of Barrington himself. Finally he carefully deleted all initials and other marks by which he had originally distinguished the graphs, and put his key-list away in his pocket-wallet. The graphs themselves he pinned together and left inside the cover of his writing-block, where, next morning, one of the Riverside's maids found them, and, being an unscientific person, formed an opinion, which nothing ever afterwards altered, that 'the Colonel' in the unwedded loneliness of his middle-age, was accustomed to console himself of nights with some complicated version of the ancient pastime of 'Fox-and-Geese.'

12

Three communications reached Gore on Thursday morning—a scrawl from Challoner, cancelling the golf arranged for that day, on the plea of a day amongst the partridges in Wiltshire; an intimation that the secretaryship of the London club had been filled; and the following reply to a note which he had despatched to Mrs Barrington before starting for Cleveport on the preceding morning:

'27, HATFIELD PLACE,
Wed., *Nov.* 8.

'DEAR WICK,—It is very good of you to have thought of me. I know nothing of my husband's business affairs, nor have I the least curiosity with regard to them. However, I suppose someone ought to go through his papers and see how things stand. The funeral, as you perhaps know, is tomorrow morning at eleven. If you can spare an hour or so on Friday afternoon—I suggest three o'clock—I shall be very grateful if you will come and talk over things. At the moment I don't know if he has left enough money to pay his servants the wages owing to them—or even his own funeral expenses. Fortunately, I have still a few pounds of the £100 a year which my most generous of parents allow me. Angela Heathman, too, has been very kind, and has offered repeatedly to title me over any money difficulties that may arise. A rather unexpected charity—but I can't afford to be proud. Forgive this long grouse.

'Yours,
'ETHEL BARRINGTON.'

'P.S.—I take back anything stupid I said to you about Barbara Melhuish and her husband. No one could be more kind or more thoughtful than Dr Melhuish has been. And Barbara wrote me the sweetest little note before she went away to Surrey this morning. I have only just got it, and am still inclined to blubber. So please forget anything silly I said to you yesterday.—E.B.'

When, about three o'clock on the following afternoon, Gore arrived at Hatfield Place, his friend Florence ushered him out to a room at the end of the hall, where he found Mrs Barrington awaiting him with—somewhat to his discomfiture—Miss Heathman. On a table stood a large tin box, the contents of which had been emptied on to the tablecloth and arranged roughly in order.

By daylight Miss Heathman's drawn, sallow pallor was still more noticeable. She departed almost immediately, having explained with her nervous, fleeting smile, that she had merely called in passing to cheer dear Ethel up a little, and to renew her offer of any assistance in her power.

'Well,' said Gore, when she had gone—slithering, as he described her mode of progression to himself, like a sick snake—'I have a respect amounting to slavish adoration for anyone who is sixpence richer when she has ended shaking hands with you than she was when she began doing it. But, candidly, if I wanted a little cheering up—'

'She does look rather dreadful, poor old thing,' Mrs Barrington agreed. 'But she has been awfully kind, really. In fact, almost overpoweringly kind. She has been here for an hour and a half this afternoon. I can't think why, exactly. I've never really known her very well. Of course she's years and years older than I am. However . . . she obviously means well . . . and I haven't so many friends that I can afford to pick and choose exactly . . .'

For a little while they chatted desultorily over a cigarette. Then she turned to the table.

'My husband kept all his private papers in that box, as far as I can make out. I couldn't find the key. But Mr Frensham very kindly borrowed a file and filed the hasp of the padlock through for me. He has looked through all those things on the table. I really don't know that there's any necessity for you to bother about them, Wick.'

'Who is Mr Frensham?' he asked carelessly.

'He was a friend of my husband's. They used to go racing together, I think. He has stayed here once or twice.'

'Then he doesn't live here?'

'No. He lives in London. But he happened to be in Westmouth . . . so he went to the funeral yesterday . . . the solitary mourner, by the way . . . And this morning he very kindly came along to know if he could help me in any way about my husband's business affairs.'

'That,' said Gore thoughtfully, 'was very kind of him. What sort of chap is he?'

'Oh . . . well . . .' said Mrs Barrington.

'I see.'

'I mean . . . he's a funny little man, but quite a good business man, I should say. Very much on the spot.'

'Oh, yes. And so he came along and volunteered to go through your husband's papers and things, did he?'

'Yes.'

'And you said "Yes"?'

'Well . . . I did. I thought it would save my having to bother you or anyone else.'

'He has looked over all these things here?'

'Yes. He went through them all most carefully.'

'Alone . . . or with you?'

'I was in and out of the room. You seem very suspicious of poor Mr Frensham, Wick. Why? You don't know anything about him, do you?'

'I? Nothing whatever. Do you?'

'No, I can't say that I do.'

'Well,' he asked, after a moment's silence, 'what is the result of Mr Frensham's investigations?'

'He says he can't find any trace of my husband's having made a will . . . so far. Not that that matters in the least . . . to *me*. I shan't touch a penny of his money. I have just two pounds a week of my own to live on. Lots of people live on less. I can do it if other people can.'

'Had your husband any relatives living? He must have had.'

'I haven't the faintest idea. I suppose that sounds incredible. But it's the simple fact, none the less. He told me so many lies that finally I reached a stage at which I preferred him to tell me nothing about himself.'

'How often has this Mr Frensham stayed here with you?' he asked, after a moment.

'Three times, I think.'

'You've no idea what he is . . . what he does?'

'None whatever. He seems to have travelled a lot. He has been to China, Japan, America, Africa, Russia, all over the Continent . . . everywhere. The sort of man who can tell you what time the trams start running on Sundays in Oklahoma—'

'Very helpful . . . in Oklahoma . . . on Sunday morning,' he said dryly. 'But I should have thought an ordinary stay-at-home Westmouth solicitor would be quite competent to deal with your husband's affairs. Sorry to seem so unenthusiastic about your friend Mr Frensham. I know nothing about him. Neither do you. But that's a lot too little.'

She played for some moments with the filed-through padlock which lay on the table beside the tin box.

'As a matter of fact,' she said at length, 'I *have* rather regretted that I allowed Mr Frensham to go through these things of my husband's. You see, a rather awkward thing turned up. I found a cheque which I couldn't understand. I think, now, that perhaps I ought not to have shown it to anyone else until I had found out something about it.'

He stared. But Pickles had said explicitly that she had always paid in cash—

'A cheque?'

'Yes. For quite a large sum. . . two hundred and fifty pounds. A cheque of Mr Arndale's—that's what I think so odd. I can't think why Mr Arndale should have paid my husband a cheque for two hundred and fifty pounds.'

Gore pulled down his waistcoat.

'Nice round little sum—two hundred and fifty pounds,' he said pleasantly. 'Cards, I suppose. Your husband had card-parties here fairly regularly, hadn't he? . . .'

'Yes. But Mr Arndale has never played cards here. I don't think he has been to the house for over twelve months . . . longer. He and his wife used to dine here occasionally during the first year or so after my marriage. But . . . that stopped. Certainly Mr Arndale has never played cards here. I'm quite sure about that. Mr Frensham suggested that it might be in settlement of racing debts.'

'Quite possibly,' nodded Gore. 'May I see the cheque?'

'Mr Frensham took it away,' Mrs Barrington said with some embarrassment.

'Took it away? Why?'

'He suggested that he should see Mr Arndale about it?'

'Why?'

'Why? Well . . . really I don't know . . . now. Except that I told him I couldn't understand it.'

'The cheque was drawn by Arndale . . . and payable to your husband?'

'No. It was drawn by Mr Arndale, payable to "self."' 'Endorsed?'

'Yes. Mr Arndale had endorsed it, and written "Please pay cash to bearer."'

'An uncrossed cheque?'

'It was not crossed.'

'And . . . you allowed this Mr Frensham to take it away?'

She was plainly alarmed by his disapproval—by some misgivings of her own, too.

'Yes, to make sure from Mr Arndale that it was all right.'

'All right?'

'Yes. All right that it should be amongst my husband's papers.'

'What was the date of the cheque?'

'November 4th.'

'That was last Saturday. When did Mr Frensham propose to see Arndale about it?'

'Today. This afternoon. He has probably seen him already.'

Lest he should alarm her further—perhaps quite unnecessarily—he left the matter there for the moment.

'Oh, well, I expect it's all right. Very probably a racing debt, as Mr Frensham suggests. However, I think I'd like to run through these things for you. It won't take me very long. May I smoke a pipe?'

'Of course. You . . . you don't think, really, Wick, that there could be anything . . . queer . . . about that cheque, do you?'

'Not for a moment,' he said brightly, seating himself at the table. 'Now let us see what we've got here. You've looked through all other likely drawers and so forth, I presume?'

'Those are all the papers I could find,' she said, turning away a little impatiently.

'Good.'

There was a large—an extraordinarily large—collection of letters, neatly tied up in bundles of varying sizes, and docketed with the writers' names. One of the bundles had been opened—by Mrs Barrington herself, it seemed—for, as he glanced at the uppermost letter, and read the words: 'My Darling Boy,—What a topping day yesterday was. Today the world seems as flat and dull as—' she laughed contemptuously.

'Pleasant, isn't it? I used to write him letters like that, too—once. But he hasn't kept mine . . . thank goodness. I shouldn't bother about those, Wick. I'm going to make a bonfire of them at the end of the garden presently. I expect they're all from women. He was simply crazy about women, poor creature.'

Barrington had evidently been a person of orderly mind at any rate; for the letters were arranged alphabetically. And it had taken Gore something less than thirty seconds to discover, half-way through one of the larger bundles, a wad of some twenty-five or thirty letters, each docketed 'Letchworth.' He nodded prompt agreement to the bonfire suggestion.

'Best thing to do with them.'

Bank-books, cheque-books, and cancelled cheques he put aside for more careful examination, restoring to the tin box a miscellaneous jumble of less interesting souvenirs—photographs of horses, an automatic pistol, a service revolver, some boxes of cartridges, five gold cigarette-cases, a small sketch in oils of a girl's head, admirably fresh and living, a pair of field- glasses, a woman's slipper, a dog's collar engraved 'Bill,' and three small note-books containing names and addresses. In a little jeweller's box, wrapped in tissue-paper, he found four unset diamonds—as far as he could judge, very fine stones— and a platinum and diamond ring. These also, in compliance with a silent gesture from Mrs Barrington, he restored to the tin box.

A large cardboard box next attracted his attention.

'What's in this?' he asked. 'Have you looked?'

'Wigs and things,' Mrs Barrington replied, and smiled at his surprise.

He opened the box and surveyed its contents for a moment or two curiously. There was, as a matter of fact, no wig amongst them. But there were a couple of beards, three moustaches, an extensive 'make-up' outfit, a pair of blue 'goggles,' a pince-nez, and two pairs of spectacles.

'What the deuce—?' he murmured in perplexity.

'I didn't know he had those things,' Mrs Barrington smiled, 'but I've always had an idea that at some time or other he had either been on the stage or had been very keen about it.'

'Oh!' Gore replaced the lid on the cardboard box. 'Bonfire?'

'Yes.'

Some unused packs of cards and a roulette apparatus were sentenced to the same fate. Four £10 Bank of England notes, discovered in an envelope, went back into the tin box. There remained a large tobacco-tin filled with some white crystalline powder, on top of which rested three little packets, each containing a small quantity of the same powder. Gore sniffed—sniffed again. A gentleman of many activities, Mr Barrington, it was evident.

Mrs Barrington had risen from her chair and stood beside him now at the table. She stopped him as he was about to replace the lid on the tin.

'There were four of those little packets,' she said. 'Have you taken one out, Wick?'

'No.'

'Then where is the fourth?'

They made the brief search necessary to assure them that the missing packet was neither on the table, nor on the floor, nor in the tin box.

'Oh, well, it doesn't matter,' said Mrs Barrington. 'Only . . . it's rather odd that it should have disappeared. What *is* that white stuff, Wick? Have you any idea?'

It seemed to Gore very much better that he should have no idea, and he said, promptly, that he had none.

'Perhaps Mr Frensham borrowed the fourth packet for some reason or other,' he suggested.

'No. There were four in that tin when Miss Heathman was here. I know that—because I showed her that white stuff and asked her what she thought it was. Perhaps *she* may have taken one of the little packets. Though why on earth should she . . . without saying so?'

'Heaven knows,' smiled Gore. Though, in fact, it had just occurred to him that the explanation might not lie at an at all so inconvenient a distance. His speculations upon the matter were interrupted, however, at that point by the appearance of Florence.

'Mr and Mrs Melville to see you, madam. I told them you were engaged, but they insisted on coming in.'

'Very well,' said Mrs Barrington frigidly.

She turned to Gore when the servant had gone out.

'This, I presume, means that my beloved parents mean to forgive me my sin, now that I have got rid of it,' she said bitterly. 'I suppose I must see them. Does this eye of mine look very awful?'

'Personally I shouldn't have noticed it,' Gore assured her, 'if you hadn't directed my attention to it.'

'Oh, mother will spot it the moment I go into the room. She'll probably fall on my neck and burst into tears of triumph. However . . . *they've* made the first move. That's something. I'm afraid we must interrupt our investigations here, Wick. There *is* nothing of any importance, is there?'

'I'll carry on here for a few minutes. I should like to see just how money matters stand. You run along now and see your father and mother. They're the most important thing just at present. I'll leave a little memo here for you, if there's anything of interest.'

Left alone, his first proceeding was to extract Pickles's letters from the bundle which contained them and to transfer them to the pockets of his overcoat; his next, to look through the bundle containing names beginning with H, and to detach from it a little wad of letters docketed 'Heathman, A.' A glance was sufficient to reveal to him their purport. All of them related to the supply by Barrington of something referred to under the disguise 'Celeste'—some specifying an hour, presumably of convenient delivery—some protesting against delay or disappointment—some enclosing sums of money whose size opened Gore's eyes considerably. He tore these communications into small pieces and consigned them to the fire by instalments, without any doubt as to the identity of 'Céleste'and the *contents* of the tobacco-tin, or as to the manner in which that fourth little packet had disappeared. The explanation of Angela Heathman's sudden and unexpected devotion to Mrs Barrington was perfectly clear. The poor, silly creature, finding her supply cut off, had hoped that some chance would enable her to lay her itching fingers on one of those little packets.

He stood for some moments regarding the bundles of letters frowningly. Curious reading, no doubt, most of them. The sooner that bonfire happened the better, obviously. He picked up one of the bundles at hazard, and ran his eye over the names which slipped past his finger. The last two letters of that bundle were docketed 'Wellmore, J.'

'My aunt,' he mused, 'is old Jimmy Wellmore at that game, too?'

Whatever the game with which Wellmore had been amusing himself, it was clear from his letters that he had declined to pay Mr Barrington for it, and had refused altogether to understand why that gentleman should take any interest in it. Both communications were of recent date; that particular deal of Mr Barrington's had been in its initial stage only when the

Fates had interfered. It was no particular business of Gore's; but since old Wellmore had given him an excellent dinner three days before, he tore up the letters and burnt them then and there.

He lighted another pipe and seated himself in a comfortable arm-chair with the bank-books. The deposit account showed on October 17th a balance of £923 11s. 4d., which had apparently varied very little during the eighteen months which the entries covered. The pocket in the cover of the book contained some slips, about a dozen in number, pinned together, each initialled at the head, recording sums received or paid—there was nothing to indicate which—on various dates. There was no 'B.M.' amongst the initials; though, by a curious coincidence, those on the second slip were 'W.G.'

The current account book showed a credit balance on October 31st of £110 2*s. id.* It showed, however, upon a little examination, some details of greater interest than that.

The entries extended over the period from June, 1921, to October 31st, 1922. During that period the lodgments amounted to nearly four thousand pounds. From whatever source Barrington's income had been derived, it had worked out at something pretty close to £3000 a year for the period shown.

The second point of interest was that all the lodgments—many of them for considerable sums—had been made by cash, and that all cheques drawn upon the account had been drawn payable to 'self.'

The third point of interest did not intrude itself upon Gore's attention until he had studied this curiously discreet account for some little while. There was a series of lodgments, made at regular intervals of two months, from the beginning of the period covered by the entries, all for the sum of £250. The last lodgment of this bi-monthly series had been made on September 2nd. No £250 had been lodged at the end of October.

Knowing, as Gore knew, of that cheque of Cecil Arndale's for £250, dated November 4th, the discovery of which had perturbed Mrs Barrington, it required no great acumen upon his part to divine the source from which that regular revenue had flowed to Barrington's banking account. The very obvious, but very amazing conclusion could only be that Arndale—for at all events eighteen months past—had been making payments to Barrington at the rate of fifteen hundred a year.

Why?

Another careful examination of the bundles of letters on the table revealed none of Arndale's amongst them. Gore was standing at the window, looking out into the narrow strip of winter-stricken garden, selecting a site for the bonfire which he had now resolved should be an accomplished fact before he left the house, when Florence ushered into the room a smiling, fresh-coloured, stoutish little man who advanced towards him with an outstretched hand of effusive geniality.

'Mr Frensham, sir,' the parlourmaid announced. 'Mrs Barrington thought you would like to see him, as you are here, sir.'

'Pleased to meet you, Colonel,' beamed Mr Frensham. 'Pleased to meet any friend of Mrs Barrington's, I'm sure. There's no lady I have a greater regard for, or would do more for, than Mrs Barrington. She's mentioned my name to you, perhaps. Poor old Cyril was an old pal of mine. Dear old chap. One of the best. Absolutely one of the best. Yes. Rotten bad luck, him getting knocked out so sudden—as you might say, before he'd reached his prime. Rotten bad luck. Yes. You didn't know him at all, did you?'

'I had met him once,' Gore replied pleasantly. 'But, no, I can't say that I knew him at all.'

'Charming feller,' said Mr Frensham. 'Absolutely charming feller. Connected with the Brazenby family, you know, and all that lot. Lord Winshamcote's mother—the Honourable Violet

Brazenby, she was, you know, of course—she was a half-sister of poor old Cyril's mother's.'

'Oh, yes,' said Gore politely. 'Cigarette?'

'Thanks, I will,' said Mr Frensham.

He lighted his cigarette and blew a cloud and watched its progress towards the window.

'Least . . . so he said,' he added; and, after a little beaming glance at Gore's amiable face, decided upon still greater frankness. 'Said more than his prayers, of course, poor old Cyril, sometimes—between you and me.'

Gore smiled the indulgent smile of a man of the world, and maintained it while Frensham's quick, bright little hazel eyes took minute stock of his person. Frensham's own personal appearance afforded little clue to his avocation. His neat dark suit and bowler hat were absolutely inexpressive. His fresh, clean-shaven face, with its humorous, quickly-darting eyes, was the face of a music-hall comedian rather than that of an associate of blackmailers and drug-traffickers. Nor was there anything in the least furtive or dubious in his air or manner. His geniality was the ordinary well-intentioned familiarity of the class to which his voice and accent and vocabulary showed that he belonged. So Gore continued to smile at him amiably until, after quite a long pause, he began to talk again.

'Funny me happening to be in Westmouth just when the poor old chap copped out,' he said, shedding the ash of his cigarette into the grate and turning to take another birdlike view of Gore over his shoulder before he straightened his burly little figure again. 'Glad I was able to roll up for his funeral. Can't say his friends here in Linwood gave him much of a send-off, poor old chap. Wasn't another soul at it except me and the undertaker's men. Nasty for *her*, that, you know, Colonel. Nasty. Wimmen feel things like that, you know, don't they? Sensitive. Yes.'

He turned and beamed at the table.

'Been having a look over those things of his, have you?'

'Yes. I've just been through them.'

'Left no will, seemingly.'

'No. So it appears.'

There was another silence, disturbed only by the slow crackle of the fire. Frensham jerked his head towards the door, coughed, and lowered his voice to mysteriousness.

'She tell you anything about this cheque?'

'Cheque? Oh, yes. Er—I believe you very kindly undertook to see Mr Arndale about a cheque—'

Again Frensham got rid of his cigarette-ash with elaborate carefulness.

'I've seen him,' he said, and nodded reassuringly. 'It's all right. That's what I've come back to see *her* about. But I hear she's got visitors with her now, eh?'

'Mr and Mrs Melville are with her.'

'Ow. Likely to stay long, are they?'

'I've no idea. Some considerable time, I should say.'

'Ow. Well, I'd better wait. She's a bit anxious about that cheque, I know.'

'Oh, I don't think so,' smiled Gore. 'I don't think there's any necessity whatever for you to wait and see her.'

'Oh, yes, there is,' said Frensham promptly. 'I'm in no hurry. I got to explain to *her*, you see. I'm a chap, when I've undertaken to do a thing, I like to do it, see? I'm in no hurry.'

He turned to the table again, and began to fidget with the contents of the tin box with the abstracted air of a man who beguiles a wait by the fiddling of his fingers. After a moment or two he took out the tobacco-tin.

'What's this stuff he had in this tin?' he asked. 'Had a look at it?'

As he spoke he removed the lid, and Gore saw his face change. It was the slightest thing—the effect of an instant—a scarcely perceptible flickering of the muscles at the corners of his lips and of his eyes. But for Gore, watching him from the hearth-rug, the warning was quite sufficient. The discovery that one of the four little packets had been removed had completely eclipsed Mr Frensham's geniality for that tell-tale moment. The beggar knew what the stuff in the tin was . . .

Gore walked over to the table and possessed himself of the tobacco-tin good-humouredly but firmly.

'If I were you, Mr Frensham,' he said quietly, 'I think I should mind my own business. I'm a very old friend of Mrs Barrington's—and in that capacity I offer you that advice. Now, you have in your possession, I understand, a cheque of Mr Arndale's for £250 which Mrs Barrington found amongst her husband's papers. Will you kindly give it to me?'

Frensham's eyes flickered swiftly up and down the tall figure that stood between him and the door. Obviously he was thinking hard. Equally obviously, however, he realised that the odds were all against him; and he fell back instantly upon an injured and surprised respectfulness.

'I should give it to you with pleasure, Colonel, of course, if I had it. But I haven't got it. I gave it to Mr Arndale.'

'Mr Arndale asked you to give it to him?'

'Yes, Colonel, he did. He said the cheque was his, and that he gave it to Cyril Barrington last Saturday morning to get it cashed for him. So, of course, I gave it to him, then, when he asked for it. Sorry if I haven't done right, I'm sure, Colonel. Hope I haven't dropped a brick, have I?'

'Not at all,' said Gore. 'You acted quite rightly.'

'I needn't tell you, Colonel, it's no concern of mine. I merely offered to see Mr Arndale about the cheque because Mrs Barrington was so uneasy in her mind, like, about it. I don't know *what* she thought. But it seemed to me she thought there was something fishy about it somehow. However, what Mr Arndale told me was that poor old Cyril was out at his place early on Saturday morning, and as he wasn't coming into Linwood himself on account of him going shooting, he asked

Cyril to get it cashed for him. Seemed to me all right. Seems to you all right, Colonel, don't it?'

Arndale's explanation appeared a curiously lame one. But, on the other hand, it was just the kind of explanation which Arndale would have been likely to produce on the spur of the moment, confronted by an absolute stranger with the cheque and asked to account for Barrington's possession of it.

'Quite,' said Gore. 'Where did you see Mr Arndale this afternoon? At his house or at his office?'

'At his house. Nice place he's got, too, out there.'

'You told him, of course, that Mrs Barrington had asked you to see him about the cheque?'

'Well, Colonel, what do you think? Think I'd walk into a gentleman's house on my own and say to him, "Here, what about this cheque of yours? What's the meaning of it? What you been paying two hundred and fifty quid to my pal Cyril Barrington for?" Not hardly likely, is it, Colonel, now I ask you?'

Upon that point Gore offered no opinion. He stared at Mr Frensham's rubicund countenance for some moments fixedly. Finally he opened the door of the room.

'Thank you, Mr Frensham. In that case, then, I think we need not take up any more of your valuable time. I will tell Mrs Barrington what you have told me. Good-afternoon.'

Again Mr Frensham did some quick thinking. But again discretion gained the day.

'Well, hang me,' he said with good-humoured resentment, 'you'd think I'd been trying to pinch the damn thing. Blow me if you wouldn't. Catch me offering to do a good turn for anybody again in a hurry. I don't think. Damme, I don't know what you'd think you thought I was. Good-afternoon.'

Gore watched his aggrieved progress to the hall door with some misgivings. Even then, however, he was still quite unable to decide what to make of him. It was not until late that night that a note from Mrs Barrington, which he found awaiting him upon his return from a theatre-party, enabled him to form that decision.

'Dear Wick,' Mrs Barrington wrote, 'I'm awfully worried about that cheque. Mr Arndale rang me up after dinner this evening about it. He says the cheque is all right, and that he gave it to my husband last Saturday to cash for him. But he says Mr Frensham refused to give it to him this afternoon, and kept it, because he said I had instructed him not to part with it. I can't understand it. What am I to do about it? Mother wants me to go away with her at once—probably to Vence—for a long rest and change. But it's fearfully awkward about Mr Arndale, isn't it?'

Further enlightenment as to the kind of person Mr Frensham was awaited Gore when he went round to Hatfield Place immediately after breakfast next morning. He discovered then that that genial gentleman had not only succeeded in retaining Arndale's cheque, but had also contrived, in the simplest manner in the world, to obtain possession of Barrington's bankbooks, the three note-books containing names and addresses, and the tobacco-tin.

After getting rid of him on the previous afternoon, Gore had proceeded forthwith with the burning of the bundles of letters at the end of the garden, much to the mystification of the Kinnairds' elderly housekeeper, who had watched his operations from an upper window until the dusk had hidden her from his view. Mrs Barrington's father and mother had still been with her when he had gone back into the house, and he had left without seeing her again, leaving behind him a brief note informing her of the results of Frensham's visit to Arndale. No doubt Frensham had watched the hall door. For, according to Florence's account, Colonel Gore had hardly gone when Mr Frensham had returned. He had explained that he had forgotten some papers which Mrs Barrington wanted him to look into, had been shown by the unsuspecting Florence into the room at the end of the hall, where the tin box still lay on the table with Gore's note on top, had opened the box, taken what he wanted, thanked Florence most politely, and departed. So little had the parlourmaid suspected anything amiss in these proceedings that she had not even mentioned them to her mistress until, late at night, Mrs Barrington had asked her to carry the tin box upstairs.

For Gore the most ominous feature of this raid was the fact that it had paid no attention to the negotiable valuables which the tin box contained. The banknotes and the diamonds had held no interest for Mr Frensham, clearly. The cool, adroit audacity of the thing was in itself significant, too—the trademark of the practised rogue. How many more such 'pals' of Barrington's were there—hovering—waiting for their chance at the offal?

The devil of the thing was that one could do nothing, and that, of course, Frensham reckoned on that for impunity. Obviously one couldn't go to the police and say: 'A box containing half a pound or so of cocaine has been stolen from me by a man called Frensham, who was a friend of my husband's.' The police would want to know all about that cocaine—and all about a lot of other things, probably, once they got started on the job. It was quite likely that Frensham had been a partner in the pleasant and lucrative business of blackmail. Quite probably he knew all about Arndale's cheque—knew enough about Arndale to let loose some filthy scandal if one drove him to it by having him arrested for purloining the cheque. It was an unpleasant conclusion to be forced to—but one *was* forced to the conclusion that there must be some very serious reason to explain the payment of fifteen hundred pounds a year to a man of Barrington's character.

The situation was complicated, too, by Mrs Barrington's ignorance of the means by which her husband had extracted a livelihood from the world. It was possible that she entertained some vague misgivings on the subject; her uneasiness with regard to the cheque had confessed as much. But it was clear enough that she had no actual knowledge of the sinister business in which Barrington had been engaged. Nor did Gore feel in any way called upon to enlighten her on the point. He contented himself with a strong warning against any further dealings either with Frensham or with any other person who might present himself as a friend of her husband's, and an equally strong recommendation to shut up her house and get away with her mother to the south of France as quickly as possible.

'Well . . . but what about Mr Arndale's cheque?' she asked. 'I'm responsible for it.'

'Nonsense,' he said curtly, Arndale is quite capable of looking after his own cheques. He can stop payment if he wants to. At any rate it's no concern whatever of yours. If Frensham or anyone else gives you any bother about it, send him along to me to the Riverside. I'll talk to him like a father—if he comes.'

At heart, however, he was perfectly aware that his heroic attitude was the merest of bluff. Not since Mrs Melhuish had first told him her story on that Tuesday afternoon which appeared now separated from the present by weeks instead of a bare four days, had he felt so uneasy upon her account. By dint of endless repetition, endless retracing of the same ground, endless failure to convince himself absolutely of the correctness of any one theory as to the manner in which Barrington had died, he had reached now a stage of mental weariness in which, so far from knowing clearly what he thought about the matter, he found himself, whenever he attempted to think about it, incapable of following one line of speculation for sixty consecutive seconds without straying off along another, the very postulates of which refused credence to those of its predecessor. On that Saturday morning he was not merely equally prepared to believe that Arndale or Melhuish or Challoner or diseased arteries, or any combination of these, had been responsible for Barrington's death. By some curious confusion of his mental apparatus he *did* actually half believe that each of these causes had been responsible for it. And it seemed to him, as he walked back from Hatfield Place towards the Riverside, just as likely that those letters of Mrs Melhuish's which had been in Barrington's possession when he had left her on Monday night were now in the possession of Frensham, as that they were in the possession of Arndale or Challoner or Melhuish himself.

For—for anything he knew to the contrary—Frensham might very well have been the man who had been at Barrington's house with him from twelve to one on Monday night, talking with him over a whisky-and-soda—discussing, perhaps, the business that lay just before them. He might very well have accompanied Barrington to Aberdeen Place in the car, and have waited outside—eager to hear what was going on inside, impatient for Barrington's reappearance with the plunder of which he was to have a share. That might very well account for the opening of the hall door. From Aberdeen Place he might very well have accompanied Barrington to some place at which they were in the habit of adjusting the accounts of their partnership—some discreet headquarters of their rascality. It was, evidently, entirely useless to indulge in vague surmise as to the habits and haunts and methods of such people. But if Barrington had had, somewhere, some place of safer keeping for his dangerous merchandise than his own house, it was only too easy to conceive that Frensham, and possibly several other 'pals' of 'dear old Cyril's,' knew all about it. If those letters of Pickles's had been left by Barrington in some such place—well, her troubles were only beginning.

There was, however, so far as he could see, nothing to be done except to wait and see what happened. He had succeeded, with unexpected ease, in recovering the other lot of letters for her, unobtrusively. With that achievement, he told himself, he could rest content for the present. The whole affair was at once so sordidly unpleasant, so difficult to get hold of, and so insidiously engrossing to the exclusion of ordinary, rational interests, that he almost succeeded in persuading himself that his one desire was to shake it off and have nothing more to do with it.

The manner in which he had discovered Cecil Arndale's financial relations with Barrington embarrassed him a good deal.

'Damn it all,' was his last thought on Saturday night, 'what should *I* say if I found some silly, meddlesome ass poking his nose into my business? I'm the remains of a soldier—not an apology for a private detective. I *will* have nothing more to do with it.'

And on Sunday he hired a motor-cycle of decayed constitution and rode a hundred miles to deliver Pickles's letters into her own hands. Pickles, however, was in bed with a bad cold and a temperature, so that he failed to interview her personally, though she sent him down a hastily-scribbled little message of gratitude. In a valiant attempt to ride another hundred miles back to Westmouth in darkness and over roads coated with grease, he snapped a chain at midnight five miles from anywhere. He pushed his mount into Salisbury, slept in one of the George's excellent beds until nine o'clock, and did not reach his quarters at the Riverside until its lunch-hour had passed.

He found awaiting him a communication informing him that the secretaryship of the golf club was no longer vacant. The next letter of the little heap on his mantelpiece was of greater interest.

> 'Dear Wick,'—Mrs Barrington wrote—'We are off this morning. Paris—then Vence. The Frensham man rang me up yesterday, and coolly proposed that I should go and see him at some place called

the Excelsior Hotel. I think it is somewhere near Broad Street Station. Of course refused. He said that I should be wise to change my mind about that, and that I was to ring him up there when I did change it. I rang off then. Horrible little beast. I can't think why I was foolish enough to give him Mr Arndale's cheque. I thought I had better let you know that he had rung me up. This is written in great haste. My packing is not finished yet. Ever so many thanks for your kindness.—
Yrs.—

'ETHEL BARRINGTON.

'P.S.—Will send address when we have one. Will you keep enclosed key, in case I should have to ask you to come here to the house while I am away. Sounds pretty cool. But I hope I shan't have to trouble you.—E.B.'

Mr Frensham was preparing to get busy, then, already.

13

The Riverside's page-boy knew all about the Excelsior Hotel. It was in Purley Square, he stated, close to the river—'not much of a place.' The shortest way to it—though the boy's manner conveyed surprise that any guest of the Riverside should require the information—was to descend by the Cliff Railway to Spring Road, take a tram to the corner of Old Cut Road, and ask there for further direction. Shortly before the arrival of afternoon tea Gore solemnly tossed a penny, and, the penny having fallen tails, went to the telephone and rang up Westmouth 1727. The manageress informed him that Mr Frensham was still staying at the Excelsior, but was at the moment out. She undertook to inform him on his return that Colonel Gore would call about half-past four that afternoon in the hope of seeing him.

It was probably most unwise, Gore admitted to himself, to give the fellow any warning. But he was not quite prepared yet to adapt his methods to those with which it was almost certain Frensham would defend himself from this frontal attack. Nor did he think it prudent to declare an open hostility just yet. The supposition that Pickles's letters were now in Frensham's hands was the merest of surmise. *They* were his real object, he reminded himself. His intended negotiations with regard to Arndale's cheque were to serve merely as a feeler—a means of getting into touch with the enemy and obtaining some definite information about him. If for no other reason than that Frensham had tricked him so audaciously, he meant to recover, if he could, Arndale's cheque as well as the other things taken from Mrs Barrington's house. That, however, was a matter of personal vanity, and of quite secondary importance. He rather regretted now that he had been so peremptory with Frensham at their first meeting. No use in taking a high hand with a chap of that sort. The thing to do was to take him quietly—keep him guessing until you had him where you wanted him—and then let him have it.

In this mood of admirable prudence he set out after tea in quest of the Excelsior Hotel. He found it without difficulty—a small, rather dingy hostelry at one side of a forlorn, threadbare little square, so close to the river that the funnels and bridge of a big cargo-boat lying just behind it rose over its roof, illuminated by the flares at her hatches. Though darkness had fallen, the riverside was still busy. All around was the fretful clamour of the cranes, the slithering rattle of tackle, the roar of falling coal, the monotonous bawling of stevedores. Gore sniffed the tang of tar and timber with enjoyment, and smiled because it still had power to catch up his spirit and ship it for the seas of buried treasure in company of Long John Silver.

A slatternly young woman informed him that Mr Frensham was in the billiard-room. There he found Frensham bent over an evening paper spread upon a billiard-table, smoking a cigar.

He betrayed no symptoms either of resentment or of embarrassment.

'Found your way here all right, Colonel, I see. Take a pew, won't you. I got your message when I came in. I'd just been up to see poor old Cyril's missus. But seems the house is shut up. Least I couldn't make anyone hear, and I must have knocked for five minutes or more.'

'Mrs Barrington has gone abroad, I believe,' said Gore agreeably.

'Ow,' said Mr Frensham, examining the toes of his boots dubiously. 'She has, has she? Abroad, eh? Ow. That's a bit awkward. There was one or two things I wanted to have a talk with Mrs Barrington about, you see.'

He folded up his newspaper regretfully and put it away in a pocket.

'Yes, now. That *is* a bit awkward. For every one. Abroad, eh? Where's abroad?'

'The south of France, I understand.'

'Ow.'

A rather gloomy silence fell. 'What's the whisky like here?' Gore inquired at length.

'All right,' said Frensham, with conviction, and, indeed, as it proved, with perfect truth.

When the slatternly young woman had delivered their drinks and departed again, he raised his glass with a sociable 'Good health, Colonel,' absorbed the greater portion of its contents, and set it down on the long-suffering cushion of the billiard-table.

'Well, Colonel, what was it you wanted to see me about?'

'Well, Mr Frensham, I'll be quite frank with you. You mentioned just now that there were one or two little matters you wanted to discuss with Mrs Barrington—and Mrs Barrington herself, I know, regretted very much that she had not seen you about them before she went away.'

'She didn't seem very anxious to see me when I rang her up yesterday, Colonel. However . . . well, you were saying—?'

'I was about to say that I have Mrs Barrington's full authority to discuss with you—in the friendliest manner, of course—any difficulties which . . . er . . . may require discussion.'

But this announcement brought no relief to Mr Frensham's gloom. His eyes remained lost in a vista of dejected hopelessness.

'That's all very well, Colonel . . . if it was a matter of discussing them. But . . . well, how it is, you see . . . well, it isn't.'

'I see,' said Gore.

Frensham finished his drink.

'Now, this here cheque of Mr Cecil Arndale's, for instance—' he began, and paused to dive a hand into an inner pocket and take forth a corpulent and grubby wallet. 'I'm in a very awkward position about that cheque.'

He took a cheque from the wallet, and held it from him at arm's length to consider it with concern.

'You see, here's a cheque for two hundred and fifty quid. And two hundred and fifty quid is a big lot of money as things go—'

The conference was interrupted at this juncture by the entry of two young men of sporting seediness who, after a nod to. Frensham, a glance at the cheque in his hands, and a stare at Gore, removed their coats and took possession of the billiard-table. Frensham watched the performance of these intruders for some moments critically, then winked expressively to Gore, and led the way out of the room.

'Those two duds 'll take from now till tomorrow to play a fifty,' he explained. 'That's the one drawback to a small place like this. You can't have five minutes private conversation without half a dozen sitting in your lap. We'll go outside, eh, where we can talk quietly and comfortably'

'Good idea,' Gore agreed readily.

'Care for another little one? No? You're like me. I'm never thirsty when I'm busy. Reminds me—this way, Colonel—reminds me of a thing I heard the skipper of the old *Waiataka* say one day to a she-missionary who came aboard at Durban. Mind that hawser, Colonel. Ah . . . pretty, aren't they, all those lights in the water—yes. The old gal wanted to wash her hair, you see—'

The story of the lady-missionary was succeeded by others equally edifying while they made their way along a busy and littered quayside, past the clangour of a flaring shipyard, to the comparative peace of an avenue of timber, at the farther end of which they decided upon seats under the shelter of one of the tall, fragrant stacks. A little way beyond them a five-master was unloading a cargo of pine. A big oil-tanker slid slowly past an ; opening between two stacks, hooting hoarsely on her way downstream.

'Well . . . about this cheque,' said Frensham. 'It's like this, you see. Mind you, I don't expect *you* to look at it the way I do, Colonel. You're a friend of Mr Arndale's, I take it, and naturally *you'd* say, if Mr Arndale says the cheque is his, it *is* his, and ought to be given back to him. That's just why I put you off that way on Saturday. I'll own up to that now. I did put you off, and I admit it. Why? Because I'm not satisfied that that cheque ought to be given back to Mr Arndale. And I'm not satisfied that I'd be justified in giving it back to him. That cheque ought to be dealt with by poor old Cyril's executors—that's how it seems to me. You may say, "Well . . . he's left no executors." Well, then, I say it ought to be dealt with by someone who'll do what an executor ought to do—and that is, look after things in a legal way and see that poor old Cyril's missus doesn't get done in the eye. You know yourself, Colonel, what women are. No idea of business. Always in a hurry. Ready to believe any fairy-tale anyone tries to stuff them up with. I don't mind telling you, Colonel, if I'd advised Mrs Barrington to give up that two hundred and fifty quid—just because Mr Arndale tells us this cock-and-a-bull story of him getting Cyril to cash that cheque for him—well, I'd feel damn silly about it. Yes, damn silly. Poor old Cyril was my pal—that's the way I got to look at it. It's my duty—mind you, my duty, I say, Colonel, so far as in me lies, to see that his missus doesn't get done in the eye. And I'm going to see that she doesn't. If that two hundred and fifty quid is Mr Arndale's money, let him stop payment of the cheque—until whoever acts as executor has gone into things.'

'I presume Mr Arndale *has* stopped payment, Mr Frensham,' said Gore, beginning to weary a little of this foolery.

'Do you?' asked Frensham. 'I don't.'

He took another cigar from his bowler hat, bit off its end, and spat the end into the darkness.

'Now, here, Colonel. Did you happen to take a squint at that bank-book that was in that box of Cyril's?'

'I had a look at it—yes.'

'Notice anything funny about it?'

'No, I can't say that I did.'

'Didn't look at it very carefully, perhaps. Well, I may tell you, Colonel, between you and me, *I've* had a good look at it. And what I think about it, there's a lot more in that cheque of your , friend Mr Arndale's than meets the blooming eye. I'm not going to tell you what I think. I may be right, or I may be wrong. But I don't mind laying you a fiver to a farthing Arndale doesn't stop payment of that cheque. I wish he would.'

'You wish he would?' Gore said patiently.

'I do. Why? Well . . . it's an uncrossed cheque—endorsed. I don't want to carry a cheque of that sort round with me, I needn't tell you—a cheque for two hundred and fifty quid. Nice business for me if I lost it, or had it pinched from me. There are plenty of folk about these days who wouldn't mind giving you a crack on the skull, if they knew you had—'

He stopped and rose to his feet abruptly, staring past Gore at the narrow gulley between the stack which sheltered them. and its neighbour. 'Look out, Colonel,' he exclaimed in alarm, 'There's a beggar there behind you—'

Gore turned his head quickly and caught a glimpse of a figure which emerged from the narrow passage swiftly and struck at his head silently and viciously with a short flexible implement whose weight broke through the guard of his upraised arm and caught his chin heavily An arm came round his neck from behind and throttled him. He heard a muffled oath from Frensham, saw the darkness split into a million stars, and fell down a very, very long tunnel of cotton wool into nothingness.

14

When he awoke some few minutes later, it was to a world whose whole content and significance had been reduced to a red-hot saw which was splitting his brain slowly but mercilessly into two sections of agonised pulp. After a little time there impinged upon this perception a monotonous babbling murmur which resolved itself at length into the voice of Mr Frensham, blaspheming in the darkness with a lurid fluency. Mr Frensham also was lying on the ground, suffering, he alleged, from a broken collar-bone. Discovering, however, presently, that he was mistaken in this belief, he got to his feet, helped Gore into a sitting position against the corner of the timber-stack, and examined his injuries by the light of a succession of matches.

'Lucky for both of us we got thick skulls, Colonel,' he grunted. 'Well . . . we're a nice-looking pair of blooming mugs now, aren't we? Cleaned you out, too, have they? I'll bet they have.'

Gore's head still swam dizzily, but he made the brief examination of his pockets necessary to inform him that the contents of his note-case and some loose silver, the only articles of value which they had contained, had been taken from them. Already he was convinced that he had walked blindly into a carefully-prepared trap, though he was still too confused of thought to conceive the purpose of so elaborate and risky a device. He had recognised the man who had first assailed him as one of the two who had interrupted his conversation with Frensham in the billiard-room at the Excelsior Hotel. Their intrusion, he divined now, had been arranged beforehand to afford Frensham a plausible excuse for enticing him to the darkness of this deserted stretch of quay. He was still speculating stupidly as to the object of the thing when Frensham burst again into vivid profanity.

'I've had my eye on those three beauties,' he declared. 'I've seen them hanging about the hotel, watching me. Those two chaps that came into the billiard-room . . . those were two of them. You saw that big chap that came for you first, did you?' Gore nodded.

'Recognised him, didn't you?'

'Yes.'

'Of course you did,' Frensham snorted. 'I recognised the beggar's ugly dial the moment I saw it popping round the corner. I didn't see the two that came round the other side . . . but I'll swear they were the two chaps that have been in and out of the Excelsior with the tall fellow—'

He considered for a space. Then he remembered that his head had nearly been split open and his collar-bone nearly broken, and indulged in various hissings and gaspings indicative of acute physical discomfort.

'Anyhow,' he said, 'they can't do anything with that cheque at this hour. The banks are closed long ago. First thing we've got to do is to get to the telephone and tell Arndale he's got to stop the cheque first thing tomorrow morning.'

Light began to dawn dimly in Gore's painful brain.

'Yes,' he nodded. 'Where's the nearest police-station?'

Frensham's head jerked round towards him sharply. 'Police-station?' he repeated coldly.

'There's one in Spring Road, isn't there?' said Gore, rising cautiously to his feet. 'That's probably the nearest. We had better go there.'

Mr Frensham did not think so. His manner, indeed, became so aloof and unfriendly when Gore persisted mildly for a moment or two with a suggestion so obviously damn silly, that his companion in misfortune withdrew it tactfully. Even then, however, Mr Frensham's resentment was disposed to linger a little.

'Course, if you want to go to the police, go to the police, Colonel. I'm not stopping you. I'm just as willing to go to the police as you are, if it comes to that—if there was any use in going to the police. Go to the police by all means—if you think that's the best thing for you to do.'

But gradually his tone softened to its old geniality.

'You see, in a thing of this sort, Colonel—well, you got to do nothing in a hurry. You got to look round you and consider everything. You'll say to yourself: "I've got a blooming fine old bump on my head, and I've lost—" What was it you had on you? Much?'

'About six pounds.'

'Well, none of us wants to lose six quid. That's a fact. But then you'll say to yourself: "If I go to the police and tell them a cheque of a friend of mine named Arndale has been taken from another friend of mine called Frensham—well, then, the first thing the police will do, they'll go along to my friend Frensham and begin asking him questions. And of course he'll have to answer the questions. And if he answers the questions, well— Well, it may be awkward for other people. Awkward for my friend Arndale. Awkward for my friend Mrs Barrington. Bloody awkward." Well, now, you don't want that sort of thing, Colonel, do you?'

'No, no, no,' said Gore.

'No. You're a sport, Colonel. The moment I clapped eyes on you up there at poor Cyril's place, I saw you were a sport. There's ups and there's downs in everything in life—and a chap that's a sport takes 'em both as they come and keeps on smiling. Doesn't he. No use crying over spilt milk. We'll just go back to the little pub and ring up Arndale and tell him to stop the cheque. That's the sensible thing to do. About your six quid— well, only thing I can say is, it's lucky you hadn't more on you. I've lost a couple of quid myself— *and* my watch that was my poor old dad's. But lorlummy, I'm not squealing.'

In the darkness, as they made their way back to the little hotel, Gore smiled grimly at the audacious effrontery of this speech. The whole affair was pretty clear to him now. This melodramatic assault was intended to serve the double purpose of scaring him off and of removing the cheque from Frensham's possession under his very eyes. His respect for the plausible scoundrel whose arm insisted on supporting his dizziness had increased very considerably. Mr Frensham, he saw now, was not a person with whom one could afford to take any chances or whom one could hope to outwit by straightforward, respectable methods. The straightforward, respectable person was just the kind of person with whom Mr Frensham and his friends loved to do business—their natural prey—the very purpose and explanation of their existence. No doubt the straightforward person might sometimes be stupid enough or desperate enough to face exposure and go to the police. But equally without doubt these scoundrels were careful to keep a finger on the pulse of their victim's fears, and prepared at the first signal of danger to scuttle to their holes. Frensham's whole poise had altered instantly at the very mention of the word 'police.' Gore wondered a little just what would have happened if he had persisted in that suggestion of his. If one could reckon on Frensham's losing nerve and clearing out, probably the wisest thing to do *would* be to go to the police. But could one reckon on that?

Besides, once set on his track, the police would find him, wherever he went. Probably the police knew all about him and his friends, especially if they were engaged in dope-traffic.

There had been an active vigilance in all the seaport towns in the south-west lately, following on the disclosures in a somewhat sensational murder-case in Cardiff.

But why not simply make a pretence of going to the police to report the incident which had just occurred? It would be impossible for Frensham to know whether the threat had been carried out or not. If he was to be scared away, that would scare him away. If it didn't, it would at all events start the operation of keeping him guessing.

First, however, it would be interesting to learn whether he really intended to take measures to have Arndale's cheque stopped. It seemed, superficially, the last thing he would want to do. The cheque was uncrossed and endorsed. Tomorrow morning, as soon as the banks opened, it could be presented and cashed. Frensham himself, of course, would not appear in that transaction. He had separated himself now from the cheque—been assaulted and robbed of it—with an entirely straightforward and respectable witness to vouch to the fact. Why should he and his friends deliberately throw away an opportunity of acquiring two hundred and fifty pounds by having the cheque stopped? Superficially, it was evident that they were most unlikely to do anything of the kind. Frensham was probably quite certain that, for good reasons, Arndale would not dare to stop the cheque. The proposed conversation at the telephone would be the merest of farces, designed solely for the edification and instruction of the straightforward and respectable witness.

But a very little reflection upon the matter suggested another view of the position. It was hardly likely, after all, that Frensham and his confederates depended upon the clumsy and primitive business of highway robbery for their livelihood. Two hundred and fifty pounds was certainly a considerable sum. But there were other methods by which very much more than two hundred and fifty pounds might be extracted—comparatively safely and artistically—from a goose that had been in the habit of laying golden eggs with such extraordinary regularity and generosity. Frensham, there could be no doubt now, had learned all about those golden eggs from Barrington's bank-book, even if he had not known all about them before. The probability was that, for him, the intrinsic value of Arndale's cheque was, at all events for the moment, far greater than its face value. Coupled with the entries in Barrington's bank-book, it formed first-class evidence that Arndale had been making those large and regular payments to Barrington, and, no doubt, was to be used as such to induce him to continue to make them to Barrington's successors in title.

The conversation which took place at the telephone of the Excelsior Hotel was, however, unenlightening. Frensham rang up Arndale's office at the Yard, and was informed that Mr Arndale was engaged. An attempt to impress the person at the other end proved unavailing. Mr Arndale had given instructions that he was not to be disturbed under any circumstances by any business, however urgent.

'Will you give Mr Arndale this message?' said Frensham, looking at his watch—to Gore's amusement. 'Mr Frensham is going along to his office—now; No. My business is private. I want to see Mr Arndale personally. You'll tell him that? Thanks.' He rang off and turned to Gore.

'You'll come along with me, Colonel, won't you?'

'I think not, Mr Frensham. I shall probably see Mr Arndale later this evening.'

'It's only across the ferry,' Frensham urged. 'Better come along.'

'I think not,' Gore said again. 'I'm sure I can rely on you to give Mr Arndale a full account of what has happened. I think, on the whole, I had better drop in to the police station in Spring Road as I go back. It's on my way. The sooner the police get busy the better, it seems to me.'

Frensham stared at him for some moments, and, as he stared, he presented an odd effect of withdrawal into himself—or rather into an entirely other Frensham. An enigmatic blankness descended as a veil over his rubicund face. Gore had the impression of having seen a very large and brightly illumined window blink suddenly into darkness.

'Very well, Colonel,' Frensham said curtly, 'I'll go with you to the station. It'll save the police the trouble of coming to me. But you realise, of course, that this means . . . well—trouble?'

Gore caressed the bump on his head with a gingerly hand.

'Trouble, Mr Frensham? Trouble for whom?'

'Trouble for Arndale—for one. Trouble for Mrs Barrington, I for another. There it is for you, Colonel—straight. As far as that goes, I believe you know it as well as I do myself.'

'You flatter me, Mr. Frensham,' Gore said pleasantly. 'You do, I assure you. I admit that I conceive it possible that trouble may ensue—for someone. But—'

'Someone? Who's someone?'

'That I leave to your intelligence.'

Frensham stared again for a little while.

'Meaning me?' he inquired at length.

'I'm afraid so.'

Frensham's response to that was a derisive noise of peculiar unpleasantness and contempt.

'Go on,' he said; 'I'm listening.'

'I really don't think there is anything more to say. Except that, naturally, if there *were* any chance of getting you into trouble I should be sincerely grieved, I simply hate getting people into trouble.'

'Oh, you do, do you?' said Frensham. 'Here—what are you getting at, Colonel? Come on. Cough it up. Let's have no beating about the bush.'

'If there is a bush,' Gore smiled, 'it contains five one-pound notes and some silver of mine—and various other things for which I'm afraid I'm responsible. I am a deplorably obstinate sort of person, Mr Frensham. I shall probably keep on beating about that bush until I—well, until I get my own back.'

'Meaning—?'

'Just that.'

'And you think the police will help you to do it, do you?'

'Unless you do.'

At that Frensham took his hands from his pockets and gave way to an outburst of righteous indignation.

'Here!' he cried wrathfully. 'What do you mean? Don't you get talking silly, that way. What do you mean saying *I* can help you? Don't you start getting fresh with me, I advise you—'

'Don't shout, Mr Frensham,' said Gore quietly. 'And don't wave your hands about so close to my face. I can quite understand that, naturally, you feel a little uneasy and anxious. But I assure you that it is quite useless to make a noise about it. If you wish to retain my esteem and regard—and I perceive that you do—you can quite easily do so without—if I may use the phrase—throwing your weight about.'

'Well, you ought to be more careful about what you say,' Frensham protested surlily. 'You oughtn't to go suggesting things when you know you can't back them up. Why, I might as well say to you: "low get me my two quid back—and my watch, that was my poor old dad's." How do I know it wasn't you set those two chaps on me? You're in a mighty bloody hurry to get Arndale's cheque into your hands, I know that.'

Gore smiled and turned his back on him.

'Very well,' he said, strolling towards the door, and lighting a cigarette as he went, 'shall we leave it at that? If my money and the other things which I mentioned just now—you know?—the things which you removed from amongst Mr Barrington's effects on Thursday last—if all those things—mind, *all* of them— are returned to me before ten o'clock tonight, well—nothing will happen. If not, something will—quickly.'

'Oh, will it?' snorted Mr Frensham. 'You go to hell.'

And there the interview terminated. It was at all events some- thing, Gore told himself, as he made his way towards the tram-lines, to have had a good look at the enemy. But that, it must be admitted, appeared to him a somewhat inadequate consolation for a racking headache, a severely abrased chin, and an uneasy surmise that Mr Frensham had learned that afternoon a great deal more about him than he had learned about Mr Frensham.

15

He succeeded in reaching his rooms at the Riverside without encountering any curious eyes—a fact upon which he congratulated himself as he inspected his reflection in the privacy of his sitting-room. A trickle of blood had found its way to his collar and tie; another had crept down his temple to his eye. His hat and overcoat were liberally besmeared with an evil-smelling mixture of mud and oil. No wonder the tram-conductor had eyed him curiously as he had climbed to the roof of the car.

To his annoyance, as he absorbed the consolation of a whisky-and-soda, the page entered the sitting-room with his customary precipitation.

'Beg pardon, Colonel. I wasn't sure if you'd come in. A man wants to see you, if you're not engaged.'

For an instant Gore yielded to a wild hope that already Frensham's nerve had failed him. But the boy's next words—delayed to permit an exhaustive inspection of the colonel's person—dispelled that illusion.

'Name of Thomson, Colonel. He was here before this afternoon to see you. But you was out. He's waiting in the hall.'

'Send him along,' said Gore. 'I'll see him here.'

The boy lingered as he departed.

'Cut your chin, ain't you, Colonel? You ain't half got your collar in a mess. My eye, an' look at your coat.'

Having elicited, however, no explanation of these interesting phenomena, he consented to withdraw, returning some minutes later with the smart-looking chauffeur who had helped to carry Barrington from Melhuish's car into his own house.

'I hope you'll forgive my troubling you, sir,' the man explained respectfully. 'I wanted to know if you'd be kind enough to help me. Dr Melhuish's man has left him—you may remember him, sir, perhaps, an oldish man called Rogers—'

'Yes, I remember him. Well?'

'Well, Dr Melhuish is in a hurry to get a man, sir, I hear, and I should like the job. I think I mentioned to you that evening I spoke to you that I was on the look-out for another job if one turned up. I called at Dr Melhuish's this afternoon, but he was busy with his patients. I'm to go back tonight to interview him. Meanwhile I thought you would forgive my taking the liberty of asking you to recommend me to Dr Melhuish.'

Gore smiled at the keen, capable face, whose habit of impassiveness did not altogether conceal the anxiety with which its owner awaited his reply.

'Well, Thomson,' he said frankly, 'you seem to me a very smart, intelligent sort of chap; but, in the first place, I know nothing whatever about your talents and accomplishments as a shover—and in the second place, my acquaintance with Dr Melhuish is of the slightest. Mr Harry Kinnaird will give you a recommendation, won't he?'

'I suppose he would, sir,' said the man dubiously. 'But he and Mrs Kinnaird are in the south of France at present. I've got his address for Dr Melhuish. But it will take at least four days for the doctor to get a reply from Mr Kinnaird. By that time—well, by that time, sir, someone else will have got the job.' 'It's as urgent as that?'

'Yes, sir. I know that the doctor wants a new man at once. Old Rogers simply put on his hat and coat and walked out of the house last evening without even leaving the car ready to go out this morning. The result was that Dr Melhuish was nearly an hour late getting off on his rounds. I'm pretty certain, sir, that if you could see your way to recommending me, I should get the job at once.'

'How long have you been driving?'

'Thirteen or fourteen years, sir. You needn't have any anxiety about the technical side of the thing, Colonel. I've driven pretty well every make of car I've ever heard of, and I put in six months in shops at a big garage in Reading before I took on my first driving job.'

'Who were you with then?'

'With Mr Arndale, sir, of Holme Park. No doubt you know him.'

'Oh, you were with Mr Arndale? When was that?'

'Nineteen-nineteen. I was with him for ten months. I went from him to Mr Kinnaird.'

'Why did you leave Mr Arndale? Better wages?'

'No, sir. Not better wages. Mr Arndale paid me four shillings a week more than Mr Kinnaird pays me. No. Mr Arndale was annoyed by something I happened to say one day, quite unintentionally. I happened to make a remark about people who had stayed at home during the war, forgetting that Mr Arndale himself—'

He paused and completed the story by a little movement of his resolute lips.

'What were you in?' Gore asked.

'Surreys to begin with, sir. Then they gave me a commission in the M.G.C. I ended up with three pips.' He hesitated. 'D.S.O. in 1917.'

'What were you before the war?'

'I was assistant science master at Tenbury Grammar School.'

The Riverside's gong boomed its first warning of the approach of the dinner-hour. Gore raised a caressing hand to his face abstractedly to ascertain whether by good fortune this was one of the rare occasions upon which a second shave could be safely omitted. The abrupt touch of his fingers revealed to him the fact that blood was still oozing from the cut on his chin, and he took out his stained handkerchief to dab at it cautiously before the mirror over the fireplace.

'Very well, Thomson,' he said, observing that the man was watching this proceeding with interest, 'if an opportunity occurs I shall be delighted to do anything I can to help you. However, I fancy that if you tell Dr Melhuish what you have just told me, he will probably require no further recommendation. Especially if he is in a hurry for a man.' He nodded pleasantly. 'Good- afternoon.'

'Good-afternoon, sir.'

At the door, however, the visitor paused.

'I don't know if I ought to mention it, Colonel—but there's a Mr Frensham who has been making inquiries about you. Perhaps you know him. He was a friend of poor Mr Barrington's.'

'I have met Mr Frensham,' Gore replied curtly. 'Making inquiries about me? Making them of whom? You?'

'Yes, sir. He came round to the garage on Saturday morning, while I was doing some vulcanising there. What he *said* was that he was thinking of making Mrs Barrington an offer for her two-seater, and that he wanted to find out something about it, as I had been keeping it in order for Mr Barrington. But, as a matter of fact, sir, I think he really came to try and pump me for information about you.'

'Very kind of him, I'm sure,' smiled Gore. 'I hope you gave him all you had, Thomson.'

Thomson smiled too, sardonically.

'I had none to give him, sir. So I concluded there was no harm in letting him have it. However, I thought I'd better mention it to you, sir, as I was here.'

'Quite. Er . . . inquiries? What did he want to know?'

'He asked a lot of questions, sir, until I choked him off and told him I was busier than I looked. He seemed especially anxious to find out whether you were an intimate friend of Mr Arndale's—and also whether you were an intimate friend of Mrs Barrington's. I said simply that I knew nothing whatever about you, except that you had just come back from Central Africa.'

'I see. Right you are, Thomson. I'm afraid I must cut away and change now. I won't forget about Dr Melhuish.'

'Thank you, sir. Good-afternoon.'

The second gong went before Gore had succeeded in restoring his chin to something approaching seemliness, and he was still struggling with an unduly starched collar when the page irrupted into his bedroom gleefully to inform him that a gentleman desired to see him.

'Who is it?' Gore demanded, and then swore briefly but heartily. The wing of the refractory collar had escaped from the strain of his fingers as he turned towards the boy, and, slipping upwards, had grazed the cut on his chin and set it bleeding again. He rent the defiled collar from about his neck and cast it from him bitterly, as Arndale's tall figure lurched into view and swept the page from its path.

'It's me, Gore,' he said sullenly and thickly. 'I want to have a word with you about something. Go on. Go on. I can talk while you're dressing.' He dismissed the page with a push and shut the door, and turned to Gore again a face of surly anger. 'Look here, Gore. There's just one piece of advice I want to give you, old chap, and that is—mind your own business. That's what I've come here to say to you. Mind your own business. Just that. You understand?'

Gore was not easily shocked; but his visitor's appearance did shock him severely. It was bad enough that he should be, if not drunk, next door to it—and at that hour. But there was a worse degradation in his face than the mere stupidity of drunkenness; a haggard, weary fear which the blustering truculence of his manner at the moment attempted vainly to conceal. His skin had lost its plump ruddiness and sagged now in muddy unhealthiness with a curious effect of deflation. His bloodshot, shadowed eyes refused to meet Gore's, and slid away to the knob of the bedstead which, to emphasise his remarks, he prodded with his stick as he spoke.

'What's the trouble?' Gore asked, when he had taken swift stock of his visitor's pose.

'The trouble is this. I hear you've been making yourself busy about my affairs. Butting in where you're not wanted. Understand? I hear you've been trying to kick up some silly fuss or other about a cheque of mine—threatening people—making an infernal ass of yourself generally. Well . . . just chuck it, my dear old chap. Understand? I'm quite capable of looking after my own affairs. Understand?'

Gore inspected his chin solicitously in his mirror.

'Cecil, my lad,' he said gently, 'you're half-screwed, so I won't throw you out into the corridor, though I should very much like to. If you've got anything sensible to say to me, say it, by all manner of means. If not . . . bung off. I'm just a teeny-tiny bit snappish this evening.'

'I've said all I've got to say,' said Arndale doggedly. 'Don't threaten me, Gore. I tell you, I won't allow anyone to threaten me.'

'Right, my dear old fellow,' Gore smiled sweetly. 'You'll save yourself a lot of trouble if you don't, I fancy.'

'What do you mean by that?'

'The most friendly of advice, Cecil.'

'Well, you can keep your infernal advice to yourself. And your infernal threats, too. Understand?'

Gore's good-humour was not, as a rule, easily disturbed. But the events of the afternoon had ruffled his normal serenity of mood a good deal; his chin refused persistently to stop bleeding; and Amdale's manner was deliberately provocative. He realised at that point that the very briefest prolongation of the conversation in the strain in which it had so far proceeded would almost certainly terminate regrettably, and resolved to terminate it there and then. He reached the door in a stride.

'I hate saying so, Arndale, but I've had enough of this. If Frensham can scare *you*—and you wouldn't come here to talk to me this way unless he *had* scared you—he's not going to scare me. You can tell him so, with my compliments. I've no doubt he's waiting anxiously to know what kind of a reception I've given his ambassador. Just tell him again, will you, that if I don't hear from him before ten o'clock tonight the police will receive lull particulars of that interesting little affair that took place this afternoon. I'm sorry for you, Arndale. I believe you're in a tight place. I've no idea why or how. But I can guess anyhow that it's a tight place. That, however, is *your* look-out. And now you know.'

He opened the door. Arndale eyed him for a little while heavily.

'Shut that door,' he said at length.

'Not unless you're going to talk reasonably.'

'All right, I'll talk reasonably, as you call it.'

Gore shut the door, but retained his hold of its handle. 'Well?' he demanded curtly. 'Buck up. I've got to get some dinner, you know.'

But Arndale appeared unable to find words for the thing he had come to say, simple as Gore knew it to be. He had abandoned now summarily his attempt to work himself into a rage, and stood staring with clouded gaze at the knob of the bedstead.

'I'm not going to give you any reasons, Gore,' he said at length, without raising his eyes, 'but I ask you not to make a fuss about what happened this afternoon—not to go to the police about it. Frensham told me you lost some money—five or six pounds—'

'I lost a good deal more than that, Cecil. However, don't worry about what I lost. I shall get it back before I've done with Mr Frensham and his pals. I'm sorry to discover that you're one of them, though.'

'Oh, don't be a fool,' said Arndale wearily. 'Cut it out, Gore. Leave Frensham alone. You'll make nothing out of him.' He made a gesture of weak exasperation. 'Damn it all. What are you *trying* to make out of him? That's what I want to know. Why are you making all this fuss about that cheque of mine? What's it got to do with you?'

'Nothing whatever,' Gore assured him—'now. But the other things which Frensham took away from Mrs Barrington's house without her permission must be given back . . . with my own money . . . to me . . . here . . . before ten o'clock. You can tell Frensham so. Otherwise—'

'What other things were taken?' Arndale asked curiously.

'Barrington's bank-books, and some other papers and things.'

'Barrington's bank-books?' Arndale repeated. He mused over that for a little while stupidly, then dismissed his speculations with another exasperated little gesture. 'Don't bother about them, old chap. There's no use in threatening Frensham. Leave it alone. You know I shouldn't ask you to—if I hadn't a reason. Anyhow, I understand Mrs Barrington asked Frensham to—'

But Gore's patience was now exhausted.

'Rot,' he said curtly. 'Leave Mr Frensham to do his own dirty work, Arndale.'

He opened the door again and his visitor passed out into the corridor.

'We're old friends, Gore,' he pleaded. 'I ask you once more not to drag the police into this.'

'Sorry,' said Gore inexorably. 'If you didn't attach such importance to your new friends, your old ones might be some help to you. Hope you'll put your head under a pump before you let Mrs Arndale see you. Cheerio.'

But even as he saw Amdale's broad-shouldered back lurch out of sight round the angle of the corridor, he realised that he had handled him quite wrongly. Instead of taking advantage of an opportunity to discover something definite about Arndale's relations with Barrington and about the hold which it was clear Frensham possessed over his fears, he had allowed the irritability of a moment to induce him to throw it away. With a little management Arndale could probably have been persuaded to talk—perhaps even enticed into clearing up the whole mystery of Barrington's death—

There, almost within his grasp, had been that interesting and useful fact to be acquired—the fact which Arndale was afraid of. But it had been allowed to escape . . . because one didn't try to inveigle people into giving information they didn't want to give.

Gore shrugged his shoulders and went to dinner. The head-waiter's eye met his solicitously as he entered the diningroom twenty minutes later; and presently the man approached his chair.

'Sorry to hear you've had an accident, Colonel. Not serious, I hope?'

'Nothing,' Colonel Gore replied chillingly, 'is serious except brunette hairs in blonde soup.'

The head-waiter inspected the colonel's soup-plate with horrified eyes, flushed a rosy pink, and bore the plate hastily away with his own hands. It was the first time the colonel had found the slightest of fault with the Riverside's cuisine; a circumstance which the *chef* upon receiving the head-waiter's report, attributed to the fact that it was the thirteenth of the month.

16

In reply to Colonel Gore's inquiry over the phone next morning—which was the morning of Tuesday, November 14th, Major Whateley, the official who presided over the local branch of the Ministry of Pensions, sent along to the Riverside an ex-sergeant of the Westshires named Stevens—a sturdy, stolid, steady-eyed man of thirty-five or thereabouts, who appeared everything that could reasonably be hoped for for five bob a day.

When Gore had listened to the inevitable story of jobs that could not be got, he explained the nature of the job he had to offer. Stevens listened attentively to his directions, undertook to find out anything that was to be found out about Mr Frensham's movements, habits, company, and personal character with the utmost discretion, and to report in two days' time—that is to say, on the afternoon of the following Thursday— such information as he had succeeded in acquiring.

'You will want some money,' Gore said. 'I don't want you to blue this two quid exactly. But you'll probably find it useful to pay for other people's drinks occasionally, and so on. If you should want to talk to me in a hurry about anything, telephone to me here to the Riverside. But don't use the telephone at the Excelsior. Keep your eyes and ears open and your mouth shut. I fancy you'll find Mr Frensham is in with a pretty hot lot.'

Stevens departed on his mission with two pounds and many expressions of gratitude. Thursday came and went without any sign from him. On Friday morning Gore received the following communication, written in block capitals on a postcard:

> 'Your friend, Bert Stevens, has hopped it to London for his health. Any spare quids you have may be posted to him c/o Sherlock Holmes, Esq., New Scotland Yard, as he is still thirsty and hopeful. Trusting you're in the pink as this leaves us at present.—From ALL OF US.'

Discomfiting as this communication was, it was in some measure a relief; for the failure of his ally to report on the preceding day had caused Gore some misgivings as to his personal safety. The allaying of that anxiety was, however, no remedy for the fact that Frensham was now thoroughly warned and on his guard. This second humiliating failure to illuminate the dark places wherein that gentleman moved so warily was even more unfortunate than the first. Frensham must have guessed now that the threat to call in the assistance of the law had been mere bluff and that he was quite safe in defying it. If the police had been put on his track, a bungling amateur like Stevens would never have been employed to supplement their professional operations. Frensham would realise that at once. He'd say to himself and to his pals: 'That's all right. They're afraid. Now we know where we are we can carry on with the good work comfortably and happily.'

But happy and comfortable were the last things that Mr Frensham and his friends should be, Gore was now determined, at all events while they remained in Westmouth. And the immediate effect of that derisive postcard was to induce him to set at once about the carrying out of a project which he had been meditating since Stevens's failure to appear on the preceding day.

He set off shortly after breakfast for Hatfield Place, armed with the latchkey which Mrs Barrington had enclosed in her last letter against some unexplained contingency, and let himself into Number 27 in the confident expectation that the house contained no one to witness the harmless burglary which he had come to commit. His surprise and embarrassment were therefore no less than those of the two people who, at the sound of his entry, emerged from the sitting-room at the end of the hall.

Mrs Barrington—whom he had supposed in Paris at that moment—had been the first to appear, and, upon perceiving him, had half-turned as if to shut the door of the sitting-room behind her. The movement, however, had been too late. Challoner already stood in the aperture, looking extremely sheepish, and, as he recognised the intruder, extremely annoyed.

Mrs Barrington was the first of the three to recover her self-possession. She had been crying, Gore saw, and looked wretchedly ill and worn; but as she came towards him along the hall she mustered up a wan, appealing smile to accompany her calm 'Good-morning, Wick. How on earth did you know I had come back?'

'I didn't,' he said frankly. 'You've caught me red-handed. Just my luck. I really came here to pinch something out of that tin box of your husband's. Do you mind very much?'

'Not in the least. But it's fortunate that you came along this morning—and so early. I took all the things out of the box before I went away and locked them up in a cupboard upstairs. If you had postponed your visit for another quarter of an hour or so I'm afraid you'd have had some difficulty in finding what you wanted. What *do* you want, by the way?'

'Lead me to that cupboard,' he said solemnly. 'There you shall see.'

'How mysterious,' she laughed. 'Well, come along. I haven't much time. I must catch the 11.15 back to London.'

As they went up the stairs she explained that the original programme of her journey to Vence with her mother had been revised, and that they had decided to remain in London until the following Monday. The discovery that in the flurry of her departure she had forgotten a fur-lined travelling coat which had appeared upon consideration indispensable, had induced her to return to Linwood for a night. Gore agreed that a fur-lined travelling coat was absolutely necessary at that time of year, and changed the subject considerately. He had seen Arndale, he told her, about that cheque. Arndale appeared perfectly satisfied about it. There was nothing whatever to worry about so far as it was concerned. The other things he hoped to recover from Frensham in the course of the next few days.

Mrs Barrington smiled vague approval and disappeared to prosecute in a bedroom an apparently complicated and impatient search for the keys of the cupboard before which she had left him standing on the landing. She reappeared at length and opened the door of the cupboard.

'His things are all together, on the bottom shelf,' she said carelessly.

The cardboard box of which he was in search lay against the back of the cupboard, and to reach it he was obliged to stoop and thrust an arm sideways into the narrow space between the lowest shelf and that immediately above it. For a moment it eluded his grasp, and, as he groped for it he was aware that, behind him, Mrs Barrington had taken something from the shelf quickly and had stepped back a little from the cupboard—he assumed to examine it. As his fingers closed on a comer of the cardboard box he glanced over his shoulder towards her with a smile.

'Got it,' he announced, and then perceived to his horror that the object which she had taken from the shelf was Barrington's revolver and that she was holding it, with a curious, awkward, lamentable determination, pointed towards her own haggard, tear-stained face. There was no time to do anything save make a sweeping blow at the weapon with his left arm. He heard the heavy explosion as the momentum of his violent movement deprived him of his balance and sent him asprawl on knees and hands to the floor. But he was on his feet again in an instant and snatched the revolver from the hand that had dropped limply to her side.

'What the hell—?' he demanded angrily.

She was shivering with fright now, and her teeth chattered as she answered him.

'I can't stick it, Wick,' she said flatly. 'You . . . you've done me a bad turn.'

Challoner came rushing up the stairs, alarmed to incoherence.

'Great Scott—what . . .?'

He put his arm about Mrs Barrington and drew her into a bedroom and shut the door. Almost immediately, however, he reopened the door to say, 'For God's sake, Gore, keep your mouth shut about this,' and slammed the door again. Gore stared at it indignantly for a moment or two, transferred his gaze to an untidy abrasion in the plaster of the wall beside it where the heavy bullet had passed in obliquely, and then went downstairs and out of the house. But he remembered to take the cardboard box with him, and also to leave the latchkey behind.

17

Mr Frensham's next appearance in the affair took place on that afternoon, about six o'clock, in unexpected proximity to the Riverside.

At that hour Gore, leaving the hotel by the back entrance on his way to the club, came to an abrupt halt in the darkness of the grounds at sight of a small, burly figure which stood by the gates, tapping its bowlegs with a cane.

He stood stock still, debating with himself the significance of this extremely curious coincidence, the most obvious explanation of which was that his own movements were now under surveillance. But this conjecture was quickly abandoned. Frensham's attitude of impatient waiting changed to one of expectant attention. Then he raised his hat and moved to meet a young woman who came into sight quickly from behind the angle of the building beside the gates.

'Am I late?' the young woman inquired airily, as they shook hands. 'Of course I went and dropped the only pair of gloves I have in the world into the water-jug. I had to dry them.'

'The only pair?' said Frensham, with gallant scepticism. 'You're not going to kid me that such an attractive young lady as you can't coax her best boy into doing better for her than that, eh?'

Miss Rodney's rejoinder—for it was her voice unmistakably that had greeted Frensham—was sprightly if inaudible, for the pair moved off together along Selkirk Place laughing. To say that the discovery of this incipient flirtation—for that was the impression which Gore had derived from their meeting—surprised him, would be, perhaps, an overstatement of his feelings with regard to it. But it did appear to him so curious that, before he went on his way to the club, he continued to stand for some little time where he had halted, endeavouring to piece together such disjointed fragments of information concerning Miss Rodney as he possessed.

His thoughts were destined to distract themselves to Miss Rodney again very shortly.

As he sat at breakfast next morning, Percival entered to deliver a note just left by Dr Melhuish's man.

Gore, having glanced at the note, which was an invitation to dine with Melhuish that evening failing any prior engagement, nodded and seated himself to write a brief acceptance.

'Heard about Miss Rodney, sir?' inquired Percival after a moment.

Gore paused, pen in hand, to look round over his shoulder.

'Miss Rodney? No. What?'

'Done a bunk, sir. Hopped it during the night. Took her trunk and all with her, and never said a word to no one. The guv'nor didn't half carry on when he heard about it. 'Spect he thought she'd cleared off with some of his cash till he'd checked over the till.'

'During the night?'

'Yes, sir. It must have been pretty well on in the night, too, when she went. 'Cause neither of the other two young ladies that sleep out there heard her going. Though you'd say she'd have made a row fetching her trunk down the stairs, wouldn't you, sir? If you ask me, sir, it's a mystery.'

But Colonel Gore was too preoccupied to offer any comment, and had resumed his chilled bacon and eggs with austerity.

It may be of interest to record here in his own words Gore's impressions as to that nocturnal flitting of Miss Rodney's, as he set them forth in that connected narrative of the affair upon which his temporary attack of detective fever had induced him to embark.

'I thought it odd, of course,' he says, 'that the girl should have gone away in that way, at that hour, without warning to the manager, and without (so I had gathered from Percival) leaving behind any indication as to where she had gone. Since she had taken her trunk with her, it seemed that some man must have assisted her to get it away. I conjectured almost at once that Frensham had had something to do with her leaving so mysteriously and giving up such a good job. It seemed possible that Frensham knew of her relations with Barrington and had been threatening exposure in the attempt to extort money from her. That might have frightened her into clearing out, in the hope of shaking Frensham off. If she had made up her mind to do that, she would probably have arranged with one of the hotel porters to remove her trunk for her. The night- porter, for instance, could have managed that part of it for her without the least difficulty—rung up for a taxi to come to the back entrance or somewhere near it, and carried the trunk to it.

'I didn't think, then, that there was anything more in her leaving in that fashion. I didn't feel sure that there was even as much. I had given up the idea that she knew anything more about Barrington's death than anyone else in the hotel did, and I didn't for a moment connect her leaving with it. I knew she was a flighty, feather-brained little piece of goods, and it seemed just as likely as not that she had gone away with one of her admirers. I knew that she had plenty of them. Though there appeared to be no reason, in that case, why she should have selected such an ungodly hour as she seemed to have done.

'It also occurred to me as possible that she had suddenly discovered that she was about to have a child, and had cleared out in a sudden funk on that account. But, on the whole, I had a feeling that Frensham was at the bottom of it. Certainly that morning I was ready to believe anything about Frensham.'

18

A little after noon on that Saturday Gore paid a visit to the Excelsior Hotel. His idea being to discover, if possible, something of Mr Frensham's ways and company, he had gone to considerable pains to transform his appearance, with, he considered, a success beyond fair risk of detection. He had shaved off his moustache. He had purchased in Oldgate, second-hand, a complete outfit of unmistakable seediness—suit, hat, boots, and neck-cloth. A beard and moustache from Barrington's cardboard box had been bleached to a dingy-gray by a chemist in St Paul's Road. These latter adjuncts—assisted by an ancient pair of spectacles, were assumed in a taxi—very much to the driver's surprise—and induced their wearer to face the shrewd eyes of the Excelsior's proprietress without serious misgivings.

Under the disguise of Mr Thomas Barker, he engaged a room for the night, paying for it in advance. Inquiry, which he endeavoured to tinge with anxiety, elicited the information that no one of the name of Metcalfe had been to the hotel that day in quest of him. Having requested that he might be informed of Mr Metcalfe's arrival at once, he partook of the Excelsior's midday dinner and adjourned subsequently to the bar in the company of a ship's steward with whom he had struck up acquaintance during his meal.

The ship's steward, it became clear, was a regular habitué of the place in the intervals between his weekly journeys to and fro across the Irish Channel. And his intimacy with the proprietress, who presided in person over her bar during its midday séance, provided Gore at any rate with a piece of information which otherwise might have been difficult of unobtrusive acquisition by a stranger to the establishment.

Mr Frensham was still the guest of the Excelsior.

'Full up, missus?' the steward inquired as he absorbed his Bass.

'Wish I was, Mr Thring,' replied the proprietress. 'No. I've only three stopping at present. And one of *them* is leaving this afternoon.' She smiled towards Gore. 'Your friend'll be bird alone, 'cept for Mr Frensham.'

'How's he?' asked the steward, emptying his glass. 'Still smiling? Been tipping any more winners?'

'He tipped himself one yesterday, by what he says. He told us last night he had a tenner on Step-Out.'

The steward whistled appreciatively.

'Sixteen to one,' he murmured enviously. 'Wish it was me. Never mind. I got a real good thing for next week.'

His conversation with the proprietress became hushed and mysterious. Gore, concluding from the fact that Frensham had not appeared at dinner-time that he was not then in the hotel, strayed out into the dreary little square in front and seated himself on a bench commanding a view of the Excelsior's front door. The early afternoon was still sunny. A horde of urchins were engaged in an ear-splitting but wholehearted football match near at hand. And with the aid of a pipe the first hour of his vigil passed quickly enough.

The second hour, however, dragged noticeably; the third was frank boredom. The football match and the sun had alike disappeared and a chilly mist had settled over the deserted little enclosure which, save for occasional passengers along the path which crossed it diagonally, Gore now had entirely to himself. Already lights were beginning to flicker out palely in the surrounding houses when Frensham at last came into view, hurrying towards the hotel along the west side of the square from the direction of Old Cut Road. Gore waited for five minutes or so, and then rose from his seat with the intention of making a tour of the square in the dusk to warm himself. His bird had returned to the nest; but it might be hours before it emerged from it again—if it did emerge from it again that day. It seemed to him easier to keep watch from without than within—though the job promised to be a chilly one—at all events until later in the evening when the bar reopened. One could take an occasional saunter round the square without losing sight of the Excelsior's door and without attracting attention.

But, as he rose from his seat and stretched himself, he saw Frensham come out again and stand before the door, slapping his leg with his cane, and looking about him. After some moments he began to promenade to and fro before the hotel, gradually extending his range, sometimes looking at his watch, sometimes pausing to gaze expectantly along that side of the square by which he had just returned. And it was during one of these pauses, which became more and more prolonged as time went on, that Gore became aware that he was not the only person for whom Frensham's movements possessed an interest just then.

Some forty or fifty yards from the Excelsior the line of squalid little houses along the south side of Purley Square was broken by a low archway and a passage, leading—as he had noticed earlier in the course of his vigil—to some still more humble cottages clustered about a narrow interior court. In the archway a man was loitering, his head protruding cautiously or as cautiously withdrawing itself as Frensham's strolling figure receded from or approached his lurking-place. Gore watched him discreetly for some little time, thinking it possible that the fellow was an associate of Frensham's and that he himself had been under observation on his seat. His prolonged occupation of it might well have attracted attention, it occurred to him, if Frensham and his friends kept a look-out for suspiciously behaving strangers hanging about in the neighbourhood of the Excelsior. He decided to move off slowly along the narrow diagonal path and to take up a fresh position by the gate at its farther end.

There he waited for nearly half an hour. Frensham had ceased to parade to and fro now, and, having dodged in and out of the hotel for some time, had disappeared into it permanently. A sharp frost had set in with the falling of darkness, and Gore had begun to regret seriously that his purchases in Oldgate that morning had not included an overcoat.

But he stuck to his post doggedly, and for that virtue was rewarded, in the middle of a sneeze, with dramatic abruptness and unexpectedness. A tall figure came striding out of the darkness on the footpath at the other side of the street—a figure which he hardly needed the illumination of a street-lamp to recognise—that of Cecil Arndale. A curious thrill of exultation consoled him for his long, cold wait. Something doing at last . . . Frensham and Arndale together. Were his elaborate preparations to make anything of that chance? Would the two talk in the hotel or out of doors—perhaps down by those timber- stacks? What a bit of luck if they selected the timber-stacks—

Arndale, however, had hardly entered the door of the hotel when he came out again, accompanied by Frensham, and a few moments later the pair passed Gore at a rapid pace on the opposite side of the street, going towards Old Cut Road. Gore's first impulse was to follow at once a little way in the rear. But, recalling the watcher whom he had detected lurking in the archway, he lingered until, as he had expected, a sturdily-built figure came cautiously into sight round the angle of the square by the Excelsior, and then, at a quickened pace, advanced towards him along the railings of the square. As he went by, the man glanced quickly and curiously towards the loiterer by the gate, and revealed to Gore's surprise the stolid, square- chinned countenance of his some-time ally, Stevens.

It was impossible to tell whether he was following the couple in front with Frensham's knowledge and by Frensham's instructions, or for some purpose of his own. Gore was inclined to take the former view of his behaviour. But in either case, since the man had proved himself absolutely untrustworthy, the prudent thing, obviously, was to allow him to go on his business, whatever it might be, and follow at a safe distance behind him.

Gore had no doubt that Frensham and Arndale were making for Old Cut Road, the principal exit from the network of small streets and lanes and alleys between Spring Road and the river. Arndale's tall figure, conspicuous in a light-coloured raincoat, could easily be picked up again, even if he and his companion were allowed to get some little distance in advance. He allowed Stevens a reasonable law of a hundred yards or so, and then moved off in pursuit.

Instead, however, of proceeding straight forward towards Spring Road, Arndale and Frensham turned down a lane half-way along Old Cut Road, and Stevens, after a little cautious reconnoitring, followed their example. All three were out of sight now, and Gore quickened his pace until he reached the mouth of the lane—an evil-smelling, cobbled little passage between two rows of white-washed cottages, unlighted, and blocked at the end nearer to him by a collection of coal-drays, ranged in file with upreared shafts for the night. Nothing was to be seen of Stevens or of Arndale and Frensham. He hurried along the lane, came to a cross-lane, hesitated, hurried on, came to a second cross-lane, turned left-hand up it in the hope that it would lead him to Spring Road and view of his quarry, came to a halt at the entrance to a brick-yard, turned back—trotting now, and pursued by the humour of a knot of young larrikins— trotted up the first cross-lane, turned a corner so abruptly that a mongrel terrier was moved to assault him viciously, and, followed by the infuriated animal with determination, emerged, after some further intricate and obscure wanderings, into the brightly lighted hubbub and bustle of Spring Road's Saturday evening. He gazed to right and he gazed to left. But the annoying truth was only too clear. His quarry had vanished. He had made a mess of it once more.

Well . . . he must only make a fresh start tomorrow, that was all—earlier in the day, before Frensham got moving in the morning. He went back to the Excelsior to retain his room for the coming week, and to inform them there that he would not sleep at the hotel that night, as the date of the arrival of his friend, Mr Metcalfe, was now uncertain. He would call, probably, early next morning, he said.

It was ten minutes to six when the taxi in which he had removed the detachable portions of his disguise set him down in University Road. His engagement to dine with Melhuish was for eight o'clock. For the sake of exercise, and because no other way of filling in the intervening time suggested itself, he decided to walk by University Road and its continuation, Blackbrothers Road, to Blackbrothers Hill, and return from there to Linwood across the Downs. It would take him, he estimated, something over an hour, walking at a sharp pace. He would reach the Riverside in plenty of time to change at leisure and get to Melhuish's by eight.

Discovering, when he reached the top of Blackbrothers Hill and came out upon the breezy expanse of the open Downs, that it was then only twenty minutes past six, he turned his face north-west instead of south-east, and walked across the grass to the farther end of Mersham Down. The wide stretch of level turf, broken here and there by little clumps of timber or of thorn-bush, was deserted at that hour of the winter's afternoon, and he met no one save an occasional early couple strolling arm-in-arm and engrossed in their own affairs. He turned back, reached the lights at the top of Blackbrothers Hill again at twenty minutes to seven, and, leaving the paths once more, struck off across the grass towards the distant lights of Linwood.

He joined one of the main roads intersecting the Downs at a point close to the top of the sharp, curving descent known as Fountain Hill, which led down to the lower level of the Promenade. Descending the hill, he passed, at one of the most dangerous cross-roads in England, the fountain which gave it its name, and, faring straight forward, entered the stately avenue of the Promenade.

A couple of Pekinese, snarling and yapping, ran across the path just in front of his feet when he had left the fountain some fifty or sixty yards behind him, and, at the sound of the voice which recalled them, he turned his head towards the direction from which it had come, believing that he had recognised it for Miss Heathman's. Her house was, he knew, almost directly opposite the point which he had then reached, across the road—one of the score of rather pretentious detached residences which bordered one side of the Promenade and represented the high- water mark of Linwood's exclusiveness. He knew, too, that Miss Heathman possessed a number of Pekinese—things which he detested. And no doubt these two facts strengthened his supposition that the voice which had called petulantly after the straying animals was hers. In the darkness, however, he could only make out the voice's owner vaguely as a blurred feminine figure standing on the grass, some little way from the path, beside a masculine one. He was not in the least interested in Miss Heathman just then, and concluded that, as was the habit twice a day of every second woman in Linwood, she was exercising her dogs, and went on his way. It was ten minutes past seven when he reached the Riverside.

19

At odd moments since the morning his thoughts had recurred to Melhuish's abrupt invitation. But if any other motive than the ordinary desire to be civil to a friend of his wife's had impelled Melhuish to it, Gore was still at a loss to conjecture what that motive was, when he shook hands with his host at eight o'clock.

He was now practically convinced, as has been already indicated, that his first suspicions with regard to Melhuish had been entirely unfounded. Melhuish, he believed now—practically—knew no more of Barrington's death than he had stated he knew—that it had been due to a heart seizure and had occurred half an hour or three-quarters of an hour before the Barracombe women had called him out to the dead man's assistance. Gore was now prepared—practically—to admit that his own impressions of Barrington's appearance after death had been exaggerated and misled. He was satisfied—practically— that, having concluded his interview with Pickles on that Monday night, Barrington had driven off in his car with Frensham, who had been waiting for him outside, to some place where they had probably spent the night together. And, upon that hypothesis, he had dismissed from his mind—practically— not merely his baseless conjecture that Melhuish's hand had caused or contributed to Barrington's death, but also his suspicion, equally baseless, that Melhuish had, wilfully or through error, diagnosed the cause of death incorrectly.

'I was dead sick,' his narrative admits, 'of that old theory of mine about Barrington. I had tried to fit it to five people, one after the other—Mrs Melhuish, Melhuish, Arndale, Challoner, and Mrs Barrington, and failed. And when I found myself trying to fit it to a sixth—Frensham—trying once more to screw the same old facts into the same old story with a new villain of the piece—I threw it overboard definitely. At all events I was so sure that Melhuish had no misgivings in the matter that I almost decided before I left the Riverside to go across to Aberdeen Place that evening, to take the little Masai knife-sheath with me, and tell Melhuish how and where I had found it, in the hope that he would then tell me how and where he had found the knife to which it belonged—a point which I wanted to clear up. At the last moment I didn't do so, because on second thoughts I decided that it was better to avoid all reference to Barrington. I left the sheath on the writing-table in my sitting- room, simply because I was too lazy to lock it up again in the suit-case in my bedroom in which I kept it.'

Melhuish, who looked tired and worried, had been very busy all day, he explained, and had feared until the last moment to have been compelled to plead a serious case as an excuse for postponing his dinner-hour. His wife was still running a temperature, still in bed, and unlikely to return from Surrey for another week or ten days. He intended to run up to see her on the following day. No, her temperature was not a serious one. There was a lot of influenza of a mild type about in that part of the world. She had sent her kindest regards to Gore.

Their talk, as they waited for the gong, strayed to indifferent matters.

As they went down the stairs they heard the clamour of a newsboy coming down Aberdeen Place, and caught his stereotyped cry:

'Evenin' Piper. 'Orrible Tregedy. *Mile an? Echo.* Evenin' Piper. Evenin' Piper. 'Orrible Tregedy . . .'

'Probably one of my cases,' Melhuish said gravely. 'A young fellow called Brook and his wife collided with a bus at the corner of Victoria Street this afternoon—motor-cycle and side-car—he was killed. His wife may live; but, even if she does, she'll be a cripple for the rest of her life.'

'Shockingly dangerous corner that.'

'Shockingly dangerous.'

The two men had reached the foot of the stairs now, and with a little gesture of a hand Melhuish offered his guest precedence. As he crossed the hall to the dining-room, Gore's eyes fell upon the trophy on the wall beside it, and perceived that, where the two Masai knives had hung at its lower extremity, there was now a bare space. Concluding that, for prudence sake, and probably in remembrance of his own advice, Melhuish had removed both knives and put them away in some place where they could do no damage, he passed on into the diningroom without comment.

'Usually,' Melhuish was saying behind him, 'they have a man on point duty at that comer. But this afternoon, for some reason, there was none. The bus came round on its wrong side—as the buses usually do at that corner—'

'Yes, I've noticed that,' Gore agreed. 'They usually put on a spurt, too, as they come round, to get up the hill. Reckless devils, some of those bus drivers. Oh, that reminds me. Have you succeeded in acquiring a new shover yet?'

'Not permanently. I've got a chap temporarily . . . as a matter of fact, one of those rather reckless individuals of whom we've just been speaking. The Westmouth tramway people supplied him to me temporarily, until I find a good man to take on the job permanently.'

'A chap called Thomson called to see me the other day, to ask for a recommendation. Rather a keen, useful-looking sort of fellow. I suppose he's been along to see you—?'

'Thomson? Oh, yes. Quite an excellent chap. I rather think of taking him on. Arndale, who had him for a year or so, before he went to the Kinnairds, spoke to me most highly of him this afternoon. I'm writing to the Kinnairds about him tonight. I hardly like to take him on, permanently at any rate, until the Kinnairds have agreed to let him go.' He turned to Clegg. 'By the way, Thomson left Mr Kinnaird's address this afternoon, you said, didn't you?'

'Yes, sir. I left it in the morning-room.'

'Get it for me, will you. I mustn't forget to write to Mr Kinnaird tonight.'

'Very well, sir.'

Melhuish turned his head towards the windows. A second newsboy was hurrying down Selkirk Place now, crying in shrill rivalry with his hoarser-toned competitor in Aberdeen Place.

'And get the evening papers, will you, Clegg.'

'Yes, sir.'

'You saw Arndale this afternoon?' Gore asked casually, when the man had left the room. 'Looking pretty cheap, isn't he?'

Melhuish nodded. 'He doesn't look well. Any golf lately, Colonel?'

They were still discussing courses and holes when Clegg returned to the room with the evening papers, which he laid on the sideboard in passing, and an envelope which he deposited at his master's elbow. While they waited for the coming of the fish Melhuish opened the envelope, glanced at the communication which it contained, and then passed the latter to Gore across the table.

'Mr Alfred Thomson writes an excellent hand at any rate, doesn't he?' he smiled. 'I sincerely wish mine were as legible.' He rose, moved to the sideboard, picked up one of the two newspapers, and then returned to his seat.

There was a little silence, disturbed only by the subdued rumble of the lift in which the fish was ascending to the expectant Clegg, and by the rustle of Melhuish's paper as he opened it and turned to its last sheet. Gore glanced at the brief note which his host had passed to him and which contained the latest address which the Kinnairds' chauffeur had been able to ascertain for his employers.

'Writes quite a good fist,' he agreed. 'I suppose he has told you that he was assistant master at Tenbury Grammar School?'

Melhuish, whose attention was fastened on his newspaper, made no reply for a moment. It was not until his sole had lain unheeded before him so long as to arouse Clegg's visible concern that he laid aside the *Evening Echo* and apologised for his abstraction.

'I beg your pardon, Colonel . . . I'm afraid I didn't catch what you said—?'

Their meal had reached the stage of coffee and privacy before Gore learned the explanation of that silence of frowning forgetfulness. Melhuish waited until the door had closed upon the servant's final exit, and then passed the *Echo* across the table, indicating two smudged paragraphs at the foot of a stop-press column.

'This is rather curious, Colonel, isn't it?' he said quietly.

Before Gore had straightened the limp sheet between his hands, the name 'Frensham' leaped out at him and warned him in some measure of what he was about to read. But as the actual truth found its way to his brain, phrase by phrase, horrified consternation fell upon him—a dismay so utter that even to his own ears his muttered 'Good God' sounded meaningless and inept.

The report was headed:

> 'Fatal Accident on Linwood Down'
>
> 'At seven o'clock this evening the body of a middle-aged man named Richard Frensham was found by two quarrymen in the disused quarry immediately beneath the precipitous point of the cliffs overhanging the river gorge, known as Prospect

Rock. From the fact that the body was still warm it is conjectured that the ill-fated man had met his death very shortly before its discovery. A letter signed "A. H." and addressed to "Mr Richard Frensham, Excelsior Hotel, Purley Square, Westmouth," which was found in one of the deceased's pockets, has enabled the police to ascertain that he had been staying at that hotel for some weeks past. The ghastly injuries to the body leave no doubt that the deceased fell, under circumstances which, we understand, the authorities are already taking steps to investigate, from Prospect Rock to the quarry two hundred feet below.

'By a curious coincidence, the corpse was found but a few feet distant from the spot where that of an unknown man was found on June 10th, 1920, and but a few yards distant from that where another unknown unfortunate was discovered on February 4th, 1919.'

20

He knew the old quarry well—had known it all his life. From the narrow, stony path which coiled amongst the dense thorn-bushes at the edge of the cliffs and led to Prospect Rock, one could, if one leaned far out over the fragile railing protecting the path at the side next to the precipice, see the boulder-littered, cup-like recess far below, overhung by the sheer, bulging wall of rock. Between the quarry and the river lay a narrow cart-track. Figures moving along that track, he recalled, were no larger than a fly on the hand of a person looking down at them from Prospect Rock. Two hundred feet? More nearly two hundred and fifty at that point. He had a vision of that headlong fall—of the annihilating crash that had rushed up out of the darkness to meet the doomed man—

But that impression was instantaneous—a sensation that came and passed more swiftly than thought. The horror that remained, that defied his best efforts to refuse it admittance to his mind, obliterated for the moment all conceptions of circumstance, all capacity for pity, all facts connected with Frensham save one.

For the first time certainty, absolute and indubitable, stared him in the face. Even if he had not known that Frensham and Arndale had met that afternoon—even if Arndale had not been, to his knowledge, the last person in whose company Frensham had been that afternoon—that certainty would have trampled all possible doubt or question under foot. The hand that had

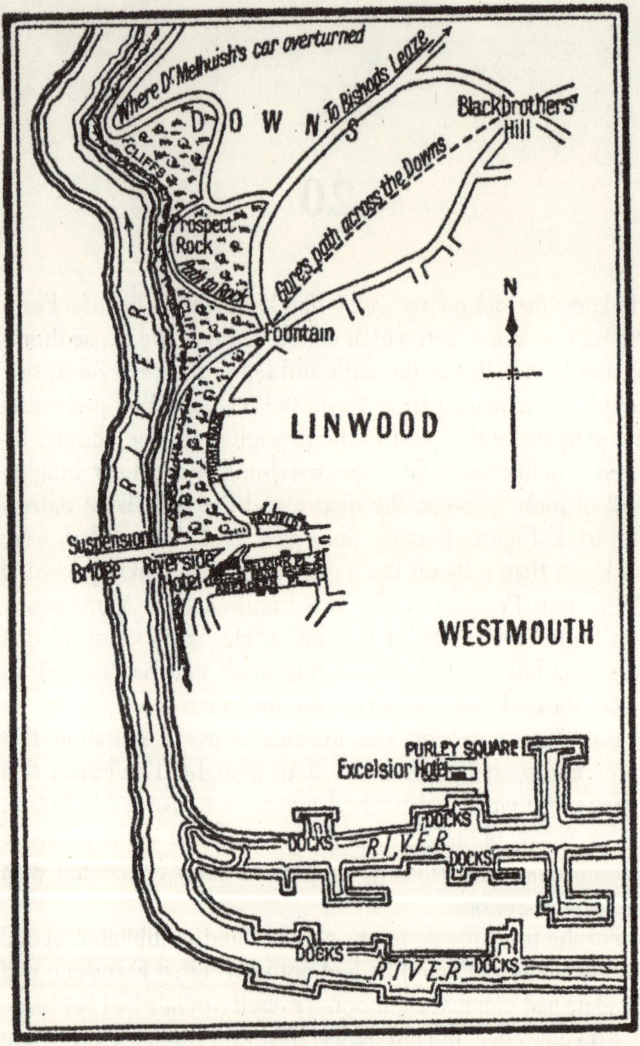

'Callins' Geographical Establishment, Glasgow.

dealt death to Barrington had found murder a safe and easy remedy. What Barrington had known, Frensham had known. For that knowledge the same hand had found the same remedy.

The folly—the desperate madness of it, staggered him. That fellow Stevens . . . *He* had seen them together, followed them. How many others had seen them together? A tall man and a small one walking together . . . how many people must have noticed them . . . The chances were that Arndale could not walk on any part of Linwood Down at any hour of the day without meeting someone who knew him at least by appearance . . .

'Good God,' he said again. 'This is terrible.'

His eyes returned to the first words of the account. Seven o'clock. He made a rough calculation hurriedly. Descending from Fountain Hill, Prospect Rock had been to his right hand, a couple of hundred yards distant, separated from the road by a stretch of rocky ground thickly covered by thorn-trees and bramble-bushes. It must have been about a quarter to seven, he estimated, when he had passed so close to the scene of the tragedy—had passed, by the Fountain, the end of the narrow path twisting away towards Prospect Rock from the road. Yes, about a quarter to seven. He had called at the Lending Library in Linwood Park Road to get a couple of books, and had gone down afterwards to the post office in King Street for a book of stamps. Ten past seven when he had reached the Riverside—yes. He had been on Fountain Hill about a quarter to seven—about the very time at which the thing had happened. 'Very shortly before' seven o'clock, the *Echo* said.

He raised his eyes to find Melhuish regarding him curiously—so curiously that for a moment or two he returned the look silently across the table. The most grotesque of imaginations had flashed upon him. For an instant he had had the impression that while he had been staring at the *Echo* Melhuish had been watching him with a vigilant, hostile apprehension, as if waiting for the next movement of some dangerous, yet blundering animal. Was it possible, he asked himself incredulously, that the man's fancy had somehow connected *him* with the tidings of those two smudged paragraphs? Could any man's fancy leap so preposterously? Impossible.

And yet an impulse beyond his control constrained him to put the matter at once to the test.

'I must have been coming down Fountain Hill,' he said quietly, watching the impassive eyes that looked across at him through the slight haze of cigar-smoke, 'at the very time the poor little beggar fell over.'

'Indeed? You were on the Downs this afternoon?'

'Yes. I walked across from Blackbrothers Hill.'

'Oh, yes.'

No. He had been mistaken, he told himself—deceived momentarily by a slight narrowing of eyelids, a slight compression of nostrils and lips—that most ordinary change of expression which a man's face assumes when the smoke of his cigar threatens to irritate his eyes and his nose a little. Melhuish's face had resumed its rather tired, rather formal smile now. The tone in which he had said 'Oh, yes,' was merely one of polite concession to his guest's interest in the discovery that he had been in the neighbourhood of catastrophe at the time of its happening.

'There have been a good many accidents and suicides at that particular spot, I believe,' he said, rising from the table and moving again to the sideboard. 'I walked round that path along the cliffs once—shortly after I came here first. I remember thinking at the time that the railing was rather inadequate protection.'

He had picked up the second evening paper. 'Let us see what the *Mail* says. The wording of the *Echo* report would almost lead one to believe—'

He paused abruptly and read the *Mail's* somewhat longer account carefully to the end before he turned his face again towards the shaded lights of the table.

'They have found a knife in the quarry,' he said slowly—"'a small, sharp-pointed knife of unusual design", this report says, "fitted into a haft of leather or hide. The police authorities preserve a strict reticence as to this discovery, which seems to point to the conclusion that Mr Frensham's death may not have been, as had been at first conjectured, due to an accidental fall from the cliffs above.

"'It is understood that the letter signed with the initials A. H., which was found upon the dead man's person, throws an important light upon this latest mystery of a spot already notorious for its tragic associations."'

He handed the *Mail* to Gore and went back to his seat. Another little silence fell until, with the gesture of a man who had come to an at length inevitable decision, he abandoned his half-finished cigar and, dropping his elbows on the table, leaned forward gravely towards his guest.

'You know,' he said, 'that this man Frensham was in some way associated with Barrington—at any rate, that he was on terms of intimacy with him?'

'I believe,' Gore replied cautiously, 'that they were fairly intimate.'

'I have known you for a very short time,' Melhuish went on levelly, 'and I can hardly expect you to indulge in confidences . . . even if I do so myself. However . . . I am going to risk a confidence—'

He paused as if arranging his ideas, and then, without warning, went on again tranquilly.

'You are aware, of course, that Barrington's death was not entirely due to natural causes. Indeed, I think it is perfectly safe to say that, but for the severe nervous and physical shock produced by certain extraneous causes, he would not have died . . . when he did die. You are aware of that?'

He spoke with the detached deliberation with which he might have addressed a clinical class across a hospital cot containing a mildly interesting case. Gore, for whom this formally-phrased revelation made a terrible certainty more terribly certain, stared at him in silence, wondering what was to come.

'I thought it possible at the time,' he decided to admit guardedly. 'Though I am bound to say it surprises me now a great deal to realise that my very vague suspicions were correct.'

'What were your suspicions?' Melhuish asked. 'What *are* your suspicions . . . *now*?'

Gore shrugged.

'Do my suspicions matter in the least, doctor—if the fact is as you say—?'

Melhuish interrupted him with a cold little gesture of impatience.

'I have been frank with you, Colonel Gore—frank, as you will admit, beyond discretion. What do you really believe to have been the cause of Barrington's death—now—at this moment? What do you believe caused that physical and mental shock of which I spoke just now?'

Where was this questioning leading, Gore asked himself. If towards Arndale, he was most resolutely determined that no slightest word of his should guide it.

'Suppose you tell me what your own idea about the matter is, doctor,' he suggested, rather stiffly. 'If your idea is . . . my idea . . . well, then, I'll say so. If it isn't, I'll say so, too. Please remember that I'm only a layman.'

Melhuish smiled bleakly.

'My idea,' he said, reaching for the *Mail* and pausing until he had found the lines he wanted—'my idea is a little sharp-pointed knife of unusual design, fitted into a haft of leather or hide.' He raised his eyes.

'Well?'

It seemed useless to fence about that point any longer.

'Yes,' Gore said, most unwillingly, 'that, I own, was my idea too.'

'Was?'

'Is, then.'

Gore sat back in his chair.

'I wish to God I had never sent your wife the infernal things,' he said with sincerity. 'I'm glad to see, at any rate, that you've taken them from your hall—'

'One of them,' Melhuish said gravely. 'Someone else took the other from my hall . . . this afternoon. That is why I have ventured to make to you—whom I hardly know—a confidence which places my professional reputation in your hands. I am not going into my reasons—now—for making that confidence. I will say, simply, that I want to be prepared . . . and to prepare you . . . for a contingency the nature of which you realise, I have no doubt whatever, as clearly as I do.'

'Someone else removed one of them,' Gore repeated at length. 'Who?'

'That I cannot say . . . with certainty. I can only tell you that at five o'clock this afternoon, Clegg—my man—pointed out to me that one of the knives had been taken from the wall . . . the second time that one of them has disappeared, as of course Clegg knows. A considerable number of patients passed in and out of the hall this afternoon. Various people called to inquire for my wife. My wife's bedroom is being done up while she is away. The men were in and out all day up to four o'clock. I suppose about thirty people, besides my own servants, were in the hall between two o'clock and five.'

Deliberately, without the slightest doubt, Gore noticed at once, he had omitted to recall Arndale's visit in reference to the engagement of the Kinnairds' chauffeur. There was nothing to conceal from this cold-blooded, cold-brained Northerner. The fat was in the fire with a vengeance—

'Which knife was taken?' he asked. 'The one with a sheath . . . or the one without?'

'The one without a sheath.'

'The one,' Gore risked hardily, 'which you found in Barrington's pocket . . . or in Barrington's car . . . that afternoon?'

'No. I didn't find it that afternoon,' Melhuish said quickly and plainly in some surprise. 'Nor did I find it in Barrington's pocket. . . nor in his car. I found it close to the gates over there leading into the hotel grounds, the night before. Monday night wasn't it . . . the 6th? Yes. I found it on Monday night—just before I met you by the letter-box in Selkirk Place. I looked about for the sheath but couldn't—'

He checked himself as Clegg entered the room.

'A cigarette, Colonel?'

'Nurse Scott has rung up, sir, to say that Mrs Brook is very bad. She wants to know if you can go to Foster Place at once. I told her you were at dinner, sir—'

Melhuish looked at his watch, then at his guest.

'Will you forgive me? It is the poor girl who—'

'Yes, yes. Of course, doctor,' Gore said hurriedly. 'Please don't delay a second on my account—'

Melhuish hastened away to the telephone, returned to find Clegg aiding Gore into his overcoat in the hall.

'Most extraordinary thing I ever heard of, sir,' the man was saying. 'I saw them both there with my own two eyes at lunchtime, both of them—'

'I go out the back way,' Melhuish interrupted, holding out his hand. 'It would take me too long to walk to Foster Place. Again a thousand apologies. May I run in and see you one evening;?'

'Do.'

As he returned to the Riverside, retracing step by step the route he had followed on that Monday night, Gore paused to look back through the laurels of the Green towards the lamp in Aberdeen Place beneath which he had seen Barrington for the last time alive. He was actually thinking that it was quite within the range of probability that he might find himself compelled to state, on oath, his belief as to the identity of the man whom he had seen standing there that night with Barrington in the light of the lamp, when that possibility was brought home to him with a rather startling unexpectedness. A policeman emerged from the gates of the Riverside's grounds as he neared them, glanced at him sharply as he went by, and then, perceiving that he was about to enter the grounds, turned and followed him.

'Excuse me, sir,' he asked, civilly, 'do you happen to be Colonel Gore?'

'Yes, I am Colonel Gore.'

'Sergeant Long and I are making some inquiries respecting a man called Richard Frensham, sir. They told us at the hotel that you were dining at Number 33 Aberdeen Place. I was just stepping across there to ask you if you'd see the sergeant. He's waiting in your rooms, sir. Seeing you in evening dress, I thought you might be Colonel Gore, so I stopped you.'

The man accompanied Gore to his sitting-room, where his superior, who had been seated at the writing-table, rose at their entry.

'Hope you'll excuse me using your table, sir. I was just jotting down some notes. I am Sergeant Long of the Westmouth City Police. I have received instructions to obtain from you any information you can give us concerning a man named Richard Frensham. I don't know if you are aware, sir, that a man of that name was found dead this evening in the quarry below Prospect Rock?'

'Yes. I have just seen the account in the evening papers. I'm afraid, though, that I haven't a great deal of information to give you about the poor man, sergeant. I met Mr Frensham on two occasions only—the first time at the house of a Mrs Barrington who lives here in Linwood—'

The sergeant had picked up a little notebook from the writing-table.

'Address, sir, please, and date?'

'27 Hatfield Place. The date—Friday, November the 10th.'

'Thank you, sir. And the second occasion?'

'At the Excelsior Hotel, on Monday, November 13th.'

Sergeant Long required to make no note of that second meeting, for the reason that he already had one.

'Yes, sir. I've got that. They told us at the Excelsior Hotel that a Colonel Gore had been there by appointment over the telephone to see Frensham on the afternoon of November 13th. Finding that a Colonel Gore was staying here at the Riverside, I concluded it was the same.'

'Sounds very simple,' thought Gore. 'Pretty quick, all the same . . . for a provincial police-sergeant.'

Aloud he said: 'Those are the only two occasions on which I met Mr Frensham.'

'Might I ask, sir, what your relations were with him? Business dealings . . . or what?'

'He was, I understand, a friend of Mr Barrington's. After Mr Barrington's death, which took place a couple of weeks ago, he offered to assist Mrs Barrington in arranging her husband's affairs.'

'What was Mr Barrington's occupation?'

'So far as I know, he had none. I myself only returned to England a few weeks ago—so that, naturally, my knowledge of the affairs of people living here in Linwood is rather limited . . . However, I believe I am right in saying that Mr Barrington had private means. Mrs Barrington is a very old friend of mine . . . I happened to be at her house one day when Mr Frensham called. That was how I made his acquaintance. I went down to see him at the Excelsior Hotel on November the 13th to get some information from him for Mrs Barrington about some business matters which he was looking into for her.'

'Can you give us any information as to Frensham's occupation or business, Colonel?'

'I'm afraid not. I rather think Mrs Barrington told me he came from London. I gathered from his own conversation that he had travelled a great deal. But beyond that, as I say, I really know next to nothing about him.'

'From what you saw of him, can you say if you know of any reason why he should have committed suicide?'

'No. He seemed quite a cheerful little man.'

'From what you saw of him, or from his conversation, did you form the conclusion that he went in fear of anyone—I mean, in fear of personal violence or molestation from any person?'

'No. I shouldn't have said so at all. I noticed that the report in the *Mail* suggested that his fall had not been accidental. It said something about a knife having been found—'

Sergeant Long compressed his lips beneath his heavy moustache.

'It was no accident, Colonel. He was stabbed in three places. It's an ugly business, this. I saw the knife myself, sir. A nasty little affair. I'd say it was a black man's or a yellow man's knife, myself. I saw a knife once something just like it with a stoker I had to take off a West African cargo boat down in St Paul's Dock a bit before the war. A native knife of some sort that was—the chap had got it from a nigger, he told us. You been in Africa yourself, Colonel, I hear?'

'Yes, I was there for a couple of years.'

The sergeant's steady brown eyes surveyed his face exhaustively—rested, Gore felt pretty certain, on the now nearly-healed but still conspicuous cut on his chin.

'Well, there's nothing more *you* can tell us about Frensham, is there, sir?'

'Nothing, I'm afraid.'

'Then I needn't take up any more of your time, Colonel. Sorry to have had to trouble you. People don't like us coming bothering them with questions, of course. However, that's our job, sir. We've got to leave no stone unturned in a serious case like this.'

'I quite understand, sergeant. Only sorry I can't be of more assistance to you.'

'Good-night, sir.'

The two large, well-drilled men saluted smartly and departed. Gore listened until their heavy footsteps had died away towards the hall. Then he crossed to the writing-table, and, picking up the little beaded sheath which lay still where he had left it before going out, on some unanswered letters beside the blotting-pad, contemplated it with grim amusement. It had lain there under Sergeant Long's no doubt observant eyes while he had jotted down those notes of his. Those no doubt observant eyes had seen . . . and remembered . . . a knife 'something just like' the knife that belonged to that sheath. Had they seen also . . . and remembered also . . . a sheath something just like that sheath? If they had, would Sergeant Long not have said so? Or would he—?

'I wonder,' said Gore.

He seated himself by the fire to follow, step by step, the progress of an imaginary Sergeant Long, possessed . . . for the sake of argument . . . of intelligence, knowledge, and observation . . . well, say, equal to his own. This supposed Sergeant Long, having learned at the Excelsior Hotel that a Colonel Gore had called there on the afternoon of November the 13 th to see Frensham, ascertained that Colonel Gore was staying at the Riverside Hotel in Linwood, went there, and made some inquiries about him. From the manager and the staff of the hotel he learned that on the evening of November 13th Colonel Gore had returned to the hotel with a badly cut chin. This supposed Sergeant Long then went into Colonel Gore's sitting-room and saw there on a writing-table a sheath which was 'something just like' a sheath he had seen with a stoker off a West African cargo boat—the sheath of a native knife. He knew, did this observant Sergeant Long, that the knife with which Frensham had been stabbed, was a knife 'something just like' the knife which had belonged to that sheath which (supposedly) he had seen with that stoker. He had found out, also, had this clever Sergeant Long, that Colonel Gore had just returned from Africa. Now, supposing all that, what more would Sergeant Long have been likely to want to know?

His first question, surely, would have been . . . almost certainly, 'When and where did you last see Richard Frensham?'

His next: 'Where were you between the hours of six and seven o'clock this afternoon?'

His next: 'Can you produce any evidence—any person who saw you, to prove exactly where on Linwood Down you were at a quarter to seven?'

His next, probably: 'Did you have a quarrel with Frensham on the afternoon of November 13th, and' (perhaps) 'another quarrel with him on the evening of November 17th?'

His next: 'Where is the knife belonging to this knife-sheath which I find here on the writing-table in your sitting-room?' And his next, probably: 'Will you accompany me to the Central Police Station?'

Surely no conceivable police-sergeant, knowing what that imaginary Sergeant Long was supposed to know, could find it in his heart to salute respectfully and go on his way with a benign 'Good-evening.'

And yet . . . how easy it might have been for Sergeant Long to make his way to that blunder. And how deucedly awkward if he had made his way to it . . . or should make his way to it. . .

Suppose one were asked at the inquest to answer—on oath—the questions: 'When you last saw Frensham, was he alone?' and 'Who was the tall man in a light-coloured raincoat with whom you say you last saw him in Old Cut Road about halfpast five on the afternoon of November 18th?'

What could one do? One would have to tell the truth . . .

Not that Arndale didn't deserve anything that was coming to him. But one didn't want to be the person who, practically, put a rope about his neck . . .

Besides, Arndale was the sort of chap who'd go to pieces when he saw the game was up. Ten to one he'd own up to having done Barrington in also. If he did that. . . Pickles *couldn't* be kept out of it . . .

Yes. A great deal depended upon Sergeant Long. A stolid, rather good-looking, ruddy-skinned big fellow—quiet, even gentle of manner . . . kindly of smile . . . But Gore had been too long a regimental officer to place any undue reliance upon the simplicity of those stolid, straightforward looking British façades.

He abandoned the strong temptation to consign the knife-sheath to his sitting-room fire and so get rid of it for good and all, and went into his bedroom to lock it up in the suit-case in which he kept possessions of special privacy and importance. Catching sight of his sheaf of graphs, as he was about to shut up the suit-case again, the thought occurred to him that one of them, at least, could now be brought to a full-stop at a final negative certainty. His suspicion of Arndale was a belief that was almost certainty, it was true; yet, after all, it was not certainty. But if he had ever been certain of anything in his life, he was certain now, he told himself, that Frensham had not had any hand in Barrington's death.

He picked up the bundle of diagrams and glanced at the key-sheet, pinned to the front, on which the number of each graph was set opposite the initials of the person to whom the graph referred. Number 7 was F.'s graph, and Gore was about to turn it up and complete it when his eyes fell on the initials facing the number 15. A. H . . . Weren't those the initials given in the newspaper reports—the initials signing that letter that threw an important light . . .?

There had been a run on the papers that evening, apparently, for it was nearly a quarter of an hour later when at length Percival succeeded in procuring a copy of the *Evening Mail* for him. His recollection, he found, however, had been quite accurate. The initials of the writer of that important and illuminating letter were A. H.

He returned to his chair by the fire and—not for the first time, as will be remembered—informed the hearth-rug that he was damned.

21

'The discovery on Saturday evening last,' said the Westmouth *Times and Courier* of Tuesday, November 21st, 'of the dead body of a man lying amongst the rocks in a disused quarry at the foot of the cliffs on the south-west edge of Linwood Down, was the subject of an inquiry held yesterday at the City Coroner's Court.

'The deceased was Richard Frensham, age, occupation, and permanent place of residence unknown. The circumstances of the tragedy, which had excited widespread attention, presented certain grave features, for the further investigation of which the police applied for and obtained an adjournment of the inquiry.

'Mrs Margaret Rummer, proprietress of the Excelsior Hotel, Purley Square, identified the body of Frensham, who, she thought, was about forty-five years of age and had frequently stayed at the Excelsior. She did not know what his occupation was, but thought he was a racing man. He was out a great deal, often from early morning until late at night. He had engaged a bedroom at the hotel on October 24th, and had slept in it every night since that date until the night of Saturday last. She did not know if he had any particular friends, but he was a jolly, friendly little man, ready to chat with anyone in the bar or about the house. He appeared to have plenty of money, and to be lucky backing horses. He appeared to be in the habit of carrying a good deal of money about with him. He had won a good deal of money, he had told her, on a horse called Step-Out on Friday last. He had had ten pounds on the horse, he had told her, and it had won at 16 to 1. She saw him in the hall of the hotel some time about five o'clock or a little later on last Saturday afternoon. He was fidgeting about. She thought he was expecting someone. That was the last time she saw him alive. He always paid his bill regularly. He paid in cash. She had never known him pay by cheque, nor seen him with a cheque-book. She always considered him a most respectable, civil man. He had never told her of any permanent address. She thought he came from Birmingham by his accent and by his knowing Birmingham so well.

'James MacMillan, quarryman, said, on Saturday evening last about seven o'clock he was returning by the track along the river with William Bishop to Westmouth from Digglesbury, where they were both in employment. Passing under Prospect Rock they heard a cry which seemed to come from the cliffs above their heads, and then a kind of smack against the ground in the old quarry under the rock. Thinking someone had fallen, he and his mate went into the quarry and had a look about, but saw nothing, and went on towards Westmouth.

'William Bishop, quarryman, corroborated the evidence of the preceding witness.

'William Edward Rose, quarryman, said he was returning on Saturday evening from Digglesbury to Westmouth a little way behind Bishop and MacMillan. He heard a cry or shout from the top of the cliffs near Prospect Rock, and, seeing MacMillan and Bishop coming out of the old quarry called out to them to ask them if anyone had fallen. They did not hear him, and went on towards Westmouth. He decided to have a look for himself, to see if anyone had fallen, and after searching about for a little while found the dead man's body jammed between two large boulders with its feet in the air. He ran after MacMillan and Bishop, and all three went to the police-station in Spring Road and informed the police of what they had heard and seen. He was certain the man was dead when he found him, though he did not touch him. He struck some matches and saw that his head was split clean open and his brains coming out. He was bleeding a lot. He looked up towards Prospect Rock from the quarry before he went after MacMillan and Bishop, but could not tell from the quarry whether there was anyone up there, as the cliff bulged out and it was then black dark.

'Elizabeth Penny, waitress at the Excelsior Hotel, said that on Saturday evening last, about half-past five or a little before, she saw deceased in the hall of the hotel. She asked him if he was waiting for his girl, and he said, "No such luck for an old fossil like me, Lizzie." Just as he said that, a tall, youngish man in a light raincoat came in from the square, and deceased said to him, "I'd given you up," and went out with him again. That was the last time she had seen deceased alive. She had never seen the man with whom he went out before. He was a tall man, younger than deceased, not very dark nor very fair. She could not say if he had a moustache. She took him for a gentleman by his look. The light in the hall was not very good, because the mantle of the incandescent was broken. The man did not speak to deceased while he was in the hall. Deceased and he went out again immediately.

'*The Coroner:* You had never seen this man before?—No.

'Had any other man come to the hotel at any time since October 24th to see Frensham? One gentleman came, named Colonel Gore. That was this day week—Monday of last week.

'But this man who came on Saturday last—the man in the light raincoat—he had never been to the hotel before?—No. At least I never see him.

'Mrs Rummer was recalled, and said that when he was in the house at night Frensham would come into the bar and chat with anyone who happened to feel inclined for a chat. There was no one he talked more often to than any of the others. His talk used to be mostly about racing or football or things of that sort, like most of the men who came into the bar. He was very jolly in his ways, but quiet. She never saw him the worse for liquor. She never knew him to have a dispute or a quarrel with anyone in the bar.

'Henry Massingham, tobacconist, Linwood Park Road, said that on October 25th a gentleman who was a regular customer of his and whom he knew to be Mr Barrington, of 27 Hatfield Place, had come into his shop about dinner time with a man whom he (Massingham) believed to have been the deceased. Mr Barrington had been buying some cigars and offered one to the man who was with him, saying: "Try one of these, Frensham," or "Have one of these, Frensham." The name Frensham had stuck in his memory because he had been born in Surrey near Frensham Ponds. On the evening of last Saturday, November 18th, this man had come into his shop again to buy some cigarettes. That was some time after six o'clock. He was sure that it was the same man whom he had heard Mr Barrington address as Frensham. The man was alone. He might have had a companion waiting for him outside without his (witness's) knowledge of it. He bought a twenty package of Virginia cigarettes, and went out again quickly. There were two other customers waiting to be served, but he could not say now who the other customers were. They were strangers. Neither of them, as well as he remembered, answered the description of the man who had called at the Excelsior Hotel to see Frensham that afternoon. Neither of them spoke to Frensham in the shop or paid any attention to him, so far as witness saw.

'Police-Constable Loderby, H147, said that in accordance with instructions he had made a careful search in the disused quarry beneath Prospect Rock on the evening of Saturday, November 18th, while the body of deceased was being removed and afterwards. He produced a knife which he had found at a distance of twenty-eight feet three inches from the spot where the body had been discovered. The spots marked A and B on the plan of the quarry (produced) indicated correctly the respective positions of the body and of the knife when found. The blood on the blade and haft of the knife were still wet when he found it.

'Police-Sergeant Yatt said, in accordance with instructions he had made a careful examination of the ground in the neighbourhood of Prospect Rock and also in the disused quarry beneath it, both on the evening of Saturday, November 18th, and on the morning of the following day. He had found no traces of a struggle in either place, but in both places the ground was splashed and spattered with blood a good deal. A struggle might have taken place on the path at Prospect Rock without leaving any trace of footmarks. The path was very rocky there and would exhibit no marks made by boots such as deceased had been wearing at the time.

"*The Coroner:* There have been complaints, I understand, made to the police during the last few years that respectable people have been accosted and molested by undesirable characters on this particular portion of the Downs?—Yes.

'The path has been patrolled regularly by the police for some time past?—Three times a day since January of last year.

A *Juryman:* At what hour was the path patrolled on Saturday last?—8 a.m., 3.15 p.m., 9.10 p.m.

'*The Coroner:* So that between the hours of 3.15 p.m. and 9.10 p.m. no policeman passed along this path?—No.

"*The Coroner:* Of course it is impossible for the police to be everywhere at the same time.

'Lt.-Col. Wickham Gore, D.S.O., stated that deceased had volunteered to assist Mrs Barrington, widow of the late Mr Cyril Barrington, of 27 Hatfield Place, in the arrangement of her husband's business affairs. At Mrs Barrington's request, witness had called on the afternoon of Monday, November 13 th, at the Excelsior Hotel, to see Mr Frensham in reference to some inquiries which Mr Frensham was making for Mrs Barrington. He knew nothing of deceased's occupation, but understood from Mrs Barrington, who was an old friend of witness's, that he came from London.

'*The Coroner*: I believe you and I have met before, Colonel Gore, under happier auspices?—I believe so, sir.

'The only visit you paid to the Excelsior Hotel to see this unfortunate man was the visit you paid on November 13th?— Yes.

'You did not call at the hotel again to keep an appointment—or to see Frensham, on last Saturday afternoon?—No.

'Police-Sergeant Long produced two bank-books and a cheque-book found in deceased's suit-case in his bedroom at the Excelsior Hotel. No other papers of any kind were found amongst deceased's effects. There was nothing to show where he came from or what his business was.

'Herbert Westropp, cashier, Linwood branch of Lloyd's Bank, said that the late Mr Cyril Barrington of 27 Hatfield Place had a deposit and a current account at that branch. The bankbooks and the cheque-book produced had been issued to the late Mr Barrington in connection with his accounts there.

'Police-Sergeant Long, recalled, said that the slips (produced) containing entries of sums of money paid or received on certain dates, were inserted in the pocket of the current-account bankbook produced when it was found by witness in deceased's suitcase.

'*The Coroner*: These slips appear to record moneys paid to or received from certain people whose initials only are given in each case. There are a number of these slips—eleven in all—each referring to payments made to or by a person with a different set of initials: J.M., W.G., L.N.P., M.G., F.T., S.McA., R.F., J.R., J.J., T.L., R.T. The payments go back for a considerable time in many cases—in some cases as far back as 1920. The latest date on any of the slips is

October 25th. That date appears on the slip headed with the initials R.F. There appears to be nothing to connect that slip definitely with deceased, though deceased's initials are R.F. It is rather curious, however, that a payment was made either to or by R.F. on October 25th—which, we know, was the day following deceased's arrival at the Excelsior Hotel, and on which date deceased was seen in the company of the late Mr Barrington.

'Lt.-Col. Gore, recalled, said he could not say definitely whether the late Mr Barrington had had monetary dealings with deceased. He thought it possible. Witness personally had had no such dealings whatever with Mr Frensham. Witness's initials were W.G.

'*The Coroner:* Initials which we were very proud of in this part of the world when you and I were learning our cricket, Colonel. I see that the dates of the payments on this slip which is headed with those initials belong to the year 1921. I think I am right in believing that in that year you were in Central Africa?—Yes.

'You had no monetary dealings with the late Mr Barrington?—None.

'Then obviously we must look for some other W.G.

'Police-Sergeant Long, recalled, said that the letter (produced) signed with the initials A. H. was found by him in a pocket of deceased's overcoat when he searched the body in the quarry, together with a penknife, some peppermints, and a used tram- ticket. No money was found, either on deceased's person or amongst his effects at the Excelsior Hotel.

'*The Coroner:* This letter, which is signed A. H., and bears neither date nor the writer's address, says: "Agree price. Shall be Fountain end of Promenade, 6.30 tomorrow Saturday evening with dogs.' The handwriting appears to be disguised. The envelope bears the postmark Linwood, Nov. 17,5.30 p.m.

A *Juryman:* The handwriting appears to be a woman's.

"*The Coroner:* That is my personal impression also. The police have been unable to trace the writer of this letter so far. I hope that the writer of it—and I trust the press will give prominence to this—I hope the writer of it, if he or she is an innocent person, will come forward without delay and explain it.

'Dr R. Tanqueray Jones detailed the injuries to the body of the deceased. In addition to the extensive injuries caused by the impact of the fall, he found three wounds, all of which, in his belief, had been caused by some narrow, sharp-pointed weapon used with great force. They might all have been caused by the knife found near the deceased. He detailed the nature and position of these wounds, one of which had been inflicted upon deceased's neck from behind, the other two in the abdomen, probably while deceased lay prostrate on the ground. It was impossible to say with certainty, he thought, whether deceased was dead before he fell or was thrown over the cliffs. It would have been quite impossible for deceased to have inflicted the wound in his neck himself. Any of the three wounds might have caused death after a certain lapse of time. He was of opinion, however, that deceased had probably been still alive when he struck the rocks in the quarry below.

'Upon the application of the police the coroner adjourned the inquiry until Friday next.

'(Photographs of the scene of the tragedy will be found on P.5.)'

Below the report of the inquest appeared the following paragraph:

'The name of Lt.-Col. Wickham Gore, whose evidence in connection with the Linwood Down tragedy is given above, will be familiar to many of our readers as that not merely of a distinguished soldier, but also of an explorer of international reputation. Together with Lt.-Col. Armstrong and Sir John Parkett he was employed during the years 1920 and 1921 in collecting materials for that most popular and successful of educational films, "The Heart of Africa." Lt.-Col. Gore belongs to a family well known for many generations in Linwood and the neighbourhood, and during his army career was perhaps the most brilliant of that brilliant combination of polo-players known to fame as "The Whoppers."

'(Photograph on p. 5.)'

22

On that Tuesday morning Gore was standing waiting for a bus at the upper end of the street when Mrs Arndale went by in a sporting little blue two-seater. She waved a hand to him as she passed, and pulled up a little way along the kerb, signalling him to approach. With the exception, perhaps, of Arndale himself, his wife was the last person on earth whom Gore wanted to talk to just then. But she had seen him standing there, obviously waiting for a bus, and no bus was in sight. He had no choice but to obey her imperious, smiling summons.

'Haven't they arrested you yet, then?' she laughed. 'We're all simply thrilled to the kernel. Why *didn't* you let us know you were to give evidence at the inquest? And why *didn't* you tell the old coroner that you were on the very spot when the murder was committed? After all, you were only a few yards away. Just think what excitement it would have created in Linwood. As it is, my cook told me in confidence this morning that she believes you'll turn out to be the "one as done it."'

This was all extremely difficult and not a little puzzling. Gore's smile was somewhat forced as he asked which of the newspapers had supplied the information that he had been 'on the spot.'

'Bertie saw you,' Mrs Arndale laughed. 'He was there, too. He was behind you all the way from Blackbrothers Hill across the Downs on Saturday evening.'

'Really? I didn't see him.'

'He saw you. He makes out that the murder must have been just in full swing as he and you were going down Fountain Hill. Where do you want to go?'

'Towards my lunch, really.'

'Let me take you there. Or are you afraid Mrs Barrington will be jealous?'

As they threaded their way through the traffic she explained that her brother had been playing golf out at Penbury on Saturday afternoon, and had accepted a lift in as far as Blackbrothers Hill, where his friends had dropped him. From there he had walked home to Selkirk Place across the Downs and along the Promenade. Apparently he had been barely fifty yards behind Gore until, at the top of Linwood Park Road, their paths had separated.

'Why didn't he shout out,' Gore asked, 'if he was so close behind?'

Mrs Arndale made a little grimace.

'Bertie doesn't love you just at present, Wick, for some reason, I gather. He doesn't love anyone just now. Perhaps he's jealous of your devotion to someone— Though I rather think Master Bertie has cooled off a good deal . . . now that the glamour of an illicit passion—that's the correct phrase, isn't it? I've never had one, worse luck—may be expected to replace itself by the dullness of legal and respectable possession. I bet Bertie doesn't marry her—though he keeps on saying that he's going to—or rather because he keeps on saying so. He comes out nearly every afternoon now to tea to tell me so. If he doesn't come to tea he comes to dinner. By the way, when do you intend to dine with us—or do you ever intend to dine with us? Please do it before they hang you, won't you. I've asked you twice, and you've told me two most shocking whoppers. Oh, that reminds me. Didn't the old *Times and Courier* simply spread itself over your career this morning? And what a topping photograph. I never realised, until I saw that photograph, what an absolutely criminal type of face yours was. I wish you'd give me one. I'm so tired of the faces of people who never do things.'

They were passing Prince Albert Square just then, and Mrs Arndale's sprightly attention was distracted to the flaring posters of the big cinema theatre there.

'You never go to picture-houses, I suppose?' she smiled.

'Sometimes.'

'They had rather a topping picture on there last week—"Dust"—Emma Dugdale told me I mustn't miss it. So I made poor old Cecil take me to the first house on Saturday. Poor old thing. I loved it—but it bored him absolutely stiff. He fell sound asleep as soon as the lights went down, and snored. Snored—I couldn't make him stop. It was most embarrassing. Fancy falling asleep at half-past six in the evening . . . and snoring . . . publicly. Of course he never sleeps a wink at night now, poor old boy, until three or four o'clock in the morning. I'm really getting frightfully worried about him. I'm so afraid he'll start taking drugs. I've a deadly horror of dopes . . . As it is, I know he's drinking far more than is good for him.'

She sighed.

'Some world . . . Rather a decent little bus this, isn't she? Cecil's latest birthday present.'

'Very nice indeed,' Gore said rather hurriedly, realising that she had turned to glance into his face curiously.

The first house at that cinema theatre began, he knew, a little after six o'clock and lasted until a little after eight. Was it possible that Roly-Poly was trying to ram an alibi down his throat? Or was it the actual astounding fact that at a quarter to seven on Saturday evening Arndale had been sitting beside her in the cinema theatre, dozing—snoring? She *had* said the first house . . .

'You must have found the place very crowded on Saturday evening, didn't you?' he asked. 'Though I suppose not so crowded for the first house—?'

'It was pretty fuggy,' she admitted, 'but nothing to what it must have been during the second house. There were two enormous queues right round the fountain, waiting for the second house, when we came out. And we came away at least a quarter of an hour before the show was over . . . when the big picture finished.'

'Did your husband stick it out as long as that?'

'I had to pinch him to waken him. Oh . . . there's Dr Melhuish . . . I wonder how Barbara is. Have you heard?'

'Not since Saturday. I dined with Melhuish on Saturday evening. Mrs Melhuish was still in bed then, he told me.'

'Poor dear. I must drop her a line. Wasn't it perfectly dreadful about the Brooks? You didn't know them, perhaps?'

The conversation concerned itself with the accident at the corner of Victoria Street and its fatal results, until they reached the front doors of the Riverside. There Gore undertook to dine with the Arndales on the following Monday.

'No whoppers, mind,' Mrs Arndale commanded—'by telephone, telegram, post, or wireless. Swear.'

'I swear. If I don't turn up,' he grinned, 'you'll know they've got me.'

She laughed as she released her brake.

'I'll come and see you in your cell. Don't forget, I want a copy of that photograph. And don't let Mrs Barrington know you've given me one. Monday, at eight—or never again. By-bye.'

She laughed again as the two-seater slid away and left him looking after her in the sunshine, beneath the interested gaze of Percival and the hall porter. Quite forced, that laugh of hers, he was inclined to think . . . artificial. Her whole manner had been forced, and . . . well, too sprightly. Not a good liar, little Roly-Poly. Poor little Roly-Poly . . . Did she know why she was to tell people that yarn about the picture-house? He hoped not. He had always been rather fond of little Roly-Poly. Nothing much in her, of course, but a thundering good little sort . . .

Rather annoying, though, if one was going to be bored with a lot of that sort of chaff...

So Master Bertie Challoner had cooled off, then. Feeling a bit silly about that unexpected meeting in Hatfield Place, of course. That probably accounted for his walking just behind for a mile and a half without hailing or trying to pick up . . .

Odd, though, that Challoner should have been the one to see him . . . suppose he had wanted a witness to prove where exactly he had been at that time. Quite odd.

And then . . . suddenly . . . it seemed to Gore perhaps not so odd . . .

A south-west gale howled and moaned and groaned in the creaking trees of the Green that night, and screamed and wailed about the flank of the Riverside, and rattled all the windows of its annexe most infernally, but none more infernally than those of a certain private sitting-room to which several references have been made already. In that sitting-room a tallish gentleman with a not unpleasing brown face—now clean-shaven—sat in extremely well-fitting evening clothes before his fire, hammering his excellent teeth with the stem of a long-extinct briar pipe of offensive odour. His forehead was creased by three large wrinkles; his eyes gazed into the heart of the fire as if the least distraction of their gaze might prove fatal. On a chair beside his own lay several sheets of manuscript pinned together, and a fountain-pen. And the last words on the last sheet of the manuscript were:

'The whole thing began to seem to me dream-like—not real— exactly like a mixed-up nightmare. I had a sort of feeling that I should wake up and discover that it was the morning after that dinner at Melhuish's, and that I'd had a bad night. The only clear, definite conclusion I had arrived at now was that, if Arndale hadn't done it, Challoner had. Stevens fitted for Frensham, partially, but only partially. For Barrington, of course, he didn't fit at all. I couldn't get away from the belief that whoever had killed one had killed the other; and that excluded Stevens. However, it didn't seem much use reasoning from any belief—'

And the fact is that a graph for Stevens was added to the collection in Colonel Gore's suit-case before he retired to rest that night.

23

But by next morning he had reverted definitely to the earliest of his theories, which had first connected Arndale and Challoner with the affair and had supposed Mrs Barrington aware of at least some of the measures which they had taken, in concert, on that Monday night.

Arndale had known that Barrington was to see Pickles on that night. It was he who had met Barrington under the lamp, had gone home with him to Hatfield Place, remained there for an hour with him, and gone out again with him in his car. They had separated then, temporarily; but, knowing where Barrington was going, Arndale had followed him and waited until he came out from Pickles. There had been a quarrel; Barrington had tried to defend himself with the knife, and had somehow received a scratch on one hand—probably without Arndale's intention. Fright, probably, more than anything else had caused Barrington's death. At all events he had died—suddenly. Arndale had put him into his car, driven it across to Challoner's flat—where Mrs Barrington had probably been at the moment— and had persuaded Challoner, probably with Mrs Barrington's assistance, to allow him to use the garage in the lane. Next day, when darkness fell, he or Challoner had driven the car and the dead man to Melhuish's door and left them there.

No doubt, with Barrington dead and buried, Arndale had thought himself safe . . . for a day.

Then Frensham had appeared on the scene, and had taken up Barrington's old game, and had paid the penalty. Arndale had remembered how swiftly the knife had worked once. He had obtained possession of it again—laid his plans carefully, and succeeded, somehow, in inveigling Frensham to a spot where he thought they could be safely carried out.

If Challoner had aided him in his first adventure, was it not quite conceivable that he had been scared into aiding him—probably by keeping watch—in the second. Probably someone had seen him hanging about there near that path leading to Prospect Rock, and he had realised that he had been seen and perhaps recognised. So he had invented this story of having walked across the Downs from Blackbrothers Hill just behind someone else—Gore, as it happened—whom he had seen from his hiding-place come from that direction and go down Fountain Hill.

This last part of the theory—the part concerning Challoner—was certainly not very convincing. But for that curious episode in Hatfield Place, Gore would have felt inclined to accept Challoner's unsuspected proximity during his walk across the Downs on Saturday evening as a curious coincidence. But it seemed to him that some extraordinary desperation must have laid behind Mrs Barrington's attempt to shoot herself. Why should she have come back from London to that furtive meeting with Challoner, if some extraordinary urgency which she shared with him had not compelled her? Something had frightened her badly—frightened them both badly, he felt sure. It was quite possible that Frensham knew or suspected the circumstances of Barrington's death, and that he had begun to threaten all the three people whom his knowledge or his suspicion had connected with it.

Certainly some much stronger fear than solicitude on Pickles's behalf must have driven Arndale to this carefully-planned silencing of Frensham. What more likely, after all, than that Frensham had got some information from the Rodney girl which had put him upon the track? She had been peeping out of her window that night—on the alert—waiting for Barrington. She *must* have seen and heard what went on. . . . practically beneath her window. She must have seen and heard the car going up the lane afterwards, too, and into Challoner's garage. Perhaps, even, she had seen the dead man in it. From her window one could see down into a passing car. There was plenty of light there at the mouth of the lane; and the car would have to go pretty slowly round the sharp, narrow corner. If Frensham had got *that* information, Arndale and Challoner and Mrs Barrington were all sufficiently explained.

There were moments when Gore accused himself—or rather, felt that he ought to accuse himself—of an undue cold-bloodedness in these speculations of his. The business was a horrible business. One ought to have been decently shocked by it. One ought to have been horrified by the thought that three old friends were involved in such a business.

But the truth was—and his apologies to himself for that truth became feebler and feebler—that the thing had now so caught hold of him that he had come to regard the actors in it as merely pieces of a puzzle baffling and engrossing to the verge of monomania. He was perfectly aware that his reticence at the inquest had sailed perilously close to the wind. He was perfectly aware that if he succeeded in establishing the fact that Arndale had committed a cruel and cowardly murder—if not two—it would be his own duty to denounce him to justice, his own grave peril not to denounce him. Nothing was farther from his intention or his desire than to be compelled to face that consequence. But he could not persuade himself to leave the pieces alone. 'I'm not going to be beaten by the damn thing,' was his defence. 'I want to know.' And so he went on shuffling the pieces of his puzzle and using so many matches that the Riverside rebelled and compelled him to purchase his own.

He came to the conclusion—once more—that all along he had made one fatal mistake for a criminal investigator. Instead of following up any one of his theories, he had allowed himself to be distracted by every red herring which chance or imagination had drawn across it. One never got any forrarder that way.

This theory—still in favour at the end of Wednesday—about Arndale and Challoner, for instance . . . One ought to begin at the very beginning, and follow it up step by step, fact by fact. One ought to start by trying to ascertain where Arndale and Challoner were, respectively, between the falling of dusk and six o'clock on the afternoon of Tuesday, November 7th—that is to say, during the time at some point of which Barrington had been driven back in his car to Aberdeen Place, dead. It was essential to the stability of the theory that one or other of the two should have visited the garage in the lane some time between those hours. If one or other of them could not be nailed to that fact, then the whole theory fell to pieces at once.

Now Challoner, he knew, had been in his flat in Selkirk Place when he had rung him up from Barrington's house some time about seven o'clock that Tuesday evening. Arndale also, he knew, had been in his own house across the Downs at that time; the servant who had answered his call on the telephone had said that Mr Arndale was in and had asked if he wished to speak to him personally.

But where had they both been earlier that afternoon—just before dusk and just after it? Now how could one find that out?

The obvious course was to make inquiries in the lane itself first of all. The rooms over the stables there which had been converted into garages were in most cases occupied—presumably by chauffeurs and their families—at all events by people with very little to look at and likely to be induced by a small douceur to say what they remembered to have seen. A fortnight had elapsed, it was true. Still, some of the women who were to be seen at any hour of the day hanging out of their windows or gossiping in the lane might be capable of remembering what had happened a fortnight ago. The ordinary witness in the ordinary trial was expected to remember things that had happened months before. At all events it was worth trying.

He tried it on the Thursday morning after the inquest.

As a result of inquiries at which the entire population of the lane ultimately assisted, he acquired the following information:

1. Mr Challoner had last taken out his car on
   - (*a*) last Friday week.
   - (*b*) last Saturday week.
   - (*c*) last Tuesday fortnight.
2. No car had come out of Mr Challoner's garage since last Monday week.
3. A tall, dark man had taken a car out of Mr Challoner's garage on—
   - (*a*) Tuesday of week before last.
   - (*b*) Friday of last week.
   - (*c*) Friday of week before last.
4. The garage from which the tall dark man had taken the car was not Mr Challoner's, but the garage next to it.
5. The tall man was not so dark, but more inclined to be fairish. Not so tall either.

For these variegated statements Gore paid seventeen and sixpence in largesse. The lane cheered him as he departed.

In the Mall, as he was about to turn into the club, Melhuish passed in his car. He had evidently overcome his scruples as to taking over the Kinnairds' chauffeur, Gore perceived, for the man was driving, Melhuish in a back seat being apparently absorbed in his newspaper. He looked up, however, as he went by, and, seeing Gore, stopped the car to ask if he might come across to the Riverside for a chat that evening.

'Delighted,' said Gore. 'How's Mrs Melhuish?'

'Much better. She hopes to get back early next week. Looks like snow, doesn't it?'

'Rather. Any time up to midnight, doctor—'

'Thanks. About half-past nine, probably.'

The club was always practically deserted at that early hour, and Gore was somewhat disconcerted to discover, when he entered the lounge, that he was to share its solitude with Bertie Challoner. They interchanged a rather formal 'Good-morning,' and for a little time remained entrenched behind their respective newspapers at opposite sides of the fire. Then Challoner rose and came across the hearth-rug with a rather uncertain smile.

'Look here, Wick,' he said bluntly, 'I expect you think I'm a frightful ass. You've probably been hearing all kinds of stories about me, I expect, from various people . . . I think I had better explain. I suppose you've been wondering about . . . what happened the other day in Hatfield Place, haven't you?'

'I have,' Gore replied with candour.

'Well. . . it's like this,' began Challoner, and seated his fourteen stone with delicate nicety in a chair beside Gore's. 'Ethel and I have fixed up to get married . . . You'd better have that straight—to start off with. We're to be married in the spring. You may be my best man, if you care to take on the job.'

'Delighted, my dear chap, if I'm in England.

'I suppose Roly-Poly had told you, hadn't she?' Mr Challoner was plainly a little disappointed that this announcement had been received so calmly.

'Your sister? Not a word.'

'It's a wonder. Well, anyhow, there it is. It's not public property yet, you know, but I thought it better to let you know.'

'Congratulations, my dear fellow.'

For a little time Challoner expanded his views and feelings with reference to matrimony in general and matrimony for him with Ethel Barrington in particular. He had evidently thought the subject out earnestly and exhaustively, and he spared Gore none of the reasons which had persuaded him to a decision which it was clear he still regarded as of the most momentous and anxious gravity. From that he passed to the reasons—equally numerous and embarrassingly intimate—which had prevented him from coming to that decision long ago—long before she had ruined her life . . . or part of it... by marrying that blackguard Barrington. The reasons were not very convincing; but their very feebleness appeared at least to afford Mr Challoner the pleasures of self-martyrdom. Then for a considerable period he dilated with fervour upon the Hell through which that blackguard had dragged one of the best... in fact, *the* best. . . little woman that had ever lived. And at length he burst into a full- blooded description of the episode on the evening of the Melhuish's dinner-party, which had culminated for the best little woman in the world in a black eye and a resolve to break the chains of her intolerable and unspeakable slavery for ever. There was no need to encourage the historian. His wrathful reminiscence flowed on now, forgetful of his audience, desirous only to find words for its denunciation and its pity.

It was a somewhat disconnected story, but a palpably authentic one; and in substance it amounted to this:

On the afternoon of that Monday Challoner had called at 27 Hatfield Place . . . for the first time, he alleged . . . 'just called in the ordinary way.' . . . Barrington had returned—unexpectedly, it was clear—and had found him 'having tea and chatting.' . . . To Challoner's surprise and outraged incredulity, the blackguard had made the most frightful scene, the most frightful accusations. Mrs Barrington had fled to her bedroom; the scene had continued downstairs until Challoner, after various speeches of the utmost nobility and virtue, and various threats and defiances of not quite so dignified a nature, had left the house.

About half-past ten that night Mrs Barrington had rung him up at his flat to say that, after he had gone away, she had had a dreadful row with her husband, who had struck her several times severely—that it was the last straw—and that she had thought it over and had decided to leave the house that night—for good—before her husband returned from the Melhuishs' dinner-party.

Challoner had thought that that was a very 'serious' thing for her to do, and had tried over the phone to dissuade her from doing anything so serious in a hurry. But she had refused to alter her decision, and finally he had persuaded her to consent to the Arndales meeting her at the Riverside. She couldn't possibly arrive at the Riverside, he had told her, at eleven o'clock at night, with a black eye, alone. She had agreed to his suggestion, and he had rung up Arndale at the Melhuishs' house and asked him and Mrs Arndale to go at once to the Riverside to meet Mrs Barrington when she arrived there, and to arrange about rooms for her.

They had met her when she arrived at the hotel, and had remained with her for nearly three hours, as she had been very worked up and excited, naturally. Arndale had left his wife with her for the greater part of the time, and had apparently been backwards and forwards between the hotel and Challoner's flat at least twice, if not more often, to report how things were going with the fugitive and her consoler. It was impossible for Gore to follow Arndale's movements in the narrative with accuracy. It appeared, however—according to the narrative—that about 11.15 he had left the Riverside by the front door, come up Aberdeen Place—past the Melhuishs'house—crossed to Selkirk Place to Challoner's flat, and remained there until a little before one o'clock. He had then gone back to the Riverside—to return again by the same route almost immediately, a little *after* one o'clock. It had been upon this excursion that he had seen Barrington's car waiting in Aberdeen Place near the Melhuishs' door, empty. He had remained at the flat until about a quarter to two—twenty to two, in fact, as Gore knew—and had then gone away finally to pick up his wife at the Riverside and take her home. The purport of these passings to and fro was not altogether clear; but the impression which Gore understood he was to gather from them was that Mr Challoner and the best little woman in the world had been on the point of burning their boats, and that his sister and her husband had busied themselves to dissuade them from a step which even Mr Challoner himself now admitted would have been disastrous.

The narrative explained, too, Mrs Barrington's prompt return to Hatfield Place on the afternoon of the following day—following Gore's conversation with Challoner over the phone. Challoner had rung her up to tell her of her husband's death—of which he had just heard from the Barracombes—and to advise her to return to Hatfield Place at once—as she had done. He had told Gore over the phone that he didn't know where she was, because—well, under the circumstances he hadn't wanted to seem to know anything about her movements—for her own sake.

At that point Gore asked one question, though he made two of it.

'By the way, did you see Arndale that afternoon, Bertie?'

'Yes. I came up from the Yard in his bus, and he came into my rooms for a bit. Why?'

'Nothing. Just wanted to know. What time was that?'

'About half-past four, I suppose . . . or five.'

A couple of men drifted into the lounge, exchanged salutations, drifted away to the billiard-room.

'However. . . what I really wanted to explain,' said Challoner, 'was that business in Hatfield Place the other afternoon. I know it's safe with you, old chap. But I can't help feeling that you must have wondered about things a good deal—'

It became clear that the best little woman in the world had been a little unreasonable. She had wanted Mr Challoner to snap his fingers at the gossips of Linwood and take her away to Italy and marry her without delay. Mr Challoner had found many inconveniences in this programme, and had been obliged to point them out. The best little woman in the world had misunderstood him—absolutely. She had gone rushing off to France with her mother still misunderstanding him—absolutely. As if any chap with a spark of honour or decency would think for a moment of throwing over the best little woman in the world . . . But she had persisted, it seemed, in believing that that was what Mr Challoner desired and intended to do. And she had come back from London to say so, once more and for the last time. And well—that was how things had stood when Gore had let himself into the hall of 27 Hatfield Place and startled both of them into fits.

'My God, Wick,' Mr Challoner said impressively, 'if She had shot Herself, I swear I'd have put a bullet into myself too.'

'That,' said Gore, 'would have been quite a jolly little picnic— for all of us. However, as it is, I assume everything is now quite satisfactorily explained and understood and so forth.'

'Oh, Lord, yes,' said Mr Challoner. 'I've explained it to death. However . . . I've been wanting to have a chat with you about things. Just to prevent your getting hold of the wrong end of the stick, you know.'

'Yes,' said Gore, 'one is apt to get hold of the wrong end of the stick, isn't one?'

'You see now how it is, old chap, don't you?'

'Quite . . . quite.'

Mr Challoner rose, surveyed his reflection, not unkindly, in a mirror, and sauntered to a window to regard the weather.

'Good,' he said. 'It doesn't look as rotten as it did, does it?'

'I think it looks rottener,' said Gore with conviction.

When Challoner had left him alone he read, successively, the interesting portions of *The Times*, *Punch*, *The Sketch*, *The Tatler*, *The Bystander*, and the *Illustrated Sporting and Dramatic*. At the end of that time it was sleeting outside. So he had a little drink and read the interesting portions of *The Field*, *Country Life*, *The Strand*, *Nash's*, *The Morning Post*, and *Punch* of the week before. He then fell into a stupor and dozed off before the fire. When he awoke snow was falling, and General Barracombe was telling a bald-headed man a story at the other side of the fire. Lest he should hear it, he dozed off again.

These particulars of Colonel Gore's behaviour are of significance. For they were the outward manifestations of a conviction that in point of brain-power he compared quite unfavourably with a bisected earthworm.

24

It was nearly ten o'clock that night when Melhuish arrived, detained at a nursing-home by a transfusion case to which, he said, he must return in an hour or so.

'However,' he said, as he settled himself in a chair, 'I have hesitated so long about coming to have a talk with you that, despite the lateness of the hour, I felt I had better come tonight . . . as the adjourned inquest is tomorrow. You'll have to attend, I presume?'

'Yes. Rather a bore. I don't suppose they'll ask me any more questions.'

'I hope not. However, to speak quite frankly, there is the possibility that they may, and that you may find it extremely awkward to have to answer them.'

Gore paused in the filling of his pipe.

'Awkward?'

Melhuish made a little impatient gesture. 'No, no . . . Don't fence with me. Let us face this thing together.'

'With pleasure,' said Gore. 'But . . . what thing? I have nothing to conceal, if they do ask me any further questions tomorrow. I assure you of that.'

'You do not expect me to take that statement seriously?'

'I do. I've no idea why you shouldn't.'

Melhuish stared in perplexity.

'You've no idea who murdered this man Frensham?' he asked at length, bluntly.

'None whatever. Have you?'

'*I know* who murdered him,' Melhuish replied coldly, 'and so I believe do you, though you refuse to admit it.'

'Well, let us face it then, doctor,' Gore shrugged. 'Who? Arndale?'

'Yes, Arndale.'

Gore shook his head with a smile.

'No. You're wrong, doctor. I thought so, too. But Arndale was with his wife at the picture-house in Prince Albert Square from a little after six until eight o'clock that evening.'

'Who says so?'

'Mrs Arndale.'

'Anyone else?'

'No. Not that I know of. But I believe it's the fact.'

'You saw the knife with which the thing was done?'

'Yes.'

'Well?'

'Yes. It was one of our knives all right... or one exactly the same.'

'I told you that Arndale called at my house on Saturday afternoon last?'

'Yes.'

'He was left alone in the hall for several minutes while Clegg came out to my consulting-room to tell me that he wanted to see me. Well?'

'You said that thirty people at least were in and out of your hall that afternoon. Why on earth *should* Arndale want to kill that unfortunate little blighter? What motive could he have had?'

'That question,' said Melhuish, 'you can probably answer better than I can. But my guess—for I can only guess—is that he killed him for the same reason that he killed—or helped to kill—Barrington.'

At that Gore sat up in his chair.

'This is extraordinarily interesting, doctor. Now how did you get hold of that idea? I'd like to know . . . because it's just the idea I got hold of myself... for a bit.'

'I saw him doing it,' Melhuish said coolly; 'though I didn't realise it at the time. Arndale, to all intents and purposes, killed Barrington—I believe I know why. And I believe he killed Frensham for the same reason—or partially for the same reason. And when I say I believe that... I mean that I'm as convinced of it as that I'm sitting here in this chair looking at you.'

Gore relit his pipe. 'Suppose you tell me just all you know, and how you know it, doctor—and then I'll tell you why you're all wrong.'

'I should be glad to hope that you could. I fear not.'

There was a silence before the level, quiet voice proceeded. 'I saw my wife on Sunday. I think I told you I intended running up to Surrey—?'

'Yes.'

'She told me that she had made you . . . as a very old and trusted friend . . . her confidant with reference to some letters . . . some letters which she had written to Barrington—before her marriage, and which she wished to recover from him. I. . . you will understand that, naturally, it has hurt me a good deal that she selected even the oldest of friends for a confidant . . . rather than myself. However . . . I am . . . capable of understanding her reasons. And you will permit me to say that I have met few men with whom I should consider a confidence safer . . .'

'Charming of you to say so, doctor,' Gore plunged hurriedly, 'I'm delighted Mrs Melhuish has unburdened her mind to you. That chap Barrington seems to have been making her life a perfect nightmare . . . though, of course, she has altogether exaggerated . . . er . . . I mean, she allowed herself to be quite too seriously disturbed by . . . er—'

'She has told me all about him . . . Some of it, I had not known until she told me. Some of it I had. I knew that Barrington came to my house that night. I saw him in my house that night myself. I heard him talking to my wife . . . in the hall. I knew . . . why he had come.'

'Oh!' murmured Gore feebly, 'you did? Then why the— I beg your pardon—'

'Why didn't I thrash him and kick him out of the house? Well, put yourself in my place. Would *you* have faced your wife's discovering that you had been watching her—spying on her?'

'Lord, yes,' said Gore heartily.

Melhuish shrugged. 'My faith in myself is not as robust as yours,' he said coldly. 'I wish it had been. If it had—these two wretched men would have been alive now.'

'What *did* you do?'

'Nothing. I remained on the stairs where I had been when Barrington and my wife came out of the dining-room into the hall . . . until Barrington went away. My wife told you of the conversation which she had with him that night?'

'The general trend of it, yes.'

'She told you that—that Barrington took one of those knives with him when he left her?'

'Yes. She told me all about that.'

'There is one thing she did *not* tell you—one thing which I haven't told her. As I came down the stairs—Barrington and my wife were still in the dining-room, then—as I came down the stairs the hall door was pushed open—Barrington had left it ajar when he came in—and someone came into the hall and stood there listening for a minute or two. Can you guess who that someone was?'

'Frensham?'

'No. Not Frensham. Arndale. He stood there listening to Barrington's voice—the dining-room door was shut, but *I* could hear Barrington from the stairs. Then, I suppose, he heard Barrington coming towards the door . . . At any rate he hurried out—just before Barrington came out into the hall with my wife.'

'But-'

'Wait. Let me finish my story—and then we'll argue. When Barrington went away, leaving my wife in the hall, I went upstairs to my bedroom. My bedroom looks out on to the Green, I ought to say. The windows were open, and after a moment or so, hearing voices below and knowing that Barrington had just gone out, I went to it and looked out. You know the little bit of cross-road that connects Selkirk Place and Aberdeen Place?'

'Yes.'

'About half-way across it I saw Barrington and Arndale struggling on the ground. Then Arndale got up and threw something away from him over the railings of the Green. Just then my night telephone rang in my bedroom, and I left the window to go to it. It was a call from a Mrs MacArthur to go and see her boy. She's a talkative nervous woman. She kept me at the telephone for some minutes. When I got back to the window, both Arndale and Barrington had disappeared from where I had first seen them. But when I leant out a little I saw Arndale lifting Barrington into a car—Barrington's car, I believe, but I'm not sure of that—which was standing a little way down Aberdeen Place, towards Albemarle Hill. I concluded then that Barrington had been hurt and that Arndale was taking him home—until I saw Arndale put him down on the floor of the car and cover him up with a rug. I guessed then that something serious had happened, and went downstairs and out. But by the time I reached the hall door the car had gone.'

'Which way?' Gore asked.

'I can't tell you. It may have gone up Selkirk Place, or up the lane, or down into Albemarle Hill. I don't think it can have gone up Aberdeen Place towards the Mall. I think I should have been in time to see it, if it had. But it was out of sight, and hearing, when I reached the hall door. So that Arndale must have driven away at a furious speed.'

'Suppose the car had simply gone across into Selkirk Place,' Gore suggested, 'and stopped a little way along there, you couldn't have seen it from your hall door—and you would have heard nothing, naturally—if the engine had stopped?'

'No. It didn't do that. I went across myself into Selkirk Place immediately. There was no car there—not a soul in sight—so far as I could see. Of course it was foggy that night. But I fancy it went down into Albemarle Hill. The intervening houses would have cut off the sound of the engine once it turned the corner there—'

'You went across into Selkirk Place immediately, you say?'

'Yes. It had occurred to me by that time that what I had seen Arndale throw away was the knife which Barrington had taken. I thought it quite possible that Barrington had tried to use it—or threatened to use it—and that Arndale had taken it from him and wounded him with it. Remembering what you had told me only an hour or so before, it occurred to me that, if that had been the case, Barrington was probably either a dead man or as good as one. You can understand that that thought alarmed me?—'

'Oh, quite,' said Gore. 'Quite.'

'And why it alarmed me. I went across at once to see if I could find the knife. And, as I told you the other evening, I did find it—almost at once—lying just inside the railings of the Green—quite close to the gates leading into the hotel grounds. I didn't find the little sheath—though I looked about for it for a little while—just to make sure. But while I was looking for it that door beside the bar—you know?'

'I know,' Gore nodded.

'That door opened and two women came out. One of them was, I think, a girl belonging to the hotel—a barmaid.'

'Quite right.'

'The other was, to my amazement, Miss Heathman.'

'*What?* demanded Gore incredulously.

'Miss Heathman. I'll explain that presently. When they saw me, they went back into the house and shut the door. I didn't care to loiter about there any longer, naturally. In any case, I thought it probable that the sheath had not been on the knife when Arndale had taken it from Barrington. I went up Selkirk Place, half intending to go and see Mrs MacArthur's child. But I was so disturbed by what had happened—and by the thought of what it might mean for—my wife—that I really scarcely knew what I was doing, or where I was going. At the Mall end of Selkirk Place I gave up all intention of going to Mrs MacArthur's that night, and turned back. I met you then—you remember— by the pillar-box.'

'Quite,' said Gore. 'But, you remember also, we both saw Arndale coming out of Challoner's flat. How do you account for that? What had become of the car? Suppose he had driven it down into Albemarle Hill, how on earth could he possibly have got to Challoner's flat in so short a time? Where had he left the car? What had he done with Barrington?'

'That I can't explain,' Melhuish admitted. 'I can only tell you what I saw.'

'You're absolutely certain that it was Arndale whom you saw in your hall?'

'Absolutely.'

'He must have worn an overcoat of some sort on a night like that. Can you remember what kind of coat?'

'Yes. A raincoat—a rather light-coloured raincoat. The coat he wore over his evening clothes. I myself helped him into it when he went away with Mrs Arndale after dinner.'

'You saw his face . . . in the hall?'

'Distinctly.'

'Well, hell,' said Gore.

'You haven't told Mrs Melhuish that you saw him?' he asked, after some moments of perplexity.

'No. I have told her nothing that might lead her to connect Arndale with what happened that night . . . or with what happened last Saturday evening.

'I know what is passing through your mind,' Melhuish went on, after a moment. 'You think my wife may have known that Arndale was there—outside the house—that she had asked him to help her to compel Barrington to give up those letters. I had thought that possible myself—until last Sunday.'

'You don't think so now?'

'No. My wife has told me everything.'

'I wonder,' thought Gore.

'Well?' he asked, after some silent meditation, 'what do you intend to do?'

'Nothing—unless I'm compelled to. I've taken a big risk already. I'm content to take a bigger one—provided I'm sure of *you*. I have no claim on your silence. It is a matter for your own conscience. I simply tell you that *I* am prepared to face any risk—any consequences—to blot out the fact that Barrington was at my house that night. You *know*. I guessed from the first that you knew—'

'How did you guess?' Gore asked curiously.

'I saw your face when you looked at Barrington in the hall. I saw your face when you came back into my consulting-room and caught me examining his hand. I saw your face in the bedroom at Hatfield Place when you discovered that his wrist-watch had disappeared—'

'I see,' said Gore. 'I sincerely trust that other people are not as observant as you are, doctor. What the deuce was the Heathman woman doing there with that girl at that hour of the night? By the way—has it occurred to you that the A. H. who wrote that mysterious letter to Frensham arranging a meeting—'

'Yes,' said Melhuish quietly. 'It was she who wrote it. She told me so herself on Monday. I have known for some time past that she has been taking drugs—though I had no idea where she got her supplies from. However, she told me all about that on Monday.'

On his return from Surrey, he explained, on Monday afternoon, he had found waiting for him a message from Lady Wellmore, asking him to go and see her sister as soon as possible, as she appeared to be on the verge of a most serious nervous breakdown. He had gone at once to the big house in the Promenade and had found Miss Heathman in a pitiable state of fright and hysteria. She had confessed to him that she had been in the habit of obtaining cocaine and morphine from Barrington for a long time back, and that a few days after Barrington's death Frensham had come to her, representing himself as a friend of Barrington's and in his confidence, and had offered to continue the supply of the drugs. She had written to Frensham on the Friday before his death, arranging that he should meet her on the Promenade; and the discovery of her letter making that appointment and the fear that its authorship would be traced to her had reduced her to such a condition of terrified apprehension that she had locked herself up in her bedroom from Saturday night until Melhuish's arrival on Monday afternoon, refusing to see anyone until he came, and barricading the door with the furniture of the room.

'Fortunately,' said Melhuish, 'Frensham had failed to obtain the drugs for her. Otherwise—'

'Did he actually turn up for the appointment on the Promenade?' Gore asked.

'Yes.'

'Did she say if anyone had been with him?'

'I asked her that question. She said she had seen no one waiting about for him—but that it was quite dark at the time.'

'Did you make any reference at all to your having seen her in Selkirk Place on that Monday night, with the Rodney girl?'

'Yes. She went there to meet Barrington. Apparently she—and, I gather, several other people—have been in the habit of meeting him there at various hours of the day and night. He was to have brought her some cocaine that night, and she waited for him from half-past eleven until just after I saw her—nearly two hours.'

'Had she seen you at the gates?'

'Yes.'

'Had she seen Barrington that night?'

'I was afraid to ask her that question. I think not. I understood that she went home, just after I saw her at the door, without seeing him.'

'Well,' said Gore, when he had devoted some little time to an attempt to digest these communications, 'now I suppose I had better tell you what *I* know, hadn't I? Suppose we have a little drink first—or perhaps a big one is indicated. Personally, I feel slightly depressed . . .'

'Rather curious, isn't it,' he said, as he let Melhuish out into the hotel grounds half an hour later, 'that they didn't discover any traces of poison in Frensham's body. Or *is* it curious to the medical mind?'

'Not in the least,' Melhuish replied. 'Both knives had a twelve- hours' boiling.'

'When did you do that?'

'The day after one of my maids found one of them under the stand in the hall. I thought it—safer.'

'Quite. Good-night, doctor. I'm glad we've had this chat. Looks as if we're going to get some more snow. Remember me to Mrs Melhuish when you write, won't you? When did you say she comes back?'

'Wednesday, I hope. She's looking forward to seeing you again, I know. Good-night. Good luck.'

25

The adjourned inquest produced one fresh witness only. A disreputable-looking elderly tramp named Leech, described as of 'no occupation,[1] stated that some time between half-past six and seven o'clock on the evening of the preceding Saturday he had seen a smallish man, whom he now believed to have been the deceased, passing the Fountain at the end of the Promenade in the company of a taller man. He had been having a drink at the Fountain, he said, and had come out through the railings surrounding it just as these two men passed, going up Fountain Hill towards the Downs, and had been so close to them that he had seen both their faces distinctly. He was unable to say whether they had continued on up the hill or turned up the path branching from it towards Prospect Rock. The taller of the two men had worn a light-coloured raincoat and spoke like a gent. After they had passed he had stood in front of the Fountain for some little time, having nothing particular 'on,' and had then seen another man cross the road and follow slowly after the other two. He had been too far from this third man to see his face distinctly in the darkness, but he had thought at the time, 'from him acting so funny,' that he was following the first pair and keeping an eye on them. There were all kinds of 'games' carried on up there of evenings, he knew, and it was none of his business to bother his head about them. When he had smoked his pipe he had gone down Valley Road towards the river. He was unable to state precisely the hour at which he had seen the three men. Nor could he describe the appearance of any other person whom he had seen in the neighbourhood of the Fountain that evening, though he admitted that he had seen a 'fairish few.' He was unable to deny that he had just 'done' six months for assault and robbery. But he was sure that the smaller man of the two who had first passed him had been the deceased.

He was a shifty-eyed, unsavoury-looking person, and it was clear that the coroner, at all events, attached no importance to his evidence. The jury returned a verdict of wilful murder against some person or persons unknown; and Gore was able to catch a train to take him to lunch at Cleveport.

On Cleveport links, about half-past three that afternoon, he topped his drive from the fourteenth tee into a ditch considerably off the orthodox route to the fourteenth green, from which no man had ever been known to extract a ball with a golf-club. The plus-two cousin to whom reference has already been made, and who was at that moment four up, smiled pityingly, and said, 'Hopeless, old chap. Have another.'

The light was failing, and they were playing without the assistance of caddies. But Gore shouldered his bag and strode off towards the ditch with determination, and disappeared from sight into its muddy depths. The plus-two cousin surveyed the darkling landscape for some little time, and then decided to go and discover what was happening. As he approached the ditch he heard his antagonist's voice utter a sound of inarticulate triumph.

'Got it?' he inquired, pausing.

'Well, as a matter of fact,' replied a cheerful voice from the depths, 'I believe I have.'

Some minutes passed and nothing happened. The plus-two cousin advanced to the edge of the ditch and looked down into it.

'Thought you said you'd got the damn thing,' he growled unsympathetically.

'Oh . . . *that,*' said Gore vaguely. 'No. Not yet.'

But a very few moments later he found his ball, half-buried in ooze, and hit it from that impossible lie with an iron a hundred and eighty yards dead on the pin. His third shot was *the* finest brassie-shot he had ever played in his life. His mashie-shot went down. He won the next four holes, and finished one up.

The plus-two cousin was inclined to regard that iron-shot from the ditch as the devil's own luck.

'Not at all, my dear fellow,' Gore assured him. 'Simply a matter of self-confidence, mental balance, and staying-power. Sorry that shot demoralised you so utterly. You were really playing quite decent stuff up to that.'

As he approached the steps of the Riverside about eleven o'clock that night, a sturdily-built man who had been loitering close to the entrance to the Cliff Railway Station came across the road and stopped him with a deprecatory 'Beg pardon, sir, could I speak to you a minute?'

Gore halted and surveyed his waylayer unencouragingly.

'Oh, it's you, Stevens, is it? Well?'

'Well, sir,' said the man shamefacedly, 'I expect you've taken it pretty bad of me having let you down over that two quid. And I'm not going to make any defence of what I did, I've been ashamed to come near you, sir—that's the truth. And I'm ashamed to look you in the face now. It was the drink did it, sir—I needn't tell you that. Drink, and having the money. I hadn't had five bob of my own for a twelve-month before that. However, no use me making a song about it now, sir. Don't think I've come to try and cadge some more money out of you. I haven't. But I've got something to tell you about that chap you asked me to keep an eye on—'

'What?' demanded Gore curtly.

'I know the man that killed him,' Stevens answered coolly, 'if that's any use to you. I been thinking it over ever since the news came out on Saturday night, wondering if I ought to go to the police, or come to you, sir, or keep out of it altogether. Anyway, I decided this evening I'd come along and see you first, as I'd done the dirty on you over that two quid. I don't suppose the police would believe me if I was to go and tell *them* that I'd practical seen Frensham gettin' done in. Look at all the thanks that chap—what's his name? Leech—look at all the thanks *he* got for his trouble. Every one laughin' at him—'cause he was one of us chaps that's down on our luck, sir. But it's right enough, sir, what he said, all the same. The two chaps he saw were Frensham and this chap Richards I'm telling you of—and the chap he see following them was me.'

'Richards?' Gore repeated after a moment.

'Well, I don't suppose that's his name, sir, but that's what he calls hisself anyway, where he's living, out at Hilpound. Him and his wife's got rooms out there, sir, over an ironmonger's shop—in Gloucester Road—right facing the police-station.'

'His wife, you say?' Gore asked sharply.

'Yes.'

'What's *she* like? What colour's her hair?'

'Sort of red, sir. Not ginger red—more of a copper colour like.'

'Tallish? Good figure?'

'Yes, sir. Does her face up a good bit, I'd say. A showy piece altogether, sir.'

Gore turned towards the Riverside's steps.

'I believe I'm good for another quid, Stevens, if it's any use to you.'

'Use, sir—' said the man ravenously.

'Just come along then, will you.'

In the light of Gore's sitting-room it was manifest that Stevens had been having, as he admitted, a rough time of it lately. He declined with a rueful grin the whisky of which he appeared in need, but munched some biscuits greedily—the first food, he said, that he had tasted that day. Following his adventures at the Excelsior Hotel, where he owned to having embarked upon a lurid 'bust' in the course of which he had no doubt 'opened his mouth' unwisely as to the source of his brief opulence, he had made his way on foot to Chippenham, where he had hoped, according to his own account, to borrow from some relatives living there two pounds wherewith to repay his benefactor. Disappointed in that virtuous hope, he had gone to Bath, and had there obtained employment for some days on the making of a new road. That job closing down, he had returned to Westmouth with a few shillings in his pocket and, discovering that Frensham was still staying at the Excelsior, had set himself to watch his movements in the hope that they might still be of interest to Gore. His account of himself for the hours between five and nine o'clock on the evening of the preceding Saturday was circumstantial.

From his hiding-place in the archway in Purley Square he had seen a tall man in a light-coloured coat go into the Excelsior, come out again immediately with Frensham, and go off with him towards Old Cut Road. Following them, he had seen them both enter a cottage in a lane off Old Cut Road—Gore remembered that lane—and had waited behind some coal-carts until they had come out again.

'See anyone pass while you were hiding behind those coal-carts?' Gore asked.

'Yes, sir. An old bloke in a trilby hat went by. Funny-looking old chap. Bit queer in the head, I think he was. I see him afterwards running and the people shouting after him. Why, sir?'

'Nothing, nothing,' said Gore hastily. 'Carry on.'

'Well, sir, they stayed in that little house for about twenty minutes. It was a place I'd seen Frensham go into before, but never with the tall chap. I never see *him* before that. They went up into Spring Road, me following behind, and Frensham got into a tram there and went into the city, and I chanced my arm, and went in with him, on the roof. I had ninepence left, so I thought I'd risk a penny of it. The tall chap went off the other way, walking—towards the Suspension Bridge. Frensham got off at Sunderland Bridge, and I followed him to a booking-office in Parr Street. Then he got on a bus, and I blew another thruppence following him out here to the top of Linwood Park Road. The bus was pretty crowded, but after a bit he spotted me and came back and sat down beside me. "Hallo," he says, "you're back, are you? Well, how's all your friends up this way?" "Nicely," I says. "I'm just going to drop in for afternoon tea with some of them." He laughed at that. "Yes," he says, "you look as if you could do with another bit of kindness." After that a lady came and forced in between us, so we said no more to one another. When he got out at the top of Linwood Park Road, I went on in the bus to the limit, and then nipped across the Gardens, and came out on the Promenade just a bit behind him. It was easy there, sir—on account of the big trees. But any way he never looked behind him once that I could see all the way along the Promenade. At the far end of the Promenade, a bit short of the Fountain, he met a woman and stopped to speak to her for a bit. Two little dogs she had, this woman I'm telling you of, sir. I crossed the road and sat down on a seat to wait until they'd finished talking, and I was too far off to see the woman with the dogs properly, to tell you what she was like. But whoever she was, I said to myself when I read the papers afterwards, it was her wrote that letter asking Frensham to meet her. What would *you* say, sir? Her meeting him just near the Fountain, and having them dogs, and all? Likely as not, she was in it with this chap Richards. Least that's what *I* think, sir.'

'Let's get on to him,' said Gore. 'I'm waiting to hear where he comes in again.'

'He come in when Frensham left the woman with the dogs, sir—that's where he come in again. He come along the side of the Promenade I was sitting on, and stood looking across the road until Frensham left the woman. I twigged him at once. You couldn't mistake him, 'cause he was such a tall, big-made chap, and you'd see the coat he had on half a mile off in the dark. Says I, I've seen *you* before, my lad, this evening. So I just sat tight on my seat and looked ornery. Then when the tall chap see Frensham going on, he crossed the road, putting on a bit of a spurt, and caught him up just before he reached the Fountain. By that time, of course, I'd got moving too, sir. But I had to go careful there, 'cause of the big lights in the centre of the cross-roads. I see a chap there, standing by the Fountain, looking at me, as I went by. I reckon, now, it was that chap Leech that give evidence this morning, sir.'

'Possibly. Carry on.'

'Well, sir, as you know, I suppose, the footpath that goes to Prospect Rock twists off to your left as you go up Fountain Hill. When I see Frensham and the tall chap taking off along the path, I was in a bit of a fix. Because it's so narrow and twisting along that path you couldn't tell when you mightn't turn a comer and run bang into them. So I thought I'd just cut on ahead of them through the bushes to the top of the path—where it comes out on to the Downs again—and find a bit of cover and wait for them to come along. Not that I thought, *then*, there was anything up. But somehow, I don't know how it was, sir, once I got following Frensham so far, I got sort of keen, if you can understand, sir, not to let him go if I could hold on to him.'

'I can understand,' said Gore. 'Carry on, Stevens.'

'Well, I went on ahead, then, sir, pretty smart. It's rough going there, over the rocks, and in amongst them bushes—but many's the night I've slept out just there, sir—I know it well. I made for a place among the bushes where I knew I could make myself comfortable and see anyone coming out at the top of the path on to the Downs. And when I'd been there, perhaps— well, getting on to seven or eight minutes, sir—not longer—I see the tall chap coming along by himself, going at a tidy pace, and making across the grass towards Blackbrothers Hill direction. "Hallo," I says to myself, "where's the little 'un got to?" So when the tall chap had got well away, I went down the path, looking out for Frensham. But of course I see no sign of him. I went as far as where the path comes out into Fountain Hill again, and then I thought to myself, well, I've lost him for now. I'll follow the big fellow and see where he goes. So I doubled back up the hill and across the grass, and about half-way to Blackbrothers Hill I see my friend in the white coat again all right, going hell for leather. "Making for the tram," I says to myself. "Another tuppence or thruppence gone west." Sure enough, he got on the tram at Blackbrothers Hill, and went down to Sunderland Bridge. There I see him gettin' on a Hilpound car. "Blimey," I says to myself, "here goes my bed for tonight." And so it did, sir, for he went till the way to Hilpound, and that's a thruppenny fare. He got off just before where the trams stop, at the near end of Gloucester Road, and I see him going into this house over an ironmonger's shop— Liversedge is the name over the shop, sir—there's a hall door beside the shop, and he let himself in with a key. Of course I couldn't tell then, sir, whether he was going to stay there all night or how long he was going to stay there. But anyhow I hung about on chance—about an hour and a half it was, before I see him come out again, and got on a tram going into the city. 'Course all I could do, sir, was kiss him good-bye, the bank being broke. However, as I'd come so far, I thought I might as well try to find out if he lived there in that house, and perhaps what his name was. So I went up to the door and knocked— there was an "Apartments" card in the fanlight, you see, sir—and asked if they had any rooms to let. The old dame as opened the door looked at me pretty queer, 'cause of me not being what you might call exactly flush-looking. However, I kidded her I was working at a big garage I see in Gloucester Road, and she took me up and showed me some rooms at the top of the house. 'Course I said I was nervous about being at the top of the house 'count of fires. So, as we were coming down the stairs again, a piece with this copper sort of hair I told you of, sir, come out on to the landing to give the old lady some money—the rent it must have been, I expect. "Oh, thank you, Mrs Richards," said the old dame. "I hopes as your husband enjoyed his tea. He had to go away again very soon, this evening." "Yes," says the other one—the young one, "he had to go back to his work. Isn't it a nuisance? I'll have to go to the pictures by myself this evening." "'Nuff said," I says to myself. So I tells the old lady I was sorry, and cleared out. 'Course I had to walk back into the city, so when I got in the boys were calling out about the murder. Fair knocked me out, that did. If I'd have stopped to look, when I went back along the path looking out for Frensham that time, I expect I might have seen the blood on the ground, dark and all as it was.'

'Where *did* you sleep that night, Stevens?' Gore asked.

The man grinned.

'Well, I was lucky that night, sir, as it happened. A watchman in Coronation Road let me doss by his fire. None too dusty that, sir—with a bit of sacking for your head. Wish I was sure of it for tonight.'

Gore smiled.

'I think we may be able to do a bit better than that for you tonight. Now, look here . . . I want you to tell me exactly how many people you've told this yarn of yours to—and who they are.'

'I haven't told one except yourself, sir.'

'You expect me to believe that?'

'I don't, sir—after what I done. But it's the truth, sir.'

'Have you been out to Hilpound since Saturday evening?'

'No, sir.'

'Are you married?'

'No, sir. That's the only bit of luck's come *my* way for a while.'

But some other bits came Stevens's way that night—a square meal, a bath, and a bed in one of the Riverside's attics. When Gore presented him with an ancient suit of pyjamas, he ejaculated a strangled 'Gawd, sir,' and wept like a child.

About eleven o'clock next morning Gore knocked at the hall door beside the ironmonger's shop and requested to be informed if Mrs Richards was in—quite unnecessarily, since he had just seen her return from her Saturday morning's marketing. Any lingering doubts which he still entertained vanished promptly when his eyes fell upon the table of the little sitting- room in which Miss Betty Rodney greeted his apparition with a stare of blank dismay.

'Colonel Gore!' she gasped, and then made a pitiful attempt to mask her fright with pleasantry. 'Good gracious. This *is* a pleasant surprise.'

He waited until, with curious eyes, the aged landlady had retired, and then locked the door and put the key into his pocket.

'What do you mean?' she demanded. 'Why have you locked that door?'

He pointed to the little bottle of marking-ink which stood, still uncorked, by the parcels which she had just laid down, and picked up a collar from amongst a miscellaneous array of soiled linen which was scattered over the table.

'Not even carefully done,' he said quietly. 'And you go and leave those things lying about for that old woman to see—'

The girl was trembling now violently.

'What are you talking about?' she demanded. 'Open that door at once, or I'll scream.'

But the threat was a mere formality. She offered no resistance when he took her arm and drew her a step or two towards the window. Outside the door of the police-station at the opposite side of the road a benevolent-looking, red-faced sergeant was conning in the sunshine the contents of a long blue envelope with official severity.

'Now, I give you your choice, Miss Rodney,' Gore said sternly. 'I want to get certain information out of you. If you're sensible, you'll let me have it. If you're not, I shall go across the road and—you'll go with me. It's no use whatever trying to bluff me. You may as well be sensible.'

Miss Rodney made a pretence of fainting, and more than a pretence of tears. But from beneath these manifestations emerged a resolute determination to save her own skin as far as it could be saved. With a very little further pressure she became quite sensible. Presently, even, she consented without demur to the unlocking of a trunk which contained the more precious intimacies of her wardrobe—and some other things which interested Gore more.

The rosy-cheeked sergeant had laid aside his helmet and the cares of office temporarily, and was smoking a pipe in the little plot of garden in front of the station, when Miss Rodney and her trunk and her visitor departed from the hall door beside the ironmonger's shop in a taxi. From the first-floor window Mrs Stone, the aged landlady, watched the taxi out of sight. Then she turned to the table and read once more the message which lay there awaiting the possible arrival of Mr Richards that evening. 'Gone away,' it said simply. And Mrs Stone's thoughts, as she gazed at it, did Colonel Gore a grievous wrong.

As a matter of fact Mr Richards did not call that evening. Until ten o'clock Mrs Stone and a crony whom she had invited to share the thrill of his discovery of that curt message sat expectant of his arrival. By that hour the snow which had hesitated for the past week or so had definitely decided to make a night of it. Mrs Stone let her friend out into a blizzard of swirling gray silence, and went to bed with her curiosity still unsatisfied—a condition in which, as regards Mr and Mrs Richards at least, it still remains and is likely to remain.

26

The church bells were ringing next morning when Gore passed out through the front door of the Riverside to survey from its steps approvingly the as yet immaculate whiteness of a snow-wrapt world upon which the sun shone dazzlingly. Behind him in the hall, Percival and the hall-porter gazed speculatively at an elaborate apparatus which had arrived late on the preceding afternoon from Messrs. Wright and Hardman, the photographers in the Mall. The hall-porter had never seen such a large camera before; and after some contemplation of it he went out on to the steps to inform Colonel Gore respectfully of the fact.

'One of my boys goes in for it a bit, sir,' he explained. 'I expect he'll be out this morning with his camera, like a good many more. Always is a lot out with their cameras when we get a bit of snow. Though it's animals my boy goes in for mostly. I suppose you did a lot of photographing when you were in Africa, sir. I see that film of yours—'

He paused as Dr Melhuish's car, its brasses winking violently in the sunlight, came round the comer out of Aberdeen Place and drew up at the foot of the Riverside's steps.

'This for you, sir?'

'Yes. Dr Melhuish has kindly lent me his car for this morning. Can you get that stuff aboard for me?'

While the hall porter and Percival carried down the camera and its stand and several plate-packs, and deposited them in the car, Gore descended the steps with a pleasant nod in return to the chauffeur's salute.

'Good-morning, Thomson,' he explained. 'I want to try to get some pictures before this sun thaws things out too much.' 'Yes, sir. So the doctor told me.'

'I rather think of trying the glens running down towards the river.'

'Beside Valley Road, sir?'

'Yes. Let's have a look round there first. All in, Percival?'

'All in, sir.'

The powerful car purred up Albemarle Hill, swung left-hand across Linwood Gardens, and descended the long, curving sweep of the Promenade. As it approached the Fountain Gore leaned forward.

'On second thoughts,' he said, 'I think I'll try that path along the edge of the cliffs. I ought to get some pretty bits along there. Carry on up the hill. Left, then.'

'Right, sir.'

Save for a few early Sabbath morning strollers, black against the snow, the expanse of the Downs was deserted. At the top of Fountain Hill the car turned left-hand, and a couple of hundred yards farther towards the river, drew up, in accordance with Gore's directions, at the head of the narrow winding path which led back through the wilderness of thorn and gorse-bush towards Prospect Rock. Gore got out, lighted a cigarette, and possessed himself of the camera and its stand.

'Now, how am I going to manage those plate-packs?' he mused. 'I wonder if you'd mind fetching them along for me, Thomson. The car will be all right here, won't it?'

'I suppose so, sir,' said the chauffeur, rather dubiously. 'I hardly like leaving her.'

'Oh, she'll be all right,' Gore assured him. 'I shan't be going farther back than the Rock.'

'Very well, sir.'

As they made their way along the rocky path—treacherous going that morning—Gore turned his head to take in with appreciation the beauty of the view across the gorge. The sky was gladdest blue. Against its gladness the sombre winter woods that crested the opposite ridges made a pleasing note of contrast. The russets and grays of the gashed cliffs that descended precipitously to the river, always admirable, were that morning delightfully diversified by clinging patches of snow. The river, in flood and swirling blackly for a while between white banks, twisted abruptly and dramatically into fullest sunshine as it swept round the foot of the cliffs to westward for a space. The gulls wheeled and swooped in the sunlight. A cargo-boat, dropping cautiously downstream, supplied the requisite point of human animation. The effect, Gore thought, was quite Norwegian that morning.

'Rather topping, isn't it?' he said over his shoulder. 'Ever been in Norway, Thomson?'

'No, sir.'

A pale, spectacled young man in very dark clothes came up the path, aimed a small Kodak at the scenery hurriedly, and went on his way.

'I'm not the only pebble on the beach,' Gore remarked pleasantly. 'Ever done any photography, Thomson? I suppose you have—like everybody else. Now, I rather think that when we get round the next bend there's a rather striking bit—'

The path, turning aside sharply as it touched the very verge of the precipice at their right hand, became a mere staircase of footholds in the flank of the outcropping ridge known as Prospect Rock. As they came in view of this slight eminence, a man rose from the seat placed there at the inner side of the path for the benefit of sightseers, and stood against the sky in the narrow passage between the railing and the bushes, looking down at them. At sight of that tall figure the chauffeur halted.

'Mr Arndale, sir—' he said doubtfully, perceiving that Gore had turned about and was regarding him with a curious intentness. Gore nodded gravely, and stood aside to allow him to pass to the front.

'Yes. Carry on, Thomson. You can put those things down by that seat on top. No . . . Don't do anything foolish. I've got a man behind. Carry on to Mr Arndale.'

Thomson cast a swift glance behind him, and saw, some thirty yards back along the path, a sturdy and very determined-looking individual armed with a stout stick, who barred his retreat in that direction. At one side was a dense tangle of thorn-bushes through which flight at any speed was an impossibility. At the other was the railing and a sheer drop of three hundred feet.

'What the hell's this?' he demanded.

'Carry on,' Gore repeated blandly. 'We'll discuss all that in a moment. If you want a scrap, you can have it—with pleasure. But you haven't a dog's chance, you know.'

It took Thomson some further moments of calculation to convince himself of the truth of that statement. Finally, however, he did accept it, with a calmness which extorted Gore's admiration. Not the faintest stir of emotion pierced through his self-control as he faced Arndale's contemptuous greeting at the summit.

'You're a pretty scoundrel,' his former employer broke forth.

'And you?' he retorted coolly.

With a gesture Gore checked Arndale's angry rejoinder.

'Let's have this out quietly. Now, first of all, Thomson—before we sit down—will you just show us this bower of love in which you and Miss Rodney were sitting about ten o'clock—I believe I am exact enough in saying ten o'clock—on the night of February the third, nineteen-nineteen? Where is that—to begin with?'

Thomson stared.

'Who the hell told you about that?' he asked. 'That—?'

'Now, now. No flowers of speech, Thomson, please. All we want is a plain, unvarnished narrative. And understand this. That's all we *do* want. Nothing more. You understand? Absolutely nothing more. You *may* swing for what you've done—you deserve to. But that's not our business. At least we're going to assume that it isn't. Understand? There is not the slightest use in calling Miss Rodney names. She has, I admit, given you away as thoroughly as it is in her power to give you away; it's only fair to tell you that. But you must realise that she finds herself in the awkward position of an accessory after the fact. You must make allowances for her. Now, where is this nesting-place she has told me about? I seem to remember that there are a good many of them hereabouts, amongst these bushes. You won't tell us? Very well, then, we'll take that for granted for the moment. Sit down there, on that seat.'

Again Thomson's narrowed eyes made a swift calculation. Then, with a shrug, he obeyed.

'Certainly.'

A nursemaid and two rosy-cheeked children came up the path and passed the three men as they seated themselves. The nursemaid lingered a moment to look down timorously over the railings into the abyss below, holding her charges each by a hand. Then, after a curious glance about her, reminiscent, no doubt, of the recent tragedy, she turned about and went back in the direction from which she had come. The children, excited by the snow and the slipperiness of the path, laughed and babbled joyously.

'Now, let us start from that night,' Gore said, when the little party had passed out of earshot, 'the night of February the third, nineteen-nineteen. At that time you were in Mr Arndale's employment as chauffeur. You were also, I understand, carrying on, more or less, with Miss Rodney. I believe there was some talk of your marrying her at that time—however, the point is not of importance. The pertinent fact is that on that night you took her for a walk, as you seem to have been in the habit of doing just then, brought her up here, and sat with her in this bower of bliss amongst the bushes. While you were in there, so Miss Rodney has informed me, you saw Mr Arndale come along this path. Your bower of bliss must have been very close to the path—otherwise you could hardly have recognised him at ten o'clock on a February night. But perhaps you heard his voice. At any rate, you recognised him. He was accosted just here by a woman—'

'He accosted her,' said Thomson.

Arndale shrugged his shoulders, and Gore passed the point. 'At all events, he spoke to a woman and a woman spoke to him. Then a man appeared on the scene, and the woman cleared off. The man made a certain accusation against Mr Arndale, and Mr Arndale struck him and knocked him down. He got up—or tried to get up—and Mr Arndale struck him again. He caught Mr Arndale by the legs and pulled him down, and they fought for a bit on the ground. Then Mr Arndale got an arm free and struck him again, and he slipped under the railing and went over the edge of the cliff. I don't know how much of all this you saw—but that, Mr Arndale informs me, is what happened.'

'More or less,' commented Thomson coolly. 'It's a matter of phrases and words. You could have saved yourself a lot of trouble by simply saying that Mr Arndale threw the chap over the cliff.'

'You suggest—deliberately?'

'I say deliberately.'

'It's a lie,' broke out Arndale. 'I meant only to get clear of him. I didn't know we were so close to the railing. If you thought I had murdered the man—deliberately thrown him over—why did you say nothing about it? Why did you remain in my service?'

Thomson laughed.

'I had a good job. I wasn't in a hurry to lose it. Besides, I always had an idea it might pay me better to hold my tongue.'

'Oh? You had that idea before you came across Mr Barrington, had you?' Gore asked. 'That's rather interesting. Well, now, let us get on to your association with Mr Barrington.'

'I never had any association with him.'

'Oh, yes, you had. You left Mr Arndale's employment at the beginning of June, nineteen-nineteen, and went from him to Mr Harry Kinnaird, at 26 Hatfield Place. Now, Mr Barrington had just moved into 27 Hatfield Place then. I presume he had a car at that time—and I presume that you must have begun to look after his car for him very shortly after you went to Mr Kinnaird. If I'm wrong, please say so. Miss Rodney has supplied me with a good deal of information—but there are gaps. Now, when did your intimacy with Barrington reach such a stage that you were able to discuss with him this affair of Mr Arndale's up here on the night of February the third?'

'I never discussed it with him. I was never intimate with Mr Barrington.'

'Yes, you were. Some time or other before the beginning of September of that year, nineteen-nineteen, either you or Miss Rodney must have told Barrington what you had seen that night. Because it was at the beginning of September of that year that Barrington began to blackmail Mr Arndale. According to Miss Rodney's account, you and she and Barrington frequently discussed what you had seen—though she denies positively that she knew anything whatever about the blackmail scheme—' 'It was she who first suggested it to me, the—,' said Thomson. 'She was carrying on then with Barrington—though I didn't find that out until a bit after that. He got her to make the suggestion to me. It was Barrington's idea from beginning to end. I had nothing to do with it.'

'Come, come. He was paying you considerable sums of money regularly from that September onwards. Why was he doing that? You don't suggest that he paid you something like five hundred a year regularly, merely for looking after his car in your spare time?'

'How do you know he was paying me considerable sums of money, as you call them?'

Gore smiled.

'Well, someone whose initials were F. T. was getting them, you know. By the way, that reminds me. If you've got any more collars or things that are still marked F. T., I should alter those F's to A's myself, if I were you. That is, if you think it at all worth while. As a matter of fact, I wasn't quite certain that you were F. T. until I discovered that Miss Rodney had been busy with her marking-ink.'

'Some Sherlock Holmes,' laughed Thomson placidly. 'I might have known that slut would give me away.'

'I quite agree,' said Gore, with conviction. 'Very well, then. From September, nineteen-nineteen, this nice little arrangement went on quite smoothly until just the other day. Barrington took the risk, and you received a dividend on the profits. I said quite smoothly, but, as a matter of fact, it didn't go on *quite* smoothly, did it? There was some little ill-feeling over Miss Rodney, wasn't there? Barrington had cut you out there completely, I understand. Also, you began to think that your dividends were not large enough—considering that you had supplied the capital, so to speak—the information upon which the bleeding of Mr Arndale depended. You had some sort of row, finally, with Barrington—at the end of October of this year—a row which ended with his death on the night of November the sixth, in Aberdeen Place. Now, why did you kill Barrington, Thomson— exactly?'

'I didn't kill him.'

'Oh, yes, you did.'

'I didn't kill him,' Thomson repeated doggedly. 'The swine had bad heart-disease. We had a bit of a row, and he got excited and drew a knife on me. I took it from him—and then I found he was dead. I swear it was his rotten heart killed him—nothing I did to him.'

'If you believed that, why didn't you get a policeman? Why did you do what you did? Why did you take him away and hide him that night and get rid of him the way you did next day? If you believed that, why were you so afraid of Frensham that you killed Am, too, to silence his tongue? Why did you take the pains to get hold of a knife like the one you had used for the first job—the one that had done the first job so expeditiously? Nonsense, man. You knew—you know as well in your heart of hearts that you took Barrington's life as you know that you took Frensham's here . . . between this seat and that railing there. Mind, I don't say you killed Barrington deliberately. I don't believe you did.'

'I've told you twice already that I didn't kill him,' Thomson said once more impatiently. 'He got a scratch on his hand from the knife. But that couldn't have killed him. I didn't want to kill the blighter. Why should I? Here—as you've found out so much, you may as well know the lot. Barrington was to have paid me fifty pounds on the last day of October. He didn't pay it. He kept putting me off with one excuse or another, and I wanted the money. He had promised it without fail for that Monday, and I was determined to have it. I knew he was dining at Dr Melhuish's house that night, so I waited outside the house until he came out—with you.'

'Where did you wait for him?' Gore asked.

'Down the area steps of an empty house, five or six doors from Dr Melhuish's. We talked there for a bit under a lamp, and then he asked me to go to this house with him. I went, and we had a drink or two. He was in a hell of a temper because his missus was out, and he gave me the benefit of it. But he said that he was to get a hundred and fifty that night from Mrs Melhuish and that I should have my fifty out of it next morning. I said that wasn't good enough, and that I'd go with him and wait for him. He changed, and went to Aberdeen Place in his car, and he told me to wait for him over by the bar at the back of the Riverside. He was to meet a friend there, he said— Frensham was the friend—and he was to come across there as soon as he'd got the money from Mrs Melhuish. I went to the door beside the bar and whistled, and Betty opened the door and asked me where Barrington was. Frensham was with her, and I spoke to them for a moment or so, and they asked me to go in and have a drink. But I wanted to keep an eye on Barrington, so I went back to Aberdeen Place again and waited at the top of the area steps of the empty house. While I was waiting there some chap came up Aberdeen Place from Albemarle Hill and stopped outside Dr Melhuish's house. Barrington must have left the hall door open, for the chap just pushed it open and went in. After a moment he came out again, and went across into Selkirk Place.'

'Any idea who he was?' Gore asked.

'No. It was too foggy then to see him clearly. He was a big fellow. I thought, when I saw him going in, that there was trouble coming to Barrington.'

'Well—after that?'

'After that I waited for a little while, and then I went down to Dr Melhuish's door. It was standing open a little, and I heard Barrington—'

'Don't bother about that. I know what you heard. After a little while Barrington came out. Then, I suppose, you asked him for this money—this fifty pounds he owed you?'

'Yes. He said that he had been paid by cheque, and that he couldn't give me the money then. I knew that was a lie, and we had a row. He threatened me with that poisoned knife—' 'How did you know it was poisoned?'

'I heard Mrs Melhuish telling him some yarn about it—or him telling her one. I forget which. But one or other of them said it was poisoned.'

'A yarn? You don't believe it was poisoned? Now—why? Did it fail to work so expeditiously the second time you used it?'

To that Thomson made no reply.

'Where did you hide Barrington and his car that night? In your own garage, of course?'

'Yes.'

'Curious what a long time it has taken me to find that out.' Gore smiled grimly. 'And yet I knew that Mr and Mrs Kinnaird and the family were away, and that there was no one in the house but yourself and an old housekeeper. I believe you were kind enough to supply me with that information yourself. Curious.'

A couple of elderly men of the shopkeeper class in their Sunday clothes, followed by two puffed fat women in furs, came up the path and paused in front of the seat.

'Must 'ave been travelling at some speed when 'e 'it them rocks,' one of the men remarked, when he had looked down over the railing.

'Well,' said the other, 'say it's three hundred feet. A failin' body acquires an acceleration of, what's it?—thirty-two feet a second, isn't it? Well, you can work it out from that. You got to take the mean velocity for each second. Well, say 'e fell sixteen feet in the first second—thirty-two and sixty-four's ninety-six, half of that—forty-eight feet in the second second—sixty-four an' ninety-six's 'undred and sixty, 'alf of that—eighty—lemme see—sixteen, forty-eight, eighty. . . that's 'undred an' forty-four . . . and so on. You can work it out quite simple. S'pose 'e was travellin' a good 'undred and fifty miles an hour when 'e landed, any'ow.'

The women, squinting at their powdered noses, made little noises of appreciation.

'I never knew such a 'ead for figures as 'Enry's got,' said one of them. 'I always say 'e's wasted in the tobacconist's business. W'ere was it they found the blood, 'Enry?'

Henry prodded the snow in various carefully selected places. For a moment the party was thrilled by the appearance of a reddish stain beneath the ferule of his stick. Discovering, however, that it was due to a fragment of crumbled sandstone, the second man, visibly a little resentful of Henry's head for figures, uttered a loud and derisive laugh.

'Wot's ticklin' you now?' demanded Henry coldly.

'Me?' said the other, smiling irritatingly at the view. 'S'pose I can laugh if I want to, can't I? Don't be so touchy.'

'Touchy?' retorted Henry. ''Oo's touchy?'

'Now, now. . . don't let us 'ave no more argy-bargyin',' urged Henry's wife. 'Kickin' up a piblic row on Sunday mornin'—'

The party went on their way, grumbling and slipping as they descended from the little plateau. Thomson laughed with cynical amusement.

'Other people get much more value out of these little affairs, don't they? How long more have I got to sit here?'

'Not very long,' Gore assured him.

'Mind if I smoke?'

'Not in the least.'

'Thanks so much. Well, now you'd like to know about Frensham, I suppose.'

'Before we come to that—again as a matter of curiosity—you drove Barrington's car back the following afternoon to Aberdeen Place?'

'Yes.'

'Had you any special reason for leaving it just where you left it?'

'Yes, of course. If the knife had killed him . . . and if it were found . . . well, it belonged to Melhuish. If he had simply died of heart disease—there was a chance that the whole thing might blow over quietly. I knew he was to have gone to Melhuish that Tuesday afternoon about his heart. He had told me so himself, while I was with him at his house the night before.'

'I see. Very carefully thought out.'

'Oh, yes. I thought it out pretty carefully.'

'Well, then—about Frensham? Frensham and Miss Rodney, she tells me, actually saw you and Barrington having this tussle. Did they see you putting him into the car and driving away with him?'

'No, they didn't actually see that. The car was over in Aberdeen Place. The fog was too thick to see across there from where they were. But Frensham suspected at once—in fact, he knew at once.' 'So he began to threaten you. Why? In order to get money out of you?'

'Yes. He knew that Barrington was to have got that hundred and fifty from Mrs Melhuish that night—and he guessed, of course, that I had it.'

'You had it?'

'Oh, yes. I had it. I have it. You'll find it in my box—all but two quid.'

'Thanks. Frensham, then, began to threaten you, because you wouldn't give up this money. Now, let us come to last Saturday evening. You had thought out everything most carefully again, hadn't you? You had got the knife—you had selected the place. How did you induce Frensham to come up here—to this lonely place—in the dark—with you?'

'Simply promised him what he wanted—half that hundred and fifty. He thought he could bluff the lot out of me, then.'

'Where did you meet him?'

'Just by the Fountain.'

'By arrangement?'

'Yes.'

'And then?'

'I offered him fifty, and we argued the matter out. He didn't know the Downs. He came up here like a lamb, arguing the whole way along. It was quite simple.'

'I see. Thanks very much, Thomson. Now, first of all, I want to leave Mr Arndale out at his house across the Downs. Then you'll drive me to Dr Melhuish's and put up the car. After that . . . you are your own master. I have only one warning to give you. And that is this: if you give anyone any trouble—you understand what I mean by those words?—if you give anyone any trouble whatever—no matter what it may cost me or anyone else, I'll hang you. Now, come along.'

The three men went back silently along the path to the car, passing Stevens, whose disappointment at so tame an ending to the interview expressed itself in an incredulous 'Wash out, sir?' as the party went by in single file.

'Yes, you can bung off, Stevens,' Gore nodded. 'I'm going across the Downs with Mr Arndale. I shall be back to lunch.'

Arndale, who, after his first angry outburst, had preserved a moody silence, hesitated before he followed Gore into the back of the car.

'What about the girl?' he asked morosely. 'What guarantee have we that she won't talk?'

'None whatever,' Gore said simply, 'except her knowledge of the consequences for herself if she does. I've explained them to her pretty thoroughly. And that's really all I or anybody else can do.'

Thomson, who had now started his engine, turned about in his seat.

'How did you find her?' he asked. 'I should just like to know that.'

'Sorry. I'm afraid you must continue wondering about that, Thomson.'

'*Did* you find her—or did she go to you, Arndale? Tell me that.'

'We found her,' said Gore. 'You made the job quite simple for us. Carry on.'

It was not until they had covered nearly half a mile of the straight stretch of road skirting the cliffs at the western fringe of Linwood Down, that Arndale's eyes turned from their dejected gaze across the gorge to look ahead with uneasiness to the sharply curving S, towards the first loop of which he car was rushing at a pace which had attracted Gore's attention also.

'Steady,' he called out. 'Don't drive so fast.'

Thomson made some inaudible response over his shoulder, and slackened speed slightly. But immediately Gore saw him open the throttle again stealthily, and they took the first bend of the S at something closer to forty miles an hour than was at all comfortable. The car executed a mighty skid in the snow, plunged back across the road, straightened, and then hurtled at headlong speed towards the low wall that guarded the road at its most dangerous turn. Arndale rose to his feet.

'My God!' he exclaimed. 'He'll have us over the cliffs.' He leant forward and struck Thomson on the shoulder heavily. 'Pull her up,' he shouted, 'Pull her up, you damned fool.'

Thomson turned and laughed up into his face.

'Don't be nervous, old cock,' he said contemptuously. 'We're all going home together.'

At that Arndale, after a panic-stricken glance towards the death that was rushing to meet them, turned and scrambled over the back of the car as Gore vaulted into the vacant front seat and grabbed the wheel. For a crazy fifty yards the car swung madly from side to side of the road. A bare six feet from the wall it swung about on two wheels, performed a somersault, and then lay extraordinarily still. A solitary figure, half a mile away across the snow, took off his hat and began to run, his dog barking joyously at his heels.

27

On the morning of the following Thursday, when Mrs Melhuish and Mrs Arndale called at the Riverside with a large quantity of chrysanthemums and solicitous inquiries for Colonel Gore, a stolid-visaged person who stated that he was the colonel's man, took them over from Percival outside his master's door peremptorily. The colonel was up that morning for the first time, he explained, and not quite dressed. The two ladies, however, declared that that didn't matter in the least, and, though with obvious misgivings as to the propriety of the proceedings, he admitted them to the invalid's sitting- room.

There they found Colonel Gore seated at his writing-table in a dressing-gown which he drew about him rather hurriedly upon their appearance, with a plaster-of-Paris-encased leg cocked up on an adjoining chair. When he had thanked them for their flowers, learned that Mrs Melhuish felt almost quite herself again, and that Mrs Arndale's husband's leg was progressing as satisfactorily as he assured them his own was, Mrs Melhuish bent with knitted brows to inspect a curious-looking diagram upon which he had apparently been working at the moment of their entry and which is here reproduced for the reader's edification.

Mrs Melhuish, it has to be admitted, could make nothing of this document. Mrs Arndale said it reminded her of the performance of a what-do-you-call-it—not a barometer—but the other thing. Colonel Gore refused, with some trifling

F.4.

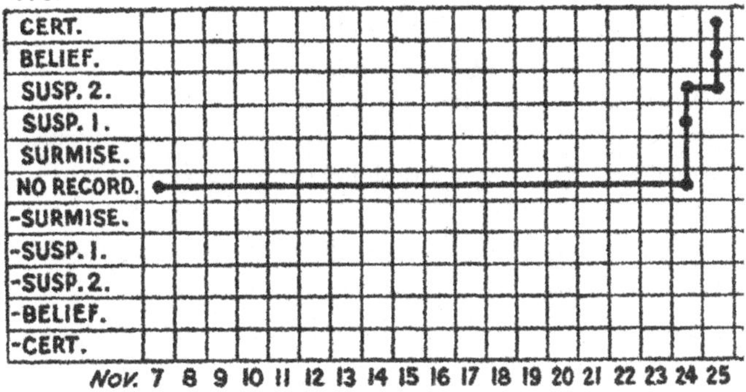

embarrassment, to explain it, and diverted the conversation to the chrysanthemums again.

Then for a little time they discussed the accident on the preceding Sunday morning. Mrs Melhuish couldn't understand it. She had often noticed the Kinnairds' chauffeur. Quite a superior-looking young man. She was sure the Kinnairds would not have kept him so long if they had thought him a reckless driver.

'Do you think he had been drinking?' she asked severely. 'One would say he must have been either mad or drunk to have attempted to take that comer at such a speed. Perhaps he was just showing off.'

'Perhaps so,' Gore agreed.

'Well, he paid dearly for it, poor fellow,' said Mrs Arndale. Left a widow, I suppose. *Was* he married, dear?'

'No,' replied Mrs Melhuish, 'thank goodness. Quite bad enough for Sidney to have his car smashed up, without having to pay a pension to a widow. Of course the car was insured—'

'Oh, then, that's all right,' laughed Mrs Arndale cheerfully. 'Now, my dearest Barbara, we must trot along. I've got to have a tooth stopped, run down a tweeny, and find Cecil a book he can read—all before lunch. Come along. See you sometime, Wick. Keep on getting better and better. By-bye.'

She waved a farewell from the door and was gone. Mrs Melhuish held out her hand.

'I'm so glad you had it out with your husband, Pickles,' smiled Gore. 'By the way, I've got those letters for you.'

'What?'

She hung towards him, still holding his hand. Her exquisite eyes filled slowly with a divine rapture. Her clear pallor warmed to the flush of a wild rose. 'Get out,' she whispered softly. 'You're pulling my leg.'

He averted his eyes hastily.

'Fact,' he said brightly. 'They're in there in my bedroom. I'll send them across to you.'

'Don't,' she smiled. 'Bum them for me. Where did you—?'

'Now—no questions,' he commanded. 'That is to be my reward.'

Mrs Arndale's voice called her reproachfully from the corridor.

'Very well,' she smiled. 'That. . . and this.'

She bent, kissed the thin spot on the top of his head, and fled laughing from the room.

28

Gore's explanation of the incident which took place on Cleveport links in that ditch near the fourteenth tee is, perhaps, of some interest.

'When I saw that ball whizzing off for the ditch,' he says, 'I was pretty sure that it had gone into the ditch, but not quite. As I went after it, the idea occurred to me: "Suppose I were to find two balls now—both new Red Kings—one in the ditch and unplayable, and the other, say, just at the edge of the ditch in a good lie. Which ball would one select as one's own?" Of course such a thing was absolutely unlikely, and the idea was a futile sort of idea enough—the sort of thing that comes into one's head without any particular reason and goes out of it and leads to nothing. And of course I *did* find no ball in a nice lie at the edge of that ditch. But somehow my mind jumped from that idea—I had nothing to do with its jumping—it just jumped, and I found myself wondering if there could have been anyone mixed up with Barrington and Frensham who was sufficiently like Arndale to be easily mistaken for him. And then my mind made another jump to the only person I could think of who had been mixed up in the business and who was anything at all like Arndale— Thomson. I had no sooner thought of Thomson than I began to think of a dozen different things connected with him, all at once. I remembered that I had seen him in a light-coloured raincoat—the afternoon he called to see me about a recommendation to Melhuish. I remembered that he had called at Melhuish's house the afternoon the knife had disappeared for the second time from the hall. I remembered that he had been connected with Barrington in looking after his car for him. I remembered that he had been in a great hurry to get away from the Kinnairds' employment into Melhuish's. I remembered that he was a big, powerful chap. I remembered his face. But I think the thing that really first convinced me that I was on the right track was my remembering that Mrs Barrington's maid had called him "Fred". I don't know why that had stuck—but it *had* stuck. I suppose I remembered everything connected with that afternoon Barrington was found especially distinctly. At all events I remembered quite distinctly that the maid had called Out "Fred" to him, and I was almost certain that he had signed himself Alfred in the note which he had left for Melhuish giving the Kinnairds' address, and which Melhuish showed me the evening I dined with him. Well, if his name was Alfred, a person who knew him well enough to call him by his Christian name *might* call him "Fred", but it seemed hardly likely. "Alf", perhaps—or even "Alfie"—if not full "Alfred", but hardly "Fred". Of course then I asked myself, why, if his name was Frederick, should he have changed it into Alfred. That puzzled me, until I remembered that one of the slips in the pocket of Barrington's bank-book which was found amongst Frensham's things at the Excelsior, concerned someone whose initials were F. T. If Frederick Thomson knew that Frensham had that slip in his possession, and if he meant to murder Frensham—it seemed to me that he might, if he was an intelligent, careful person, decide to alter his name to Alfred Thomson. The Kinnairds were away— that made it easier. It was a long shot—but, as a matter of fact, Thomson *was* quite an intelligent sort of person up to a certain point. Still, I admit I rather patted myself on the back when I found that the Rodney girl had been altering the F's on his collars and things to A's.

'So I was actually getting somewhere near the bone when Stevens turned up. Though of course it was really Stevens who recovered those letters for me. If he hadn't—'

But that hypothesis of Colonel Gore's is clearly of no importance.

There is a sergeant of the Westmouth City Police who sometimes, in his spare moments, wonders a little about Colonel Gore. His name is Long, and he is an extremely intelligent and thoughtful officer. As, however, he has a wife and a large family, and has long ago learned the imprudence—in the Westmouth City Police Force at all events—of doing anything in a hurry, it is probable that he will continue to wonder for some time to come.

THE END

Bonus Novella:

Too Much Imagination

1

INTO THE NET

'I cannot understand, Gore,' said the junior partner of Gore and Tolley, as the senior partner made a tranquil and unobtrusive entrance at five minutes past ten precisely, 'how any intelligent human being can arrive at his office *every* morning exactly five minutes late.'

The senior partner lighted a pipe without resentment and turned the twinkle of a pair of kindly if exceedingly shrewd gray eyes upon his colleague.

'System, my dear Tolley,' he said blandly. 'Highly specialized system. My existence is saturated with it. As to the particular point under discussion, I may say that in all human probability I was born five minutes late.'

'Don't be an ass,' said Mr Tolley. 'Guess what's in the net this morning!'

'I know,' said Colonel Gore placidly. 'Sir Maurice Gaul, I understand, desires to enlist our distinguished services. I had a note from Lady Pauncefield this morning telling me that she had recommended us. Very sweet of the dear old thing. I'm glad we got back that gold plate of hers for her. Well, let us hear what our friend Sir Maurice has to say for himself.'

Tolley picked up a crested sheet of delicate azure from his desk and read:

Tel. 33 Mortfield.

Telegrams.	Oast. Surrey.	The Oast House.
Stations.	Guildford.	Mr Mortfield.
	Famham.	Surrey.
	Milford.	May 14.

Sir Maurice Gaul would feel obliged if Colonel Gore would arrange an interview here at any hour either tomorrow, Thursday, May 15, or next day—preferably tomorrow. Sir Maurice would feel obliged if Colonel Gore would arrange day and hour by telephone tomorrow, Thursday morning, by which time he trusts that his telephone will be in order—if not, by telegram.

'Good,' smiled Gore. 'We're getting on, Tolley—even if the great Sir Maurice Gaul can only address us in the third person.' His hand went to the telephone. 'It's a lovely day for a run down into Surrey. And most fortunately I put on a very beautiful new suit this morning. Double-three Mortfield, isn't it? This may be quite a good thing for us, old chap, with a bit of luck. Find a train for me, like a darling. I'm going to it right now.'

And, in point of fact, six minutes later the junior partner was once more alone. Colonel Gore's system was sufficiently elastic to adjust itself to the emergencies of the Southern Railway Co. And the first train that could get him to Sir Maurice Gaul was the only train that interested him in the least.

For the fish that had strayed into Gore and Tolley's net that morning was a very big and desirable fish indeed—a fish which had been celebrated for quite a long time and was something more than celebrated at the present moment.

2

TOO MUCH TO SWALLOW

The career of Maurice Gaul had been an idyll of literary success. The son of a Christian police court solicitor, the grandson of a Jewish tailor, at a bound he had emerged—somewhere in the early nineteen hundreds—from the obscurity of reporterdom into the full blaze of fame.

A first novel, written in six weeks, had done that for him; a second, dramatized with brilliant success, had supplied him with food and clean collars for the rest of his life. For the following twenty years he had produced best seller after best seller—not all equal in quality to his early work, but all entirely satisfactory to the enormous public for whose literary palate he had never failed to supply just that soothing blend of sentiment and sensation it hoped for from him.

Good-looking, self-confident and suave, with no illusions save that of success, at thirty-six he had fashioned himself into a social personage of dignity if not of importance, had married a wife with ten thousand a year and hosts of influential friends, and had found a seat in Parliament.

The war had made him special correspondent to the *Daily Mercury*, and four years stay-at-home England, no less than England at the front, had largely depended upon him for its hopes and fears. Four times a week his picturesque pen, gifted with a talent for facile emotion, had brought its column of actuality from France or Salonica or Mesopotamia or Russia to the British breakfast table—authentic stuff, pointed with piquant detail, and beyond doubt turned out by a man who knew everything and every one worth knowing.

Other special correspondentships had followed with peace, and had subsequently supplied excellent copy for more novels, more articles, more Parliamentary Committee work. He had an excellent idea of the value of his wares and had inherited the business ability of his breed; his income from his literary work had probably exceeded that of his wife considerably.

He had been knighted—he had been adorned with distinguished orders—English, French, Belgian and Italian—he had built himself a magnificent house in one of the most beautiful parts of Surrey—and, having thus achieved success at forty- seven, had sealed it by writing a book telling how he had done it.

And then, a few days before, upon this favourite of the gods, disaster, utter and devastating, had fallen like a thunderbolt.

On May 2, Maurice Gaul had left his Surrey residence, the Oast House, and for a week exactly had disappeared from the ken of his large household. According to the account which he had subsequently given to the police, he had spent those seven days in Bristol, collecting local colour for a projected novel, a portion of which was to deal with the experiences of a 'down-and-outer' in the capital of the west.

His story was that, for purposes of realism, he had begun his adventures in Bristol with the sum of one shilling, that by the fourth day he had been absolutely destitute and had remained practically so until the end of the week of his experiment. He had accounted thus for the fact that neither on May 6, 7, nor 8 had he seen a newspaper, being unable to afford to buy one.

He had thus remained until the morning of May 9 in absolute ignorance of the terrible tragedy which for three days had set all England agog.

About ten o'clock on the night of May 5, a Mr John Arling, who resided about a mile from the Gauls, and who had known Lady Gaul since her childhood, had received, upon his return to his house from the golf club at Mortfield, where he had been playing bridge, a telephone message which had arrived about half an hour before and had been taken by his butler, Robert Ellis. Lady Gaul had rung up, the butler had said, to ask that Mr Arling would go up to the Oast House as soon as possible, as she wished to consult him upon a matter of very great urgency and importance.

Mr Arling had put on his cap again and started at once for the Oast House, which he had reached about twenty minutes past ten. The drawing-room was on the ground floor, the house, though of wide frontage, being of two storeys only. Its blinds, as usual, had been up and, as he passed its windows, he had seen Lady Gaul, seated with her back to the windows, apparently reading. He had tapped at a window, but she had not turned at the sound.

He was a constant visitor at the Oast House at all hours of the day and, as was his habit, he had entered the house by the front door—which was always left open until eleven o'clock during the summer months—without knocking or ringing, and had gone into the drawing-room.

He had begun an apology for his delay in complying with Lady Gaul's request, when his attention had been attracted by something odd in her attitude. At first he had believed her asleep. But upon approaching her chair he had discovered to his horror that she had been stabbed between the shoulder-blades and that the back of her frock and the upholstery of the big armchair in which she sat were saturated with blood.

It had been only too evident that she was beyond all help. But he had rushed out of the room in search of the servants and, after some delay, had found the housekeeper at the end of the garden chatting with the head gardener. These two had been the only servants then on the premises, all the rest of the staff having been given permission to witness a night attack on Farnham by tanks and airplanes in connection with manoeuvres then in progress on the other side of the Hog's Back.

From the garden Mr Arling had rushed to the telephone to summon the Mortfield doctor and to inform the Mortfield police. He had then gone back to the drawing-room where he had found the two servants standing gazing in stupefaction at their murdered mistress.

In the clench of the dead woman's hand, rolled into a wisp, they had found a blood-flecked letter signed with the initial 'C,' but without other indication as to its writer. The contents of that letter had not been published in the newspapers, but the press had conveyed the impression that its purport lent a note of additional painfulness to the affair.

The medical evidence at the inquest had gone to show that Lady Gaul had probably been murdered about an hour before Mr Arling had found her, that two savage blows had been inflicted from behind with a heavy, wide-bladed knife and that her death had been instantaneous. No fingerprints had been found by the police, no footprints. The passing tramp theory had been, of course, suggested, but without conviction.

There had been several dogs about the house and the grounds that night as usual. But neither the gardener nor the housekeeper could recall having heard any unusual barking—though they had admitted that the dogs were all friendly dogs and made no fuss even about tramps.

The tragedy, owing to the social position of the victim and of her husband, had created an immense sensation—a sensation increased by the fact that not until nearly four days later could any trace of Sir Maurice Gaul's whereabouts be discovered.

On the morning of May 9 he had received from a newspaper purchased at Temple Meads terminus his first tidings of the terrible catastrophe which had befallen him. He had at once communicated with the police and had returned to Surrey by road in a hired car to avoid the delays of the cross-country railway journey.

When he had reached his house it had been to discover that a fire which had broken out in the small hours of the morning the reeking debris, had been a police inspector in whose pocket—though he had not actually produced it then—had been a warrant for his arrest. From that indignity his explanation of his movements during the preceding four days and the inspector's caution had for the moment saved him.

But all England, reading its newspaper that evening, had shaken its head and, with a thrill, told itself that that 'lost-in-Bristol' story was altogether too much to swallow and that the solution of the four days' mystery of the Oast House was, for any intelligent and fair-minded newspaper reader, as clear as daylight.

3

THE NOTE IN HER HAND

The crested limousine which had met Gore at Guildford station swooped up a steep and sandy road through the sombre silence of a pine-wood, swooped over a crest and swooped down on the sunlit glory of the Surrey heaths in mid-May. Gore gazed with benignity upon the view thus suddenly revealed to him. Typical Surrey on a typical spring morning—what more agreeable?

The gorse was blazing gold, the tender green of the young bracken pointed the brown of the heather, the air was filled with balmy fragrances and the twitter of larks. Curve after curve, pine- clad or striped with the silvery slimness of the birches, fell away, mile upon mile, to the blue distance of Hindhead and Blackdown. To the left a sheet of swan-decked water sparkled among the trees. To the right, three miles away, the telegraph posts of the Hog's Back marched in procession against the skyline.

Gore caught sight at that moment of the house which the fortunate man of his thoughts had builded for himself—a black, gutted skeleton, in silhouette against the southern sunlight that pierced it through and through mercilessly and showed it a mere empty, hollow husk. One small portion only—an annex built out toward the gardens to house the servants—had escaped.

Sixteen thousand pounds that house had cost Maurice Gaul to build, so the newspapers had said. Quite a good deal of money to burn. A fused wire, however, had apparently done the job promptly and thoroughly. The fire engines from Guildford and Farnham and Godalming had had between them just enough water to wet a fair-sized hay-rick fairly thorough.

The car passed an elaborate gate whose pillars bore the inscription 'The Oast House' in Old English lettering, and drew up before a pretty, hawthorn-embowered cottage, a hundred yards or so farther down the road. There Gore alighted and was received by a pale, prim little man who ushered him into a delightful little book-lined sitting room.

'I am Sir Maurice Gaul's secretary,' he explained. 'Sir Maurice asked me to say that he regretted that your interview must take place in these comparatively humble quarters of mine. But as a matter of fact, with the exception of the servants' quarters, Sir Maurice, at the moment, has no other place to receive anyone.'

'He had only built the house quite a short time ago?'

'About twelve months ago.'

'A curious name—The Oast House.'

'He built it on the site of an old oast barn. There were extensive hop-fields along this slope forty or fifty years ago. Some of the old buildings have been left standing. You may have seen them as you came in. Lady Gaul had a taste for the picturesque. Here is Sir Maurice now.'

The secretary opened the door to admit a stoutish, still youngish man, with curling black hair, liquid eyes, curved spine and strongly-marked features. The adjective sleek, pervaded Gore's first impression of him, despite the shadows beneath his eyes, and the almost lugubrious gravity of his air. He bowed solemnly, dismissed the secretary with a glance and consigned, with a rather fleshy white hand, the visitor to the chair from which he had risen.

'I don't know at all if you can do anything to help me, Colonel Gore. However, Lady Pauncefield—who is a very valued friend of mine, and to whom, I understand, you have recently been of very great service suggested that you might be able to do something for me. Perhaps I may also say that I recall very clearly the part which you played in that terrible business down in Wiltshire—the Powlet case.'

Gore bowed politely and waited.

He found Sir Maurice Gaul so far, frankly, a little disillusioning, and a little pompous. But, no doubt, under more than trying circumstances even a celebrity found it necessary to stress the fact that he was one.

'You have, I assume, read the newspaper accounts of my wife's death. I think, however, that I had better begin by giving you my own account at first-hand. I have asked Mr Arling to come up and see you personally also. He will be here very shortly. You will, also, if you wish, see every member of my household staff and ask them any questions you may think fit. They are all entirely loyal to me. I can at least promise that you will be supplied with all the available facts.'

His succinct narrative of his visit to Bristol supplied Gore with one new and significant detail. So far neither his own efforts nor those of the police had been able to discover a single person in Bristol who could testify to having seen him at any place there between May 2 and May 9, though plenty of witnesses could be found to vouch for the afternoon of the former date and the morning of the latter.

On arriving at Bristol on May 2 he had deposited his luggage and his money—with the exception of the sum of one shilling— at the Grand Hotel. On the morning of May 9 he had reclaimed them. In the interval he had wandered about, in shabby clothes purchased specially for his adventure, looking for casual employment in East Bristol. Day after day he had taken his place in one or another queue of applicants for work.

Once only had he reached a foreman—to be turned away promptly upon the discovery that he belonged to no union. He had rubbed elbows with scores of unfortunates engaged in the same quest as himself, but not one of these had it been possible to find. He had slept in the open every night—on Clifton Downs most often; no lodging house keeper could vouch for a single night of the seven.

He had begged in the streets of Clifton and had extracted pennies from sundry elderly ladies; but none of the elderly ladies could be discovered. He had revisited, in the make-up of his adventure, a dozen cheap restaurants and shops where he had purchased food; but at none of these places had the people undertaken to recognize him.

'It seems incredible,' he smiled forcedly. 'But they were all, naturally, places frequented by seedy customers like myself. One seedy customer is very like another. And the people at these places are not violently interested in their customers, as you are no doubt aware.'

'Then there is only your own statement to cover the interval from May 2 afternoon to May 9 morning.'

'That is so.' Gaul glanced at his watch. 'Before Mr Arling comes, I think I had better go into a very painful matter which, naturally, I prefer to discuss with you alone—from *my* point of view. You are aware that a letter was found in my wife's hand. This is a copy of it.'

The last words which Lady Gaul had read had been these:

> I can only say again what I said last night. Almost certainly your husband suspects. I hope and believe that so far it is merely suspicion. But for both our sakes, we must run no further risks. As we have often agreed, we have been mad. But for the sake of the wonderful sweetness of the madness that has been ours, there must be no hideous and disastrous anticlimax.

> This must be final. Bum this letter. Burn every scrap of mine you have kept, if you have kept any. Be careful of that sly-faced little secretary of your husband's. I feel pretty sure that he has been spying on us for some time back. I managed to leave my undervest behind last night. I hope you discovered it before the maids did.
>
> Snip off the name tab and any laundry marks at once. I can get it some time. But don't send it back—don't write—don't telephone. This is the end.—C.

'You were away on the night of May 4?' Gore asked after a pause. 'Was that undervest found?'

'Yes. By the police, in one of my wife's bureau drawers. The name-tab and the laundry marks had been cut out.'

4

GORE IS FRANK

'You must not expect emotion from me, Colonel Gore,' Gaul went on, when Gore had handed back the copy of the brutal letter to him. 'I am past emotion—and you have no use for it. I will simply say that at this moment I have no faintest idea who the writer of that letter is, and that its contents came to me as an utter and overwhelming surprise. I was passionately devoted to my wife. I had always believed that she was devoted to me. But that letter was found in her hand by Mr Arling and my servants.'

'I ask the question without apology, Sir Maurice. Is there anyone whom you can imagine capable of writing that letter—I mean, apart from any actual knowledge of such a person?'

Gaul hesitated, seemed to brace himself to conviction.

'No.'

'You must be entirely candid with me, Sir Maurice. Lady Gaul, it has been stated in the press, was engaged to Mr Arling prior to her engagement to you.'

'Yes. But all that was quite finished—done with—long ago.'

'You had no faintest suspicion of an affair with Mr Arling?'

'None.'

'Nor with anyone else?'

'None. There is Mr Arling's car. There is one other point. On my last birthday my wife gave me a case containing three cigarette holders of various lengths—amber and meerschaum. For the past year I have taken the case and the three holders with me wherever I have gone. Just before I left here on May 2, my valet handed me the case. I opened it, not a hundred yards from my gates, on my way to the station. I never smoke cigarettes without a holder.

'I found then that there were only two holders in the case. On the night of May 5 the police found the third holder in an ash tray on a table just beside my wife's chair. The point they make is that, as I admit, hitherto I have always taken the three holders away with me in the case. My man says that he did not open the case before he gave it to me, but simply picked it up off my dressing table, taking it for granted that all three holders were in it as usual.'

'Had the third holder been seen by anyone in the interval between that and the night of the murder?'

'No.'

The door of the room opened and Spain, the secretary, ushered in a big, bronzed, middle-aged man, with wide-open blue eyes which contemplated the world with the mild, good-humoured puzzlement of a child—a type, Gore reflected, whose apparent simplicity was probably entirely misleading. Having introduced the new arrival as Mr Arling, Gaul, without unnecessary explanation, left Gore alone with him.

Arling, too, it seemed, had little to add to the information already published in the press. There had been a partially smoked cigarette in the holder found in the ash tray beside the murdered woman, he said; but he could not recall whether there had been any loose ash in the tray.

'About that telephone message from Lady Gaul, Mr Arling?' Gore asked. 'Your butler took it?'

'Yes.'

'It occurred to you, of course, to ask him if her voice had sounded agitated or distressed?'

'Yes. He said that her voice had seemed to him rather excited and rather shrill.'

'He knew her voice well?'

'Oh, yes. He was in Sir Maurice Gaul's employment for five years before they came here. Shortly after they came here—well Lady Gaul thought a smaller place would suit him better. I happened to have lost my old butler just at the time. So Ellis came to me.'

'You were out until ten o'clock on the night of May 5?'

'Yes. At the golf club. I dined there.'

'And Ellis? He was in at half past nine, when the message from Lady Gaul arrived? Where was he for the hour before that?'

Arling smiled.

'Out, I believe. But you had better see poor Ellis before your imagination does him any injustice.'

'I should like to very much. Perhaps, some time this afternoon?'

'Any time.'

'You were a very old friend of Lady Gaul's. Had she ever mentioned to you before that she was in any trouble?'

'Never.'

'I may take it then, Mr Arling, that the contents of the letter which was found in her hand came to you as an utter surprise?'

Arling stiffened.

'Of course.'

'You were at one time engaged to Lady Gaul?'

'Yes.'

'You are a man of the world, Mr Arling. You realize that the British public has quite made up its mind that you were the writer of that letter?'

Arling shrugged.

'Realize? I have always realized that there are plenty of idiots in the world.'

'Quite. However, I ask the question directly. Did you write that letter?'

'Good God, man, no.'

'I take it that the original letter is at present in the hands of the police?'

'I believe so.'

'I should like to see the original. The police, I presume, have discovered resemblances between its handwriting and your own. Many?'

Coolly as the question was asked, the reply was given as coolly.

'Oh, yes,' said Arling. 'The handwriting was quite an excellent imitation of mine. By the way, I suppose that Gaul has told you that the police found two letters of mine in Lady Gaul's escritoire, together with a third letter which I did *not* write, but which they are quite convinced I did.'

'No. Sir Maurice did not mention that.'

'He probably left it to me to tell you everything that concerned myself. At any rate, such is the fact. The two letters which I did write to Lady Gaul were both solely concerned with plants and cuttings which I gave her for her garden and so on. The one which I did *not* write is a note making an appointment—not to mince matters—to spend a night with her at the Savonia Hotel on a date in last April—the fourteenth, I think. It is curious that Gaul did not tell you about it.'

'Not in the least,' Gore said curtly. 'Either Sir Maurice believes that you murdered his wife—or he murdered her himself. Either supposition would explain his silence reasonably.'

Arling's blue eyes stared.

'You are certainly frankness itself.'

'I wonder,' Gore smiled amiably, 'if *you* are, Mr Arling?'

'I have grown rather callous to people who wonder about me during the past week or so,' Arling said frigidly. 'I'm afraid I must leave you to wonder.'

Gore sighed.

'Very well, Mr Arling, thank you. I shall continue to wonder— until I find out.'

5

BLOODSTAINED LINEN

So the interview terminated. Arling left the room, and was succeeded by a defile of the servants, each of whom was solemnly ushered in and out by a dignified butler. Gore interviewed, first, eleven miscellaneous servants, none of whom could tell him more than that Sir Maurice and Lady Gaul had always appeared on excellent terms, that Mr Arling had been a frequent visitor at the Oast House, but a perfectly open one, both during Sir Maurice's presence and his absence, and that he or she, as the case was, had gone to Farnham to witness the night attack on the night of May 5, and had reached home shortly after eleven o'clock in the small char-a-banc which had been hired for the purpose of their outing.

A housemaid gave it as her opinion that for the last weeks—two or three or so—Mr Arling had not come so much to the house. The butler explained that Mr Arling had been away a good deal during those weeks, and got the housemaid out of the room as soon as he could.

Then followed the housekeeper and the head gardener. They were both most respectable and intelligent servants, and they both told their story briefly and lucidly. The fact emerged that the head gardener was 'courting' the comely housekeeper—a detail which accounted, no doubt, for their lack of interest in night attacks, and their being found together at the end of the garden by Mr Arling.

Gore asked them both the two questions which he had asked Arling concerning the cigarette holder, and smiled upon learning that they had been asked the same questions by the police inspector.

'That,' he said, 'proves how exactly alike great minds can think.'

The gardener stated that there had been a half-smoked cigarette in the holder, and that the police had found that it was one of the brand which Sir Maurice Gaul usually smoked—a Russian cigarette made by Torrance & Co. He could not say that he had noticed any loose ash in the tray.

The housekeeper, however, stated definitely that there had been no ash in the tray. By order of the police everything in the drawing-room had been left absolutely untouched for two whole days. On the third day she had been permitted to go into the room with a housemaid shortly before lunch time.

She had looked round the room then carefully to estimate what amount of cleaning up the housemaid should be instructed to perform after lunch. She remembered distinctly seeing the ash tray still on the small table and noticing that the holder had been taken away. She was perfectly clear in her mind that there was then no loose ash in it. She was almost certain that there had been none in it when she had first seen the cigarette holder lying in it, on the night of the murder.

'Why, sir,' she asked, 'what has that to do with it? That's what I can't make out.'

'Well, Mrs Colfin,' Gore replied, 'some people, you see, put their cigarette ash in the ash tray. Most people, however, put it on the carpet. Now, I suppose you would not have noticed if there had been any ash on the carpet that morning, would you?'

The housekeeper, bridling a little, supposed she would certainly have noticed. It *was* one of the things she was paid to notice. Lady Gaul had always been very particular about ash on the carpets, and she had to notice it, because Sir Maurice threw ash about everywhere.

'I mentioned that to the police inspector, sir. But there was no ash on the drawing-room carpet that morning. I'm quite certain of that. The police inspector said just the same as you, sir. He wanted to make out that there might have been, without me seeing it. But it wouldn't pay me not to have my eyes open, sir, in my position.'

'You are probably quite right, Mrs Colfin,' Gore said soothingly. 'Now, you were in the garden that evening chatting with the head gardener, Robertson. How long?'

'From about nine o'clock on, sir. I took my knitting out, as I often do. And when the light went Robertson and I went on chatting about things.'

'So that from about nine until about twenty minutes past ten—when Mr Arling came in search of you—Lady Gaul was absolutely alone in the house?'

'Well—alone—well, yes, sir. Except for whoever murdered her. The dogs were about, sir, of course.'

'Quite. But you heard no sound from the house while you were down there in the garden?'

'No, sir. Except the noise of the motors on the road, when any passed.'

As Mrs Colfin and the head gardener left the room, the butler appeared once more, followed by Spain.

'That, sir, is all the staff. Shall you require any of them again?'

'No, thank you, I think not.'

'I suppose,' Spain said, when the man had gone away, 'that I ought to be included in the household staff. Though I'm afraid I'm unlikely to be of much assistance to you. I was out when the dreadful affair took place. I spent the evening in Guildford with some friends and didn't get back until nearly eleven.

'The police insisted on getting the names of my friends, and the hour I left the house to return here, and all that—I gave them a written statement. If you'd care for a copy, here is one.' Gore smiled as he glanced at the neatly-typed sheet of foolscap.

'I don't think I want this, Mr Spain, thank you. Not being a police inspector, I am permitted to use such meagre intelligence as the Lord has given me. When Sir Maurice went away on May 2, did he give you any address in Bristol?'

'No. I understand he gave Lady Gaul one.'

'Curious that he should not have given you one—I suppose there were letters to forward?'

'No. Sir Maurice detests any kind of interruption or disturbance when he is working on a book or a story. I have known him to leave most important letters unanswered—unlooked at—for weeks.'

'You have never seen anything to indicate that Sir Maurice and Lady Gaul were not on the best of terms?'

'No.'

'And you have been in Sir Maurice's employment for a considerable time?'

'Nine months.' The little, pale, dejected man flushed into a sudden vehemence. 'I trust, Colonel Gore, that you are not one of the many who have allowed themselves to be misled by a few absolutely deceptive appearances. I admit that there are circumstances which, unfortunately, chance may render it absolutely impossible to explain by proved facts.

'But for anyone who has known him intimately, even for the short period for which I have known him, the idea that he could have committed this terrible crime is ludicrous—absolutely and merely ludicrous. I do assure you of that. Forgive my speaking with such emotion. But I have just been speaking to that idiot of a police inspector who has practically lived on the premises for the past week.

'He told me that some boys found some pieces of linen stained with blood this morning, on the heath, down near the pond. They brought them to the police sergeant, and he went to the spot and poked about and found, in a rabbit hole which had practically been filled in with packed heather, a bloodstained kitchen knife and some other pieces of bloodstained linen. The pieces, put together, he says, make a handkerchief.

'When I left him he was about to go through the things which Sir Maurice saved from the fire—what he had in the suitcase which he took away to Bristol—hoping, of course, to be able to make out that the handkerchiefs are of the same kind of linen and pattern as the pieces he found in the rabbit hole.

'"This will swing him," he said to me, smacking his lips. I—well, I'm afraid I said more than I ought to have said. But isn't it outrageous that a bumpkin of a village policeman should be allowed to say such a thing—in the hearing of Sir Maurice's own servants?'

'Rather unnecessary,' Gore agreed. 'What about the knife?'

'The sort of knife they cut up meat with in the kitchen. The cook says it may have been one of his.'

'Well,' Gore sighed, 'it is certainly a most difficult business, Mr Spain. Fortunately Sir Maurice remains perfectly cool and collected.'

'Isn't he wonderful?' the little secretary exclaimed fervently. 'Marvellous courage, marvellous self-control. He reminds me of the protagonist of a Greek tragedy—the favourite of Fortune, the man who had everything—struck down suddenly—robbed of everything—his wife, his honour, his house, his liberty—perhaps his life—humbled to the dust—and yet, undefeated.'

'As you say, quite a tragic figure,' agreed Gore, impressed by this view of his client.

'Absolutely Sophoclean,' said the secretary.

6

ARLING MAKES A CONFESSION

Arling appeared at the door. Beyond him, Gore had a glimpse of a purple-faced police sergeant in mysterious colloquy with a lily-white constable. The two turned and peered in curiously at him, then, exchanging a smile of amusement, turned away and went up the road toward the house.

'The force is mildly annoyed by your arrival on the scene, Colonel Gore,' Arling smiled. 'They'll show you anything they have in their possession. But on the whole they think they'd like you to mind your own business and leave them to get on with theirs. You said you'd like to meet my butler; perhaps you'll walk down with me to my house and have lunch. Though I don't know if it is quite delicate on my part to invite you to eat with me.'

'Sir Maurice has arranged that Colonel Gore will lunch here, Mr Arling,' said Spain.

Arling appeared relieved. The two men chatted of indifferent subjects as they went down the road that wound among the gorse. Their walk was nearly over when Arling stopped and turned to face his companion abruptly.

'Look here, Colonel Gore. Do you believe that Gaul did this?'

Gore shrugged.

'I am here to ask questions, Mr Arling, not to answer them.' 'Oh, damn that. Have you heard that they found the knife and a handkerchief of Gaul's with it in a rabbit hole?'

'Probably.'

'It's one of Gaul's handkerchiefs all right, you know.' 'Probably. Well, Mr Arling?'

'Well—there are a couple of things you had better know. I think. First—about Lady Gaul. About three weeks ago Gaul came into the drawing-room from nowhere while I was sitting talking with Lady Gaul—about the slump in cross-word puzzles, I believe. He made a frightful ass of himself—delivered a regular little oration about the danger of our seeing so much of one another and so on and so forth. Of course, I simply roared.

'But he was perfectly serious. As a matter of fact, I *had* cut down my visits to the Oast House a good deal during the last few weeks, because of that little scene. I need hardly say that he simply made a fool of himself. I don't know why I didn't tell you about this straight off. But—well, they hadn't found that handkerchief then. Had Gaul himself said anything of it?'

'Nothing.'

'Well—there it is. And there's another thing you had better know. I mean—I think you ought to know how things stand—and this thing has been on my conscience. You know that letter? Well, when I found Lady Gaul dead, I saw that she had a letter in her hand, as I believed, in my handwriting. I took it out of her hand, read it hurriedly and, like a fool, lost my head and decided to suppress it.

'Lady Gaul always called me Claud, you see—principally because my own name is John. The imitation of my handwriting was so infernally clever that I got scared and, as I say, lost my head. That's the only excuse I can give you. I stuck the letter in my pocket and went out to get the servants. After I had found them—it took some time—I went to the telephone to ring up the doctor. When

I went into the drawing-room again, I saw, to my amazement, the gardener taking a second letter from Lady Gaul's hand.

'*That* was the letter of which Sir Maurice showed you a copy. But the extraordinary thing—the devilish thing—is that *that* letter was also in an exact imitation of my handwriting, and was, word for word, a replica of the first letter, which I had pocketed. Of course, I ought to have spoken out—admitted that I had done a silly thing. But like a fool, I didn't. However, I'm going to do it now. I *have* done it now. I've told Gaul, and I've told you I shall send a written statement to the police after lunch.

'Of course,' he went on, when they had walked some way in silence, 'that second letter couldn't have been *written* in the interval—say five or six minutes by the time the servants got to Lady Gaul. It was a long letter. It must have been written beforehand. But can you conceive any human being writing two such letters exactly the same? Why, he even went to the trouble of smearing them both with blood.

'Here, I'll show you the first letter. Can you conceive anyone doing such a thing?'

'Oh, yes,' said Gore. 'All you want is a person with a practised imagination who was also able to foresee that you would pocket the first letter.'

'Precisely,' said Arling curtly. 'And there's only one person I know who fits both ways.'

He took a sheet of note paper from his pocketbook and handed it to Gore. A long brown smear ran across its middle, encircled by smaller brown spots. Gore examined it carefully through a lens.

'If it's a forgery,' he said, 'it's dashed well done. Not a quiver. Usually a glass gives the game away. But this was written slap off. I should like to see some of your own handwriting.'

But the lavish specimens which Arling submitted to him when they reached his house quite clearly did nothing to affect his opinion.

'Dashed clever,' he said simply. 'And dashed awkward—perhaps.'

7

TASTES OF A SECRETARY

Ellis, Arling's butler, was produced—a butler of the unctuous, refined type. He repeated, rather sulkily, his statement that Lady Gaul's voice over the telephone that night had sounded shrill and excited. Requested by Gore to give an imitation, he refused at first, produced some ludicrous squeaks from an unwilling throat, refused finally and definitely to make a fool of himself. But Gore thanked him with such grave sincerity that he was visibly mollified.

'You had no difficulty with Lady Gaul before you left her service?'

'I have never had any difficulty with my employers in any place, sir. I esteemed Lady Gaul most highly. I did not quite suit her requirements—so I looked out for another place.'

'Is it not a fact that Lady Gaul dismissed you because you drank too much?'

The man's face changed. The cast became a malevolent permanency. He turned to Arling.

'I'll answer no more questions from this gentleman, sir. Let him go ask those who have reasons of their own for telling lies about me.'

But Arling displayed no sympathy with offended dignity.

'*Were* you dismissed for drinking too much, Ellis?'

'I was not. I left of my own free will.'

'Where were you on the night of the murder?' Gore asked placidly. 'From nine to nine thirty?'

'I've told you I will answer no more—'

'Where were you, Ellis?' Arling demanded.

'Lying down, sir, in my room.'

'But you told me that night that you had been out for a walk.'

'I was lying down in my room, sir. I didn't feel very well that night.'

'Two lies,' said his employer, abandoning him. 'Do you want to hear any more?'

'Not from him,' Gore replied curtly. 'I shall probably hear as many as are likely to be of any help before the day is done. I should get that statement to the police at once, if I were you, Mr Arling. It will give them plenty of opportunity for attending to their own business.'

He found on his return to the Oast House that they had lost no time in doing so. Spain was standing in the road outside his cottage waiting with the news that the expected blow had fallen at last and that Sir Maurice had been arrested. Apparently the discovery of the morning had precipitated the disaster.

Spain was utterly dejected.

'It seems to be the basest kind of treachery and disloyalty on my part,' he said mournfully, 'but I can't help it. Do as I will, the fact that he has been arrested persuades me to believe that perhaps the impossible is possible, and that he did kill her. I suppose I must not ask how *you* feel, Colonel Gore?'

'I?' said Gore brightly. 'I feel remarkably hungry, if I may say so. This Surrey air—'

'A thousand apologies,' said Spain. 'Lunch is ready. Will you forgive me if I leave you to be your own host? I have to get into Mortfield on my motorcycle at once to send off a lot of telegrams for Sir Maurice. Shall you stay the night—or do you think that, now, you will return to London this afternoon?'

'No idea yet,' Gore replied succinctly. 'You can put me up here if necessary?'

Spain assured him that a room was at his disposal and left him to an excellent lunch. Presently, through the window of the sitting room, where the butler had brought his coffee, Gore saw him depart on his motorcycle.

'A sad little gentleman, sir,' the butler commented. 'I'm afraid, like the rest of us, he's going to lose a good job.'

When the secretary returned it was to find Gore browsing among his books.

'Your literary tastes are severely classical, Mr Spain, I perceive. Rather too classical for me. I've been looking for a nice, bright, jolly modem novel to help my digestion. I have been able to find only three novels that could be called modern—all by the same man, by the way—a man of whom I never heard before.'

He reached out a hand and selected one of three novels which stood in a clump between a set of George Meredith and a set of Hardy.

'Silas Furlonger. No. I don't believe I ever even heard of Mr Silas Furlonger.'

The secretary smiled faintly.

'Probably not. He is not a popular person.'

Gore turned over some pages.

'This one appears to be about a dipsomaniac. Not jolly things, dipsomaniacs. I've known two or three of them in my—'

He paused to read some lines.

'Um,' he said, and replacing the novel, picked out one of its fellows.

'Birth control. Most interesting—but not utterly jolly.'

He replaced the second volume and picked out the third, glanced at its title page, said 'um' again, and put it back in its place.

'No, I'm afraid I'm not quite up to Mr Furlonger. A favourite of yours, Mr Spain?'

'Well, yes. I was for a time Mr Furlonger's secretary before I came to Sir Maurice.'

'Indeed. Has he written many novels?'

'No. Those three only. He doesn't write at all now, I believe.'

'A curious name. A *nom de plume*?'

'No.'

'Really. Quite an unusual name.'

Gore glanced at his watch. 'A quarter to three. I wonder if you have a timetable, Mr Spain. I shall not stop the night, thank you. I find I must go back to town.'

Spain, if a little resentful at the sudden change of programme, provided a timetable promptly. Gore caught a train at Guildford and spent a penny on a special edition.

'The Oast House Tragedy,' he read. 'Startling Developments. Arrest of Sir Maurice Gaul.'

The only other occupant of the compartment, a stout woman, obviously bound for a garden party, distinctly heard the military looking gentleman in gray tweeds in the opposite corner, emit a snort. He appeared otherwise perfectly harmless, but at the last moment she decided to change into another compartment.

8

SPAIN WAXES VEHEMENT

The middle-aged gentleman in gray tweeds reached the Oast House again shortly after eight o'clock to find Spain and the butler paying off the servants, all of whom, by Gaul's instructions, were to leave his service, temporarily at least, next morning. Spain explained that it was his employer's wish that, in view of developments now probable, they should feel in no way fettered by any notions of loyalty to him.

'They don't want to go, sir,' said the butler. 'But they've got to go. So have Mr Spain and me. However, I'm not going far. I'm taking a room down at the Jolly Farmer. I have my own ideas about this business, sir. And there's a certain person I mean to keep my eye on. I'll mention no names—but I know he had it behind his eyes for poor Lady Gaul. I've heard him say so himself, when he was drunk.'

Spain left the worthy man to complete his regretful task and accompanied Gore to his cottage, too depressed by the loss of an excellent position, Gore concluded, to display any curiosity or surprise as to his return.

'The butler means the man who was butler before him,' he explained. 'But they've always been bitter enemies. He was talking nonsense just now. You intend to stay the night?'

'No. I shall not detain you very long, Mr Spain. I wonder if you have any specimens of Mr Arling's handwriting available. Possibly among Sir Maurice's papers—'

'No. Mr Arling never wrote to Sir Maurice. But, as a matter of fact, I have several sheets of manuscripts in Mr Arling's handwriting. He has been working for some months back upon a book of nature studies. He is an ardent "ist" of various sorts—and I have been typing his manuscripts for him in my spare time.'

While he went to the desk which occupied one comer of the sitting room, Gore strolled over to the bookcase to stand looking at the three novels of the uncelebrated Silas Furlonger.

'By the way, Mr Spain, I think you said this afternoon that Silas Furlonger was not a *nom de plume*?'

Spain was absorbed for a moment in his search for Arling's manuscript. He turned then with a taped bundle of sheets in his hand.

'Pardon? Oh—Furlonger. Yes, it's a *nom de plume*. His real name is Ferdinand Miler. I think I told you that I had been his secretary for some time before coming to Sir Maurice. This is Mr Arling's manuscript.'

Gore took the bundle of sheets, and, having lighted a pipe, retired to an armchair with them. His interest, however, appeared, to be rather in the matter of the manuscript than its handwriting, for he read a couple of pages with close attention.

'Mr Arling, too, is an imaginative person, apparently,' he said musingly. 'This opening of his is quite lyrical.'

'Oh yes,' smiled Spain, 'nature study is a passion with him. As you probably detect, he has been strongly influenced both by Maeterlinck and Fabre. To that extent—I suppose, one would call him imaginative.'

'It's rather odd to find that streak in him—too.'

'Too?' Spain repeated vaguely.

'You see,' Gore explained, 'there are at all events two things which I knew for certain about the person who murdered Lady Gaul. He was a person of what I described to Mr Arling himself this afternoon, as practised imagination, and he was also, necessarily, a person who knew that there had been a disagreement between Mr Arling and Sir Maurice Gaul with regard to Mr Arling's intimacy with Lady Gaul.

'Then there is the question of times. I have verified Mr Arling's statement that he dined at the golf club at Mortfield and played bridge afterward. But I have ascertained from the secretary that in fact Mr Arling left the club at nine o'clock, having merely finished after dinner a game of bridge begun before it. The Oast House is not more than twenty minutes walk from the club.

'He *could* have murdered Lady Gaul and reached his own house by ten o'clock—easily. Of course, one has to suspect him of quite unusual cleverness, if one is to suppose that he wrote that letter and left it in Lady Gaul's hand to point, obviously and inevitably, to her husband as the murderer. But there are lots of quite unusually clever people in the world. And, glancing at this manuscript, it would occur to anyone that Mr Arling was one of them, wouldn't it?'

Spain's eyes had hardened.

'I can at all events tell you that Mr Arling has taken considerable pains to distort every possible fact against Sir Maurice. It has been most marked—most gratuitous. As for imagination— well, frankly, does that matter? Does it require much imagination to stab a woman in the back?

'Not that I suppose for a moment that he murdered Lady Gaul,' he added with a shrug. 'He *could* have done it, no doubt. But—why? Because he quarrelled with Lady Gaul over that letter he had written her?

'I don't think that letter would ever have been found, if that had been the case. Mr Arling is a sensitive, cautious man—a man with a perfect dread of anything like notoriety—'

He paused. Gore had risen and had come across the room toward him tranquilly, yet with a deliberation that had caught the other's attention.

'Thank you, Mr Spain.' Gore smiled faintly. 'Now, will you kindly sit down again in that chair and listen to me.'

As if every drop of blood had fled from his body, the secretary's drawn little face went, in a flash, livid white. An odd little ejaculation of terrified dismay choked itself in his twitching throat. He sat down again in the chair from which, divining the truth, he had half risen, and stared at Gore helplessly.

9

WHAT REALLY HAPPENED

'On the evening of May 5,' Gore said quietly, 'you left this cottage on foot at five o'clock and arrived at the house of your friends, the Taits, on the outskirts of Guildford, at six. You dined there, and left at half past eight, saying that you had to walk most of the way back to reach here by eleven. The distance is about nine miles—uphill most of it.

'Two and a half hours was a reasonable allowance. And as you explained to the Taits, no bus ran westward along the Hog's Back to help you between 7 and 9 p.m. Off you went then at eight thirty—and, so far as is actually known, you reached this cottage a little before eleven.

'Of course you didn't walk, though—either to Guildford, or back from it. You have a motorcycle and a clever brain. I needn't guess exactly how you kept the motorcycle in the background, from the Taits in Guildford and the housekeeper and the head gardener here. But I'm quite sure you managed it, quite simply.

'You got back about nine. That gave you ample time to complete your preparations—if they had not already been completed. You had only to make sure that the two servants, who never probably entered the drawing-room in the evening, were safely out of the way at the end of the garden. You went into the drawing-room, made a pretext of some sort for disturbing Lady Gaul, got behind her, and stabbed her.

'You smeared your ingenious forgery of Mr Arling's handwriting with blood—or was it already smeared? Probably you also dabbed one of Sir Maurice's handkerchiefs with blood then. You put his cigarette holder with a half smoked cigarette of his special brand, in an ash tray beside Lady Gaul, and then you switched on the lights—or were they on all the time? Of course, nothing could be seen from the road. That would have been a risk—but a small one.

'Then you went to the telephone, rang up Mr Arling's house, and produced an imitation of Lady Gaul's voice good enough to pass muster with Mr Arling's butler—who, by the way, had, I rather think, drank more than was good for him that evening, and had been sleeping it off, his master being out. At any rate, he delivered your message to Mr Arling at ten o'clock, and Mr Arling came up to the Oast House and found what you had left for him to find. I don't know where you were hidden—but the blinds were up.

'You could have seen every movement of Mr Arling's from outside. But more probably you were inside. You saw him put your forgery No. 1 into his pocket, and then rush out of the room. You had known just what Mr Arling would do—you had forgery No. 2 ready—bloodstains and all. You jammed it into Lady Gaul's hand and cleared off.

'You probably went to where your motorcycle was hidden, probably among the gorse somewhere on the heath. You lay low there until about quarter of eleven. Then you walked out on to the road and arrived here, on foot for anyone who wanted to see you doing it.

'I don't know when you put the piece of the handkerchief and the knife in that rabbit hole. Probably very early next morning. You would recover your motorcycle from its hiding place then, too. Then—this morning you left those guiding pieces for someone to find. Quite clever of you to select a rabbit hole on the path by which the children go across the heath to school.

'I'm still wondering about the fire? Did that wire fuse accidentally—or did you help it?'

Spain paid no attention to the question.

'Go on,' he said, curiously. 'Where did I blunder? *Did* I blunder—or is this just guesswork?'

'Just guesswork. But you did blunder. You used a quite unnecessary adjective this morning—the adjective Sophoclean. Unfortunately for you, I came upon that adjective as I was glancing through the pages of one of your friend, Mr Furlonger's novels. That struck me as odd.

'I asked you if Furlonger was a *nom deplume*. You took just a little too long to say that it wasn't. That was a blunder, too. Because it started me just guessing quite seriously about you and your motorcycle. I couldn't very well ask you to hang yourself. So I went back to London and saw Mr Silas Furlonger's publishers.

'They also told me that his real name was Ferdinand Miler—which would have been a keen disappointment if they hadn't described his personal appearance with perhaps unkind accuracy. They passed me on to Messrs Wright, his literary agents. I found Mr Wright an extraordinary kind-hearted and sympathetic person—quite unfitted, I should have thought, to be a literary agent. He told me all about Ferdinand Miler and his books.

'"Very original, very clever" he said, "but absolute failures." He told me also about the plays which had not been produced, and the poems and stories and essays which could not be sold.

'But I had to keep on just guessing until Mr Wright told me of Ferdinand Miler's worst failure. His wife left him, I understand—for someone who could feed her—a scoundrel, no doubt—but he did feed her—for a while. Then she came back to you—I believe?'

'I was living on half a crown a week, then. Why should she stay?'

There was a silence.

'Then you discovered that Sir Maurice Gaul wanted a secretary. You contrived to get the post—by representing yourself as Mr Spain who had already acted as secretary to another literary man—Mr Silas Furlonger, whose real name was Ferdinand Miler?'

'Yes.'

'Weil—at that point I had to jump to a conclusion. One nearly always has to in this job. I wanted the why of the thing. So I put one foot on Failure who had lost everything—even the little fortune had given him—and the other foot on Success who had everything—and I jumped.

'I don't know how much envy, how much hatred, how much despair made of Maurice Gaul for you an incarnation of Success—always there before you, sleek, prosperous, self-satisfied—an infuriation from morning to night. But—if I had been you, that is how he would have seemed to me. Am I right?'

'Quite,' Spain shrugged. 'After all—how deplorably obvious.'

'By the way—that fused wire—?'

'I had luck with that.'

'Another little blunder,' mused Gore, 'was that accurate little summary of Arling's character. But your attitude with regard to Sir Maurice was admirably thought out. I'm afraid I must ring up Mortfield police station now.'

'Well,' the secretary said. 'I am willing to pay. Every chance was in my favour—Gaul's absence, the servants' outing, everything. But I forgot that there are people in the world who regard the adjective Sophoclean as unusual.'

'Lots of us are very stupid,' said Gore grimly. 'Perhaps that's why we sometimes succeed.'

THE END

A fan of Sherlock Holmes?
Then meet Solar Pons

The original fan fiction from the great August Derleth—the Sherlock Holmes of Praed Street.

"the best substitutes for Sherlock Holmes known."
– Vincent Starrett

"an excellent series of adventures in detection in their own right." – *The Chicago Tribune*

For more details and a full list of titles:
visit https://www.hachetteindia.com/home/yellowbacks